CLOUD
CUCKOO
LAND

CLOUD CUCKOO LAND
a novel by Lisa Borders

RIVER CITY PUBLISHING
Montgomery, Alabama

Designed by Lissa Monroe. Printed in the United States.

Library of Congress Cataloging-in-Publication Data:

Borders, Lisa, 1962-
Cloud Cuckoo Land : a novel / by Lisa Borders.
p. cm.
ISBN 1-57966-030-4 (alk. paper)
1. Women singers—Fiction. 2. Homeless women—Fiction. 3. Rock musicians—Fiction. 4. Blues musicians—Fiction. 5. Country musicians—Fiction. 6. Texas—Fiction. I. Title.
PS3602.O73 C55 2002
813'.6—dc21
2002002502

Parts of this book have been previously published, sometimes in slightly different versions, in the following periodicals: Chapter 1 as "The Day Prairie Rose, Texas, Disappeared From the Map" in *CrossConnect*, Chapters 2 and 3 as "Easter" in *Bananafish*, part of Chapter 41 as "Shoes" in *Snake Nation Review*.

River City publishes fiction, nonfiction, poetry, art, and children's books by distinguished authors and artists in our region and nationwide. Visit our web site at www.rivercitypublishing.com.

For my beloved friend, Barbara J. Durkin (1961–2002).
And for Steven Tiberi, Calla Durkin Tiberi, and Chase
Durkin Tiberi.

ACKNOWLEDGMENTS

First and foremost, I would like to thank my mother, Ruth Creter Borders, for always being there and for always believing in me. Although my father, Bert Borders Jr., died when I was a child, one of the many legacies he left me was in the stories he told me of his childhood in East Texas. I'm grateful to him for that, and for so much more.

For gifts of financial assistance as well as time and space, I am indebted to the Pennsylvania Council on the Arts, the Massachusetts Cultural Council, Hedgebrook, the Blue Mountain Center, and the Writer's Voice of the West Side YMCA.

I also wish to thank Nassim Assefi, Diane Caouette, Pat Conroy and Cassandra King, Jim Davis and everyone at River City Publishing, Barbara Durkin, Sarah Freligh, Gitana Garofalo, Denise Gess, Becky Hemperly, Eileen and Steve Hopkins, Teresa Leo, Bret Lott, Bill Lyon, Lisa Markowski, Matthew, Dan O'Brien, Craig Rancourt, John and Susan Rockefeller, Bill Van Wert, and David Walsh, as well as my many friends in the music folders of America Online.

Willie D. Little and Meryl S. Sussman of Youth Emergency Services in Philadelphia were instrumental in helping me to understand the mindset of a homeless teenager. The memoirs *Runaway* by Evelyn Lau and *Travels with Lizbeth* by Lars Eighner were also invaluable. Margaret Moser of the *Austin Chronicle* provided additional assistance.

Excerpt from *The Song of the Lark* by Willa Cather (Boston: Houghton Mifflin, 1983).

Finally, I'd like to thank all the bands whose music has sustained and inspired me over the years. Many—but certainly not all—of you are mentioned in these pages.

" . . . that stream of hungry boys and girls who tramp the streets of every city . . ."

—Willa Cather

PART I

CHAPTER 1
OCTOBER, 1977

My Grandma was the thriftiest woman in Prairie Rose, Texas. This was a self-proclaimed title. Thrifty is not the same as cheap, and it's not stingy, she'd tell me as we rode clear to Beaumont in her ancient New Yorker, seventeen miles just to visit a store that had paper towels five cents cheaper than the store near her home. Cheap is, however, exactly what Wendell at Wendell's Garage seemed to think of her when she'd bring the car in for yet another repair.

"Ma'am," he'd say, taking off his cap and smoothing his curly brown hair, "if you don't mind my saying so, you're being penny wise and pound foolish. It's time for you to invest in a new vehicle."

"That's the trouble with you young people today," Grandma would say. "You throw everything away." Remember now, this was 1977 or thereabouts, long before anybody except a handful of leftover hippies ever thought about recycling.

She'd look at me and say, "You witnessing this, Miriam? This young man wants to take all my life savings so he can sell me a new car, when my New Yorker's been doing right by me since your Momma was a girl."

"But Ma'am," Wendell would say, still working those curls with the palm of his hand, "I don't even sell cars here. I just fix 'em. And I make more money off *you*, Ma'am, than anybody in town. I just hate taking it from you, is all, when it feels like robbery."

"You hear that, Miriam?" Grandma would say. "Smooth, that's what they call that kind of talk. You know, Wendell, when your Daddy owned this garage he'd never have questioned but that a fine automobile like mine should be fixed and fixed until it up and died. You don't just abandon things, you know."

It was that word, abandon, that always made me sad, and Grandma didn't seem to notice it, but Wendell did. He'd give me a cold Coke if it was hot out, which it usually was in Prairie Rose. Sometimes he'd put the quarters in the machine for me, and sometimes he'd open it with a key. I had a crush on him almost from the first time I saw him, which would have been shortly after Grandma took me in, when I was eleven.

Wendell's hair was thick and curly, the color of sand on the beach. It was always mashed down in a cap, a different cap every time I saw him: Valvoline, Goodrich, Conoco, Lone Star Feeds. He wasn't tall, but his hands were huge, the skin on his palms rough and thick and tanned brown as baseball mitts. His fingers and under his nails were always stained with grease.

It didn't take long for me to decide that Wendell was my long-lost father. Never mind that his light blue eyes didn't match my dark brown ones, never mind that Wendell's last name, Hewlitt, didn't even come close to the name I was given on my birth certificate, Ortiz. I decided that Annmarie, my mother, had lied about who my father was, like she'd lied about so many other things in my life before the night she drove me in the pitch dark to Grandma's, leaving me half-asleep on the doorstep for Grandma to find with the milk and the morning paper.

Not that dumping me at Grandma's was the worst thing Annmarie'd ever done to me. In fact, it turned out to be the best. Grandma's house was the smallest and most weatherbeaten on Sour Lake Road, but it was a royal palace compared to the apartments and trailers I'd lived in with Annmarie. By the end of the first week I was at Grandma's, she had taken me shopping to three different towns for new clothes on sale, started me in school, and given me a list of chores to do—washing the dishes, taking out the trash, making my own bed. In exchange for this, I woke up every morning to a closet full of clean outfits, the smell and sound of flapjacks sizzling in the kitchen, a sandwich sitting in a bag, waiting for me to take. I knew a good deal when I saw one.

By the end of the second week, Grandma had me signed up for the church choir, after she heard me singing while I was doing the dishes one night. It was an old Bessie Smith song one of Annmarie's boyfriends back in Corpus Christi had taught me.

"Lord, child, where'd you get a voice like that?"

I shrugged, brushed my bangs back with my forearm so as not to get suds on my face. "Tommy Clayton taught me the song."

"Who's Tommy Clayton?"

"Annmarie's boyfriend," I said, leaving out the fact that he was about eight boyfriends ago. I didn't want to see Grandma get agitated.

"Now Miriam," she said, putting her hands on my shoulders, "you forget about all your Momma's doings. You're here with me now."

I wanted to ask her for how long I was there, but I knew better than to push my luck. Instead I said, "Is it okay if I still sing the songs Tommy taught me?"

She laughed. "I didn't mean you had to forget all that. You sing whatever songs you like."

I started practicing with the church choir the following week. Thanks partly to my voice, partly to the frequent gallbladder attacks that kept the church's best soprano away from too many rehearsals, within a month I became the youngest soloist ever at the Home Sweet Home Bible Church.

School and homework and choir practice and household chores still left me plenty of free time to wonder about Wendell. Once I'd decided he was my Daddy, I could think of nothing else but him. I imagined myself making change for the customers in the garage, wearing one of Wendell's caps, whistling the way he did to call Duke, his German Shepherd, whose black-and-tan coat always felt greasy from brushing up against the machinery. I could even see us down at High Island Beach, me throwing a frisbee for Duke to catch in the surf, Wendell laughing from the spot where I'd buried him in the sand.

Soon Grandma's car troubles were not frequent enough to suit my needs, and I had to find another reason to go visit Wendell on my own. One Saturday I hopped on my bike, an old no-speed of Annmarie's that Grandma had resurrected from the back shed, and rode it past the garage seven times until I thought up an excuse: I needed air in my tires.

"Is that right?" Wendell said, and he was smiling as he guided my bike over to the air pump.

When he was finished, he got me a Coke and sat me down on a chair in a corner of the garage.

"So Miriam," he said, wiping his hands with a grease-stained towel, "how do you like Prairie Rose?"

"I like to be called Miri," I said. One of Annmarie's boyfriends had made up the nickname because I hated Miriam so much, and it just stuck. "Prairie Rose is okay."

"Miri, is it?" Wendell laughed. "Fits you better. Your Grandma treating you okay?"

I nodded. "I like living with Grandma," I said. "Everything in her house has a place it belongs. When I lived with Annmarie, everything just ended up on the floor, or piled on the kitchen table." I threw Annmarie's name in to see what effect it would have on Wendell, if he'd gasp at the sound of it, sit me down and tell me how he was my Daddy and he and Grandma and I would all live together now, like a family.

Wendell just looked surprised, though, and I realized for a second that he might not be my Daddy, he might not even have known Annmarie when she lived here, and yet I was talking to him like he knew my whole life story. I hadn't been at Grandma's long enough to realize that everybody in Prairie Rose did, in fact, know my whole life story, and each other's.

"Annmarie's my Momma," I added.

"I know," he said. "I was just surprised you called her by her given name."

"She didn't like me to call her Momma."

Wendell shook his head. "That would be Annmarie for you," he said.

I felt my palms get sweaty then, and I rolled the cold Coke can in my hands to cool them down. I knew I'd been right. Wendell was going to claim me, and he would buy us a house with big windows and a sun porch for Grandma, a huge backyard for Duke. He'd be in the front row of the church every Sunday, beaming with pride at my solos, and after the service he'd accept compliments about my fine singing voice with a simple, "That's my girl." I rubbed the Coke can like it was a magic lamp that would grant me these wishes.

"I knew your Momma," he said, "in high school."

"Did you date her?" I blurted.

"Date her?" Wendell chuckled. "I wouldn't have had a chance. I was two years younger than your Momma, and she was dating seniors when she was still a freshman. I liked her, though. We all did." He had his cap off again, smoothing that hair.

"Why?" I wanted to shout, but it came out as a whisper. I felt anger flashing through my hands to the Coke can, a hot and bitter pain that seemed to turn the can instantly warm. It was a feeling I'd had many times toward Annmarie, but this time it was at Wendell, for not being my father. I imagined the can was a weapon I could use against all the people who'd hurt me in my life. That didn't leave too many still standing.

"Why what?" Wendell asked, innocent to the fact that I was about to destroy him with my mighty can.

"Why'd you all like her?"

"Well, Miri, your Momma was beautiful. You know."

I shook my head. Not even my powers of imagination could place Annmarie as a beautiful girl. By my earliest memory she looked hard and mean, and she probably wasn't even twenty yet.

"How long's it been since you seen your Momma?" Wendell asked.

"Not that long," I said. "It's just she was never beautiful, is all."

"Was when I knew her, honey," he said. "She had this long, shiny brown hair and these big old dark eyes, just like yours. Real sad eyes."

That was the final insult, worse even than him not being my Daddy. I looked nothing like Annmarie, at least not the Annmarie I'd known, and no one had ever before dared to say that I did. Wendell's fate was sealed.

"Her hair's blonde now," I said, putting the Coke can down like a grenade on the bench where he was sitting. "Bleached."

I ran for my bike, hopped on, and pedaled as fast as I could, my voice working up and down the scales they taught me at choir practice as my legs pumped the bike.

When I thought I was far enough away I let loose with my secret weapon, my high note, a sound so clear and piercing it could surely ignite an explosion that would take the whole town up into the sky, splitting it into pieces so small that even Grandma couldn't put them back together, pieces that would slowly bleed down like raindrops and then disappear, one by one, into the Gulf of Mexico.

CHAPTER 2
APRIL–DECEMBER, 1979

We angels had our instructions, straight from Mrs. Hallie Higgins, choral director at the Home Sweet Home Bible Church: we were to do whatever was in our power to keep Mrs. Evelyn Sprague from ruining the annual Easter play.

"She shouldn't even be in the play this year, let alone have the part of Mary," Mrs. Higgins told us angels at a dress rehearsal the day before the play. "If we weren't second cousins once removed, I'd tell her so in no uncertain terms." Mrs. Higgins fanned herself with a book of sheet music, peered down the hall to see if Mrs. Sprague was on her way back from the john yet. "But I couldn't do that to kin."

Mrs. Sprague was the lady with gall bladder trouble who I'd already replaced as star soloist in the choir. For twenty-five years she'd been the best soprano in the church, and although her health had been poor in recent years, Mrs. Higgins had worked around her. Once I had moved in, though, Mrs. Higgins lost her patience. I was only twelve, but could sing the sweat off Mrs. Sprague, and everyone in the church knew it.

The play we were rehearsing for was called *The Hammer and the Cross*, and it had been performed at the church for as long as the oldest living person in Prairie Rose could remember. It went through Jesus's life from his good deeds to his death on the cross to the resurrection.

According to Grandma, the old version of the play staged the resurrection as the grand finale, but one year—Grandma thought it was shortly after she was married—some pranksters started making horror-movie groans and whistles from the back of the church just as Christ rose from his cardboard grave. They were just kids playing around, Grandma said, but the minister was so upset that he and the ladies of the church rewrote the ending. Rather than an eerie figure of Christ arising from the grave, they switched to Mary lifting the baby

Jesus from his creche, and inserted at the end a song they took from an old Christmas play, "Sweet, Sweet Child of Bethlehem."

Since this song required a star-quality voice, it made the role of Mary—previously just a bit part—one of the most important in the play. The role went to the soprano with the most beautiful voice in the church, and for the past twenty-five years, that had been Mrs. Sprague.

Problem was, Mrs. Sprague had been getting sicker with each practice, some days looking pale and wrung out, others pink and feverish. The closer we got to the day of the play—which was performed, by tradition, the Sunday before Easter—the longer and more frequent her trips to the john became. By the day of the dress rehearsal, Mrs. Sprague was having a hard time just staying onstage with us long enough to warble out a weak version of the grand finale song. After the rehearsal was over, Mrs. Higgins took me aside as the others filed out of the church.

"If Mrs. Sprague faints dead away or can't sing, you pipe in with the song, Miri," she whispered in my ear.

And the next day, I did just that. Mrs. Sprague barely made it standing to the end of the play, and when the piano intro for the song started up it was clear we had a problem. Mrs. Sprague had to lift little Billy Spross—that year's baby Jesus—out of his cradle and hold him in her arms, casting adoring looks in his direction while she sang the song. Propped up by the chorus of us angels, Mrs. Sprague, who Grandma later said looked spent and green, more like a victim of some awful plague than the serene Mary, bent over to pick up the baby. Sweat dripped down her neck and onto me, the littlest angel, who was doing my best just to stay out of her way so as not to get crushed. Mrs. Sprague was, after all, a big woman. Lolita Clack, the five-foot nine-inch high school bombshell who stood at the far end of the angel chorus, tried to fan Mrs. Sprague with her cardboard wings, but her efforts were in vain. As I watched with a mixture of horror and fascination, Mrs. Sprague began to sink to the floor, the baby in her hands.

This was where Lolita and I became heroes: Lolita for saving Billy, me for saving the play. As Mrs. Sprague went down and little Billy seemed to float in the air, her hands dissolving beneath him, Lolita used her wings to knock two angels out of the way and made a wide-receiver's dive for Billy, just catching him before he hit the stage. We all stood dumbstruck for a second, and I peeked behind the curtains to Mrs. Higgins for guidance, but she was not there. I turned back around and, with all the courage I could muster, stood in front of the empty cradle, took a deep breath and began the song. Lolita stepped up beside me, the baby in her arms, and the picture of the two of us looking adoringly at little Billy Spross made the front page of the *Liberty County Justice-News* the following week.

I'd been in Prairie Rose for more than a year before that play, and in all that time I'd been something of an outcast. Annmarie had been notorious there, not so much for doing all the things a girl's not supposed to do in a small Texas town—drinking, drugging, sleeping around—but for doing it all so openly. When she had me at sixteen, she caused a small scandal by refusing to give my father's name, or, when pressed, by offering up a variety of possibilities: Bobby Kennedy; John Lennon; her high school algebra teacher, Mr. Branford. Best as I could tell she had no idea who my father was.

I don't know if folks continued to talk about her after I was born, when she took a job waitressing two towns away from Prairie Rose and moved us out of Grandma's house and into a trailer. I doubt they knew about the boyfriends that came and went from the trailers and apartments we lived in over the course of my life, for neither of us ever told Grandma. But I do know that the day my mother left me in Prairie Rose, the talk started up again, with a fervor that gave the impression folks were making up for lost time.

But that play changed everything. When I walked into the Kountry Kitchen for an after-school milkshake the next day, I was not greeted by the disapproving glances, the frozen half-smiles and nods I'd become used to. Instead, folks looked up at me and smiled, genuinely smiled, and I heard murmurs and whispers not about my trailer-trash mother, but about my beautiful voice. "Where'd such a little girl get such a big set of pipes?" the owner of the Kountry Kitchen asked as he handed me my milkshake, refusing to take any money for it. And as I tried to head out the door, an old couple seated in the corner booth begged me to sing "Amazing Grace" before I left, and when I finally did, everyone in the restaurant applauded me so hard their hands surely must have calloused.

Of course, Lolita Clack got the star treatment as well. When she took the court with her fellow cheerleaders at the high school basketball game that Wednesday night, it was said she got a standing ovation, even catching in mid-split the doll baby some prankster threw from the bleachers.

The topping on the cake came a few weeks later, when Mrs. Higgins, who also taught music at Prairie Rose Elementary School and directed the chorus there, asked me to stay after rehearsal one day.

"How old are you now, Miri?" she asked.

"Twelve," I said, not sure what her point was.

"And when will you be thirteen?" she asked, looking me up and down like I was a pair of slacks she couldn't make up her mind on buying.

"August, Ma'am," I said, throwing that last word in for good measure.

"August," she said, like the word had a lot of meaning. She tapped her ruby red fingernails on her desk. "So by the time of next year's Easter play, you'll only be a few months away from turning fourteen, is that right?"

"Yes, Ma'am," I said, and I couldn't help but smile. Now I knew what her point was.

"You'll be Mary next year," she said, giving voice to my thoughts, but she was frowning as she said it. "I'm sure you'll have a growth spurt soon." She winked at me. "When you become a woman."

I thanked her and scooped up my books, not having the heart to tell her I'd been a woman since I was eleven.

I turned thirteen that summer and started eighth grade in the fall, but still I did not grow. Other girls in my class shot up and out like crabgrass while I remained looking like a child. I'd been a woman, as Mrs. Higgins put it, for almost two years, yet I was still under five feet tall, had no titties to speak of and was so thin that Grandma had to buy my clothes in the children's department while other girls my age shopped in preteens and juniors.

I was now the shortest girl in my class, and some of the other kids saw fit to tease me about it. I was asked on more than one occasion if I was a midget, and finally had to sit on a girl and pull her hair until she begged for mercy, to get her to take it back. I told the other girls who witnessed this fight that the next one who called me a midget would have her hair pulled out by the roots and would be wearing a wig from Weiner's Five-and-Dime for their eighth-grade graduation, and this seemed to put an end to the talk around school.

But there was no hair-pulling that could stop the Blue Hairs, the old ladies who made up the main gossip squad of Prairie Rose. They said my growth had been stunted due to Annmarie's not feeding me right when I was little. Stale peanuts from the bars where she picked up men and crusts of bread not fit to throw out to the birds, that's what people said Annmarie had fed me. While this talk didn't bother me much, it greatly disturbed Grandma. She took me to the doctor several times that year, trying to find a reason why I wasn't growing.

All the women on Grandma's side—her own mother, Mathilde, as well as both her daughters, Annmarie and Melissa—stood over 5 feet 7, and had been way over five feet by the time they were my age. We came from good strong German stock, Grandma explained to the doctor, and so there had to be a physical reason why I was so tiny. Doctor Busbee would listen to Grandma, nodding at what she said while winking at me when she wasn't looking. He'd give me a shot of vitamin B complex to set Grandma's mind at ease and tell her not to worry. He said I was simply petite, called me a "little bitty flower," and told Grandma that what I lacked in height I made up for in the size of my singing voice.

But mere compliments about my voice could not throw Grandma off track. She read an article on calcium deficiency in the *Ladies' Home Journal* and decided that was why my bones weren't growing. She started me on a diet that included two glasses of milk, a cheese sandwich, and a whopping helping of green leafy vegetables each day. She measured my height every Sunday after church and dutifully recorded the numbers on the back page of her Bible, but in ten weeks I still didn't grow, not even a quarter inch. Grandma stopped measuring me after that, blaming my height on my grandfather's Cajun genes. Though he himself had not been a short man, Grandma said he had cousins over in Louisiana who stood only a bit over five feet, and that's men cousins she was talking about.

Of course, there was the question of who my father was, but neither me nor Grandma would make mention of that. Back when I was real little and used to ask Annmarie about my Daddy, she'd buy me a box of Milk Duds or give me a Coke and change the subject. When I got to be about six I started calling her boyfriends Daddy, just to get a rise out of her, but I soon outgrew that phase.

The real moment of truth had come in the third grade, when my teacher asked me to help her explain the Cinco de Mayo holiday to the class.

"What do you mean?" I asked, unnerved by all the eyes fixed on me.

"Well, how does your family celebrate it?" she asked helpfully.

"We don't," I said, still not sure what she was getting at.

The teacher dropped it there, but my curiosity got the better of me. After class I went up to her and asked her what she'd meant.

"Well, your name is Chicano," she said. "I thought you'd know something about the holiday."

Far as I'd known up to that point, I was half-Cajun and half-German, like my mother. Although I'd asked about my father many times, I'd never before connected that I had this last name, Ortiz, which must have been his. When Annmarie got home from waitressing that night, I bombarded her with questions. She listened impatiently while she rubbed her swollen feet.

"Ortiz isn't really your name," she said. "I picked it out of the phone book."

That was Annmarie's idea of humor, but flip answers like that just fueled my fire. I kept after her until she sighed loud enough that I knew I'd worn her down, and then she launched into a story that was probably the closest to truth I'd ever get: she said I simply had no Daddy. Some people had daddies, she said, and had them all their lives; others had daddies and lost them, like Annmarie did when she was twelve and my grandfather was electrocuted at the top of a utility pole he was fixing for the power company; and some people, like me, never had a Daddy in the first place, and never would.

Of course, by the time I was thirteen I knew Annmarie was no Virgin Mary. I'd had some kind of Daddy, even if all he'd had to do with my life was getting Annmarie pregnant. I tried to ask Grandma once, but she told me not to worry about such things, that I was her girl now and that was all that mattered.

I tried pumping Wendell for information, but he didn't seem to know anything.

"Not sure your Momma ever told your Grandma who it was, honey," he said, adjusting the hand brakes on the bright yellow ten-speed bike he and Grandma had pitched in on for my thirteenth birthday.

"But you must know, Wendell," I said, handing him a rag to wipe away the excess oil. "You knew Annmarie back when."

"Didn't tell me, either," was all he'd say. I thought what he really meant was she couldn't tell him because she didn't know herself, it could have been any boy in Sam Houston High School, classes of 1963 to 1967 or thereabouts. But I never let on that I thought so.

By this time I'd long ago forgiven Wendell for not being my Daddy. For some reason we just took to each other, Wendell and me, and since Grandma thought it was good for me to have a male figure in my life she encouraged our friendship. She'd known Wendell since he was a baby and trusted him with me, just as all of Prairie Rose trusted him with their cars.

Wendell's cousin, however, was a different story. Guy Thibodeaux was his name, and he lived over in Lake Charles, Louisiana. He started turning up in Prairie Rose the summer I turned twelve. First time Wendell introduced me to Guy was the first time I'd ever heard Wendell was part Cajun, and I told him so.

"On my Momma's side," he said. Wendell must have looked like his Daddy's side, for he and Guy didn't appear even remotely related.

"Me, too," I said, "my Granddaddy was Cajun. That's something we have in common, Wendell." I liked the thought of having some kind of common heritage with Wendell, the possibility that we could be oh-so-distantly related. I wanted Wendell to be family.

After the first time I met him, we started seeing a lot of Guy in Prairie Rose. He was a high school drama teacher over in Lake Charles, but began visiting many a weekend with his cousin Wendell. They spent Friday and Saturday nights at the Silver Moon Inn, Wendell told me when I asked, and I would imagine them dressed in their best cowboy boots and new jeans, talking up girls who wore as much makeup as Annmarie. I didn't much like the thought of it, Wendell and Guy and the trashy girls at the Silver Moon, but I never said so. Sundays Wendell would go to church to make up for his weekend sins, he would say, winking at me. Guy wouldn't attend with him, though. He'd walk down to the church toward the end of the service, and when it was over we'd find him outside, smoking a cigarette he'd rolled himself, waiting to have breakfast at the Kountry Kitchen with Wendell and me.

Grandma didn't like Guy one bit. She said he was "funny," but she wouldn't tell me what she meant by that. She did say it was proof of what a fine person Wendell was that he'd undertake to straighten out a cousin like that, but still she wished Guy didn't have to spend so much time around Prairie Rose. Grandma said Guy should stay over in Louisiana, where he belonged. I decided finally that Grandma just didn't like Cajuns, despite the fact that she'd been married to one.

I thought Guy was funny, too, but in a good way; he was one of the most entertaining people I'd ever met in my life. Guy could do three different kinds of English accents alone, explaining to me the differences in the parts of the country they came from. He knew all the lines to every movie ever made in the history of Hollywood, and he also knew all the blues songs Tommy Clayton had taught me, from Big Mama Thornton to Etta James. Sometimes after our Sunday breakfasts we'd put on Wendell's blues records and sing along with them, but Guy said that even though my voice was "gutsy" it was too high for blues. Instead he taught me some of Patsy Cline's songs and coached me more closely than Mrs. Higgins while I sang them.

The first time Guy set foot in the Home Sweet Home Bible Church was for the Easter play, the one Lolita and I saved. He told Grandma that I had "star quality," and this made her like him a little more, but not much. After Mrs. Higgins told me I'd play Mary, Guy learned the finale song himself just so he could coach me in private. He said he wanted me to blow the roof off the church. Wendell got so sick of hearing "Sweet, Sweet Child of Bethlehem" in his living room that sometimes he'd take Duke and go for a ride in his truck, just to get away. Guy and I didn't care that we'd kicked Wendell out of his own house; we had a mission.

Despite all the extra work I was doing with Guy, I noticed around Christmas that year that Mrs. Higgins had started frowning at me while I sang my solos. I knew my singing wasn't off, but it started gnawing at me that something was on her mind, and I worked up the courage one Sunday after services to ask her.

She looked startled. "I'm sorry, honey," she said. "Nothing wrong with that gorgeous voice of yours. I'm just trying to figure out how to make you Mary, you being so little and all."

By this time Grandma'd given up on my calcium diet, and I thought people would more or less get used to my size. But I could see that was not to be.

"Maybe Mary was short," I said.

She shook her head. "You just look so young, honey," she said. "It would be . . . well, it just wouldn't look right, having such a young-looking girl as a mother."

"But I thought Mary was a virgin," I argued. "What's the difference how old she was?"

"People would talk," she said, nodding to a group of the gossips as they hovered nearby and tried to listen in. "But don't you worry, honey. I'm fixing to have you sing 'Sweet, Sweet Child of Bethlehem' if it kills me. I'll figure something out."

CHAPTER 3
FEBRUARY–APRIL, 1980

What she finally figured out, as she announced when we started rehearsals in February, was that Mary would no longer sing the finale song. She told us players that she'd decided it made more sense for one of the angels looking down from heaven to sing that song. And the choice she'd made was the littlest angel: me.

Mrs. Sprague had already bowed out of the play, so there was no argument from her end. Problem was that Mrs. Higgins had bumped Lolita Clack, last year's tallest angel, up to the role of Mary. And although the whole town knew that my voice on a bad day was a hundred times better than her voice at its finest, Lolita's mother caused a fuss about her daughter getting the star role and not getting the star song.

To understand how truly petty this all was, you'd have to know something about the Clacks. They were the wealthiest family in Prairie Rose. Mr. Clack had a big cattle ranch on the outskirts of town which he'd bought with the oil money his granddaddy had made in the big booms at the turn of the century. It was said that any oil well you saw pumping from Houston to the Louisiana border was a Clack rig, and this was not entirely true. But they had fistfuls of money and a vacation house on the Bolivar Peninsula. Grandma said they only stayed in Prairie Rose to rub our noses in all they had.

Lolita Clack was one of those seventeen-year-olds who looked about twenty-five. She was captain of the Sam Houston High School Rebels cheerleaders, homecoming queen, and vice-president of the senior class rather than president only because she'd let her boyfriend run for the top spot. It was said she had other boyfriends, too, college boys at Lamar University down in Beaumont. But nobody knew if those rumors were true.

To be fair to Lolita, she didn't care a lick about singing that song. She was leaving at the end of the summer for a college in California, and she told me privately that she didn't even want to play Mary.

"It's all so much bull," she said, waving her hand regally in the air as if to dismiss the whole townful of us petty subjects. "I can't wait to get out of Texas." She looked around to make sure nobody had overheard. "Don't tell anyone I said that, 'kay, Miri?" She twisted a strawberry-blonde ringlet of hair around her finger. "My Momma'll kill me if I don't get Bluebonnet Queen this year." She walked out of the church and headed for her boyfriend's waiting sports car, tossing her long curls with each step.

The Prairie Rose gossips went into overtime with this business of the play. They said Mrs. Higgins had no right to change the play, that in fifty years it had only been altered once and that was to keep blasphemers from besmirching the good name of the Lord. To hear them talk, you'd think Mrs. Higgins had undertaken to rewrite the Good Book itself. Grandma said it was all Mrs. Clack's money talking, that people sided with her because they all wanted an invitation to the summer house on the Peninsula.

One day in early March—a day we had a break in the rains that fell over Southeast Texas throughout the late winter and early spring and got a taste of the sun that would bake us in the summer months—Grandma and I ran into Mrs. Clack and Lolita's little brother, Jimmy. They were headed out of Chappy's Market, and we were headed in. Grandma took my hand and tried to snub Mrs. Clack, but she said something that made Grandma stop in her tracks.

"Lot of nerve," she said, "girl who's only in town 'cause her Momma dumped her here, taking my Lolita's part in the play."

Grandma turned and stood, red-faced, in front of Mrs. Clack. Jimmy shifted uncomfortably from foot to foot, and smiled at me shyly. He was fourteen, a grade ahead of me in school.

"Why, what's the matter, Aurelie?" Grandma finally said. "Mrs. Higgins wouldn't accept your bribe money so your no-talent daughter could sing the song?"

Mrs. Clack started sputtering and screaming about how Lolita was the most talented girl in all of Southeast Texas, Grandma shouted back that Lolita's talent was all bottled in that jar of strawberry-blonde hair dye she used once a month, and in the midst of all this Jimmy walked away, motioning me to follow him. We walked down Main Street in silence for a minute, the voices of the two women now drawing a crowd.

"My sister doesn't even want to sing the song," he said finally, scuffing his feet on the narrow sidewalk.

"I know," I said. "She told me."

"She said your voice is better than hers," Jimmy added. "She told Momma one night at dinner to stop interfering in her life, and Momma slapped her hard on the cheek. She didn't go to school the next day 'cause her face was red." Jimmy stopped talking and put his hands in his pockets, a guilty look on his face for revealing too much.

I shrugged. "I don't care what your Momma says about me," I said. "But it gets Grandma real upset."

He nodded, and I noticed for the first time that Jimmy was short for his age. I'd never paid attention to other people's heights much; they were always bigger than me, and that was all I ever saw. Jimmy was only a couple inches taller than I was, but his lack of height didn't look natural on him. He looked like someone who'd been squashed down, compacted, but would spring up and stretch out one day when it was least expected. He was the kind of boy who would go away to summer camp for a month and come back six inches taller, with the voice of a bullfrog.

"That's all them fighting, you know," he said. "Got nothing to do with you or Lolita." He kicked at a stray bluebonnet that was growing by the side of the road. "Or me," he added, his voice real soft.

From that point on, it was said that Jimmy and I were going steady. What this meant was that he waited for me outside my school, carried my books and walked me home, being careful to leave me just before Grandma's property so she would not see him. Once when his Momma had to take Lolita somewhere after school Jimmy had me over to his house. There was a room with a pinball machine and a real soda fountain, and we ate so much ice cream and played so much pinball that by the time I went home I was shaking from the sugar, my fingers sore from banging on the flippers.

We kept it secret for about three weeks, but one Saturday afternoon we walked into the Kountry Kitchen hand-in-hand and came face-to-face with two of the Blue Hairs. We knew it'd get back to our families soon enough, so we decided to tell them ourselves at church the next day.

It did not go well. Mrs. Clack asked Jimmy if he'd lost his mind, being seen with a girl like me. Grandma wanted to know exactly what she meant by that, and the two of them started up all over again, Lolita rolling her eyes at her boyfriend while Jimmy and I sat on the steps, waiting for them to sort it all out. Finally Wendell stepped in, and I must give him credit for saving the day.

"Seems to me," he said, "the surest way to keep them together is to tell them they can't see each other."

Both Mrs. Clack and Grandma stopped in mid-sentence, and seemed to ponder this a minute.

"Wendell, you're a good mechanic, but what makes you an expert on teenagers?" Mrs. Clack finally asked, with that air of hers.

"Was one myself, Ma'am," he said. "Weren't you?" He sauntered away to where Guy was waiting by his truck, and winked at me as he passed.

Mrs. Clack and Grandma certainly did not make up that day, but they seemed to call a kind of truce. Mrs. Clack stopped reminding everybody about what Annmarie was like and how I came to live in Prairie Rose, and Grandma stopped her public speculation on what number Miss Clairol Lolita used. We were even allowed to visit each other on occasion, Jimmy and me, and that was what led to the final blow that set the families at war for as long as I remained living in Prairie Rose.

The day before the play, Jimmy's father had promised to take him out to their cattle ranch, and Jimmy had gotten permission for me to come along. Because I'd always liked petting the cows and sheep I passed on the way to school, I thought it would be fun to see a whole big cattle ranch. I imagined all the steers lining up behind a split-rail fence so I could kiss their thick grass-stained lips, one by one. When we got out to the ranch, I was surprised by how the cattle were sectioned off in different areas, and how funny the ranch hands looked at me when I talked to the animals in the baby voice I'd used on Mittens, the cat I'd had when I was little.

"They're not pets, honey," Jimmy's Dad said. "But you want to see something, we got a newborn calf in that barn back there."

He was pointing off to the right, but my eyes wandered to another part of the ranch where I saw cattle being driven into chutes. I asked what was happening there, and Jimmy and his Dad both looked at each other.

"You don't want to see that, Miri," Jimmy said. "Let's go look at the calf."

I went with them, and I did enjoy fussing over that calf. The ranch hand gave me a bottle to feed it with, and when it was done I let the calf suck on my fingers, his gums strong and hard on my hand. But still I was curious about what was happening on the other side of the ranch, and I kept asking until Jimmy finally told me.

"Those steers are ready for market," he said.

"What does that mean?" I asked, pulling my fingers from the calf's mouth and wiping them on my jeans.

"They're being slaughtered."

"Slaughtered?" I knew what the word meant but didn't want to understand it.

Jimmy took his index finger and ran it across his neck like his throat was being cut. "Slaughtered," he said.

I looked down at the calf. "Will he go for slaughter, too?" I asked.

"Sure," Jimmy said, patting the calf on the head. "It's natural, Miri. I mean, how else would we get steak and hamburgers?"

Now I liked my hamburgers as much as the next girl, but I'd never before connected that there was an animal the hamburger once had been. I let the calf suckle my fingers again, and tried to imagine it growing up and being ground up into burgers. My mind refused to connect the two pictures, and so I didn't feel much of anything about the whole business.

"I want to see," I blurted.

"What?"

"I want to see what it's like when they're slaughtered."

"You sure?" Jimmy looked around like he wanted to ask his Dad, but he was off talking to one of the ranch hands.

"I think I should see," I said, matter-of-fact. I had the compulsion of someone passing a bad car crash, to crane my head and take in as much death and destruction as I could.

Jimmy looked uncomfortable, but he walked with me around the back of the ranch, past the chutes, where wide-eyed, panicked-looking animals were being driven forward with prods and shouts from the ranch hands. I could feel the animals' fear, and it made me nervous, but I didn't let on. Jimmy stopped as we got to the door of the slaughterhouse.

"You don't faint at the sight of blood, do you?" he asked me.

33

I shook my head no, though the only blood I'd ever seen was when I'd skinned my knees learning to ride a bike. Jimmy opened the door, and it took my eyes a minute to adjust to the darkness in the barn.

What I noticed while my eyes adjusted were sounds—the high-pitched cry of an animal, the deep-voiced grunts and shouts of the men—and a terrible, rancid smell. It was a mix of blood, cow dung, and urine, but I was sure I smelled something else beyond that. I smelled death.

I felt light-headed already as the inside of the barn came into focus. Once I could see I understood why the men were all shouting: a barely grown steer had gotten loose and was running around the far side of the barn, chased by the ranch hands, its cries of fear mixing with the frustrated shouts of the men in an eerie chorus that echoed from the rafters. Jimmy tugged at the sleeve of my t-shirt for me to leave, but I stood rooted in my spot, and watched in horror as the men cornered the animal. One of them hit it between the eyes with a mallet, and they all hustled to lead the staggering animal over to a wooden platform before it collapsed. The last thing I saw before that steer and I both went down was the confusion and terror in its eyes as the shiny blade came across its throat.

When I woke up I was in the back seat of Mr. Clack's Lincoln Continental, a blanket pulled over my legs. I heard Jimmy speaking to me, but before I could answer Mr. Clack hit a dip in the road just as the picture of that steer's eyes came back to me; my stomach lurched, and I threw up all over the powder blue leather seat the two hot dogs I'd had for lunch. When I looked at the chunks of hot dog and thought about what they were, I threw up again. Jimmy was screaming at his father to stop the car, but I imagine by then he just wanted to get me home. He drove faster, I threw up over and over until there was nothing left inside me to wretch out, and finally Mr. Clack delivered me, red-eyed, pale-faced and covered in my own vomit, to Grandma.

As you might imagine this did not go over well. Grandma started drawing me a bath even as Mr. Clack and Jimmy were trying to explain through the bathroom door what had happened, but she barely seemed to pay attention. She got me in the tub, left and came back with a ginger ale for me to drink to settle my stomach, and asked me if I'd be okay for a few minutes. I nodded yes, and she closed the door with such a firm push that I knew she was now going to take on the Clacks.

I was careful not to splash any water so I could hear what was said, but I didn't have to be so cautious; Grandma was so mad that her voice boomed through the house, echoing so loud in the bathroom it was like she was in there with me.

"Now let me see if I have this straight," Grandma said. "The day before the Easter play that my granddaughter's set to star in, you took her to a slaughterhouse and exposed the child to such horrors that she pitched up a week's worth of lunches? Do I have this right?" Her voice shook with anger.

"It wasn't like that, Ma'am," Mr. Clack said. "The kids wandered in there, and . . ."

"Miri wanted to see it," Jimmy offered helpfully, but this did not set right with Grandma.

"You're trying to tell me that the sick little girl in that bathtub wanted to see such horrors?"

"No, Ma'am," Mr. Clack said, and I guessed he didn't know what Jimmy had said was true. "It was a mistake, a misunderstanding. They shouldn't have been in there. I'm terribly sorry."

"I bet you're sorry," Grandma said. "So sorry that you'll offer your daughter to take over the star solo in the play tomorrow."

"Now, Ma'am . . ."

"I know all about you underhanded Clacks," Grandma yelled. "I know how you operate. Get out of my house."

"Now hold on a minute, Mrs. LaCroix, I don't want you to get the wrong idea . . ."

I heard footsteps, and a sound like something slamming shut. Then Mr. Clack yelled, "Whoa! Now watch where you point that thing, Mrs. LaCroix."

I knew that Grandma had gotten her pearl-handled revolver—a gift, she'd once told me, from her Cajun mother-in-law—from the nightstand where she kept it beside her bed. I wanted to leap out of the tub to see Grandma holding the gun on the Clack men, but when I tried to get to my feet I felt dizzy and weak and sunk back into the tub.

"Now, you two best leave my house before I lose my good judgment and fire this thing," she said, her voice low and even.

I heard the front door creak and then slam shut. Then I heard footsteps, Grandma putting the gun back in the nightstand drawer. As the footsteps drew closer to the bathroom I began soaping my arms, trying to look casual.

Grandma bent down and looked me in the eyes. "Should I call Mrs. Higgins and tell her you won't be up to doing the play tomorrow?" she asked gently.

I shook my head no, reached up a wet hand and tugged at her housecoat for emphasis. But I didn't feel like talking or explaining myself.

"Okay, honey," she said. "We'll see how you feel in the morning."

News of my afternoon at the Clack ranch made a Prairie Rose all-time record for traveling through town, thanks to Mrs. Verna Owens, an official Blue Hair whose back property bordered on Grandma's. Mrs. Owens must have seen the Clacks drive up with me, and the condition I was in. She probably walked over to investigate just as Grandma was threatening the Clacks with her pearl-handled revolver, and waited at a safe distance until they'd left, biding her time to give Grandma a chance to cool down, before knocking on the door and asking what had happened.

"They took my granddaughter to their ranch and tried to kill her so Lolita could sing the star song in the play," Grandma said and, in her state of agitation, asked Mrs. Owens to please leave or else she'd have to go back and fetch her weapon.

Mrs. Owens wasted no time getting the word out. As best I could figure, she went straight into town and told all the cashiers at Chappy's Market, so they could spread word among the customers. That's how Miss Nelda Seale, the town librarian and fringe member of the Blue Hairs gossip squad, heard about it. The story had taken on many twists and turns by the time she met up with Wendell out in the store's parking lot.

"Little Miriam is in intensive care over at Liberty County Hospital," Miss Seale told Wendell. "Lolita Clack threw her in a bull pen and she got kicked nearly to death."

Wendell immediately called Grandma, who told him the real story, and by suppertime he and Guy were standing at the foot of my bed, asking me how I was feeling. By then I was in a clean cotton nightgown between cool, crisp sheets and no longer felt sick. But I didn't want to talk about what had happened. I was afraid if I saw that animal's face again I'd throw up all over the pink-and-white afghan Grandma had crocheted especially for me.

"Are you okay, honey?" Wendell asked, taking my hand in his.

I nodded, but tried to look a bit sicker than I felt. I was liking the attention.

"You don't have to sing tomorrow, you know," he added. "You got nothing to prove. Everybody knows you got the most beautiful voice in town."

I shook my head violently, but still I didn't feel like speaking. I looked at Grandma helplessly.

"I think she's planning on singing tomorrow," Grandma said. "But we'll see if she's up for it in the morning."

"She'll be up for it," Guy said, grabbing my foot and squeezing it, blankets and all. "Miri's a pro."

I lay in bed that night and tried to think about anything other than the cattle ranch. Grandma always said to think pleasant thoughts if I couldn't fall asleep, to picture fields full of beautiful flowers or an endless beach packed with starfish and seashells, but I found that night I could only think of things, people, I knew. I pictured Wendell and Guy at the foot of my bed; Mrs. Higgins, and Lolita in her angel costume; I imagined what Grandma had looked like, holding her gun on the Clack men.

Eventually my thoughts drifted to Annmarie. I pictured her in bed, different the way she sometimes was on mornings after she'd been drinking real heavy. She'd ask me to get her a glass of water and some aspirin, and after I brought it to her I'd sometimes crawl under the covers with her and just talk, tell her anything that crossed my mind, and those were the only times she ever seemed to really listen, the only times she gave me more than flip answers. I'd never understood why those were the best times with her; why, lying in bed with a head she said pounded worse than a teenager learning the drums, with dark circles etched so deep under her eyes they looked like they belonged there, she was more interested in hearing about school, or who I was friends with, or what piece of music they were teaching me in chorus, than she was when she felt better and, you'd think, would have more patience.

But now it made sense to me. Sick time was different than real time; it seemed to stretch as endlessly as the days of a summer drought, your head thick and dry like it was baked in the sun. It was simply too much trouble to talk, feeling this way, and whatever people were saying to you seemed removed, like something you weren't really part of. You could forget all the things people whispered about you, true or not, forget all the voices in your head of people who wanted you to succeed, and those who wanted you to fail. You could be, without effort, whatever people wanted you to be. Whatever they needed you to be.

I didn't speak at all that night or the next morning, but I would not let Grandma call Mrs. Higgins despite how sick she said I looked when I got up.

I had saltines and ginger ale for breakfast, put on my angel costume and made eyes at Grandma to get her to drive me to the church extra early. I wanted there to be no mistake but that I was singing that song.

When I got there, Mrs. Higgins looked relieved, having heard rumors about me that I could only imagine. Lolita tried to apologize for her brother, and I graciously nodded my head but still didn't speak. I practiced my scales, working my voice to loosen it up, but had no wish to make words or answer direct questions. Two of the other angels whispered that I must be in shock from getting kicked in the head by that bull, but I took no steps to correct the story. I was still on sick time.

But when show time came I took the stage as the littlest angel, moving stage left or stage right with the chorus when I was supposed to, and, when Lolita picked up the baby Jesus and the piano intro started for the finale song, I cleared my throat, opened my voice up full throttle and sang straight from my guts, empty as they were, a song of pain and fear and triumph that sounded only remotely like the hymn as Mrs. Higgins, or even Guy, had coached me to sing it. It was the song Annmarie might have sung when I was little, the day she packed us up, thinking she could leave the voices of the town behind; it was the song she might have sung the day she left me here to take on a burden that was really meant for her. It was the song that young steer might have sung if he could have broken free and kicked the daylights out of all the ranch hands, bounding out of the slaughterhouse and tramping down all the barbed wire in the state of Texas, turning it into an open plain where he could devour the sweet wild clover and nudge the cows with his gummy green-tinged lips. That Easter, I sang for us all.

CHAPTER 4
APRIL, 1981

I stood on Grandma's front step, not quite ready to go in despite the fact that I was a good half-hour late. Possible excuses ran through my mind: a trip to the library; a special church choir rehearsal; an extra-long practice with the Sam Houston High School Glee Club, where I'd made another Prairie Rose first by being the only freshman to solo in the history of the school's music department.

In truth, it was none of those things that had made me late. It was Troy Wilson, a junior and the star pitcher of the high school's baseball team. Troy's baseball practice had ended just about the time I got out of music rehearsal, and he'd offered to walk me home. It had turned out to be as long and slow a walk as he could possibly manage, looping the outskirts of town twice before making it to the end of Sour Lake Road. There, in the shadow of the boarded-up old farmhouse that Grandma swore attracted wild animals and was a public health threat, with the sun setting over the tall reeds and shoot grasses of the swamp land across the street, Troy had given me my first real kiss. My lips were still humming as I put my key in Grandma's door.

The front vestibule was pitch dark, which was unusual because Grandma always put the wall lamp on for me as soon as the sun began to set. I flipped on the light switch and walked through the short hallway that led to the kitchen. The house was so quiet I could hear the soft buzz of the ceiling fan in the parlor; I could smell the lemon Pledge Grandma dusted with in the afternoons. By this time of night, I should have smelled some macaroni and cheese baking, or something frying on the griddle—corn fritters, maybe, or green tomatoes—and any sounds from the kitchen should have been drowned out by the blare of the TV in the next room. Grandma wouldn't admit she was hard of hearing and refused to wear her hearing aid; in the three years I'd been living with her, she'd been turning the TV up louder and louder, to the point where Wendell once joked that he could hear it clear across town at the garage, that Duke sometimes had to put his paws over his ears to block out the noise.

I knew something was wrong, but I thought at first it was just that I was in trouble. Maybe Grandma had gotten worried because I was late, and had gone out to look for me. Maybe she'd been watching out the window, waiting for me to come home, and had made out our two figures down the road, kissing in the dusk. Maybe she had taken her pearl-handled revolver and gone after Troy.

After the whole Jimmy Clack thing, Grandma had sat me down to have a long talk about boys. She'd told me that the male organ had a mind of its own and that, once a boy hit puberty, that second mind took over, simply using the boy's body to do its dirty work. She'd said all I had to do was look around at the women in our family—my own mother, Annmarie, who'd had no help in raising me, and Aunt Melissa, whose husband, rumor had it, snuck away from work Tuesdays and Fridays to an apartment he kept in Houston for a girl who'd once been his secretary—to bear witness to what she was saying. Grandma said the only good man she'd ever known had been my Granddaddy, and he had been struck down in the prime of his life—either by the devil for refusing to do his handiwork, or by God, to punish Grandma for marrying a Catholic. She wasn't sure which.

"Tommy Clayton was a good man," I told Grandma. "He was nice to me."

I'd learned most of my blues songs from Tommy nights when he'd stayed with me, when Annmarie was nowhere to be found. This was back when I was eight or nine, when Annmarie's drinking had gotten real bad. Tommy, who sold illegal fireworks from a shack off of Route 35 but was otherwise clean-living, had already broken it off with Annmarie, but he made an agreement with me: if I needed help, I could call him. And since I had no one else to turn to— we lived in Corpus Christi by then, too far away from Grandma—I did call him, once or twice a week. I tried to space the calls out so as not to become a pest. He'd come over with his guitar and get me to sing, tell me not to worry, my Momma would make it home, just like she always did. Tommy eventually got a construction job in El Paso and moved clear across the state, but he was a good man while he was around.

"And Wendell," I added. "Wendell's a good man, Grandma. I know you think so."

Grandma looked at me, a clear, piercing look, and sighed. "He is good, Wendell is," she said. "He's just seen too much."

I asked her what she meant. "In the war, honey," she said. "I think that's why he'll never marry. But he's a good boy; always was, from the time he was little."

I knew that Wendell had fought in Vietnam; he'd given me his dog tags, which I sometimes wore like a necklace. He'd said if I ever got lost, I could always be found that way. But I'd never thought about the fact that he was in a war, about what he might have seen, or done.

After our talk about boys, Grandma had said she felt I was a sensible girl and would not give in to the devil's temptation, but, just to be safe, I was not allowed to date until I was seventeen—a year older than Annmarie was when she had me. I knew this was crazy strict, but I didn't give her any backtalk about it. Truth be told, knowing I had a crazy strict Grandma with a pearl-handled revolver in her nightstand drawer had kept Troy walking me home for almost a month before he'd even tried to kiss me, and I liked making him take his time. It wasn't that I believed in the devil or any of that; I just didn't want to end up like Annmarie.

I called out for Grandma, there in the quiet of the house, but as I expected there was no answer. I had a real fear she'd gone after Troy, and headed for her bedroom to see if her gun was still there. But as I made my way past the parlor doorway, I heard a sound that stopped me. It was the sound I'd thought was the buzz of the ceiling fan, but as I got closer I realized it wasn't the ceiling fan at all. It was the chirping sound the phone makes when it's been off the hook for a while.

As soon as I stepped into the parlor I saw her there, on the floor, the phone in her hand. She was wearing her favorite housecoat—a print, pale yellow with big bright sky blue morning glories all over it, a silky nylon thing I'd given her two Christmases ago. Her back was to me, but I knew right away she was dead; I can't explain how, something about the way her hand curled around the phone receiver, something about how empty her body seemed. It wasn't like she was sleeping, like a body with a person inside who's just taking a rest; she was gone from her body, Grandma was. I knew it like I knew my own name.

Later, Wendell and Police Chief Davies would say I was in shock from the minute I saw her, and would use that to explain the accusations I made that day. But I wasn't in shock. I saw the whole thing way too clear: Annmarie had called and aggravated Grandma into a fatal heart attack.

I sat down and tried to imagine Grandma's last minutes on this earth, to sort it out so I could tell it clearly to the police. The smell of the lemon Pledge meant that she had dusted, which she usually did between 3:00 and 4:00 in the afternoon. At 4:00, she always sat down to watch *The Merv Griffin Show*. And at 5:00, she started dinner. That meant that she had died during Merv. The phone rang; she shut off the TV so she could hear better, picked up the receiver and heard the voice of her no-account daughter. And it was that voice that had killed her.

Other thoughts came to me in those moments before I called Wendell: for one, the idea of Grandma in pain, feeling the same fear and panic of that steer in the Clack slaughterhouse; worse, maybe. I wondered how much it hurt to die. I thought, too, about myself, about where I'd live and who would take care of me. I knew right off I was up a big creek, but I pushed this and all other disturbing thoughts as far back as I could get them. Instead I decided to focus on getting Annmarie convicted of murder.

The first thing I had to do was get the phone out of Grandma's hand. Her fingers had already started to stiffen, but not so much that I couldn't gently uncurl them from the receiver. When I got the phone free, her arm fell to the floor with a dull thud.

"Sorry, Grandma," I said, looking down at her face. Her gray hair capped her head in soft swirls and dips, like frosting. Her eyes were as blank as a teddy bear's.

I clicked the phone down until the dial tone came back up, and called Wendell at the garage, hoping he hadn't already closed for the night and gone to dinner at the Kountry Kitchen. When I heard his voice was the first time I felt tears come to my eyes.

"Wendell, Grandma's dead," I said. "Annmarie killed her."

"What? Miri, honey, that's not the kind of thing you should joke around about." I could hear the clanking sound of the garage door being pulled shut.

"I'm not kidding," I said, and the tears started to flow freely. "Grandma's dead, Annmarie killed her over the phone. Wendell, I don't know what to do."

"I'll be there in ten minutes," he said, and hung up the phone before either of us could say anything else.

While I waited the longest six minutes of my life, Wendell running red lights clear across town trying to get to me in a hurry, more and more unwanted thoughts came to mind. Like: what if I hadn't gone to school that day? Or, what if I'd skipped glee club practice and come home early? I might have answered the phone myself and hung up on Annmarie, saving Grandma the aggravation that surely had killed her. Or I might have found her still alive, called the rescue squad, and saved her myself as I waited for the ambulance, by blowing in her mouth and pressing on her chest as they'd taught us in school. The very next week she could have been back at home in her own bed, listening as I read to her the account of my life-saving heroics in the *Liberty County Justice-News*.

Wendell pulled into the driveway with a screech of brakes, like a man with the law on his tail. He left Duke in the cab of the truck and I led him inside, to Grandma's body. Wendell felt her neck for a pulse, then shook his head softly. He wanted to call the rescue squad, not the police, but I wouldn't let him. I explained to him about Merv Griffin, and the TV being shut off, and how it all proved that Annmarie had killed her.

"No one is touching Grandma until the police get here," I said through tears. "This is a crime scene." I admit maybe I'd watched one too many *Starsky and Hutch* episodes, but I was convinced of what had happened.

"Okay, honey, I'll call the police," Wendell said, and the way he touched me so soft and kind on the shoulder made me cry that much harder.

He led me out of the parlor and sat me at the kitchen table. "Stay put," he said, and there was that hand on my shoulder again. He went back in the parlor to call the police, and even though I could tell he was trying to keep his voice low it wasn't hard for me to hear him.

"Listen, Chet," Wendell was saying, and I knew he was talking to Chet Davies, chief of Prairie Rose's five-man police force, "Adelia LaCroix is dead. Looks like a heart attack."

There was a pause.

"I wanted to, but Miriam insisted I call the police. You know Miriam. Annmarie's girl."

The next pause gave me time to feel a flash of anger at him for linking me with Annmarie like that. I hadn't been Annmarie's girl for a long, long time.

"Right," Wendell said. "Anyway, she's convinced her Momma somehow killed Mrs. LaCroix. Can't talk her out of it." Wendell said something after that, but he whispered it so low that I couldn't make it out.

"Thanks," Wendell said after another pause, "we'll be here," and I scrambled to take my seat at the table before he got back in the kitchen. He found me there with my hands folded atop Grandma's embroidered lace tablecloth.

"Honey, Chief Davies'll be here in a few minutes. You want something? A Coke, maybe?"

I shook my head, and took a deep breath. "Wendell, where am I going to live? Annmarie doesn't want me back, and even if she did she'll be in jail for life on this murder charge."

Wendell shook his head. "Your Momma's not going to jail, Miri. Chief'll explain it all to you."

"But she doesn't want me."

Wendell sighed. "Miri, your Grandma told me once she had an arrangement worked out in case anything happened to her. Your Aunt Melissa'll take care of you."

"Oh, no way, Wendell!" I was out of my seat, shouting. "No way in hell I'll live with her and her snooty kids."

I'd never really talked about Aunt Melissa to Wendell; just hadn't come up. So Wendell didn't know how much I'd dreaded Christmases from my earliest memory, all because we spent them with my snobby aunt and uncle and my cousins.

Back when I was little—when Annmarie and me lived in an assortment of trailers and run-down apartments in Vidor, Liberty, and Beaumont, before we moved out to Corpus Christi—Grandma would drive over from Prairie Rose on Christmas Eve and take me to church. She thought it was a disgrace that Annmarie never took me. After services she'd drive me back to Annmarie's and stay with us overnight, reading me bedtime stories that had something to do with the baby Jesus. Personally I didn't care so much for those stories, but I loved the attention. She'd leave a cup of hot cocoa by my bed and tell me that Santa had left my presents over at Aunt Melissa's, and that was always where the holiday went downhill.

The three of us would drive up to La Porte in Grandma's car, Annmarie bad-mouthing her sister the whole way there. Aunt Melissa was only two years older than Annmarie, but they couldn't have been more different. No sweaty nights with juvenile delinquents in the flatbeds of pickup trucks for Melissa. As a teenager my aunt had spent her Saturday nights at sleepovers with the other prissy girls of Sam Houston High School, manicuring each others' nails, setting their hair on cardboard containers that once held orange juice concentrate, turning their noses up at the dirty biker crowd Annmarie ran around with. This was all according to Annmarie, but I could see the evidence in Grandma's photo albums: Melissa with her flipped-up *That Girl* hair, frosted lipstick, and peter pan collars, Annmarie in a suede fringe jacket and tight jeans, her black eyeliner smeared beneath her lower lashes.

Aunt Melissa had gone on to junior college, and it was there she snagged Uncle Tom, who was going into his father's hardware business. It doesn't sound like much, except it grew into the biggest hardware chain in Eastern Texas and Louisiana; most anyone who grew up around those parts in the '70s and early '80s would remember the low-budget jingle from the radio ads: Spears Hardware, Fixin' What Ails You. Aunt Melissa and Uncle Tom acted like they were embarrassed Annmarie and I existed, but they graciously allowed us in their home once a year because Grandma wouldn't come without us.

At the Spearses', I'd watch their three kids—two boys and a girl, all with the lackluster straw-colored hair and scary Nazi blue eyes of their father—tear open piles of packages. They had so many presents that some years I couldn't count them. They tore the wrapping off like wild dogs ripping through garbage and dismissed the gifts so quickly that I couldn't keep tabs on all three kids and keep count at the same time.

For me, aside from the presents Grandma brought, there'd be one gift under the tree—a box marked "from the family." It always contained the same thing: a few pieces of clothing outgrown by my cousin Mary Gay, who, even though she was younger than me, always stood at least two inches taller than I did. I knew the clothes were hers because she'd usually find a chance to get me alone and tell me, to remind me of what trash I truly was.

I tried to think of a way to explain this to Wendell, but I felt it reflected bad on me. After all, I had my pride. Instead I said, "I really don't think Aunt Melissa will want me."

"She'd be lucky to have you," Wendell said. "Nice girl like you."

"What about you?" I asked, grabbing his wrist. "Wendell, I could live with you. I'd cook you dinner every night, and pack you a lunch in the morning." Living with Wendell was a fantasy I'd had ever since I'd met him. When I was eleven, I'd wanted him to be my Daddy. Now I pictured myself as his wife.

Wendell laughed, but he looked at me sweetly. He knew exactly what was on my mind. "I bet you would do all that," he said. "But Miri, folks here in Prairie Rose wouldn't take too kindly to me taking a child bride."

"Then you could adopt me!" At this point, I didn't care what he was to me, so long as I could live with him. I knew what a bad fix I was in. "Come on, Wendell, you know I wouldn't be any trouble."

Now Wendell looked down at the floor, and didn't speak for a time. "Miri," he said slowly, "I don't have a wife. They'd never let me adopt you. A man all alone taking in a fourteen-year-old girl? People'd think bad of it."

"Then we could move," I said, my words fast and desperate. "We could move to Nashville. I'll become a famous country singer, and you can be my manager."

Wendell shook his head, but before he could answer me the doorbell rang. "That's the chief, honey," he said, and went to let him in.

Chief Davies went right in the parlor, me following, trying to explain about Merv Griffin and the TV being off, and my suspicion it was Annmarie who'd called. The chief listened, feeling Grandma's wrist for a pulse while I spoke. When I was all done, he picked up the phone and called the rescue squad.

"Chief, wait a minute!" I pulled on his arm. "They'll destroy the evidence."

The chief gave our address to the rescue squad and hung up the receiver. "Now Miriam, I want you to listen good to me," he said. "Your grandma probably was trying to call for an ambulance."

"No, Chief," I said. "I told you. The TV was off. If she was trying to call the rescue squad, I don't think she'd waste time walking all the way over to the TV and turning it off first. She turned it off because somebody called." I wondered how the chief could hold such a job when he seemed to pay no attention to important details.

He sighed, took off his hat and drummed his fingers along its hard blue rim. "Okay, let's say you're right. Your Momma called up and got in a fight with your Grandma, and that fight brought on a heart attack."

I nodded.

"Well, sweetheart, your Momma still wouldn't go to jail. She wouldn't have meant to kill your Grandma. Would have been an accident."

I thought about this for a second. "What about when drunk drivers kill people? That's an accident, right? But they still go to jail."

The chief shook his head. "It's not the same thing, Miriam."

46

"Why isn't it the same thing?" I asked, but I was crying by then and I could tell by the look on his face he wasn't taking me seriously. "You tell me how that's different." Wendell put both his arms around me. "She did it on purpose, Wendell," I sobbed. "Annmarie couldn't stand me being happy. She killed Grandma so I wouldn't have a place to live."

"Shh, Miri, it'll be okay," Wendell whispered, but I knew better than that.

Wendell stayed there in the house with me that night, after Aunt Melissa told him she couldn't make it down until morning. When I heard her car pull up outside the next day, it was early, and I was still in bed, Duke stretched out next to me. As Wendell and Aunt Melissa began to talk I stroked Duke's big furry head and stayed real quiet, so I could hear what they were saying.

"I've already taken care of the funeral arrangements by telephone," Aunt Melissa said in the finishing school diction Annmarie once told me she'd copied from old movies.

"I'm not worried about the funeral arrangements," Wendell said, and he sounded tired, like he'd slept even less than I had. "I'm worried about Miri."

"Well, she can't stay with my family," Aunt Melissa said. "She doesn't get along with my children."

"Now Melissa," Wendell's voice raised a bit, "your mother told me she'd worked this out with you. If anything happened to her, you'd take Miri."

Aunt Melissa sighed, loud and exaggerated. "Yes, I did tell her that," she said. "But come on, Wendell. My mother was only sixty-five years old. I just never thought she'd die before Miri was grown up. Or run off with some low-life."

"Miri is not Annmarie, you know," Wendell said, slow and deliberate. "She's a good girl. Folks around here respect her for her singing voice."

"Don't I know it? That's all I ever heard from my mother. Miri's in the church choir. Miri's soloing in the school chorus. My daughter Mary Gay sings like a nightingale, but did my mother ever brag about her?"

There was a pause. I could picture Wendell smoothing his hair like he did when he was trying to figure what to say next. "Melissa, this girl's in an awful fix. She's got nowhere to go."

"Yes, she does," Aunt Melissa said. "I've already talked to Annmarie. Let me tell you, I was up half the night tracking her down in New Orleans. She's on her way here as we speak."

With that, I pushed Duke aside and jumped out of bed. I pulled on a pair of jeans, took a whiff of the t-shirt I'd slept in and decided it could stay on. I paced the floor in a panic, wondering how my life could turn into such a mess so fast.

It had been three years since I'd seen Annmarie, that night she'd left me at Grandma's. Those last few months we were together, she'd started doing cocaine—a lot of it. I still don't know exactly how she got the money for it; don't really want to know. She was in the worst shape I'd ever seen her; her mood swings were wild, screaming and throwing things and shaking with anger one minute, crying and trying to hug me the next. Tommy Clayton was long gone by then, and I spent as much time as possible at the home of Sharon Wilson, a girl in my sixth-grade class whose friendship I'd sought out mostly for this purpose. Sharon lived in a two-story house with a pool in the backyard, and parents who liked to play Scrabble after supper in the evenings. I saw Sharon's potential as best friend material as soon as she'd turned up in my class that fall; she was both pretty and smart, and it didn't take the other girls long to decide they hated her. She was labeled "stuck-up" and ignored in the lunch room, and so it didn't take me but a few weeks of being nice to her to work my way into a standing weeknight dinner invitation at the Wilsons', with Friday night sleepovers implied. As Annmarie started acting crazier I spent more and more time at the Wilsons', until I was practically living there and Sharon's parents became suspicious.

One Saturday morning after driving me home from a sleepover, Mr. Wilson insisted on coming in to meet Annmarie, rather than dropping me off the way he usually did. The building where we lived wasn't in the best part of town, but it didn't look too bad from the outside. Inside, though, was a different story, and I tried my best to keep Mr. Wilson from coming in, but this time he wouldn't listen to any of my excuses.

I opened the door with my key, calling out Annmarie's name to warn her in case she was smoking pot, or on the couch with some guy. She didn't answer. I opened the door, and as we walked into the kitchen I saw it through Mr. Wilson's eyes—the table, piled with old newspapers and bills Annmarie hadn't yet paid, dirty ashtrays, beer bottles, and a fly swatter that I hoped Mr. Wilson wouldn't figure out we used for the roaches; the sink, overflowing with dirty dishes; the wallpaper, badly singed from a time Annmarie had tried to cook when she was wasted and nearly burned the place down; the ancient spills on the stove and the floor, leaving odd-colored lumps too numerous to count. I left him there and walked through the living room to Annmarie's bedroom, opening the door without knocking, shutting it firmly behind me.

She was in bed, half-dressed, half-passed out. I said her name and tried to shake her awake; she muttered something I couldn't make out. Her breath didn't smell, so I figured it was drugs she'd done the night before—Quaaludes, maybe. She sometimes did those when she hadn't slept for nights from the cocaine.

I went out and told Mr. Wilson that my mother had been waitressing late the night before, that she was sleeping and I didn't want to disturb her. He asked if I wanted to stay the weekend with Sharon, but I said no, and continued to say no when he asked if I was sure. He finally left, telling me to have Annmarie call him as soon as she woke up.

She slept most of the afternoon. By the time she got up, the Wilsons had already called twice. The last call, they'd wanted to know if I had any relatives in the area. I knew they were thinking about calling somebody—the police, maybe, or Child Services—but I was afraid to tell any of this to Annmarie. I knew she'd make it into my fault somehow.

I made coffee and waited for her to drink it and smoke a cigarette before I brought the subject up. We were sitting in the living room, on the couch. A bong, a bag of pot, and two more dirty ashtrays sat on the coffee table in front of us.

Annmarie's eyes got wild as I filled her in on what had happened. "Let me get this straight," she said. "He was in here? In the living room?"

"I don't think so," I said. "I think he stayed in the kitchen."

"But you don't know for sure," she said. "Shit, Miri, what's wrong with you? All this pot is just sitting here. He could get the cops over here any minute."

"I don't think he would do that," I said. It was a lie.

"You don't think," she said. "Well, ain't that the truth. You never think, Miri."

Cigarette in hand, she paced the room furiously in her short red kimono, which she swore was silk but which was actually polyester. After a couple of trips around the living room she stubbed out the cigarette and pulled a white paper packet from her purse, then a mirror and a straw.

"You said you were going to stop doing that," I said. She promised to quit all the time, and of course, I never believed her; I just wanted to make her feel bad about it.

"I just need to clear my head," she said, cutting a line on the mirror with the edge of a matchbook.

By the time she finally called Mr. Wilson, Annmarie was wired. She told him a long elaborate story about how her teenage son had had a party when she was at work, and how he was cleaning up the mess as she spoke. I just shook my head; the Wilsons knew I didn't have a brother. When she hung up the phone, I told her this.

"Why the hell didn't you let me know?" she yelled. Her eyes darted around, her hands flailed, and I knew she was looking for something to throw, so I got out of her way. Her hand landed on an empty beer bottle, which she pitched against a wall. "Why do you tell people so fucking much about us?"

There was no sense in answering a question like that, and so I waited to see what she'd do next.

"He wouldn't call the cops," she muttered. "Would he?" She sat down and did another line of coke. "Maybe he didn't see the bong." She licked her finger and ran it along the insides of the coke packet, then sucked the white powder off. "Possession of cocaine—is that a felony, Miri?"

Before I could think of an answer to that, we both heard a loud knock on the door of the apartment next to ours. It was probably just someone visiting our neighbors, but Annmarie and I looked at each other and at that moment we were both thinking the same thing: cops. They were at the wrong apartment, Annmarie whispered; God was looking out for us. Annmarie only mentioned God at times she thought she was in real trouble.

"One bag," she said, and I knew what that meant. Within five minutes we were packed and heading, each of us with a duffel bag in hand, down the fire escape, to the parking lot behind our building, where the beat-up old Cutlass Oldsmobile Annmarie had inherited from one of her boyfriends was waiting for us to make our escape.

Once Annmarie had turned onto Route 77, I knew we were headed for the Mexican border. I asked her why we were going to Mexico, but she just shook her head and lit a cigarette. I turned the radio onto a rock station I knew she liked; they were playing her favorite Lynyrd Skynyrd song, "Tuesday's Gone," and I was hoping it would calm her down. Just before Brownsville she pulled over to the side of the road and climbed in the back seat, started digging through her duffel bag. She came up with the bong, the bag of pot, and a vitamin bottle that I figured held something other than vitamins. She got out of the car and laid it all down by the side of the road, then got back in and just sat there, her whole body vibrating the way it did when she'd had too much coke.

"Don't just sit there," I finally said. "Drive. Before somebody comes."

She started the car back up, put it in drive, then back into park. She licked her lips nervously, and glanced over at the side of the road. Finally she got out, gathered up all the drugs, threw the stuff in the big leather purse she carried and turned the car around.

"We'll go see Tommy," she said, and headed back to Route 10, toward El Paso. I knew better than to say a word about it. We lost the rock station eventually, and all we could get was country. I sang along with George Jones, Loretta Lynn, Hank Williams, and when I didn't know the songs I made up the words. I sang low enough that it didn't bother Annmarie.

We drove for hours, and eventually I fell asleep. I woke once or twice with the feeling we'd turned around; I was sure at one point I saw a sign for San Antonio, when we'd already passed through there hours before. But I was too sleepy to ask, and let myself sink back into the darkness. The next thing I knew, we were parked in front of a small house, white or off-white from what I could tell. It wasn't light yet, but the sky was that dark brown color it turns just before the sun rises. I could hear the birds already starting up.

"Where are we?" I asked, rubbing my eyes.

She led me out of the car by the arm, my duffel bag in her other hand. I was still sleepy enough that I thought maybe it was a dream.

"This is the best I can do, Miri," she'd said, and she stood and stared at me as I came awake enough to recognize the house—my grandmother's. I hadn't seen her since we'd moved to Corpus Christi, more than two years before. For a second I thought she was going to hug me, or say, "I'm sorry," scoop me in her arms and carry me back to the car. But she just stood there, looking at me like she was taking a picture, and then she was gone, and as always I was the one left with the explaining to do.

Wendell and Aunt Melissa were still talking in the parlor, but I knew all I needed to know. I was not going to wait around to see what kind of shape

Annmarie was in this time. I pulled the old duffel bag from the bottom of my closet and began packing.

Wendell came in when I was halfway through. "Miri, you awake?" he asked, and then he saw me standing by the window, folding a couple of t-shirts. "Honey, what are you doing?"

"I'm leaving, Wendell," I said. "I'm not waiting around for Annmarie to get here."

"You heard all that, did you?" He sat down on the foot of my bed. "Honey, let's just see what your Momma has to say when she gets here."

"She's got nothing to say I want to hear," I said.

"So where you planning on going?"

I looked at him out the sides of my eyes.

"Guess if you told me it wouldn't really be running away, huh?"

I nodded, pulled a few pair of tube socks from my drawer.

"Look, why run off now? Maybe your Momma will decide to settle here. Then you'd still see me all the time."

The thought that Annmarie might stay in Prairie Rose hadn't occurred to me. By the way she'd always talked about the town, I knew it wasn't likely. "She won't settle here," I said. "She hates it here. She'd rather live in that whorehouse in New Orleans." I threw that part in to shock Wendell, but he just looked pained.

"Your Momma doesn't live in a place like that," he said, stroking Duke's muzzle. "Look, just sit tight until she gets here. If you don't like what she has to say, you can always run off later on, right?"

It did make a kind of sense. There was no time limit for when I could run away, or from who.

I looked at the socks in my hand, stuffed them in the duffel bag. "Alright, Wendell," I said, "I won't go right off. But I'm leaving my bag packed, in case I have to go in a hurry."

He nodded. "You want to say hi to your aunt?"

I shook my head. "I hate her," I said. "She's stuck-up."

Wendell laughed. "Always was, honey," he said. "Some folks never change." He ran his hand through his hair for a minute, then added, "But some do."

I nodded like I agreed, but I didn't. None of the people I'd known in my life had ever changed. Especially not Annmarie.

Chapter 5
April–June, 1981

Annmarie pulled up late that afternoon in a beat-up old Cadillac the color of Pepto-Bismol. Wendell and I watched out the window as she leaned against the car, smoking a cigarette, staring at the house like she couldn't believe she was there.

"It's her pimp's car," I said to Wendell, to break the silence.

"Come on now, Miri. Where'd you learn a word like that?"

"High school," I said. I thought a minute, then corrected, "TV."

Wendell shook his head. "Your Momma always did like flashy colors, though. Wonder how she drove in those shoes."

I looked out the window again and realized that Wendell's comment about flashy colors had more to do with Annmarie's get-up than it did the hot pink car. She was wearing blood-red jeans, a size too tight, and a stretchy top with red and gold stripes. Her shoes were open-toed, gold, with about three inches of heel. Her hair was dyed red now, but not reddish-brown like mine was natural. Hers was bright orange. I watched her throw the cigarette butt down on Grandma's driveway and grind it into the asphalt with the ball of her shoe. Grandma wouldn't like that, I thought.

When she turned and headed for the door, I retreated back into the parlor. Let Wendell deal with her first, I figured.

"Hey there, Annmarie," I heard Wendell say.

"Who? Holy shit! Wendell Hewlitt! Is that you?"

Wendell laughed. "Glad you could recognize me. Guess I'm not getting too old."

I couldn't believe it. Wendell was flirting with Annmarie. Probably wanted to sleep with her, like every other man who'd ever met her. I felt a stab of anger at him. Of all the people I'd ever known, I thought Wendell was one who'd always be on my side. And he was, but just then it seemed to me there were two opposite sides in the world: mine, and Annmarie's. And if you were on hers, you couldn't be on mine.

"What are you doing here?" she asked. Her accent sounded a bit off—more New Orleans, I guessed, less Texas.

"Staying here with your daughter. We've become real tight since she came back here."

"I don't mean that. My mother told me all about that. I mean, what the hell are you doing in Prairie Rose? Why'd you stay? You were one person I thought sure'd get out. Thought you'd be at least in Houston by now."

"Things happen, Annmarie. Got drafted right out of high school. When I came back from Vietnam, easiest thing to do was go into my Daddy's garage. Wasn't in the frame of mind to start a new life somewhere."

"You got sent to Vietnam? Damn, Wendell, I didn't know that. Sorry."

It was quiet for a minute. "So you want to see Miri?" Wendell asked. I couldn't hear her answer.

I'd imagined arranging myself on a chair so that when she walked in I'd be staring longingly at a picture of Grandma, or turning the TV up loud so she'd know I didn't want to talk to her. In the end, though, I was just sitting there, picking at the piping on Grandma's couch.

"Hey there, Miri," she said, standing in front of me.

I shrugged, wouldn't look her in the eyes.

"You're real pissed at me, huh?" She twirled her right foot around on the three-inch heel like it was a compass. "Guess you think I deserve the silent treatment for leaving you here like I did."

That was what I hated most, the way she had of twisting things around, making it look like I was the unreasonable one. Grandma was the only one who'd ever seen through her bullshit.

"No," I said, standing up and meeting her gaze, "I wasn't pissed at you for leaving me here. Best thing you ever did for me. I'm just pissed you're here now, is all."

In truth, my feelings were a lot more complicated than that. There was a part of me, a part I couldn't even believe existed, that wanted to throw my arms around her and tell her I forgave her, like the long-lost daughter in one of those women-in-distress made-for-TV movies that Grandma used to like to watch. But the rest of me was the eleven-year-old girl who'd taken that all-night ride back and forth across Texas, only to be dumped on the doorstep of a grand-mother who she, at that point, scarcely knew.

She sniffed and tossed her orange hair back. "You don't cut anyone a break, do you, kiddo?" she said.

"Haven't been given too many myself," I shot back.

She pouted her glossy red lips and planted her hands on her hips. "Well, I see you haven't changed much."

"You haven't neither."

We just stood there, one more stubborn than the other, staring at each other until Wendell stepped in and ended the standoff. "You must be hungry, Annmarie, after your drive and all. What say we all go get some pizza."

We rode in Wendell's truck down to the Pizza Boy, where enough people gaped at Annmarie that I knew her appearance would be all over town within an hour. I whispered to Wendell, "Can't we get it to go?"

He didn't seem to understand. "Well, we're here now, honey," he said. "Might as well sit down and eat."

Annmarie ordered a large pizza with pepperoni, without asking us what we wanted, then waited for Wendell to pay. As we stood at the counter, a group of girls I knew from school came in. They were the prissy girls, and I didn't much care for them, but still I didn't want them spreading all over school how trashy Annmarie looked.

"I have to go to the bathroom," I said, and ran to the back of the restaurant. I sat on the toilet for ten minutes, hoping the girls would be gone when I came out.

I peeked out of the bathroom and scanned the restaurant. The girls were still there, but they were at a table up front, a good distance from the booth where Wendell and Annmarie were sitting with the pizza. I had a shot at sneaking over to their booth unnoticed, and so I moved quickly, sliding in next to Wendell, my back to the girls.

"Got some good news, Miri," Wendell said as I picked up a slice of pizza.

"Could use some," I said, glaring at Annmarie.

"Your Momma's agreed to stay on in Prairie Rose for a spell. You two can probably go on living in your Grandma's house, once her affairs get settled."

I looked at Annmarie in disbelief. There had to be a catch. "Really?" I asked.

She nodded. "I'm going to try and stand it here, Miri. That's all I can prom-ise."

I began picking the pepperoni off the top of my pizza. "Could you do one thing if you stay here?" I asked, trying to think of a tactful way to say what was on my mind.

"Don't know until you ask," she said.

I stacked the pepperonis like poker chips on the side of my paper plate. "Could you just dress a little less . . ." I searched for the right word.

"Colorful," Wendell finished. "I mean, you look terrific, Annmarie, but you know how folks around here talk. Not used to anything different than what they see every day."

I was beginning to think Grandma had been right about Wendell. He was a smooth talker.

Annmarie laughed, but her eyes got dark and hard. "They'll get used to me," she said.

The thought of continual humiliation at the hands of Annmarie was not appealing, but at least I'd still be close to Wendell. I took a bite of my pizza, and saw Annmarie's bird eyes zoom in on my pepperoni stack.

"What's the matter, you don't like pepperoni now?" she asked.

Truth be told, for the past year I'd been picking all forms of meat off of and out of every dish put in front of me, ever since my visit to the Clack ranch. Grandma had never said a word about it; she'd simply started making macaroni and cheese as a side dish for nearly every meal. But I was not about to tell Annmarie this. I figured she'd just laugh at me.

"Not really," I said, taking another bite of pizza.

Annmarie sighed. "Don't expect me to indulge you like your Grandma did, Miri," she said, and Wendell got a pained look on his face but he stayed quiet.

In the days that followed there were visiting hours at the Walker Funeral Parlor, and then the funeral itself. I only remember a couple of things from these few days, just images really, like little snapshots: Troy giving me a hug inside the funeral parlor, and Jimmy Clack coming up to me outside and doing the same; Aunt Melissa's loud sobbing as they lowered Grandma's casket into the ground, and Annmarie's crack that she should have been nominated for Best Actress; Wendell asking me if I was okay, and it seeming like he asked me this over and over, even in my dreams; and the food. All manner of cakes and pies and casseroles arrived at Grandma's house from the moment word got out that she'd died, and they were still coming in a week later as I went back to school, started up my choir and chorus practices, and tried to settle into some kind of routine with Annmarie.

For a couple of weeks there, it almost looked like it might work out. The night after Grandma's funeral, Annmarie and I sat up in the parlor after everyone had gone, picking at the leftover food. She caught me up on the plot of *All My Children*, a soap opera that we used to watch together sometimes but which Grandma had forbidden because of all that rolling around under the sheets those people in Pine Valley did. Once Annmarie'd got me up to speed on Erica Kane and all her doings she cleared her throat the way she did when she had something important to say.

"I know you got stuff on your mind," she said, cutting herself a piece of the lemon Bundt cake Mrs. Seale had made. "We might as well hash it out now."

I studied her face closely. There was a sadness in her eyes I hadn't seen before, and more lines than I remembered. Even though she'd wisecracked about Melissa throughout the funeral, Annmarie herself had teared up more than I'd expected. Some of it, I thought, had to do with being stuck taking care of me again, back in Prairie Rose. But there was more. Despite all their fighting, she was genuinely sad about Grandma dying.

"Well, I thought maybe you called Grandma and gave her that heart attack," I said, matter-of-factly.

She finished chewing a bite of the Bundt cake. "Wendell told me you thought that. I wasn't on the phone with her, Miri."

I shrugged. "Guess we'll never know, huh?"

She smiled, but it was a thin, bitter kind of smile. "We will when the phone bill comes in. You know I always called collect, deadbeat what I am."

She was trying to make a joke out of it, but all I could do was nod and stare down at the piping on the couch.

"I really didn't do it, Miri," she said.

It sounded like she was being straight with me. I could usually tell when she was lying, by her tone of voice—she went up an octave when she lied. Generally she lied so much that it was rare for her voice to be down as low as it was right then.

"Okay," I finally said. It came out as a defeated little whisper.

Annmarie pushed the cake across the table towards me, but I just shook my head. People had been pushing food at me all afternoon and evening, and I couldn't understand how they all could eat so soon after putting Grandma in the ground.

"You should eat something, you know," she said.

I could have made a comment about how she'd never worried about feeding me before, but I was too tired to fight with her. I just shrugged.

She sighed and lit a cigarette. "Well, just so you know," she said, taking a puff and blowing the smoke out, "I'm on the wagon. I haven't touched anything harder than these Marlboros in almost a year."

I eyed her carefully, suspicious of what she'd just said. Her voice had stayed low, but it was possible she'd become better at lying in the past three years.

"You don't believe me," she said. "You have that look on your face you get when you think I'm lying."

It killed me how she could read me as well as I read her. "Guess the proof is in the pudding," I said, using an expression that Grandma had always favored.

"Guess it is," Annmarie said, and we sat in the parlor like that, looking through and past each other, until she finally finished her cigarette and went to bed.

I was surprised to find her up before me the next morning, a pot of coffee already made. She was sitting at the kitchen table, the Help Wanted section of the *Justice-News* open in front of her. She motioned toward the coffee pot.

"Want some?" she asked.

I looked from her to the pot and back. "Grandma said I was too young for coffee," I said. "She made me tea."

Annmarie sighed. "But do you want some?"

I'd never had coffee, and didn't really know if I liked it or not. I didn't want to disrespect Grandma, but I thought that maybe after all I'd been through, I was old enough to drink it.

"Okay," I said.

"Help yourself," she said, circling an ad with a red felt-tipped marker.

I got myself a mug and poured half a cup. It was darker than how Grandma used to make hers.

"Better put some milk and sugar in that, or you'll choke," she said, her face still buried in the paper.

I put three spoons of sugar in and a fair amount of milk, and tasted it. It wasn't bad, kind of like a weak, warm milkshake. I put in a little more milk and another spoon of sugar and stirred it good.

"I'm going to look for a job today," she said. "I don't know when your Grandma's affairs will be settled."

"Affairs?" I asked, slurping the sweet coffee.

"Her money," she said. "She owned the house, but it looks like she borrowed against it the last few years. Wendell's getting a lawyer to look into all that for us."

The last few years, she'd had to feed and buy clothes for me, as well as herself. Annmarie knew this as well as I did, and so I just kept quiet, sipping my coffee.

"Chappy's Market is looking for a checkout girl," she said. "I could do that."

"You should go down there today," I said. "Folks'll still be feeling sympathetic."

Annmarie looked up at me and smiled. "That's exactly what I was thinking. See, we don't always think so different, you and me."

This was about the hardest I'd ever seen her try with me. Even though part of me wanted to see her leave, taking with her the dirty ashtrays that had already invaded every room of the house, I figured it'd be best for me to play along. If I could just keep her here for the next three years, I could finish high school and be off to study music at the University of Texas, where Mr. Duggan, my high school music teacher, had already assured me I'd blow away the vocal arts department. Mr. Duggan was just five years out of that college himself and, rumor had it, was all kinds of wild.

I thought briefly about trying to fix Mr. Duggan up with Annmarie—I knew if I wanted to keep her in Prairie Rose for three years I'd have to find her a man—but last I heard he was dating Miss Curtis, the hippie art teacher who tried, unsuccessfully, to get everyone to call her "Ms." Neither Mr. Duggan nor Miss—Ms.—Curtis fit in much in Prairie Rose, but they seemed to have found each other. I needed to find someone like that for Annmarie, an outcast like herself.

"What are you going to wear for the interview?" I asked.

"Oh, I thought maybe my gold lamé tube top and some cutoffs," she said, looking at me for a reaction. She swiped me on the leg with part of the newspaper.

"I'm kidding," she said. "Lighten up, will you, Miri?"

"You should wear the dress you wore to the funeral yesterday," I said. "They'll think you're half-crazed with grief and hire you on the spot." I didn't know if this was true or not, but I did know that the dress she'd worn to the funeral was the only thing in her suitcase even remotely appropriate to be worn in Prairie Rose. Annmarie didn't have even a plain pair of slacks and a nice blouse; everything she owned looked like a hooker get-up, except for that one navy blue dress she'd worn the day before.

"Really?" she said, eyeing me intently. "You don't think it'd be overkill?"

"Nope. You wear that dress to Chappy's and they'll hire you on the spot."

My instincts turned out to be right. Annmarie was hired as a checkout girl at Chappy's; when she started dipping into her regular wardrobe, the owners issued her a red smock to wear and kept her behind the deli counter so folks wouldn't complain about her skin-tight pants.

As the days went on I got the idea of fixing her up with Guy; I told him and Wendell this one Sunday afternoon as we sat in the Kountry Kitchen, nursing milkshakes. It sent them into fits of laughter, which hurt my feelings more than a little.

"I thought you liked Annmarie, Wendell," I said when they'd finished. "You said you thought she was pretty."

"In that case, Wendell, I think *you* should take her out," Guy said, starting off on a laughing fit once again.

Wendell was still smiling, but I knew he could see I was getting upset. "We're not laughing because of your Momma, honey," he said. "It's just that we're not the settling down kind."

"Neither is she," I said, and this started Guy laughing again until I saw Wendell poke him in the ribs. "It's not like I'm looking for a husband for her, Wendell. Just somebody to keep her here for a while."

Wendell patted my hand. "She's here for you, Miri," he said, and I shook my head but gave up on trying to make him understand.

Annmarie went through the motions as best she could for those few weeks. She even went with Wendell and Guy to the year-end concert at my high school, a Beatles tribute Mr. Duggan had cooked up in honor of John Lennon's death that past December. I wound up singing "Blackbird" after the principal nixed Mr. Duggan's first choice for me, "Imagine," saying that it promoted Communism and godlessness. Mr. Duggan had suggested—more than once— that I could break into "Imagine" up on stage if I wanted to, but I was not about to rock the boat that way, not even for him. I had enough problems without getting the principal of Sam Houston High School mad at me, and so I just sang "Blackbird" in a way that Wendell and Guy swore brought a tear to Annmarie's eye, but which she would not admit to.

As school let out that year and the temperature began to soar, I started see- ing the signs of Annmarie's growing restlessness. She paced around Grandma's house like a caged panther in spandex, smoking furiously, looking like she would break and run as soon as she could figure out how.

One Saturday at the end of June I came home from a pool party at the Clacks'—a birthday party for Jimmy who, gossip had it, had invited me over his mother's objections—to find Annmarie packing. I wasn't especially sur- prised; we'd just found out that Grandma had borrowed heavily against the house and, after funeral expenses, there was not much money left. I'd been har- boring a dread that I'd come home one day and she'd just be gone.

"Pack your bags, Miri," she said, glancing at me over the top of the suitcase. "We're going on a road trip."

"A road trip?" I was skeptical but interested to hear more. Maybe she wasn't taking off on me just yet. Maybe she just needed to get away from Prairie Rose for a spell.

"Isn't that what I said?" She pulled her fancy black lace underwear from Grandma's dresser drawer, stuffed it into the suitcase.

"Where are we going?"

She sighed. "You just have to know everything, don't you? We're going to visit a friend of mine, Miri."

"A friend?"

"He lives in Sugar Land. Down near Houston." She closed the suitcase and lit a cigarette, her fingers shaking. I mistook this nervousness to be the excited energy she got when she was expecting to see a boyfriend.

"He?" I asked, arching my eyebrows just like Grandma or even Aunt Melissa would have. "I don't want to go see one of your boyfriends, Annmarie. I'll stay here with Wendell while you're gone."

Annmarie blew smoke out, her gaze fixed level on me. "He's not my boyfriend anymore. He's your Daddy. And don't ask me any more about it until we're on the road."

It took me five minutes to pack; I knew the drill, and besides, I'd had a bag half-packed since Grandma had died. I waited until we got on the highway, and then I started up with my questions: Who was he? Why hadn't she told me about him before? Why were we going to see him now? Why hadn't he wanted to see me before now? Annmarie took the questions calmly, blowing smoke rings as I spoke, one hand on the steering wheel. An eight-track tape of Pink Floyd's *The Wall* played softly in the background.

"You done with your questions?" she asked finally, glancing over at me, and I nodded my head.

"Okay. Yes, I always knew who your father was. I'm not the slut everyone thinks I am," she said, and then added, "at least, I wasn't then." She laughed at her own sad attempt at a joke. I just stared at her, waiting for her to go on.

"He wasn't there for us when you were born, so I put him out of mind. But things have changed." She steered into the left lane, cut around a slow-moving Chevette.

"What's changed?" I asked.

"Our needs."

"Our needs?" I looked over my shoulder nervously as she cut back into the lane too soon for my taste.

"Look, I figure he can give us enough money to stay set up at your Grandma's for a while. He's rich, Miri. He owns a whole big trucking company."

I thought this over for a minute before speaking.

"If he's so rich, how come he never helped us before?" I asked.

"Because I didn't ask before," she said.

"Why not?"

Annmarie sighed, nudged up the volume on the tape deck. "I told you, I put him out of my mind. I was pissed off, and too young and stupid to realize I couldn't make it on my own. Now I figure it's time for him to help us out. He owes us."

"And he said we could stay with him?" I asked, trying to sort the story out. It didn't make sense that this father I'd had no contact with all my life would suddenly just open his doors to us. Annmarie was hiding something, but I couldn't figure out what.

"No," she said. "The bags are for after."

I sighed. When she was being cagey like this, prying the real story out of her was a chore. "After what?" I asked.

"After he gives us the money," she said. "I figure we'll drive around a little, see the country. We could ride out to Hill Country, you know, out past Austin. Stay in a motel with a swimming pool. How's that sound, kiddo?" She took a long drag on the remains of her cigarette, stubbed it out in the ashtray.

"Sounds dumb to me to blow our money like that," I said.

She sighed and turned the volume up loud, a signal to me that the conversation was now over. I listened as she sang along; Annmarie had no pitch whatsoever. It was clear I hadn't got my singing voice from her.

There was a pit in my stomach, and it grew as the signs for Sugar Land appeared. Back when I'd lived with Annmarie, the pit was always there; there were days I couldn't eat lunch in school, I was so sick from it. I thought of it as a peach pit back then, its wrinkles and creases sharp against my soft insides. After I settled in with Grandma, it shrank down to the size of a cherry pit, then a watermelon seed; sometimes I couldn't feel it at all. But after Grandma died, it seemed to grow back overnight, and right then, watching the traffic rush by, the ancient air conditioner blowing out lukewarm air mixed with Annmarie's smoke, Pink Floyd blaring from the car's tinny speakers, the pit felt as big as an avocado. I imagined it took up all the space in my belly. I tried hard not to get sick.

Once we pulled off the interstate past Houston, Annmarie kept making wrong turns. She would drive for a few minutes, mutter that she was going the wrong way, then pull a U-turn and double back, still obviously confused. Finally she pulled over on the side of the road and dug a beat-up-looking map from the glove compartment. "Let's see," she muttered. "Alamo Lane. Where is it?"

"You didn't get directions from him?" I asked, irritated.

"I thought I'd remember the way," she murmured.

"Remember the way? You mean he's always lived here and you never told me?"

She didn't answer. After a few seconds she cried, "Here it is!" and she put the car in gear and took a sharp left.

"Don't even tell me you've known all along where my father lived," I said, my voice low and even. "Don't even tell me that."

She shook her head but refused to answer, just kept smoking with one hand, steering with the other. After a few miles we pulled up in front of a huge stone-front house. It reminded me of Aunt Melissa's house in La Porte; it had the kind of perfectly sculpted green lawn that usually isn't real, a bunch of rose bushes growing beneath a big picture window. I spotted the name Ortiz—my name—on the mailbox.

"It's really him?" I asked, watching her face carefully.

"It's him," she said. I couldn't tell if she was lying or not.

I looked back at the house, the mailbox. "He's expecting us, right?" I asked.

Annmarie laughed, but it was a nervous laugh. "Course he is," she said, her voice a falsetto. The pit in my stomach was now the size of a coconut. She put the car in park and shut off the engine. "Come on," she said. We got out of the car. She started up the flagstone walkway that led to the front door; I walked behind her, wishing I could shrink myself down to nothing. At the front door, she hesitated for a second, then pressed the bell.

A girl who looked only a year or two older than me answered. She had long dark hair and jet black eyes. I wondered if she could be my half-sister, but it was impossible to tell. I hid behind Annmarie, who stood with her hands on her hips, her back arched, like she was ready for a fight.

"Yes?" the girl asked.

"I'd like to speak to your father," Annmarie said.

The girl narrowed her eyes, looking Annmarie up and down and then glancing at me behind her. Annmarie was wearing the same get-up she'd worn the day she arrived in Prairie Rose after Grandma died, and so I could easily imagine what this girl was thinking. Finally she went away and called to someone in Spanish. After one of the longest minutes of my life, a man—the man Annmarie claimed was my father—stood in the doorway.

He was short for a man, about 5-foot-5, with thick dark hair that was graying at the sides, a gray-black mustache, and the same black eyes of the teenage girl. He was wearing a suit, like he'd just come home from work. He walked to the door with a smile on his face that disappeared when he saw Annmarie.

"I told you to leave me alone," he said, and the pit in my stomach throbbed with his words. He stepped outside and closed the door behind him. He had a Spanish accent, but only a slight one.

"I thought you might want to meet your daughter in person," Annmarie said, nudging me toward him.

He looked at me, and I pictured what he saw: a stringy little girl in a pair of faded jeans and a bleached-out yellow tank top, her long hair ragged from the day's sun and chlorine. I'd dressed in such a hurry that I hadn't thought about looking good, and Annmarie hadn't had the sense to tell me to change. I looked down at the ground, unable to meet his gaze. The pit had now invaded every inch of my body; turned me to stone, it had. I tried to steady my legs and toppled slightly backward, barely catching myself before falling into the rose bushes. My movements all felt stiff, exaggerated.

"Nothing has changed since we talked on the phone," he said to Annmarie. "I told you when she was born, I tell you now. Prove she is my daughter, and I will support her."

I looked at Annmarie in disbelief.

"You hear that, Miri?" she said to me. "He wants you to have a painful blood test before he'll do what's right."

With that, the door opened, and a woman who looked like an older version of the teenage girl began shouting at Mr. Ortiz in Spanish. She was wearing a dress the color of celery; it looked like real silk.

Mr. Ortiz answered her in a sorrowful tone and closed the door again.

"If you thought that bringing her here and destroying my family would persuade me to give you money, you thought wrong," he said. "Not without a blood test."

At that point, an anger that had been burning in the tips of my toes bubbled through my body, turning the pit instantly to a steam that began to seep through my skin. I wiped the sweat from my forehead, planted my feet more firmly, and faced Annmarie.

"Why don't you want me to have a blood test, Annmarie?" I said, my voice shaking. "Is it because you're not sure he's really my father?"

Mr. Ortiz turned and looked from me to Annmarie, who was staring at me in disbelief, too stunned to react.

"You lied about everything!" I was yelling now, caught in the heat of my own rage. "He's not going to give us anything. He didn't even know we were coming."

"Shhh," Annmarie whispered.

"I bet he's not even my father," I screamed. "I bet you did pick his name out of a phone book!"

My face was hot, the blood pulsing in my temples. I knew I was going too far with her but I couldn't stop myself. All my anger for everything she'd ever done to me came together at that moment, hardened like bits of broken glass into the sharp words that came out of my mouth.

"Well," Annmarie sputtered, "you little shit. This is the thanks I get for giving up my life to come back and take care of you?"

"Thanks for what? For embarrassing me with your hooker get-ups? Why do you think they make you wear that apron at Chappy's? Everyone in town thinks you look like a streetwalker."

Her face was contorted with anger, her mouth a sideways question mark. She backed up and clenched her fist, and for a second I thought she was going to take a swing at me. I was too terrified to move. I'd gotten her mad before, but I'd never seen a look on her face like this. She glanced from me to Mr. Ortiz and back at me, her eyes blazing, and then she turned and ran down the flagstone path. I stood still until I heard the car start up, and then I realized what she was going to do. I ran down the path, screaming her name. When I got to the curb she was already backing the car up, and I ran around to the driver's side. Our eyes locked for a second; the look on her face was stone-cold, like she'd buried any hints of feelings she'd ever had for me, locked them away in a place so deep it would never be reached. It was a look that said she was through with me for good.

She rolled down the window and tossed my duffel bag at my feet. I started to cry, and she watched for a second but her expression didn't change. She gunned the car in reverse, backed into a neighbor's driveway, and took off back for the highway with a screech of rubber.

I was too ashamed to walk back to the house. I sat down on the curb and pulled the duffel bag up on my lap, buried my face in it. I knew crying wasn't going to help me any, and so in my mind I worked my voice through the scales to give myself something else to think about. In my mind I sang "Sweet, Sweet Child of Bethlehem," and then "Blackbird," and then Patsy Cline's "Crazy" as

I listened to the fighting and screaming in Spanish that was coming from inside the house. The woman was yelling, the man was pleading, and I could hear crying that was probably the teenage girl. I just sat there and sang songs in my mind and waited for them to sort it all out.

It was starting to get dark, and I was running out of songs. I pulled my tank top up and wiped my face with it, and kicked at my duffel bag, wondering how I could have been so stupid—to come along with Annmarie in the first place, and then to piss her off to the point where she left me. I was thinking about walking out to the highway and trying to hitch a ride back to Prairie Rose when I heard footsteps behind me.

"Are you all right?" Mr. Ortiz sat down on the curb next to me. His shoes were dark brown, a shiny good leather. Even in my state I noticed things like that.

I shrugged, said nothing.

"Do you think your mother will come back?" He was looking off in the direction where Annmarie's car had been parked.

"No," I said. It was the only thing I knew for certain.

He sighed, fingered his watch band. "So she told you that I was your father?"

I nodded, and looked him in the eyes. I was looking for something of myself in there, my own dark eyes looking back at me. But I just couldn't tell. "Are you?" I finally asked. It came out as a whisper, and I cleared my throat. "I mean, could you be?"

He took a deep breath, blew it out. "I don't think so. I—I don't see how."

I saw right off that this was not a flat-out denial. "But you could be?" I asked.

He kicked at the ground, getting dust on his shoe. "It's—well, it's just not very likely," he said. I waited for him to go on. "Your mother—how old are you?"

"Fourteen," I said, still looking right at him.

"Fourteen," he said, shaking his head. "My own daughter is sixteen." He seemed lost in thought. "I hope my wife will forgive me."

I had to get him back on the subject at hand. Right then I needed to know more than anything else in the world if there was any chance he could be my father. I needed to know if I had a possibility of a home, for it was clear I'd never again have one with Annmarie.

"Did you sleep with her?" I asked. His eyes flashed at the bluntness of my question, but he was quiet for a minute.

"Once," he finally said. "When your mother was a teenager she used to work at my company after school, sometimes on Saturdays. She did a little filing, answered the phones. Did she ever tell you about that?"

I shook my head no.

"She was very young when she worked for me. About my daughter's age." He put his head in his hands for a minute, then lifted it back up. "I don't know why I did it."

"So you might be my father," I said, and he looked me over for a good long minute.

"Who knows?" he said quietly. "I don't want to hurt your feelings, but your mother had a lot of boyfriends."

"You mean she was a tramp." I was getting bolder out of exhaustion and anger. I just wanted a straight answer, and I couldn't seem to get one.

"That's not what I said." He sighed. "But she did have many boyfriends. And with us, your mother and me, there was only that one time."

"It only takes one time," I said. "They taught us that in health class."

He smiled tensely. "You—Miriam, is that right?" I nodded. "Miriam, your mother came to me after she had you and claimed you were my child. I told her to have a blood test. I said that if the child—you—were mine, I would support it. You."

"So what happened?"

"I never heard from her again. Until three weeks ago." He took a handkerchief out of his pocket, dabbed at the sweat on his forehead. "She called and said she needed money, that I should support you. I told her again to have a blood test, and she refused. I'd hoped that would be the end of it."

I kicked at a chunk of asphalt beneath my feet. It was clear to me I was never going to get a straight answer to the question of who my father was, and I decided from that day on to put it out of my head. Right then, looking out at the street, at the spot where Annmarie'd been parked, I realized I was truly alone in the world, that no one was going to pop out from behind some curtain and rescue me. That if I wanted a family, I'd have to make my own.

"So she has no idea who my father is," I said, my voice so calm and clear it surprised even me. "She just picked you because you had the most money."

He looked down at his shoes, said nothing.

"Could I use your phone, please?" I asked, and went inside—despite the glares of both his wife and his daughter, who could have been, but probably wasn't, my half-sister—and called the only person I knew in the world who would come to pick me up: Wendell.

CHAPTER 6
JUNE, 1981–APRIL, 1982

For most of the summer I lived with Wendell in the little clapboard house he shared with Duke, two miles down the road from the garage. Child Services had agreed to this arrangement, temporarily, while Wendell tried to adopt me. Mostly they let me stay with him on the word of Aunt Melissa, who, motivated by guilt and a burning desire not to get stuck with me herself, testified that Wendell was a dear family friend and that she knew her mother would have wanted me to live with him.

It seemed like everyone in Liberty County was impressed with Aunt Melissa, who wore tailored pastel pantsuits like Krystle Carrington on *Dynasty*, and talked like Katharine Hepburn in *The African Queen*, a movie I imagined she'd seen with Grandma as many times as I had. Aunt Melissa spent a lot of time in Prairie Rose that summer, talking to people at the Child Services office, and to the attorney she'd helped Wendell hire, and folks in town commented on everything from the cut and color of her hair to the size of the diamond on her finger. Out of Adelia LaCroix's two girls, Melissa had never been the pretty one, the talk around town went, but look at her now. Mothers of plain-looking girls held Aunt Melissa up as an example of what a little hard work in self-improvement could do; she looked like a Clack, they said, like she'd been born to the money, the pantsuits.

Wendell and I were visited during this time by an endless parade of girls in pressed seersucker suits and single strands of pearls, older ladies in polyester pants-and-jacket outfits, sweat beading out from underneath their sprayed-up hair. They interviewed me and Wendell, separately and together, writing fast and furious on the clipboards they carried. We were supposed to have a hearing before a judge at the end of August, and Wendell had warned me to be on my best behavior in the meantime. Since a social worker could stop by at any moment, I lived in the kind of dresses I hated—flowered, lace-collared hand-me-downs from my cousin Mary Gay—and made sure my nails were trimmed and clean at all times, my long hair caught up in a ponytail so as it wouldn't look so wild. No girl could be as perfect as it seemed Child Services expected, but the Lord and Grandma know I did my best.

It seemed Wendell, too, was expected to be a different person during this time. Guy stopped coming over, and when I asked Wendell why he couldn't have visits with kin he simply said, "Wouldn't look good." We met Guy sometimes at High Island Beach on Sundays, when the garage was closed. He and Wendell would talk in hushed tones while I hovered at the water's edge, trying to listen. Once, I heard Guy say something about moving to San Francisco, but try as I might I could not hear Wendell's response. I imagined it was Guy's idea for us to become fugitives from the law, and I sure liked the thought of the three of us and Duke piling in Wendell's pickup truck and heading west, outwitting the ladies from Child Services at every turn.

There was a drought in Southeast Texas that summer. Water restrictions were in order; lawns and wildflowers burned up in the sun, cars went around dirty, and folks' skin began to dry up like armadillo armor. People in town seemed spent, and the girls and ladies who came to talk to me and Wendell seemed more and more short-tempered, but I was not at all concerned. I figured I was set with Wendell, and that the drought, like the Child Services investigation, would pass.

As temperatures stayed fixed around the 100-degree mark, I spent many a day at the county pool. Sometimes I'd catch a ride with Mrs. Higgins, who had three boys all under the age of seven and liked to bring me along as a mother's helper; other days Wendell would come home at lunchtime and drive me over to the pool, picking me up there after the garage closed.

One Saturday in August it got so ungodly hot that two kids fainted from heat exhaustion and one of the teenage lifeguards threw up in the bushes, and so they closed the pool early. Mrs. Higgins dropped me off at Wendell's, and I walked in thinking that maybe I'd fix supper for him, seeing as I had some time before he'd get home from the garage.

I knew right off that something was wrong, just as I had the day I'd found Grandma dead. This time, it was the cool air that hit me as soon as I opened the front door; I could hear the loud whine of the clunky old air conditioner in Wendell's living room. Wendell was home, more than two hours early. In all the time I'd known him he'd never left the garage before closing.

I found him sitting at the kitchen table, a bottle of Budweiser opened but untouched in front of him. His eyes were red and wet, his shoulders hunched, his hands knotted like an old man's. Even Duke looked depressed, lying there at Wendell's feet, but whether his expression had to do with Wendell being upset or just the unbearable heat, I couldn't really tell. I stood in the kitchen doorway in my tank bathing suit and cutoff shorts and looked at him, as if by keeping some distance I could avoid whatever had happened.

"Honey," he said, "sit down."

I walked in and took the chair next to his.

"I've got some bad news, Miri," he said, the words sounding like they were stuck in his throat and he had to work hard to get them out. "Some real bad news."

Duke got up and lapped at his water dish. I said nothing, just waited for Wendell to go on.

"They won't let me adopt you," he said. He began cracking his knuckles, and I noticed as his fingers moved how dark his skin had tanned that summer; it was a red tan, though, a tan with some burn underneath.

"What do you mean?" I asked. "I thought we wouldn't know until we went in to talk to the judge next week."

He shook his head. "I got a call from the lawyer, honey. Got back from talking to him a little while ago."

"What did he say?" I asked. I wished he'd just tell me what had happened, instead of making me drag it out of him.

"Child Services is going to tell the judge you shouldn't live with me," he said. "Even if we fight it, they're fixing on taking you out of here until the hearing date." He pulled a red bandana from his pocket, wiped sweat from his forehead.

"What do you mean, 'if' we fight it?" My voice sounded high and loud.

"Honey, there's just no point," he said, his eyes tearing up. "The lawyer says it's hopeless now."

"But why?" I asked. "We've been acting like perfect people all summer long. Why wouldn't they want me to live with you?"

"Acting," Wendell repeated, rubbing his eyes with his fingertips. "Miri, there's things you just don't understand."

"What things?" I asked, my hands tightened into fists.

He shook his head. "It's over, Miri. There's nothing else I can do."

"But I thought the judge was going to ask me what I wanted," I said. "Why can't we just go to him and tell him Child Services is wrong?"

He sighed, looked off in the distance. "They're taking you tomorrow," he said.

I fell against the back of my chair, too stunned to speak.

"I've been trying to get hold of your Aunt Melissa," he added.

"Aunt Melissa!" I spit her name out like it was a pill on my tongue. "Wendell, I'm not going to live with Aunt Melissa. No way."

"Miri, you better hope you can go live with her," he said, raising his voice a notch. "It's either that or a foster home."

At that my own eyes filled up with tears. Back when I'd lived with Annmarie, when I was little, I used to worry that I'd be put in a home like that, especially when teachers questioned me about my unbrushed hair, my mismatched clothes, my falling asleep in class. And I had worried about it again after Grandma died, and when Annmarie left me in Sugar Land; but I hadn't really thought about it since Wendell had taken me in. I could see just then how stupid I'd been, counting on Wendell so much.

"Don't worry," he added, studying my face, "it won't come to that. I'll get hold of Melissa if we have to drive up there tonight ourselves."

"Don't worry?" I asked, the anger in my voice causing Duke to scramble to his feet and stand between us. "You're telling me I might have to go live with strangers, and I shouldn't worry?" I stared him hard in the eyes.

"I'm sorry," he said. "You know I wanted you here, Miri."

"So then how come you're ready to just give up without a fight?" My voice sounded like it was coming from somewhere outside of me. The pit in my stomach was huge as ever, but rather than weighing me down, this time it felt like a balloon, filled with helium. I had the strange sensation that I was floating, that I could rise slowly in the air, hover there for an instant and then shoot suddenly over the table, out the front window, gliding like a human hot-air balloon through the skies above Prairie Rose until the winds shifted and I landed somewhere else—another town, maybe, another house.

Wendell started to cry openly. I'd never seen a grown man cry before; it made some wounded part of me glad, that I could hurt him as much as he was hurting me.

"I can't fight this," he said softly. "You don't know what all's going on here."

"Then tell me," I said, rising to my feet while somehow keeping myself from floating up and away.

"Can't," he said, his elbows on the table, his hands knotted up in his hair. "It's not for you to know."

I fixed a look on him as hard and mean as it was in my power to summon up. "I don't need you," I said, holding onto a corner of the table to anchor myself. "I'll find my own place to live." I let go of the table, and was surprised to find that it didn't take the wind but rather my own two legs to carry me to my room, where I curled up in bed and stared at the wall until I could figure out what to do next.

I called Mrs. Higgins a little while later and told her what had happened. I was hoping she would offer for me to live with her—in fact, I even swallowed my pride and asked her outright—but before she would answer she said she wanted to talk to Wendell. Her going over my head like that made me want to cross her off my list, too, but seeing as hers was the only name still on the list, I didn't have much choice.

The next day, Mrs. Higgins, two ladies from Child Services and Aunt Melissa all met at Wendell's house. One of the Child Services ladies insisted on taking me out for ice cream, and I sat at the Kountry Kitchen with her, watching a hot fudge sundae melt in a silver dish as my fate was decided back at Wendell's. When we returned, Aunt Melissa was gone; but Mrs. Higgins was still there, and I was told I could live with her temporarily. I smiled at Mrs. Higgins to say thank you, but she just looked worried. As

Wendell put my bags in the car, I went in the kitchen and hugged Duke, fighting the tears I knew could spill out any second. On my way out the door, Wendell tried to apologize again, put his arms out to hug me.

"I hate you, Wendell," I said. "I hope I never see you again."

I worked to keep my face blank as sun-baked clay until the car pulled away from the house, then lost myself in sobs that felt like they'd rip me in two.

It was clear to me from the moment I arrived at Mrs. Higgins's that it was only a way station. Her house was no bigger than Grandma's, but she had three little boys and a husband all living in it with her, and now me. There were two bedrooms—one for Mr. and Mrs. Higgins, one for the boys—and I would have to sleep on the living room couch until they could fix something else up for me. I didn't think the ladies from Child Services would like this, but they didn't say anything as Mrs. Higgins took them through the house. Maybe it was because Mrs. Higgins was well known throughout the county for the piano lessons she gave to the sons and daughters of the wealthier folks; maybe it was because Aunt Melissa had vouched for her. Maybe, I thought, the ladies from Child Services just didn't know what else to do with me. They said it would be okay for me to stay there "for now," emphasizing those last two words in a way that told me not to unpack my bags.

After a few days of eavesdropping on the Higginses' whispered bedroom conversations, I figured out that a deal had been struck at Wendell's house that last day. The idea was that I was supposed to be at the Higginses' until Wendell and Child Services could convince Aunt Melissa to take me in. Fat chance, I thought, leaning up against the Higginses' bedroom door, my ear pressed to the crack. It was clear from their conversations that the talks with Aunt Melissa were not going well; and it was also clear that Mr. Higgins didn't want me there, that he felt they didn't have enough room for an extra kid.

My fifteenth birthday came and went during my first week there. Mrs. Higgins seemed to have forgotten all about it in the commotion of having me in her home. Wendell tried to call me twice that day but I refused the phone each time. If he thought taking me out for a piece of cake or a milk-shake was going to make up for abandoning me, he was wrong. Instead I ate dinner with the Higginses, did the dishes afterward, and sat out on the back step, trying to pretend that it wasn't really my birthday at all.

As school started up that fall, the rumors flying around town about me were much wilder than the truth. There was talk that Mr. and Mrs. Higgins were taking me in as a babysitter for their boys, like a live-in servant; and there were rumors that Aunt Melissa was on her way to pick me up in her Mercedes and whisk me off to that big house of hers where they'd cut my hair so it would look proper and throw me a coming-out party when I turned sixteen. There was even talk that the Clacks were thinking of taking me in, what with Lolita heading back to California for her second year of college and her room being empty and all. In the end, though, all the rumors seemed to cancel each other out. Aunt Melissa could not be convinced, and my best efforts to make myself as small and unnoticeable to Mr. Higgins as possible failed miserably when he came home early from work one day and found me blasting Patsy Cline from his stereo, singing along as loud as I could. No one else stepped up to claim me, and so, after three weeks at the Higginses', a social worker's blue sedan pulled up one day to fetch me. Mr. Higgins wasted no time carrying my bags out to the car; Mrs. Higgins cried and apologized to me at the door, just as Wendell had. I said nothing, not even "goodbye."

In less than a year, I became an expert at making foster parents' lives ungodly miserable. It seemed I had a knack for finding just the right thing to drive them crazy. In the first home, the little things did it: letting slip with the odd cuss word, leaving the milk out to spoil, washing whites and colors together in hot water and coming out with rainbow-streaked clothes. Truth was, I didn't start out doing any of it on purpose, but by the end it felt right to screw up; it was what they expected of me.

The first home I was sent to was in Daisetta, just far enough outside of Prairie Rose to force me to change schools. I was so depressed that I didn't even try out for my new school's chorus; and since the foster parents said I'd have to quit my church choir as they couldn't be taking me all the way to Prairie Rose twice a week and on Sundays, I had lots of free time to focus all my energy on making them as unhappy as I thought they deserved.

Once those foster parents gave me the boot, I was officially "between placements," which was Child Services talk for being down-on-your-luck, flat-out homeless. I spent a week in the Liberty County Youth Facility, which felt like a cross between a jail and a high school. As I sat in my social worker's office one day, listening as she called around trying to find me a home, I snuck a look at the file folder on her desk.

Uses foul language, it said. Destroys food and clothing. Refuses to eat meat.

That was all I could make out before the social worker saw me looking at my file and I had to turn my head, all of a sudden very interested in the half-dead aloe plant on her desk.

The second home was more of a challenge. The parents had taken in several other foster kids as well as me; they were both psychologists, and something about their attitudes just pissed me right off from day one. It was like they were doing me this big favor by taking in a problem kid like me, when my only real problem was that nobody wanted me. I tried the spoiled milk, the laundry, the cuss words, but the Mom would just talk to me about my "motivations." I couldn't tell her my only motivation was to get the hell out of her house, so I tried other tactics. I announced loudly at dinner one night that I did not eat meat because I'd seen how they killed baby cows, and that anyone who ate the roast in front of us was a murderer. This sent one of the younger kids crying from the room; the other two shrugged and ate it anyway. I sat back and waited for an explosion from the Mom and Dad. After all, this was Texas, Cattle Country. I figured they put people in jail for saying less than what I'd just said.

The Dad simply shrugged. "We don't have a problem with eating meat, Miriam. But if you do, you don't have to eat it."

That was the other thing I hated about them; no matter how many times I corrected them, they always called me Miriam.

It took me almost six months to figure out just the right thing to get me booted out of there. One night, I overheard the Mom and Dad fighting about some flirting the Dad was supposed to have done with his secretary.

I waited for the right moment, then sat myself on the Dad's lap and told him how handsome I thought he was—and believe me, with his combed-over bald spot and his pock-marked cheeks, it was not an easy thing to say with a straight face. He pushed me off his lap, but not before looking at me with a quick appreciative smile that the Mom did not fail to notice. I was out of there by the end of the week. She seemed to have lost interest in my "motivations."

Truth be told, I wasn't really interested in guys. The thing with Jimmy Clack had been nothing more than hand-holding, and I hadn't spent any time alone with a boy since Troy Wilson had touched his lips to mine the night Grandma died. But it was easy for people to expect the worst from me, once they read in my file about Annmarie and all, and so I let them think what they wanted.

I wasn't expecting much, then, from the fresh-faced young social worker who sat across from me one year to the day of Grandma's death. While she was on the phone setting up my third home, I took a peek at my ever-thickening file.

Abnormal attachment to animals, it said. Sexual acting-out.

"I have good news," the social worker announced, hanging up the phone. "We've identified this new home as a good match for you. You should get along much better there."

I shrugged and fingered the plastic name plate on her desk, which identified her as Miss Staples. She wore a gold add-a-bead necklace with a few too many beads, and two sports shirts, one atop the other, both with the collars turned up. Her clothes and her blue blue eyes reminded me of my snooty cousins, the Spears kids, who I'd had the misfortune of seeing that past Christmas out of some kind of lingering guilt on Aunt Melissa's part. My new foster parents, Miss Staples told me with a big smile, were Mr. and Mrs. Ramirez. I hated Miss Staples for the way she smiled.

The Ramirez house was a two-story with faded yellow siding and a big vegetable garden in front. Tucked among the vegetables were all sorts of wooden cut-out figures: a donkey pulling a cart, a fire hydrant, a little girl bending over and showing her polka-dot bloomers. Mrs. Ramirez greeted me at the door in Spanish, then ran and got the other foster kids, two little girls and a teenage boy with a bored look on his face.

"*Hola,*" one of the little girls said.

"Hi," I said. The girls looked at each other, then at Mrs. Ramirez, who went on to tell me what seemed to be a long and rather complicated story, all in Spanish.

I turned to the social worker. "What did she say?" I asked.

"You mean you don't know?" Miss Staples asked me, her eyes widening slightly. She nervously fingered the clipboard in her hand.

"How would I know? I don't speak Spanish."

"You don't speak Spanish?" Miss Staples asked in a voice that was a crisp impersonation of calm. She began flipping through the pages on her clipboard. "But it says here that you do."

"Well, I don't care what it says on your paper. I don't speak Spanish."

"But you're Chicana!" she cried in protest, her voice now a good octave higher than it'd been before. "Your last name is Ortiz."

"She looks pretty *gringa,*" the teenage boy chimed in, "to be an Ortiz."

I shot him a look that said, I will deal with you later. To the social worker I said, "My mother didn't know who my father was. She picked Ortiz out of the phone book to put on my birth certificate."

"But wasn't your mother Chicana?" she asked, the pages now being flipped hard enough that I thought they might just rip off the clipboard.

"Don't you have my mother's name on there?" I asked, knowing the discovery of that name just might put Miss Staples over her personal edge.

"Let's see—here. Annmarie LaCroix." She looked from me to the clipboard and back, as if to confirm that I could really be part Cajun. "Shit," she said. It was the first thing she'd said that had made me want to like her.

Miss Staples then started sweating, and I mean Texas sweating, rivers of water soaking her honey-blonde hair, running down her face. She put down the clipboard and rubbed sweat out of her blue eyes with her fists, smearing her black eyeliner and mascara into bruises underneath her eye sockets. I stood back and admired the effect. Mrs. Ramirez ran to the sink and brought her back a glass of tap water.

"*Gracias,*" the social worker said in an accent that even I could tell was not authentic. She uttered a few more words, but Mrs. Ramirez shook her head, pushed the teenage boy toward us.

"She only understands Spanish," he said to the social worker.

"But that's what I was speaking," she said.

"Not really," the boy said.

"Are you the only person in the house who speaks English?" she asked him.

"Mr. Ramirez does, but he's at work. The little girls speak some."

The social worker wiped her matted bangs from her forehead with the back of her hand. Her face was red as a chili pepper. "Let me make a few calls," she said to me. "I'll try to find you another home." To Mrs. Ramirez she said, in a slow, loud voice, "*Tel-é-fo-no?*" She put her hand up to her ear just in case Mrs. Ramirez didn't get that she wanted to make a call. The boy laughed and pointed into the kitchen.

I put my bags up against a wall and sat on the floor next to them. If I wasn't even going to stay the night, I didn't want to sit in a chair, I didn't want to touch anything in the house. That was the best way to stay as unattached as possible.

Mrs. Ramirez began talking fast and excited, motioning to me. "She wants you to come sit in the living room," the boy said. "She wants to get you some cookies."

I shook my head no, and I must admit I felt tears in my eyes. Not that I really wanted to stay there; I knew I'd just get myself kicked out eventually, as I'd done in the other homes. I was crying because of the whole situation, because I wanted Grandma back, I wanted Wendell back, I wanted the whole dinky, gossipy little town of Prairie Rose back. I'd been somebody there, the little girl with the big voice, the lead soprano in the Home Sweet Home Bible Church choir, star soloist in the Sam Houston High School Glee Club. Now I was just Chicana female number L01-22583, ward of the state of Texas. And I didn't even know if I was really Chicana.

The boy sat down on the floor next to me. "Hey," he said. "I'm Juan."

"Miri," I said, doing my best to keep my voice from cracking.

"Mary?" He unzipped the big black shoulder bag Grandma had bought me for my books when I started high school, which I now used as an overnight bag. He began digging through it.

"Miri," I said, pulling the bag from his hands. "M-I-R-I. Miri."

He laughed. "Okay, okay. Miri. Listen, you can stay here, you know. I could translate for you."

I shrugged, fingering the snap on the bottom of my denim jacket.

"What grade you in?" he asked. "Me, I'm a sophomore. Should be a junior, but my teachers like me so much they want to keep me in school as long as possible."

"I'm a sophomore, too."

"Well, there, you see? We could ditch school together. Hitch a ride down to the beach, go swimming. I know a place so quiet you can swim naked. Nobody ever find you there."

By now this Juan was making me feel a little bit better. I turned a smile on him, one of the many smiles I'd developed in foster care. There was the grateful smile I used on social workers; the well-adjusted, carefree-girl smile I used on school counselors and teachers; the innocent shy smile I used on foster mothers, up until the point where I decided to drive them crazy. The particular smile I turned on Juan was one that worked its magic only on males.

"What makes you think I'd be caught swimming naked with you?" I asked. I could tell the smile was working.

"You wouldn't be caught," he said, and now he was smiling too. "Mr. and Mrs. Ramirez are really nice. You should stay here."

I looked into the living room, where Mrs. Ramirez was sitting on the couch, talking in Spanish to the two little girls while she occasionally cast worried glances in the social worker's direction. The room had dark, paneled-wood walls, but there was a big picture window across from the couch that let in a lot of light. The little shelves behind the window were filled with colorful figures: blue-and-green painted birds, hot-pink-and-yellow angels. I realized looking at the three of them in there that they did, in fact, resemble a family, a lot more than the other two I'd been placed with. Maybe, I thought, Juan was right.

I got up and walked over to Miss Staples, who held her right hand up to me in a gesture that meant I should wait a minute, her left hand gripping the phone receiver so hard I thought surely something would crack—the phone, at least, if not her hand.

"Yes," she was saying, "I understand, but how can I leave the girl here? The mother speaks no English at all."

I poked her in the arm, and she covered the mouthpiece. "I don't mind staying here," I said.

"What? How could you communicate?"

"Juan said he would help me."

She looked over at Juan, and he flashed her a smile that was obviously a stock from his own repertoire. I knew right then I was going to like him.

"Okay," Miss Staples said into the phone, "just temporarily," and she hung up the receiver. To me she said in her best sincere social worker voice, "I promise you I'll find you an English-speaking home just as soon as I can. You won't be here long."

I shrugged and smiled, thinking, I won't be, one way or the other.

But as it turned out, I liked living with the Ramirezes. In the beginning, Mrs. Ramirez and I communicated through Juan, or Mr. Ramirez; if neither of them was home, we combined the little bit of English she knew with a series of elaborate hand gestures and facial expressions. It was fun, like living in another country.

The Ramirezes didn't lay down any rules when I first arrived, unlike the other two homes where I'd been lectured like a prisoner. "We believe in clear and consistent discipline, and a reward system for good behavior," the Dad in the second home had told me when I'd first arrived. A reward system, like I was Duke offering up a paw for a Milk-Bone. Fuck your reward system, I'd thought to myself as I smiled my grateful smile at the Dad.

But here, I wasn't even given chores to do. By the end of the second week, this started to bother me, so when Juan began doing the dishes after dinner one night I grabbed a towel and started drying.

"Wow, Miri, you got sucked in quick," he said. "Took three months before I started helping out."

I opened the dish cabinet above my head. "You mean they wouldn't have made me?"

He shook his head. "The way Mrs. Ramirez told it to me, they think kids shouldn't be expected to act like family until they feel like family."

I stacked a dry dish in the cabinet. "You mean I don't have to do anything?"

Juan laughed. "Now you do," he said. "You blew it. They saw you get up to help me. Now they'll give you stuff to do."

I shrugged. "It's okay. I don't mind doing my share. Long as I like the people."

"You like it here, then?" he asked.

I nodded, drying another dish. "Best place I've been since my Grandma died."

He stuck his arms in the sudsy water up to his elbows. His upper arms were brown and muscular. "I lived with my grandmother for a while, too," he said. "But she went back to Mexico."

I made a stack on the counter of the dishes that went on the high shelves I couldn't reach. "What happened to your parents?" I asked.

His hands moved around under the water, and the muscles in his upper arms rippled a bit. I resisted an urge to reach out and touch those muscles. He stared out the kitchen window for a minute. The sun was just starting to set.

"My Dad's a good guy," he said. "I mean, he was good with us, you know. But he got mixed up in some heavy shit. Went to jail." He handed me a bunch of spoons. "My Mom got a bad boyfriend after that. Fucked us all up." He pulled a hand from the sudsy water, turned on the tap. "Almost killed my little brother," he added. "They took us away after that. Split us all up."

I dried the spoons and put them in the drawer. "Sorry," I said. I didn't know what else to say.

He shrugged. "It's okay. What about you?"

I'd become so used to badmouthing Annmarie by then that lies tumbled out of my mouth easier than the truth. "My mother works in a whorehouse in New Orleans. She drives a big pink Cadillac her pimp gave her." When this didn't get a reaction from Juan, I added, "She tried to sell me to a child prostitution ring."

Juan laughed and flicked suds at me. "Cut the shit," he said.

I felt insulted by his laughing at me, but now I was trapped in my story. "Don't laugh. It's a big business over there in New Orleans. They pay a lot for young girls."

"Yeah?" he asked, looking me up and down. "Even for short little girls with no titties?"

"Fuck you," I said, my face growing hot with anger. I began slamming the dry glasses into one of the cabinets.

"Hey, I was just kidding. Don't get mad."

I ignored him, and stood on my tiptoes to try and get the plates up on a high shelf I couldn't really reach.

"Let me help you with that," he said. He stood behind me and took the plates from my hands, rubbing his body against mine as he put them on the shelf, taking a lot longer to get them up there than he really needed.

"I was just kidding 'cause I knew you were bullshitting me, Miri," he whispered in my ear. "I think you're real pretty." He kissed me behind the ear, so soft I'd never be able to forget the feel of it, then moved away quick when Mrs. Ramirez called out something in Spanish from the next room.

"*Sí, sí*," he called back, and pulled the drain from the bottom of the sink. He looked at me, the same way he'd been looking at me since I'd arrived there, but for the first time I understood everything that look meant and wanted to be part of it.

"She wants us to do our homework," he said, his eyes still fixed on me.

Then I did something that surprised even myself. I reached over and put my hand on his arm, the firm part where I could see the muscle. I just left my hand there for a minute, moving my fingers around the muscle as Juan got still as a statue, not even breathing in or out. We stood like that for what seemed like a long time, until I heard Mrs. Ramirez's footsteps approaching the kitchen. I squeezed his arm then, hard, and ran upstairs, shut the door to the room I shared with Rosa and Lupita and lay on my bed for the rest of the night staring at a water spot on the ceiling, but seeing in that ceiling Juan's arms, his eyes, and a hungry smile it seemed he'd developed especially for me.

CHAPTER 7
APRIL, 1982–MARCH, 1983

Didn't take us very long to fall in love. Of course, we tried to hide it from the Ramirezes, best as we could. At dinner we tried hard not to exchange lingering looks of desire over the warm tortillas. Tried hard not to lock fingers as we passed the salt or the butter. We tried, but did not really succeed, and Rosa, the older of the two little girls, picked up on it quick enough. She'd make kissy faces at Juan whenever she caught him looking my way; at me she'd sigh and close her eyes, rolling her head to one side as if swooning.

The Ramirezes didn't say anything to us about it right off, but they did seem to try keeping a closer eye on us. They started checking on all of us several times during the night, as if to see that we were all in the right beds; and after a couple of weeks of this, Mr. Ramirez suddenly insisted that we all keep our bedroom doors open. He directed his words at Juan, but I'd picked up enough Spanish by then that I got the drift of what he was saying.

"*Por que*," Juan asked, and Mr. Ramirez began speaking in a soft voice, so soft I couldn't make out the Spanish words. Juan looked down at the ground and muttered, "*Sí, sí*," and then added, "*Yo se!*" and shuffled from the room with his hands in his pockets.

I followed Juan down the hall. "What was that all about?" I asked, and he motioned me into his room, carefully leaving the door open.

"We have to be cool, Miri," he whispered. "He just gave me a lecture about not taking advantage of you."

I laughed. "Pretty hard to do," I said, "what with me taking advantage of you and all."

Juan shook his head. "This is serious. We really have to act cool for a while. They'll split us up if they think something's going on."

Truth was, we'd been in love for most of that summer without even coming close to sex. The physical side of our relationship was mostly those stolen glances at dinner, the lingering of our hands. Sometimes Juan would pull me in a doorway when no one was looking and kiss me, softly but intensely, his hands up and down my sides, but it never went further than that. We were too scared to do anything more in the house.

Somehow, Mr. Ramirez's lecture to Juan had the opposite effect it was supposed to have. It was mostly the timing, I think. Things had been heating up between the two of us for a while by then; Juan had finally gotten his driver's license and was allowed to use the family's barely running Pontiac on occasion; and I, as a present to myself for my sixteenth birthday, had taken the bus to Beaumont and got myself some birth control pills. No way was I having a baby at sixteen like Annmarie had me.

When I got the pills I wasn't even sure I was going to have sex with Juan, at least not yet; but once I started taking them, it seemed a waste not to, like making up a bed no one ever sleeps in.

We stopped talking much in the house, except what we thought passed for normal family chit-chat. Juan and I did, however, develop an unusual interest in our school work that fall. It seemed our junior-year courses were overwhelming us, and we needed to visit the library almost every evening, and on weekends.

Of course, we never set foot in the library. Juan took me instead to his swimming spot, a secluded beach that had been closed years before for pollution and never reopened. He claimed it was okay to swim there now, but we never went in the water.

Even though I could put on a good show, the thought of sex hadn't interested me much before Juan. All I could picture was Annmarie at my age, sashaying around in her skintight jeans and the halter tops Grandma surely did not want her wearing. I pictured her with a different guy each night, in the flatbeds of beat-up old trucks, rolling around amidst stray bits of hay, a rusty tool box, a couple of two-by-fours. Or on the leather backseat of a Lincoln Continental like the one the Clacks had; Mr. Ortiz, a man twice her age, grunting and sweating on top of her.

Before the first time we did it, Juan had tried to make it sound like he'd had lots of girlfriends. He mentioned these girls by name—Milagro, Elena,

Laura—and hinted around that he'd slept with them without coming out and saying it. But when we finally made love, I could tell it was his first time, too, though I never let on that I knew.

It was the way he touched me that clued me in: carefully, almost religiously, his fingertips and lips barely brushing my skin, as if I might break if he dared for more. He kept asking me if I was okay, if what he was doing was okay, asking permission for every place he touched me. When we were done, I wasn't sure if I'd liked it or not, but I knew he had; he had a look on his face I'd never seen before, a look full of emotions I didn't yet understand. He never mentioned any of those other girls again; they seemed to disappear from his mind the way dreams do upon waking.

It took me a few times to develop a taste for it, but once I did it became more than a desire; it became a need, this closeness, this touching, something I couldn't live without. In the beginning we did it on an old blanket that we spread behind some scrubby trees above the shoreline. After a while, I lost my fear that somebody'd come by and we'd spread the blanket out on the oily sand right near the water.

Juan would often bring with us an old guitar that had been his father's, and after we made love he'd play for me, teach me to play; or he'd put the guitar down and pull me to my feet, grasp me around the waist and dance with me on the sand, singing a Spanish love song into my ear, repeating each line in English so I'd understand the words. Sometimes after we went to the beach we'd go visit Juan's older brother, Ramon, who had an apartment a few towns away; but only during the daytime, because the neighborhood was bad and Juan said Ramon was into some "heavy shit," the kind that got their father sent to prison.

I wonder sometimes what would have happened if I'd been able to stay with the Ramirezes. Juan might have gone on as a carpentry apprentice with Mr. Ramirez, like he wanted to do; I might have finished high school. The two of us might have gotten married, bought a little place in a town not unlike Prairie Rose. But things didn't work out like that.

Just about the time my Spanish had gotten pretty good, just when Juan and I were so in love we pledged it nightly at dinner with silent gestures in the air that only we understood, Child Services called. They'd found me an English-speaking home.

The Ramirezes were mad. They spent the next two weeks fighting with Child Services, telling them that I'd already been there for eight months and that I needed stability. Or something like that. They got so angry and spoke so fast that I couldn't always make out what they were saying, and I suspected Juan hid some of it from me. He wanted to protect me, I guess.

For my part, I had Juan drive me down to talk to the new social worker, Miss Garton. She claimed that Miss Staples never should have left me there in the first place, and that the case got "lost in the system" when Miss Staples left social work several months later.

"But I'm happy there," I told Miss Garton. "And I'm doing well in school." That last part wasn't entirely true, but I hoped it would impress her.

She shook her head. "But you're not Chicana," she said, poring over my file. "You don't speak Spanish."

"I do now," I said, and threw a few phrases at her: *Buenos días. Hasta luego. Cómo está usted.* I wanted to say some of the cuss words Juan had taught me, but I held back.

She flipped a page in my file. "You told Miss Staples that your mother picked your name out of the phone book. That you weren't really Chicana."

I smiled my forgive-me-father-for-I-have-sinned smile. This was one I'd learned from Juan. "I was a very troubled girl before I lived with the Ramirezes," I said. "I used to lie all the time. But my father is Mexican." I looked up at Miss Garton to see if she was buying this.

"Where is he now? It says here your father's identity is unknown."

I looked down as if embarrassed. "Truth is, he was an illegal alien. They sent him back to Mexico."

"What part of Mexico?"

"Huh?" I hadn't expected her to ask for more specifics.

"Where does he live?"

"I don't know," I sighed, regaining my sad posture. "I haven't seen him since they sent him back."

"Give me his name. I can check immigration records and find out where he went." She was looking me right in the eyes, a direct challenge.

"Never knew it," I said, an anger in my voice that blew my act.

She let out a little exasperated noise. I hated her for it. "Well, Miriam, whether or not your father was Mexican is irrelevant now. You didn't grow up in that culture. It makes more sense for you to be with an Anglo family."

I felt tears start to leak from my eyes, but I wouldn't give her the satisfaction of seeing them. "It makes more sense for me to change schools again?" I asked, fighting to keep control of my voice.

"You'll stay in the same district. You won't have to change schools."

"No," I said, "just families."

"I'm sorry, Miriam, but the matter is settled. You'll be going this Saturday."

I started out the door, hiding my face from her, but she called out for me to stop.

"They're good people," she said. "I'm sure you'll be happy there."

If I'd had a weapon, I would have killed her right there and been happy to take the electric chair for it. Like she knew anything about me or what would make me happy. I tried to get a grip on myself because Juan was waiting in the hall, but when I saw his hopeful face I just started crying that much harder.

He put his arm around me and steered me out of the building. "Don't cry," he said. "I have an idea."

"Yeah?" I doubted there was anything more that could be done.

He opened the car door for me, closed it once I was inside. When he'd gotten in and shut his door, he said, "I've been thinking a lot about this." He fingered the steering wheel. "You only have to be seventeen to be married in this state, you know."

I watched the nervous way he ran his fingers along the wheel grips. "What are you saying?" I asked.

"Look, you'll be seventeen in like six or seven months, right? I'll be eighteen by then."

"Yeah?"

"So," he reached over and took my hands in his, moved as close to me as he could get in a bucket seat, "we could get married then."

I thought I'd explode with the way I felt for him at that moment. "You'd want to marry me?" I asked.

"Course I would," he said. "I love you, Miri." He touched my cheek with his hand. "But we'd have to hang on for a while."

I smiled. "I can do it if you can," I said. "If you don't fall for the next girl who comes to the Ramirezes." I was kidding, but he got a serious look on his face.

"No way, Miri. There's nobody else for me." He kissed me hard, a desperate kiss, and we drove in silence back to the house.

The new Mom and Dad were some kind of fundamentalists. The Mom was a small timid hamster of a woman whose eyes darted around a room without ever landing on anything or anyone; the Dad was a preacher. He talked a lot about Jesus and the Bible the first week I was there, but neither of them laid down any rules or regulations. The house was in perfect order, everything within it scrubbed to sparkling: the pots and pans in the kitchen, the sinks, the bathtub, even the floors. I got the feeling at first that if I just played along on the religion stuff and maybe helped out around the house a bit they'd pretty much leave me alone, and the months until I turned seventeen would pass with reasonable speed.

But I knew I was in trouble when I went to hear the Dad preach that first Sunday. In the course of his sermon he'd denounced rock music, all forms of dancing, alcohol, drugs, liberal politicians, and people who live in New York City. While I could agree with him on some things, like drugs, having seen what they'd done to Annmarie, I couldn't see what harm there was in rock music or dancing. I also thought that Jesus would not have condemned all the residents of an entire city, but I kept this to myself, nodding and smiling at the Dad, and saying "Amen" when everyone else did. When he asked me that night what I'd thought of his sermon, I told him he was even better than the Reverend Wilson Baylor, my old pastor back in Prairie Rose. The Dad smiled at me then, a creepy, otherworldly smile I imagined he'd developed to scare the devil out of his parishioners.

Truth be told, I'd never thought much of the Reverend Baylor's sermons. Annmarie had more than once referred to Grandma's religion as "a crock of shit"; and although I tried hard to disagree with her, I had to admit that I never once heard a word at the Home Sweet Home Bible Church that I could relate to my life. After my first few weeks of services there I'd start-ed pretty much blocking out what the reverend was saying, and concen-trated instead on my singing. I wasn't the only one; Grandma, who con-sidered herself devout, oftentimes nodded off during services; and Wendell, far as I'd been able to tell, went to church there only because he'd done it all his life and couldn't shake the habit. I'd heard Guy tease him about it, more than once.

When I first started living with the Ramirezes, they'd wanted to drive me to church in Prairie Rose every Sunday, but I refused. Once I'd left I did-n't want to see anyone in town; especially not Wendell, who still tried to contact me through Child Services on occasion. Instead I went to church with the Ramirezes, who were Catholic, like my Cajun granddaddy. I'd sit in the hard-backed wooden pew and study the stained-glass windows while Juan and the rest of the family all took communion. The priest there did-n't reach me any more than the Reverend Wilson Baylor had, but of course I didn't say so.

When I saw Juan in school on Monday and told him about the Dad's sermon, I knew it just sounded like me exaggerating again. He shrugged, told me to play along and to ask if I could go to the library some night that week. Going to the library, of course, was our code for sex on the beach.

I asked several times over the next few weeks if I could go to the library to study at night, but Preacher Dad just gave me the runaround—he would answer me with a scripture passage, and I was expected to sit around and figure out what he meant. I've never had much patience for folks who won't just come out and say what they mean, and so I took his responses in the spirit they were offered, as his way of saying no.

I gave up on the idea of seeing Juan outside of school for the next few months; instead, school became our sanctuary. He would leave love notes in my locker, and once a week he'd slip in a card from the *Loteria* game we used to play at the Ramirezes. He said that by the time I got card number 23—*la luna*, my favorite because the moon is supposed to be for lovers—we'd be together again. Sometimes we'd cut a class and sneak down to the boiler room to make out, or skip school altogether and go to his brother's place, for it was still winter then, too cold to spend the whole day on the beach. But we tried not to do that too often. We were both good at forging notes, but we didn't want to push our luck.

I was in a sort of prison, living with the Bible-thumpers, but since I was able to see Juan in school I settled into a routine at the new home. As long as I helped with the chores, attended sermons, and didn't ask to do anything a normal teenage girl would want to do, the Mom and Dad were nice to me, and I thought I could take it knowing that I'd be with Juan soon enough. I lived for school days, for the hand-holding between classes, for the quiet lunches we spent in a corner of the cafeteria. I developed a new smile, one that displayed my modesty and utter devotion to God.

One morning about two months into my stay with the Bible-thumpers, I had a hint of the trouble that was to come. I went downstairs for breakfast to find the Mom at the kitchen sink, scrubbing so hard I thought she'd surely crack through the enamel. There was no food on the table, no bowls or glasses, not even a carton of milk or orange juice. I walked over to the sink and watched her for a minute.

"You just go get ready for school, now," she said without looking up. As she turned her shoulder to scrub a corner of the sink I saw that the whole right side of her face was bruised, swollen. I started to say something, but she cut me off.

"You'll be late," she said. "Go get dressed," and with that Preacher Dad came down the stairs. Our eyes met for a few seconds, his and mine. I hadn't heard anything the night before, or earlier that morning; whatever had happened hadn't been loud enough to wake me up. As I tried to imagine possibilities other than the obvious—some kind of accident, a walk into a wall, a door, a banister—he did something that chilled me to the bone: he smiled. It was a quick smile, a fleeting upturn of the lips, there one second and gone just as fast; but it was enough to tell me everything I needed to know. I went upstairs, got dressed as quickly as I could and headed off to school, before he decided to shift his attention to me.

After that, I started noticing things about the Preacher Dad, things I'd chosen to put out of my mind before: how his voice shook when he gave a sermon, like he was about to lose control of himself; the reddish cast to his little round brown eyes, which made them look like there was fire behind them. Crazy eyes, Grandma would have called them. There was a nervousness to him, too, a manic edge that reminded me of Annmarie at her most strung-out. It was like he had the devil inside his own body, and because of that he was trying to drum the evil out of everyone else. Once I'd started noticing these things, I was having trouble keeping up my smiles, and I was afraid he'd pick up on what I thought of him. I just tried to stay out of his way without becoming so distant as to draw his attention. I never told Juan about what had happened; I knew he'd just worry, and there was nothing he could do about it, not until I turned seventeen.

The real trouble came that spring, just a few weeks before the one-year anniversary of the day Juan and I first met. We were hanging out in front of the school, waiting for my bus, when one of the prissy white girls came by, looking me and Juan up and down. She was in my music class, and hated all the attention I got there.

"What are you doing," she said to me, "holding hands with that wet-back?"

Juan started to laugh at her, but the comment unleashed some kind of beast in me. Nobody was going to talk about Juan in my presence and get away with it. I ran at the girl full-force, jumping on her as she turned and tried to scurry away. We both hit the ground, me on top, and I began slapping at her. That was all I did, just sit on her and slap her face. I didn't really know how to fight. I could hear Juan laughing behind me, and one of the other boys asking, "What's she going to do, *slap* her to death?" Those boys were still laughing when a teacher came and pulled me off. All that girl had was a rip in the back of her blouse and a red face, but they made it out like I was some beast who'd tried to rip her apart with my bare hands.

Of course, the school notified the Bible-thumpers. The Dad sat me on a chair in the kitchen and interrogated me like a prisoner of war.

"Why did the girl's comment make you so angry, Miriam?" the Dad asked, his fat hands clutching a leather-bound Bible.

I tried the modesty-and-utter-devotion-to-God smile. "It's wrong to judge people because of where they're from," I said. "We're all God's creatures." I searched the Dad's puffy face, his beady fiery eyes, to see if he was buying this.

"The girl you fought with referred to that Mexican boy as your boyfriend," he said, his face growing redder by the minute. "She told the principal that the two of you 'make out'—to use her words—in the hallways."

I squirmed a bit in my seat. Those prissy girls had nothing better to do than keep tabs on everybody else. "Not really," I said. "We're just good friends. We used to be in the same home." I tried an innocent smile, but his upper lip twitched with anger.

"Don't lie to me, Miriam," he said, those red-hot eyes of his cutting holes right through me.

"I'm not," I said, fumbling for a different smile that might work on him. "Juan and I are close. But that's all. He's like a brother to me." I sat back and waited to see what would come next.

"That's good," he said, slowly and deliberately. "I know you know how grave a sin it is to give your body to a man before marriage."

Don't I know it, I thought. Wouldn't be sitting here listening to your shit if Annmarie hadn't done just that. I smiled modestly and nodded.

"And I'm sure you know the consequences would be—well, pretty severe," he said. His hands were fisted around the Bible as if he were about to strangle it.

"I know," I said, still trying to look innocent. But I was scared. This guy was crazier than anybody I'd ever met; it was in his eyes, like a rabid dog. I couldn't believe Child Services thought Wendell wasn't fit to raise me, but this guy was.

The next day at school, I motioned Juan to follow me to the boiler room. I told him what had happened.

"I have to keep them convinced nothing's going on," I said. "I'm kinda scared of the Dad."

"What do you mean?" he asked, his words barely loud enough to hear over the noise from the machinery. "You think he'd hurt you? I thought he was religious."

I didn't know how to answer that. "He's scary, Juan," was all I said.

That afternoon I knew I was in trouble right off when I saw the Dad's car in the driveway. He usually wasn't home from work that early. I considered just taking off without going inside, but I had nothing with me, no clothes, no money. Maybe nothing had happened, I hoped, and went inside.

The Mom and Dad were sitting at the table over an open Bible, holding hands, praying aloud. My birth control pills were on the table next to them. I'd hidden the pills inside the lining of my rain jacket; I realized they must have turned my room upside down to find them in such a place.

The Dad closed the Bible with a snap, then turned and looked at me, and when I saw his eyes I knew I had to get away. I ran for the door, but he caught the back of my long hair and pulled me inside by it. I screamed.

"I'd better go upstairs," the Mom said, giving me a look of pity as she headed out of the room.

"Look," I was trying to stall him, "I can explain . . ." Before I could finish there was an explosion in front of my eyes. I couldn't see for a minute, but I put my hand up and felt something sticky coming out of my nose. When I could focus my eyes again I saw it was blood.

He'd been so quick the first time I hadn't seen it coming, but when his fist came crashing down toward my face again I ducked, and he just grazed the top of my head. He muttered something under his breath that I couldn't quite make out, that didn't even sound like English.

"They're not mine," I tried to say, but his fist landed on my cheek before I could twist away. He still had my hair wound around his free hand.

I knew I couldn't take much more of this, and something took over in me, some instinct far greater even than the one that had made me attack that girl at school. Self-preservation. I reared up like a horse and shot my knee out as hard as I could, aimed right between his legs. It hit square on and he let out a low groan, doubled over, and staggered backwards. I grabbed my black bag and ran out of there fast as I could go, blood still trickling out of my nose, my head throbbing with each stride of my feet. I flagged a woman down at the main road, told her I'd been attacked by somebody who'd jumped out of the bushes, and asked her to take me home. I gave her the Ramirezes' address.

The woman who picked me up turned out to be a teacher—special education, she told me, kids with learning problems—and she spent most of the drive trying to get me to talk about what had happened. I just kept shaking my head and telling her I wanted to go home. She offered to take me to the police or the emergency room first, but I told her my parents would handle it. I thanked her when we got to the Ramirezes, jumped out of the car quickly and ran around back, knowing she'd want to come in with me if I lingered for a second. I wasn't sure what I was going to do, but I knew that she would just complicate things. I heard her car idle for a few minutes in front of the house; finally, she pulled away.

The back door was open, only the screen latched shut. I could hear Mrs. Ramirez and Rosa singing from the kitchen—Mrs. Ramirez always sang when she cooked—and as I listened to them I realized I couldn't go in. I couldn't face the Ramirezes. I knew they'd fight with Child Services for me and try to get me back, but in the course of events they'd hear the whole story. They'd know I was sleeping with Juan. I was afraid they'd think we'd been doing it in their house, and that I was a tramp, just like Annmarie. It mattered to me, what the Ramirezes thought about me.

I walked around the back of the house and sat in the wooded lot beyond the edge of the yard, just watching them through the back window. I saw Rosa and Lupita set the table; Juan, helping Mrs. Ramirez carry the food out from the kitchen; Mr. Ramirez tickling and joking with Lupita before they sat down to dinner. They all bowed their heads to say grace, and even though I couldn't see the look on Juan's face I knew he was rolling his eyes like he always did. I felt my own face. Both my nose and my right cheek felt bigger than normal. But the bleeding had stopped.

I stayed in those woods long after the sun went down, long after they'd finished dinner. The crickets were chirping all around me; the only light I could see came from inside the house. I should have been scared, but I wasn't. I had one of those moments again, like I'd had on Mr. Ortiz's step the day Annmarie left me for good. If I was going to get through all this, to make some kind of life for myself, I'd have to take matters into my own hands. Nobody could rescue me, not Juan, not the Ramirezes, not Child Services. I had to save myself.

I decided I'd head for Austin. I'd heard tales of that town both from Mr. Duggan, who'd wanted me to study music there, and from Juan, who'd run away there once from a foster home he didn't like. Juan had described it as a college town full of hippie artist kids, a place where it was pretty easy to hustle spare change on the street, to find a dorm or an abandoned building to sneak into and sleep come nightfall.

The little bit of money I had left from the sale of Grandma's house—$973.24—was in a bank account, and my passbook was still at the Bible-thumpers'. No way I was going back there. I figured I'd get Juan to lend me a little, just until things had blown over and I could get into my account. Also, I wanted to say goodbye to him.

Once all the lights had gone out, I gathered a few pebbles from the ground. I waited what I thought was long enough for everyone to fall asleep, then I walked into the backyard, and began pitching the stones up at Juan's window. He was up by the third pebble.

"Huh? Who is it? Miri?" he whispered out the window. I knew he couldn't see me too well in the dark.

"It's me," I whispered back. "Don't wake anybody else up."

He disappeared from the window. I waited by the back door, turning my head away as I saw him unlocking it. I had a feeling I looked pretty bad.

Juan stepped outside and turned my shoulder with his hand. He touched my swollen cheek in a way that was so gentle it made my eyes fill up with tears. But I didn't have time for any display of emotions. I felt like I had to get out of town before the Bible-thumpers found me, and the Ramirezes' home was the first place they'd look.

"I just need to borrow some money, Juan," I said. "I'm leaving."

"He did this to you? That preacher?"

I nodded. "I can't stay here," I said. "They'll look for me here."

He took my hand and started to pull me into the house. "We'll tell the Ramirezes. They'll make sure you don't go back there."

I shook my head. "I can't do it any more, Juan," I said, pulling my hand free of his. "I can't count on other people taking care of me. Never seems to work out."

He looked in my eyes, touched my hair. "What do you want to do?" he asked.

"I'm running away," I said. "To Austin."

He smiled, kicked at the door frame with his foot. "Austin, huh? You think you know your way around there?"

I shrugged. "I'll figure it out."

"Well," he said, "you'll need a guide. Somebody who knows his way around."

I shook my head. Truth was, I felt a little mad at him. We'd both done the same thing, but I was the one who had to pay for it. "I don't need anybody," I said, fighting tears. "I don't need you."

Juan looked at me for a moment, ran his hand along the edge of the doorway. "I'm not letting you go by yourself," he said.

"I'm going," I said, and now I was crying full on. "You can't stop me."

He reached out and pulled me to him, put his arms around me. "You're not going without me, you know," he whispered in my ear. "Can't get away from me that easy."

We stood like that for what seemed to be a long time. I half expected the sun to start rising, but the quarter moon remained in place overhead, giving off its tiny sliver of light. Finally he said, "Come on, let's go in and fix up your face."

I turned away. "We'll wake them up," I said.

"Downstairs," he said, and steered me into the little bathroom behind the kitchen. He sat me on the toilet and washed my face with cool water, a soft cloth. The way he felt my nose to see if it was broken, the way he held the cold cloth over the swollen parts and dabbed peroxide on the cuts, he reminded me of a doctor. He had that kind of assurance, like he knew what he was doing.

"Your nose isn't broken," he said, taking the cloth off my face, drying it gently with another towel.

"How do you know?"

"I just know," he said. He wadded his hands into fists. "We went through this, Ramon and my little brother and me."

I remembered then his stories about his mother's boyfriend. "I'm sorry, Juan," I said, and started crying again. I wasn't sure who I was crying for, him or me.

"What are you sorry for?" he asked.

"I don't know," I sobbed.

He shook his head. "You didn't do anything wrong, Miri," he said. "Not to deserve this." He draped the wet cloths on the edge of the sink. "Wait here. I'll be packed in a few minutes."

I pulled at his sleeve as he turned to go. "You don't have to do this, you know," I said. "You have a good place to live here."

He smiled. "Not so good since you left," he said, and headed off into the darkness of the house. By the time I'd filled my black bag with food from the kitchen—a couple of apples, two boxes of pop-tarts, a jumbo bag of tortilla chips—Juan was at the foot of the stairs. He had everything he thought we'd need: an overstuffed knapsack, a rolled-up sleeping bag, and the old guitar he'd gotten from his father. We wrote a note to the Ramirezes, stuck it to the refrigerator with a hot-pink "L"—one of the alphabet magnets Lupita liked to play with—and stepped out into the night.

CHAPTER 8
MARCH–JULY, 1983

Juan and I walked down to Farm Road 770 and hitched a ride to the Interstate with three teenage boys out joyriding. They dropped us where we asked, at the entrance ramp to the highway, and we waited there for more than an hour before salvation arrived in the form of a timber truck, pulling an overnight to El Paso. The driver said he could go by way of Austin, that he'd be happy for the company, and so Juan climbed into the cab first, then helped me up. I did my best to keep my head turned away so as we wouldn't have to explain the bruises on my face.

Juan asked the driver a few friendly questions to draw him out and put him at ease, and pretty soon that man was going on and on about his wife and kids in Port Arthur, how the labor unions and the government were all in cahoots to screw working men such as himself, and which rest stops along I-10 had the most fiery chili. I listened and stared out the window, trying to make out some landmarks; I wanted to get a feel for what I was leaving behind. But all I could really see were the lit-up green highway signs, appearing in the darkness every few miles or so. After a spell we passed a sign that gave the number of miles to Austin—152—and I felt sure I'd seen that same sign when Annmarie had taken me on that wild ride across Texas, years ago. I started to feel sick from the motion, and closed my eyes. I would not allow the pit to form in my stomach. I was leaving the pit behind, back where it had first taken root, in Liberty County. A new life was waiting for me in Austin, and though I had no real idea of what that life would be, I thought it couldn't be much worse than what all I'd been through.

By the time that trucker dropped us near the edge of the University of Texas campus, it was nearly 3 A.M. We walked a few blocks, and then turned onto a deserted but well-lit street, a block of storefronts to our left, a grassy slope with trees and buildings to our right. I could hear a dog barking in the distance, and the sound of paper rustling in an alley between two of the stores. We passed a row of shops that looked like they catered to the college kids, with expensive-looking used clothes—"vintage," the sign said—mixed with even more pricey-looking newer stuff. The darkness inside the stores made the mannequins in the windows look eerie, like they might come to life at any second. I squeezed Juan's hand, exhausted, my nose throbbing, just now beginning to realize what we were facing.

"I know a place we can sleep," Juan said, "if I can find it."

We crossed the street and headed up the grassy slope, through the trees, Juan leading the way like a tour guide. As we cut across footpaths, passed between buildings, I realized we were on the U.T. grounds. The front entrances of the buildings we passed were well lit, but inside they looked mostly dark, except for the odd faint light in a window here and there. The dry grass crunched beneath my feet, and as I looked around at the sleeping campus, I wondered if I might have been there looking at the school, fixing to go to college, had my life taken a different path. Grandma would have liked that, I thought, seeing me go to college to study voice, or music, or maybe something she would have considered more practical, like business, or finding a husband. I wondered what Grandma would think if she could see me now, my nose swollen, hiding in the shadows of Austin in the middle of the night, looking for a place to sleep. She'd give it to both Annmarie and Wendell but good for not taking care of me. I hoped she was watching over me, or at least haunting them as punishment.

We circled several buildings, Juan inspecting basement-level windows and shaking his head each time. Finally we stopped at one that seemed to satisfy him.

"Here," Juan said, crouching down low and motioning me over. "We're in business." He pointed to a window, partially hidden behind some bushes. It was made up of nine small panes of glass, one of which was broken out.

"I hope you don't expect me to fit through there," I whispered.

He shook his head and reached his hand through the broken pane, working the window up from the inside until he could get his other hand beneath it and push it all the way up. He sat in the window frame, took a little jump, and hit the basement floor. I watched as he grabbed a wooden crate and stood on it, reaching his arms up to me so I could hand him our stuff. Once we had it all in, he helped me down.

"I haven't been here in a long time," he whispered. "I was scared they cleared everybody out by now."

I didn't know what he meant by "everybody" until my eyes adjusted to the darkness and I saw huddled forms lining the walls of the basement. There were at least twenty people in there, and they all looked to be kids; some were wrapped in frayed blankets or grimy sleeping bags, others covered with plastic trash sacks and old newspapers. Many of them slept with their arms around their backpacks or duffel bags. As Juan led me across the basement I felt something squish beneath my tennis shoe; I tried hard not to think about what that something might have been.

"Here's a spot," Juan said, unrolling the sleeping bag he'd brought for us. The two of us squeezed into it, using for pillows the clothing Juan had packed, and under different circumstances it might have seemed romantic. It was the first time we'd ever been able to spend the night together, but all I could do was lie there motionless, awake, my eyes closed so Juan would think I was asleep and also because I didn't want to see anything that might be crawling down the walls. The back of my head was wedged into Juan's armpit; my left arm felt paralyzed, crushed beneath his weight; and my legs were cramping from curling them around the guitar case. When I finally did drift off into a kind of sleep, the musty smell of the basement had settled into the back of my throat, and I woke up every so often feeling like I was choking.

I heard shuffling sounds and whispers with the first shafts of sun that reached us through the tiny window panes, but Juan and I were too exhausted to move. By the time we got up, the basement was empty. I looked around, amazed; there were no traces of the kids who'd slept there, no blankets, no newspapers, not even an empty Coke can. Juan said everybody took their stuff with them so it wouldn't get stolen, and they cleaned up their trash so the building's janitor wouldn't figure out the basement was being used as a squat. As far as he knew, there had been squats like that on campus for two years, maybe even more, though not all of them in that same basement—the kids moved around, he said, to avoid suspicion.

"Best thing is to try and leave early in the morning, before the college kids are up," he said. "We're gonna have to sneak out real careful so nobody sees us."

We rolled the sleeping bag back up and tied it into a tight roll. I pulled my brush from my black bag and ran it through my matted hair, wondered how bad I looked with so little sleep and a busted nose.

Getting out was more difficult than we'd thought it would be. Juan had to stand on a crate and lift me, holding me by my legs and pushing upward until I was able to grab onto the window frame with my hands. I scrambled out the window and tumbled into the bushes, and Juan tossed our bundles out after me, then followed.

"We're lucky no one's around," he said, peering past the bushes. "Come on."

"Where?" I asked. "Where do we go now?"

"We're gonna go make some money," he said, thumping his hand on the guitar case.

We staked out a spot on Guadalupe Street that was near the boutiques where the college kids shopped, but also a fair distance from the arcade where the younger kids—the kind that, like us, squatted in basements—hung out. Most of them had run away years ago, Juan said, had grown up on the streets and been hardened by years of living hand-to-mouth. He wanted us to distance ourselves from them as much as possible; he said people only gave money to buskers who looked like young musicians trying to make a name for themselves, not teenagers with no place to sleep who were looking to scrape together enough change for a couple of tacos.

I sang my lungs out those first few days, but despite my efforts, our busking career did not get off to the greatest start. For one thing, I knew all the words to only a handful of tunes that Juan could play—a couple of old Beatles songs, and Elvis Presley's "Love Me Tender"—and we played those same songs over and over. Between that, my busted-up nose and Juan's difficulties keeping the guitar in tune—it was old, and being tossed through a window each night didn't help it much—the few people who did throw coins into our guitar case appeared to do it more out of pity than anything else. The food I'd taken from the Ramirezes' kitchen didn't last us a week, and the few dollars we'd each had in our pockets when we left for Austin we quickly spent. Soon we had no choice but to scavenge: we'd hang out in the back of fast-food places at closing time and wait for the uneaten tacos or French fries or burgers to go out in the trash. Dumpster diving, it was called. We sometimes met other street kids like this, kids we recognized from the basement where we slept; but we saw our share of down-on-their-luck older folk as well. It was at a dumpster outside the Pizza Mia late one Saturday night that we met the Balloon Man.

I called him that because he wore a hat made of sausage-shaped red and green balloons, twisted together into a kind of crown. He was in a wheelchair and claimed to be a disabled veteran, but nobody was sure how old he was or what war he'd fought in. I thought World War II; he looked so old with his ruddy, dirt-smeared face and his filthy gray beard, like a giant dust bunny catching every bit of debris that blew down Guadalupe Street. He had deep lines like sidewalk cracks around his eyes and mouth. Juan said he wasn't that old, that it was probably Vietnam he'd fought in and he only looked so bad because he'd been on the streets for so long.

The Balloon Man spent the better part of his days ranting and shouting cuss words at no one in particular, though if you asked him a direct question or handed him a taco that you'd just pulled from the dumpster he'd get real polite and ask you how you were doing, only occasionally interrupting the conversation to holler at some passerby he didn't care for the looks of. He kept a little bag of balloons tied to his wheelchair, and when someone impressed him in particular he'd blow a few of them up and twist them into a hat or an oblong dog with the quick wrist twists of a real pro. It made me wonder what his life had been like before he'd wound up on the streets.

It was the Balloon Man who helped us get our busking career off the ground. After the first time he heard me sing, he'd beg me to perform every time he saw us; because of this, Juan and I started playing for him after dumpster dives. We experimented with songs we didn't entirely know, songs we'd played together for fun during those times we'd spent alone at Juan's swimming spot—"Brown Eyed Girl," "Heart of Gold," and "Me and Bobby McGee," which I sang in a low, bluesy voice that the Balloon

Man claimed made me sound just like Janis Joplin. Places where I didn't know the words, I made them up; guitar parts that Juan didn't know, he'd just skip over. The only country songs Juan liked enough to play were "King of the Road" and "Crazy," and since he didn't really know "Crazy" he just strummed along a bit while I sang. Sometimes he'd play one of the Tejano songs he liked, and I'd kind of hum with the melody. His guitar still went out of tune on occasion but he became quicker at covering up for it, getting it back to sounding okay.

As we played for the Balloon Man those nights, our daytime performances improved, to the point where people started tossing us enough money that we could buy actual meals on occasion. The kids from the college seemed to like the way we sounded; sometimes, one of them would bring a guitar or a set of bongos and join us. We learned more songs from those kids—Neil Young songs like "Comes A Time" and "Sugar Mountain"; Grateful Dead songs that I recognized as old blues and country songs Wendell had played for me, such as "Deep Elem Blues" and "El Paso"; and some New Wave stuff: "Alison," "Brass in Pocket," "Heart of Glass." When we did the punkier songs I always made Juan slow them down to showcase my voice more.

Days we made out well we'd also buy a jar of peanut butter and a loaf of bread, which helped us get through the days when we barely scraped together a few coins. Those loaves of bread never lasted as long as we hoped they would, mainly because we'd wind up making sandwiches for the Balloon Man and the younger street kids. On Guadalupe Street there were kids only twelve and thirteen who'd been there for more than a year, and talking to them made me feel fortunate. At least I'd had a home with Grandma for as long as I did.

One night late that spring, after a particularly good feast at the Pizza Mia—the boy who worked there had taken to just setting the pizzas out back for us so we wouldn't plow through the dumpster—the Balloon Man insisted that Juan and I were ready for the big time. He was going to take us to 6th Street and get us a job playing in a club. The Balloon Man gave us some piece of advice every time we saw him, and while once or twice it turned out to be sound—like when he told us how to sneak into the U.T. gym to take showers—most of the time he didn't make a lick of sense.

"I discovered Janis," he said, motioning us to follow him as he wheeled himself down the alley to the front of the restaurant and onto the sidewalk. "I discovered Elvis."

"Wow," I said, hoping the way it came out it didn't sound sarcastic. Juan rolled his eyes at me. We could have just walked away, Juan and me, but there was no reason not to go with him; we didn't have anything better to do.

"What are you looking at?" the Balloon Man screamed at a couple of college girls who walked past us. "You never seen a man with shrapnel in his spine before?" The girls had looked at the three of us, me and Juan and the Balloon Man, but they'd looked away quickly, and I could tell they hadn't meant to be rude. The two of them quickened their pace and looked down at their leather sandals.

"You just listen to me," the Balloon Man went on, as if he didn't realize he'd just yelled at the girls. "You get a fancy job in one of these here clubs, you'll be set for life."

I looked at Juan, who just shook his head. The 6th Street clubs were anything but fancy; we'd spent enough nights that spring hanging outside them to know. We'd heard a lot of great music, just from standing at the doors: the Fabulous Thunderbirds, Lyle Lovett, Roseanne Cash, Steve Earle, and even some punk and new wave bands like the Dead Kennedys and New Order. With bands like that, it wasn't likely that any of the club owners would give two underage street kids an opportunity to play.

We never did hustle an audition that night, but the bouncer at Club Foot took pity on us after the Balloon Man left and let us in to see R.E.M. play. Like most of the bands I heard in Austin, they were new to me—I was just beginning to realize how stuck in the '60s and '70s Liberty County was—but I liked them, how they were kind of a cross between country and punk. Juan dismissed it as "arty college boy music," and made fun of everything from the singer's mumbling to his hair, which hung in a thick curly V down one side of his face.

Standing in the back of the club, watching the band, it hit me that the Balloon Man wasn't so far off; those boys on stage were doing exactly what

I wanted to do. I want to start a band, I thought, write my own songs. It wasn't a new dream, exactly, but it was one I hadn't thought about in some time.

I was still thinking on it after Juan and I left the club, as we walked back toward the university. Our basement had been boarded up a week before, but we'd found another place on campus—a storage shed with a loose board in the back we were able to pull up and squeeze through. I hated that shed; it smelled of gasoline, dried grass, and mildew, and if I rolled over in my sleep I'd get poked in the ribs or leg or back with some scary-looking power tool. I hated that shed so much I'd make Juan look for a new place every night before I'd get tired enough to give in and sleep there. But that night I was distracted, lost in thought, and we were at the shed before I had time to protest.

"What are you thinking about?" Juan asked me, after we'd climbed inside the shed and located our sleeping bag in the darkness.

I almost told him, but part of me was afraid he'd laugh, or tell me how impossible it was. Part of me was afraid he'd think I was as crazy as the Balloon Man.

"Nothing," I said, curling myself next to him in a position that, while not exactly comfortable, had become familiar. "Just thinking."

After a couple of months of hustling like that—playing on Guadalupe Street during the day, hanging on 6th Street at night, sharing pizza with the Balloon Man and buying some of the younger kids burritos when we had enough money and it looked like they hadn't eaten in a while—summer came, and the university emptied out. The area around Guadalupe Street quieted down, the sun grew hotter by the day, and our income from busking dwindled to almost nothing. We still had about a month to wait before Juan would turn eighteen, when he would no longer be a ward of the state and could apply for a job without lying about his age and living in constant fear that Child Services would show up one day. The storage shed soon became too hot to sleep in, and we took to dozing under trees during the day, wandering the streets at night.

It was in the course of our nighttime wanderings that we met Robbie, a boy I remembered having seen around Guadalupe Street that spring. He would have been hard to forget: he wore eye shadow, blush, and purple nail polish, and even in a big city like Austin you didn't see too many boys walking around like that. Robbie remembered us, too, and complimented me on my voice, which made me like him right off. Juan wanted nothing to do with Robbie, and walked away with a look of disgust on his face every time I talked to him.

"Your boyfriend doesn't like me," Robbie said to me one night as he watched Juan amble away. Juan never went far from me; he'd just stand in the shadows, talking to the Balloon Man or some of the other street kids, waiting for Robbie to go.

I shrugged and smiled, not knowing what to say. Robbie looked to be about my age, and was clearly in the same fix as Juan and me. Make-up or no, I couldn't see a good reason to be unfriendly to him.

"He's cute," Robbie added, glancing over in Juan's direction. Juan threw a scowl back at him that was enough to wither a rose in full bloom.

"It probably wouldn't be the best idea to tell him you think that," I said.

"No," Robbie said, with a sad little smile that told me he was used to Juan's kind of reaction. "If I thought your boyfriend wouldn't kill me," he went on, "I'd tell y'all to come with me to a warehouse party tomorrow night."

I'd heard talk about these parties among some of the college kids who crossed our path, but I'd never found out anything more about them. After a few minutes, I got the whole story from Robbie: how the parties were usually put together by an older crowd—U.T. dropouts, art or music grad students, people in their twenties who'd gone to college for six years on their parents' money and were now working in 7-Elevens—and that they really got going in the summer, when the university was quiet. The parties were held in abandoned warehouses, Robbie said, and moved from place to place as police or the buildings' owners caught on. He said they tended to go all night, with various people playing music or reciting poetry; it was easy to crash in the warehouses, he said. He'd been living in them off and on for a year.

It took some work on my part, but I got Juan to agree that we'd go to the party, once I assured him it was not a hangout for male prostitutes, which was what he was convinced Robbie was. Truth be told, I didn't know that for sure, and I just hoped what Robbie had told me would turn out to be right.

That first party was the weirdest thing Juan and I had ever seen: there were poets whose entire works seemed to be hysterical rants at ex-girl-friends, performance artists who were usually naked and screaming about things we didn't understand, and musicians who played and sang an awful lot worse than we did. There seemed to be all types of people, from hip-pies to punk rockers to more regular-looking folks. But Juan and I soon discovered that if we played at these parties and stayed long enough, we could either sleep in the warehouse or, better yet, find someone we could scam.

It was Robbie who showed us how to scam, at that first party: we watched how he pretended he was part of the crowd, tried to blend in, as we'd always tried to blend in with the students when we were busking. He'd tell a variety of stories about himself; some nights he was an art stu-dent, others a bongo player or a U.T. dropout. He'd usually find some guy to take him home, and what happened after that was something Juan and I disagreed on. Juan was convinced that these guys paid Robbie for sex; I thought that if he was actually making money off it he'd have a roof over his head. Whichever way it was, I felt that whatever Robbie did with those boys wasn't really any of our business, and I'd tell Juan this when he made flip comments about it.

Juan and I put our own spin on the art of scamming. Sometimes we pre-tended we were brother and sister, from a nice family but down on our luck in a variety of ways, just in need of a meal or a place to spend the night. Other times we were a young married couple who'd just been evict-ed from our home. For some reason, people seemed more willing to help folks when they believed their lives had just recently gone off track, not a couple of runaways from foster care with nowhere to go. By the end of that month, we had a couple of stories we'd cooked up that could, if we pitched them just right, get us everything from a dinner at the Chili Palace to a place to stay for a whole weekend.

. . .

Juan finally turned eighteen at the end of June, and got a job bagging part-time at the Lone Star Supermarket, but still it wasn't enough for us to pay any kind of rent. I thought about getting a job of my own, but had nightmares that the second I gave over my social security number it would go into a file somewhere and get spit back out onto the pages of the Bible-thumper Dad's Good Book. Then he'd show up at one of the warehouse parties and give me the full beating I'd deprived him of by running away.

Round about this time Juan got back in touch with his brother Ramon. He sent us bus fare so we could go visit him in Southeast Texas, but I was afraid to set foot in Liberty County and we wound up blowing the money on two nights at the Adobe Inn in South Austin. It was rundown and not exactly clean, but we could shower and even do laundry in relative peace. And it felt great to sleep on a real bed after so many months of sleeping bags and couches. We made love—really made love—for the first time since we'd run away together.

A couple of weeks after that, Ramon showed up unannounced at the Lone Star Supermarket one night. I was waiting outside for Juan to finish his shift so we could go down to 6th Street and try to talk our way into a club where Lucinda Williams was playing. I hadn't seen Ramon in a while, but I recognized him right off, for he looked just like Juan, except his hair was shorter and his eyes weren't as warm.

"Hey, Ramon," I said as he started into the store.

He turned around. "Miri?" He gave me a hug. "Shit, you haven't grown up any at all. You still look about twelve."

"Well, I'm almost seventeen," I said, batting my eyes at him to prove my age.

With that Juan came out and saw the two of us talking. I thought he'd be excited to see his brother, but he looked uneasy, hugging Ramon with stiff arms, his eyes cast downward. It was then I remembered the money we'd blown at the Adobe Inn.

Ramon wanted us to eat at some restaurant on Lavaca Street he and Juan remembered their father taking them to on a trip to Austin when they were little; but we couldn't find it and, after cruising up and down Lavaca in

Ramon's Corvette until I just about got car sick, we finally stopped at the Chili Palace.

Juan and I ate until we were near bursting. After we were done, I left to go to the bathroom; when I came back, Juan and Ramon were in a serious discussion, their heads bowed over the table, voices so low I couldn't make out what they were saying.

"Miri, go play something on the jukebox," Ramon said, handing me a dollar.

This did not sit well with me. True, I was still only sixteen, but I wasn't some little kid who could be sent off with a pat on the head. I'd been on my own for a long time, and felt like an adult, even if I wasn't one by law. I started to tell Ramon what I thought of him trying to send me away like that, but Juan cut me off.

"Miri," he said, "please, just let us talk a little while. Okay?"

He sounded so serious, looked at me so pleadingly that I had to agree, though I was not at all happy about it. In fact, I was truly pissed. When I walked over to the jukebox I spotted a table full of college boys checking me out, and I went right over and sat down with them, just to make Juan jealous. But he was so deep in conversation that he didn't seem to notice.

"Hey, didn't I see you at a warehouse party last week?" one of the boys asked. He was white, clean-cut, with feathered blonde hair and cheeks so red and round and shiny they reminded me of scrubbed apples.

"Probably," I said. "We play a lot of parties."

"That's right," one of the other boys said, "you sang, with that Mexican kid playing the guitar. You have a great voice."

Now, I like flattery as much as the next girl. I stopped looking over at Juan and relaxed.

"Thank you," I said, smiling my male-magic smile at that second boy. His hair was longer and scruffier than the other boy's, his clothes clean but rumpled. He had a sweet-looking face.

"That's your guitar player over there, right?" the third boy asked. He was sitting on the same side as me and could see Juan and Ramon huddled in the corner.

"Yeah," I said, and then, in a bold move, added, "they're my brothers."

"Your brothers?" the apple-cheeked boy asked. "I thought that guy was your boyfriend."

I shook my head.

"You don't really look Mexican," the boy next to me offered.

I gave him an icy glance out the corner of my eyes. "Half," I said, "on my father's side." I glared at him, wondering what made him think he was an expert on identifying what people were. For all I knew, I was half-Mexican.

"My name's Miri Ortiz," I added, to prove my case.

"How old are you?" the scruffy-haired boy asked. He had big brown eyes and an easy smile.

"Eighteen," I said.

"You look younger," Apple-Cheeks said.

"People always tell me that," I shot back.

"Are you a student?" Scruffy Hair asked, and I was relieved he ignored the other boy's comment.

I liked that he thought I could be a student, that Juan's plan had worked and these college kids thought I was one of them. "Sure am," I said.

"What are you studying?" Apple-Cheeks asked. "Music?"

I'd been about to say social work, it being, oddly, the first thing that sprang to mind. But his own suggestion made more sense.

"Yeah," I said, "voice," and the thought of it made me smile a little.

With that Juan and Ramon came over to the table. It seemed they'd finally finished their conversation.

"What are you doing, Miri?" Juan asked. His eyes flashed at the college boys.

"Just letting you boys talk, like you asked me to," I said. I narrowed my eyes at him so he'd know not to treat me like a child in the future.

"Are you ready to go, or do you wanna stay here with your . . . friends?" he asked, nearly spitting out the last word.

"Hey, no problem," Apple-Cheeks said, picking up on Juan's hostility. "We saw y'all play at a party last week. We were just chatting here with your little sister, is all."

"My little sister?" I thought Juan would laugh, but he looked like he wanted to hit somebody. "Come on," he said, tugging at my elbow. I could tell he wanted to pull me out of the booth and drag me from the Chili Palace by the hair, but he was holding himself back.

"'Kay," I said, and got up real slow, just to torment him. "It was nice meeting you boys," I called over my shoulder as we left.

When we got out front, Juan kicked the brick wall of the restaurant hard, his fists clenched. He stared at the wall for a minute, and Ramon got in the car without a word.

"Juan," I said, softly, apologetically, and started to go to him, but he shook his head. There was a look in his eyes I'd never seen before. He looked like he wanted to kill someone. I wondered if that someone was me.

He turned from side to side as if searching for something, then headed a few steps down the road. He stopped in front of a wooden utility pole and punched it, punched it hard. That had to hurt, I thought, as he turned and walked back to me.

"Why'd you do that, Miri?" he asked. "You like one of those guys? You want to be with him?" The scary look in his eyes was gone, replaced by a look so full of hurt that right off I felt bad for what I'd done.

I shook my head. "I was pissed off," I said. "You get back with your brother and all of a sudden you're whispering stuff so I can't hear." I glanced at Ramon, who was watching us from behind the windshield. "He thinks I'm a little kid."

Juan shook his head. "We just don't want you involved, Miri. *I* don't want you involved."

"Involved in what?"

He sighed, ran a hand through his black hair in a gesture that reminded me of Wendell. "Ramon has an idea. If I go to work for him here in Austin, we could get a decent place to live, maybe even a car."

At first, this sounded great to me, and I couldn't understand why Juan looked so unhappy at the thought of us finally getting off the streets. Then I remembered him telling me that Ramon was into the same shit that got their father sent away.

"What does he want you to do, Juan?" I asked.

He shook his head. "Less you know, the better."

"No," I said. "Whatever it is, don't do it. You'll get on full-time at the Lone Star, and I'll get a job soon. You don't have to do this." Juan had never told me what exactly Ramon was into, but I'd always assumed he was dealing drugs. I'd seen this from both sides—from Annmarie as a user, and from the dealer boyfriends she'd brought to the house on occasion. I couldn't stand the thought of Juan having anything to do with all that.

"It wouldn't be forever," he said, like he was thinking out loud. "Just 'til we get on our feet."

I scuffed my foot on the sidewalk. "I don't like it. It's a bad idea."

He reached out, put his hand on my shoulder. "Just for now, Miri," he said. "Just for a little while. This is no kind of life, sneaking in and out of places, spending half the day looking for somewhere to wash up. I don't want to live like this. I don't want you to." He wrapped his arms around me and pulled me close to him. I started crying without really knowing why. It was just a bad, bad feeling I had about all this.

CHAPTER 9
JULY–DECEMBER, 1983

It happened just like Ramon had promised: within two weeks, we had a little apartment off of South Congress Street, and a beat-up old Chevy Juan
bought from a used car lot. At first I slept worse than I had in the basement, what with Juan's nighttime comings and goings and his refusal to tell
me exactly what it was he was doing. I tried to convince myself it was just
pot he was selling, nothing worse, surely not cocaine or heroin or anything
that destroyed people's lives, and I spent weeks searching the apartment,
looking for his stash so I could confirm this. After I'd just about given up
trying, I found the evidence one night by accident.

It was late July, and it was so hot in the apartment that night—the tiny
air conditioner in the living room window was old, and only blew warm
air—that I was wandering around dazed in an old undershirt of Juan's,
opening and closing the refrigerator door to try and cool off. I washed out
one of the two glasses we owned and filled it with ice, held the glass up to
my cheeks, my neck, rolled it back and forth across my chest. I moved the
glass as if it were dancing across parts of my body, and then I started to
dance myself, and pretty soon I was waltzing around the kitchen, the glass
in my outstretched hands. I started to sing "Crazy," my fallback song when
I couldn't think of anything else to sing, and as I whirled around the room,
gaining speed, momentum, I hit a loose floorboard near the pantry and
stopped in my tracks, toeing the floor until I found the spot again.

I got down on my hands and knees and saw that the board had been
neatly cut along its natural edges. It came up easily; beneath it was a fold-
ed-up piece of newspaper, and underneath that, a metal box with a tight-
fitting lid. Inside the box was a plastic baggie filled with a dense white
powder.

It wasn't a surprise, but it was something I'd been hoping wasn't true. I was living with a drug dealer; I was in love with a drug dealer. And the worst part of all was that I couldn't give him a single good reason to stop it. I closed the box and put it back the way it had been, with the newspaper over it, the board dropped into place.

Juan got home a little after 3 A.M. I was lying in bed by then, tossing around with the heat and the worry of what I'd discovered. I sat up as soon as he came into the bedroom.

"Juan," I said before he even had time to put his keys on the nightstand. "You're dealing cocaine, right?"

He looked at me, then turned away, pulled off his shirt. "Don't ask me no questions, Miri."

I got up out of bed and stood so I was facing him.

"Do you use it?" I asked, searching his eyes to see if I'd get the truth.

"No," he said, meeting my gaze. I believed him.

"If I ever find out you do, I'm out of here," I said. "Annmarie was into all kinds of shit. I'm not going through that again."

He shook his head, took off his shorts and underwear. "I'm not into it," he said quietly, and lay down naked on the bed, staring at the ceiling. I flopped next to him but rolled on my side, facing away, not touching. I was glad he wasn't using, but that wasn't enough. I wanted the stuff out of the apartment; I wanted him to get a normal job. It didn't seem so much to ask that we could live like normal people, like the people I'd known in Prairie Rose.

We lay like that for a long time in the heat, too sweaty to sleep, and then his voice cut through the stillness. "I'm doing this for you, you know," he said.

I turned around and faced him, ready to argue, but realized, as quickly as my anger had flashed, that what he said was true. If he hadn't run off with me, Juan would be going into his last year of high school, working with Mr. Ramirez on the weekends, well on his way to being a union carpenter. I'd screwed up his life but good, just like Annmarie had always claimed I'd screwed up hers.

"I know," I said, and he looked surprised, ready as I'd been to do battle a second before.

I didn't know what else to say after that, and so I laid back down in the darkness, feeling like I wanted to cry. Juan touched my hair, and I felt his lips on my neck.

"It's okay," he whispered, his breath no hotter than the air around us. "It's just for a little while."

By the time I turned seventeen a few weeks later, I'd buried my feelings about what Juan was doing. When he went out at night, I practiced playing his guitar, I exercised my voice, and tried hard not to think about where he was, that he might get caught, or killed. Juan threw a party for me at one of the warehouses, a surprise—I thought we were playing there, like we had earlier in the summer, before he'd started dealing—and when people asked how old I was turning, I looked them in the eyes and lied, "Nineteen."

Those last few weeks of summer were a good time for us. During the day, Juan wasn't busy like he was at night, and we'd go swimming in Barton Springs, or take a ride into Hill Country if it wasn't too ungodly hot to be in the car. We'd pack a lunch, find some pretty spot off the map somewhere, and just sit in the grass, just be together.

Once the students came back in September, Juan became busier than ever, even during the daytime. I took to hanging out on Guadalupe Street like we used to, even though Juan frowned on it because he said we were above that now. But I had nothing better to do, and I felt comfortable there. Some days I'd take Juan's guitar and sit by myself in our old spot, playing and singing a mix of songs Juan and I used to do together and a few I'd made up myself in the sticky heat of those long nights when Juan was out. My playing wasn't great but it got better as the weeks went by, and often people didn't seem to care. I took many compliments on my voice, and sometimes would just put the guitar aside and sing *a capella*. The guitar case often filled up with change and I tried to split it with Juan, but he told me to keep it, said I'd earned it myself. I didn't really need it, either—Juan now always had a wad of twenties in his pocket, and he'd peel a couple off any time I asked—but I liked the idea of that change I came home with each night. It was honest money; it was my money. When I did laundry at the Washateria I would use only the quarters I'd earned and it felt good, the clothes felt extra clean. I took to buying sandwiches for the street kids with enough regularity that the younger ones began calling me "Mom." It was a joke, but I liked the fact that I was set apart, that I was no longer one of them.

The day before Thanksgiving I went shopping for what I hoped would be a feast. I hadn't cooked much for Juan, didn't really know how, but I was determined to make a nice Thanksgiving dinner and prove to him that when we finally did get married, I could be an actual wife. Problem was, the rows of frozen turkeys I saw in the poultry section of the Lone Star Supermarket, heads chopped off, legs tucked under their pale plucked bodies, reminded me of that steer at the Clacks' ranch. Although I was still eating chicken and turkey at that point and thought my sympathy didn't extend to birds, there was no way I could take that dead frozen headless animal inside our apartment and pull the guts out from its stomach cavity in the little plastic bag I'd seen Grandma handle many a Thanksgiving. She used to fry up the gizzards, and although I never ate them I also never thought much about them. Now the idea of it gave me the same queasy feeling I'd had that day at the Clack ranch. Shit, I thought, another thing I can't eat. I was sorry I'd even gone in to the poultry section, that I'd started thinking about it again. It was a pain in the ass, thinking about food as animals, looking at a steak and seeing that steer's eyes or, now, looking at a turkey salad sandwich and seeing some poor old bird clucking around a pen. Juan had sometimes teased me about how I wouldn't eat hamburgers, or chili con carne, and with all the fixes we'd been in I knew it seemed flighty of me to turn my nose up at any kind of food. But thanks to the Clacks, I was cursed with seeing the world this way, and knew I would be for the rest of my life.

My work was cut out for me: I had to put together a feast so great that Juan wouldn't notice there wasn't a turkey on the table. I spent about two hours at the Lone Star, poring over the vegetable aisle, trying to remember the few holiday dishes of Grandma's that didn't have meat in them: mashed potatoes, black-eyed peas, cornbread. I had no idea how to do any of that, so I settled for canned cranberry sauce, a box of instant potatoes, a loaf of bread and a pecan pie from the bakery department. I threw a couple of frozen burritos and three bags of potato chips in for good measure, and I walked home with two big sacks of groceries, my arms so full I could barely see over the tops of them. That's why I didn't notice the cop cars until I was almost at the front door of our apartment.

Once it registered to me what was going on, I put the groceries down and hung back with the other handful of neighbors who were standing at the side of the building, waiting to see what would happen. My legs shook with panic, but I tried to tell myself that they might not be there for Juan, and even if they were, he might not be home. He was hardly ever home anymore, and I stood there with my grocery bags at my feet, making deals with God to be a better person and get Juan to stop dealing if he'd just not be home, just this once.

The front door of the building opened. It was Juan, in handcuffs, a cop on either side of him. If I'd been thinking clearly I would have stayed and hid, gotten a lawyer for him without the cops seeing me or wondering how old I was. But I was hysterical at the sight of him in handcuffs. I ran at the cops full force, thinking, I guess, that I could charge them like a bull and Juan would be set free. All that happened was that I got grabbed by the shoulders, manhandled a bit more than I personally think was necessary, and taken down to the station with Juan, who kept insisting that he had no idea who I was, I must be some crazy girl who lived in the building, no, officers, she does not live with me, there's no reason to take her in, too.

At the station, I gave them the name and address of a girl I'd met once at a warehouse party. I told them I was just a friend of Juan's, and that I'd lost my head momentarily when I'd seen them taking him away. I added I thought it was a case of mistaken identity, that there was a drug dealer in Austin who looked just like Juan, but they didn't seem interested in my story. I called Ramon, who would not come himself but sent a lawyer over. I hadn't really expected Ramon to come in person, I knew he didn't want them to nail him too, but it still pissed me off. Ramon had gotten Juan into this, and now he was sitting back in Liberty County with his feet up on the coffee table, sending some Austin lawyer to clean up his mess.

It turned out to be a mess beyond words, for the cops wanted to cut Juan a deal in exchange for him turning over the name of his supplier. But Juan was not about to rat out his brother, and so he was looking at five-to-ten for possession with intent to distribute. It seemed like the whole rest of our lives, five to ten years, but I didn't have much time to worry about it. The next day, Thanksgiving, when I went to visit Juan and bring him the pecan pie I'd bought, the cops nailed me. They'd checked up on Juan in Liberty County, and figured out my true identity. They brought me back to the apartment so I could pack a few things—I filled my black bag, put the overflow in a shopping sack, and grabbed Juan's guitar—and then took me into custody for the crime of running away. I wound up spending that Thanksgiving in a juvenile shelter, picking at the lumpy mashed potatoes and wrinkled peas that were the only part of the shelter's holiday meal I'd even consider eating.

I got shipped back to Liberty County. The family they placed me with wasn't too bad this time; mostly they stayed out of my way, I guess after reading all the bad things about me in my Child Services file. I started back in the same school Juan and I had gone to, still a junior, but I hardly went to a class. Instead I sat in the girl's bathroom or the boiler room and fretted, made up song lyrics and music to kill time as I waited for Juan's case to come before a judge. If he somehow got off, I was planning to run away and be with him. If he went to jail, I'd run away so I could visit him. Either way I wasn't staying in Liberty County very long.

I talked to Juan on the phone every night. Ramon had bailed him out, and put him up in Austin while he waited for the case to come up; he wanted to keep Juan as far away from him as he could. I wanted Juan to give up Ramon, told him that if Ramon really loved him he wouldn't let his little brother go to jail for doing his dirty work. But Juan said no, he couldn't, I didn't understand, and anyway five-to-ten wasn't so bad, he could be out in three-and-a-half for good behavior. When it was clear to me he wouldn't turn on Ramon no matter what I said, I tried to talk him into slipping the border to Mexico, said I'd go with him. He refused, said we'd run off together once and look where it had gotten us.

We talked the night before his case came up, and even then I still held some foolish belief that he'd get out of it, it would all be dismissed and we'd go back to our nearly married life in Austin. But there was a sound in his voice that night, something new, a sound I'd heard in others' voices before, but never in Juan's. It was a tired sound, a sound of giving up and giving over. Juan had accepted his fate, and he seemed to think I should accept it, too.

When I got the call from Ramon telling me they'd sentenced Juan to ten years—the judge had been one of those tough-on-crime types, and had given Juan the maximum to make an example of him—I was too numb even to cry. He could still get out in less than ten years for good behavior, Ramon said, adding that they were sending him to San Antonio, visiting days were Saturdays, and if I wanted I could ride out there with him, but he couldn't go that weekend, maybe the next one. I said thanks, maybe I'd take him up on it, but the truth was I already had my own plan.

That Friday night I packed everything I could fit in my black bag—a few changes of clothing, a toothbrush and toothpaste, a bar of soap, a washcloth, mascara, lip gloss, a hairbrush—and sat on the narrow little bed in the dark, hugging my bag and Juan's guitar, waiting until I was sure the family was asleep. Then I crept downstairs, took the two twenties I found in the Mom's purse, and hit the road. I'd planned to hitch a ride, but with that kind of money I could go first-class. I could go Greyhound.

I spent the night in the station waiting for the next bus to San Antonio, which left at 6:30 A.M. To pass the time I strummed on Juan's guitar, real soft so no one would notice, for I didn't want to call attention to myself. I prayed the Mom and Dad I'd been staying with wouldn't find I was missing before my bus left, and for once my prayers were answered. The bus came, and left with me on it.

It was a four-hour ride, and you'd think with all that time on my hands I would have thought about my future, what I'd do beyond visiting Juan in prison. I guess I was just overloaded from all that had happened, for my mind seemed to have shut down from worrying. It was raining, and I stared out the window at the dreary landscape, the bayous, the dead armadillos. The gray sky seemed low to the ground, like if we drove fast enough and far enough I could reach up and snatch down a corner of it, wrap it around me like a sticky sheet.

I got lucky at the bus station in San Antonio. I overheard two women talking about going over to the prison, and managed to hitch a ride with these two, though they agreed reluctantly and watched me like hawks for the whole ride. Don't know what they thought I was going to do to them; each one of them was twice my size, and we were going to a *prison*. It wasn't like I was going to misbehave in a place like that.

The true horror of the situation finally settled in my gut when I saw Juan walk out in navy blue coveralls, talked to him on a phone with glass between us, our fingers matched up on either side of the window like in movies I'd seen.

"Did Ramon bring you here?" he asked, and I shook my head.

"He's coming next week," I said.

"How did you get here? The family you're with, they're okay with you coming out here?"

I shrugged, smiled as much as I could muster.

"Shit, Miri, you ran away again?"

"Wasn't much to do back in Liberty County, without you around," I said.

"You have to go back."

"No," I said.

"Miri, I mean it. Living on the street is no kind of life. Go back and finish school. Maybe you could really go on and study music then, like you always wanted. Maybe you could be in a real band."

That last part left me truly speechless, for I'd never told Juan about those dreams, about how Mr. Duggan had said I was practically guaranteed a spot in the university's vocal arts department. How I'd seen those bands on 6th Street and wanted to be up on stage with them.

Juan was smiling, seeing, I guess, the surprise on my face. "I know that's what you want," he said, and right then, I thought, this must be what love is: someone knowing you like that, way down deep, things you haven't even told them.

"What'll I do without you?" I asked, looking away from him, struggling to keep my voice even.

Juan sighed, and tapped the glass so I'd look at him. He looked long and hard in my eyes; it was a look I'd seen before. He was trying to memorize my face, trying to find a way to say goodbye. A guard came up behind him, said his time was almost up.

"I'm not worried about you, Miri," he said finally. "A cat, that's what you are. You'll always land on your feet."

He stood up, the phone still in his hand. "I love you," I said quickly, afraid the guard would rip him away before I'd get a chance to say it.

"Love you too," he said. "Don't ever come back here, okay?" By the time the full impact of his last words had hit me, all I could see of him was a blur of blue coveralls, "Texas Department of Corrections" stenciled across the back, being led away from me.

CHAPTER 10
DECEMBER, 1983

I stumbled out of the prison in a daze, my mind still on Juan. I walked to the parking lot where I was supposed to meet the women who'd given me the ride, back at their car. It was a badly dented Renault, one of those boxy little things that had the words "Le Car" painted in huge black letters on the side; you'd think a car like that would be easy to spot, but I couldn't find it. After circling the lot twice I realized they'd taken off without me.

The prison was on a back road pretty far off the main highway, but I decided to start walking it anyway. Didn't care much how long it took me to get back into town; it felt like I would spend my whole life walking roads like the one I was on, wandering from place to place just hoping to find somewhere I could stay put. I knew it was the last time I'd ever see Juan, not just because he'd told me not to come back but because I couldn't bear seeing him like that. I was completely on my own now.

I walked for an hour, maybe two, and didn't seem to be getting any closer to civilization. If anything, it looked like I was walking into the wilderness. I passed stands of plum and oak trees, and the street went from smooth pavement to clay dirt. The sun was bright, but still it was December, and there was a chill in the air that made me pull my jeans jacket tighter around me. My feet began to ache, and though I hated to admit it I knew I'd gone off in the wrong direction. I sat down on the side of the road for a minute, took my tennis shoes off and rubbed my toes. I was tired enough that I considered, for a second, lying down in the scrubby grass there and closing my eyes; but the sound of something scurrying through the woods behind me changed my mind. I imagined it was a copperhead or a coral snake, maybe even an alligator—I'd seen them in the bayous of East Texas, and had no idea if they lived in the creeks of San Antone as well. At any rate I wasn't waiting around to see what it was. I put my shoes on and headed back toward the prison. If I could make my way downtown I could try and find a place to sleep there. Better yet, I could hitch a ride to Austin.

By the time I got back to the prison, the guards were changing shifts. Cars came and went; men and women in uniforms piled in, piled out. I just kept on walking, too tired to deal with asking one of them for a ride. They were, after all, the law; I was scared they'd ask questions I was too exhausted to give the right answers to.

About a quarter mile past the prison, a dust-covered white Chevette slowed down beside me.

"Where you heading?" He was wearing a uniform, but I was relieved to see his dark eyes, his thick black hair and caramel-colored skin. Ortiz or no, after being with the Ramirezes and then Juan for all that time, I'd come to think of myself as Mexican, at least half. I'd also taken on Juan's general distrust of Anglos, and felt better right then not getting in the car with one.

"Just need a ride back downtown," I said.

"No problem," the guy said, leaning over and opening the passenger's door.

It was a relief to sit down. My feet were throbbing by then, blistered where the tennis shoes had rubbed against my ankles. I'd been walking for miles, and hadn't gotten more than an hour's sleep at the bus station the night before. I closed my eyes and might well have nodded off if he hadn't started talking.

"Where do you live?" he asked. "I can give you a ride home, if it's not too far out."

I shook my head. "Just drop me at the bus station, if it's not out of your way. My brother's picking me up there." It amazed me sometimes, how these stories just rolled right out of me.

"You visit somebody at the prison today?" he asked. He was looking straight ahead, at the road. I couldn't tell what he was thinking.

"Yeah," I said. "My boyfriend." I hadn't planned to tell the truth; I almost said "my brother," but I'd already invented a brother to pick me up at the bus station.

He nodded. "You been to see him there before?"

"No," I said. "They just brought him here."

"What's he doing time for?"

I knew what he'd think if I told him the truth. "For trying to take care of me," I said. It was true, another kind of truth.

He shook his head again, smiled a little, his thick mustache curving upward like a smile on top of a smile. "How old are you, anyway?"

"Nineteen."

"You don't look nineteen," he said, glancing over at me.

"I don't look a lot of things I am." When he didn't ask me what I'd meant by that, I added, "I'm half-Mexican."

He shrugged.

"People say I don't look it."

He glanced at me again. "You kinda do," he said.

"Really?" I was relieved to move the conversation away from Juan, the prison.

"Sort of. I mean, why not? People who are half-this, half-that, who can tell what they're gonna look like?" He stroked his mustache, stared off in the distance.

"You are, right?" I asked.

"What?"

"Mexican, I mean. You're Mexican, right?"

He shook his head. "My parents came from Panama."

"Oh." I thought about this for a second. I'd heard of Panama, the Panama Canal. I had no idea where it was. "I never met anybody from Panama before," I said.

He laughed. "You still haven't. I grew up here, San 'Tone."

We were on the downtown highway loop by then, and the traffic was heavy. He looked around to the left and cursed softly, then swerved hard into the next lane.

"Sorry," he said to me, and we were both quiet for a few more minutes. He turned on the radio, a country station, the kind that Juan hated. Juan always said that all country music sounded alike, that the women whined about wanting to be loved by drunks and the men singers boasted about how bad they treated their women. He'd told me once that his stepfather, the one that beat Juan and his brothers, listened to country all the time, and so I never argued with him when he went into one of his rants, not even to defend Patsy Cline. I just let him go until he got it out of his system. I wondered what he'd say now if he could see me in the car with this guy from Panama who was tapping the steering wheel to a Hank Williams tune.

"You know," he said, "you shouldn't stay hung up on a guy in jail. I seen it over and over. Never works out good."

I shrugged, not knowing what to say.

"You seem like a nice girl, you know? You should go find yourself another boyfriend." He glanced in the rearview mirror. "Just my opinion," he added.

I looked out the window, watched the billboards and exit signs go by. "Doesn't matter," I said. "He told me never to come back." I rolled the window down a little, felt the cool air rush in on my face. "I think he blames me," I said. I hadn't expected to tell this much truth, especially not to someone who was practically a cop.

"He told you not to come back?" he repeated, and I nodded, still facing away.

"Must care about you, then," he said. "Most of these guys try to keep their women hanging on. It's all they got."

I could see the bus station up ahead. "Anywhere around here is fine," I said.

"No, I'll pull in." He turned off the highway and drove up to the front of the station. I was relieved that there were enough cars and people to cover my story.

"You see your brother?" he asked, squinting at the cars.

"He said he'd park around back," I said. "He's waiting for me inside."

"You sure?" He looked at me like he was going to ask or offer something, but I cut him off.

"Will you do me a favor?" I asked, and he nodded.

"His name's Juan Quinones," I said, opening the car door and swinging my bag onto my shoulder. I pulled the guitar case from the back seat. "Would you . . . look out for him, or something? He really doesn't belong there."

He smiled at me, a smile so thin it was nearly smothered by his mustache. "I'll try. I can't promise."

"Do what you can," I said, snapping my jacket closed against the wind. "Thanks for the ride." I slammed the door and lost myself in the crowded bus station, never looking back.

First thing I did inside that station was to lock myself in a bathroom stall and count what was left of my money. $14.95. Sure, it'd cover a one-way ticket to Austin, but I'd be left with barely enough for a few days' worth of sandwiches. Seemed the smarter thing to do was to try and hitch a ride, save my money. Who knew, maybe there'd be a warehouse party going on, it being a Saturday and just before Christmas and all. Maybe I'd get lucky, get somebody to put me up for the night. I really wasn't looking forward to sleeping in some dorm basement or that awful storage shed, especially without Juan.

I heard a girl raped in that basement we used to sleep in, at least I think so. Can't be sure, scared as I was of what I thought I was hearing, trying at the same time to hear and not hear what was going on. Juan slept through the whole thing, snoring softly like he did, but I was wide awake. I couldn't see a thing in the darkness, but from across the basement I was sure I heard a girl's voice say "no." Then it was quiet for a while, and I thought maybe somebody had just been trying to take her sleeping spot, maybe she'd just been talking in her sleep, just dreaming. Then I heard her cry out. It wasn't a loud cry, nothing like a scream, just a little grunt of pain, like she was trying not to attract attention but it had just slipped out. After her cry, I thought I heard a deeper voice, a male voice, but I couldn't really make out what was said. I considered waking Juan, but then it was quiet again. I buried my head in Juan's chest and tried to convince myself it was nothing, just normal noises I'd heard, maybe even imagined. Maybe I was dreaming. By the time we got up the next morning there was no girl in the basement, no evidence there'd ever been a girl.

I packed my stuff back up and left the bus station, walked down and across to the northbound side of the highway. I stood with my thumb out right beneath a billboard advertising the Festival Guadalupano, which was already over, and truth be told I stood there for a long time without anybody even slowing down, much less picking me up. It was dusk, starting to get dark, and just when I began thinking maybe I should give up and buy that bus ticket to Austin after all, an eighteen-wheeler slowed down, pulled onto the shoulder, and came to a stop a ways past me.

The driver was greasy-looking and white and his fingers twitched nervously on the steering wheel as he asked me where I was headed. I had a bad feeling about him right off, but when he said he was driving straight to Austin I felt it would be foolish for me to turn down the ride. I wasn't having great luck there in San Antonio, and I thought, sooner I get to Austin, the better. Least I knew some folks there.

The trucker said his name was Leroy Lawless, that the last name had fit his Daddy and Granddaddy but that he was going the straight and narrow, working for a living, not some scab but a bona fide union trucker was how he put it. He chattered so many details of his life so fast, I finally decided he was on speed. It explained his nervous twitching, and how much he was sweating in December.

"So then my old lady says, 'You give up that gal on your Tyler run, or you get the hell out of my house,' and I tell her I'd like to see what she's got on the side, that last kid don't look like nobody in my family . . ."

He went on and on, a non-stop white trash autobiography. I knew there were some who would have called me white trash, too, and maybe back when I lived with Annmarie I might have thought of myself like that. But not anymore, not after living in Prairie Rose with Grandma, starring in the choir and attracting the interest of wealthy boys and baseball players. Not after being Juan's girl.

I stopped listening to the trucker and looked out the window, his chatter becoming background noise, like the sound of the road rushing by. The lack of sleep was catching up with me, and I must have dozed off for a second, because it didn't register right off that his hand was on my thigh; I tried at first to brush it away, like a mosquito. I only came fully awake when he grabbed my wrist and twisted it.

He looked at me and smiled, showing a mouthful of crooked teeth, yellowed from what I imagined as years of smoke and bad hygiene.

"Now you give me a little something, I drop you off in Austin and nobody gets hurt," he said, although my wrist was already hurting.

I remembered a time when I was ten, not all that long before Annmarie left me at Grandma's. I'd woken up in the middle of the night to the sound of screams: a man's screams. I stayed in bed for a minute, afraid to move; but curiosity got the better of my fear, and I peeked out my bedroom door just in time to see Annmarie slamming the front door to the apartment, locking it and sticking a chair under the knob. A man yelled "You fucking bitch!" and pounded on the door a few times, but then it was quiet.

"What happened?" I asked her, rubbing my eyes. "Who was that?"

She went in the kitchen, filled a glass of water from the tap and drank it down. I picked some album covers off one of the kitchen chairs so I could sit. "That asshole came over to—to sell me something," she said. I knew, of course, that this meant drugs. "But he wanted more than money."

"What did he want?" I asked.

"What do you think, Miri? He wanted to fuck me."

"And you didn't want to?"

"Now don't you get fresh with me. I've been through enough tonight." She filled the glass of water again, took a few more sips.

I hadn't meant to be fresh; it just seemed like she slept with every guy I saw her with, so it hadn't occurred to me that she might not always want to. "So what happened?" I asked.

"He started giving me a hard time," she said, "so I grabbed him between the legs and twisted and squeezed, as hard as I could. I walked him to the door like that." The idea of this had made me laugh, and she laughed a little, too, but I could see, as she sipped the water, that she was still shaking.

It hit me that this might be the first thing I'd ever learned from Annmarie that was useful, and I looked at the trucker, wondering if it was something I could do with only one free hand. His jeans were tight across his crotch; I couldn't imagine how I could get a good enough hold to really hurt him. Instead, I thought back on the scams Juan and I had pulled at the warehouse parties, and came up with a different plan.

"Look," I said, "I haven't eaten all day. If you'll pull off and get me some dinner, then I'll do whatever you want."

Anyone with half a brain would have seen right through this plan, but fortunately for me Leroy Lawless didn't have the sense God gave a goat. He let go of my wrist and gunned it down the highway, licking his chappedup, scarred lips as he looked from me to the rearview mirror to the high-way and back. An exit came up for San Marcos, and he took it, pulling us off the interstate and into the first truckstop diner we saw. My original plan had been to head for the bathroom as soon as we got inside, to slip out some back door or window, but I no longer saw Leroy as someone to fear; I saw him as someone I could scam. I decided I would get a free dinner for my trouble.

I shoveled down a big plate of spaghetti, Leroy watching me the whole while like I was going to be his dessert. He talked more about his trashy wife but I barely listened; my eyes were on the "Rest Rooms" sign, the arrow that pointed to "Ladies." When I'd eaten my fill, I told him I'd be right back, then grabbed my stuff and headed where the sign was pointing. I was afraid even a fool like him might actually figure it out soon enough, and my heart was pounding at the chance I'd taken; I should have tried to slip away the minute we got there. But I made it to the bathroom, locked myself inside and, as luck would have it, there was a window I could fit through easily. I had a little trouble getting the screen up, but finally it gave and I was outside, looking around for the best place to run to and decid-ing to stay off the main highway; I was sure it was the first place he'd look. Instead I ran down the road the diner was on, glancing over my shoulder every so often to see if he was after me.

Once I slowed down to a walk and had a chance to think about what had just happened—not only what the trucker had wanted from me, but the crazy risk I took to get a free meal—I started to shake. It was uncon-trollable, my teeth chattering, my whole body quivering. The shaking bounced Juan's guitar in its case, making little hollow thumping sounds that echoed off the strings. Up ahead I saw something called the Big Tex Family Restaurant, and I decided to hide out there for a while.

Inside, it was a slightly nicer version of the truckstop diner I'd just escaped, with new-looking booths, a jukebox at each table. I headed straight for the bathroom, splashed cold water on my face and fought a feeling that was beyond tears—a feeling like I wanted to give up. I even had a dark moment where I thought about calling Wendell, telling him all that had happened and asking him if maybe I could just sleep in the garage, unbeknownst to Child Services, until I figured out what to do next.

But Wendell had made his decision about me long ago, and I was not about to beg him for a place to sleep. I hadn't sunk that low, not yet. I ran a brush through my hair, frowned at the circles under my eyes, and headed back into the diner.

I took a booth far in the back and faced the door, so I could see if the trucker came in looking for me, and ordered a piece of pecan pie and coffee. I hadn't had coffee since those few weeks I'd lived with Annmarie in Prairie Rose, after Grandma died, and, when it came, I savored its strong smell. It was earthy and sweet and reminded me of better days.

The waitress put the check on my table right off: $1.86 with tax. That left me with 13-something dollars and not a whole lot of options. I asked her how far we were from Austin, and she said about seventy miles, give or take.

Even though I was near-broke I played a quarter in the jukebox, thinking, what the hell, it wasn't going to make or break me. I punched in the numbers for Johnny Cash, and for a Tejano song I knew Juan liked. First, though, I had to listen through other people's music, hit singles mostly: "Bette Davis Eyes," "Edge of Seventeen," and "Do You Really Want to Hurt Me" by Culture Club, a band whose lead singer was a man who dressed like a girl and pulled it off better than a lot of actual females, including my cousin Mary Gay.

Another batch of songs came on, this time the kind of stuff the kids at the warehouse parties liked: Elvis Costello, the Talking Heads, the Clash. I was surprised that kind of music was even on the jukebox in a little out-of-the-way diner like this, and I looked around to see who was playing it. Three booths away, I saw my salvation.

It was the scruffy-haired boy I'd flirted with at the Chili Palace, sitting opposite another boy I didn't recognize. After all I'd been through that day, it looked like my luck was finally changing. I glanced at myself in the chrome of the jukebox, dug around in my bag for the mascara and lip gloss I'd lifted from the Mom in that last home. She'd had so much makeup lined up on her nightstand, huge palettes of eye shadows with as many colors as a box of Crayola crayons, blushers and eye pencils and tubes of mascara that looked like they'd never been opened, that I doubted she would miss what I'd taken. I put on the mascara and lip gloss, ran a brush through my hair for good measure, and marched over to those boys without a moment's hesitation.

Scruffy Hair recognized me right off, and introduced me to his roommate, Kevin, inviting me to join them. They said this weekend was their last blowout before finals, and they were making the most of it, having gone to visit some friends of Kevin's down in San Antonio, and now heading back to Austin to hit some 6th Street club. I still didn't know Scruffy Hair's name, but it didn't much matter; by the time their burgers and fries had come, I had them eating out of my hand with a long and very sad story of how my brother'd been taking care of me since we were little, was even putting me through college, but now he'd gotten in trouble with the law and I'd been evicted from the apartment we'd shared.

"Doubt I'll even be able to go back to school next term," I threw in, stealing a couple of fries from Scruffy Hair's plate.

"That's awful," he said, his brown eyes large and sympathetic. "Where are you living now?"

"Don't know where I'm staying tonight," I said, the first truthful thing I'd told him in the past half hour. "Got relatives in Southeast Texas, that's where I've been staying since this all happened. I tried hitching a ride back to Austin, and this is as far as I got." I reached for Kevin's untouched pickle, waiting for him to nod okay before I picked it off his plate. "I at least want to take my finals," I added, chomping on the pickle.

"You don't have anywhere to stay tonight?" Kevin asked.

"Nope." I considered adding a more detailed answer, but I could tell by their faces that this was working just fine, as is.

"Well, you can stay with us," Scruffy Hair said, Kevin nodding in agreement. "We share a house with three other guys. It's filthy dirty right now, but if you don't mind picking a few beer cans off the couch you can crash long as you want."

"At least get you through finals," Kevin added.

It was like I'd pulled an arm on a slot machine and wound up with the jackpot.

"Well, that's mighty nice of you boys," I said. "You sure your roommates won't mind?" I batted my eyes at Kevin and worked a wicked smile on Scruffy Hair.

"Can't imagine any objections to having a pretty girl stay on our couch. Can you, Kev?"

Kevin shook his head, and added, "We're going to see our friends' band open for Ian Oliver tonight. Wanna come?"

"Who's Ian Oliver?" I asked, as if it mattered. I'd go, long as they were paying.

"The guy who used to be in that '60s band, Woolly Mammoth," Scruffy Hair said, and he and Kevin laughed.

Now Woolly Mammoth I had heard of. They were sort of a second-rate Led Zeppelin; when I was little I used to get the bands confused, since they sounded alike to me and Annmarie loved them both. The nights she came home from her waitress shift without a man—and believe me, those nights were few and far between—she'd put on Woolly Mammoth, loud enough to wake me up, though to be fair I was a light sleeper when she left me alone at night. I'd hear the harsh bass lines, the pounding drums, the lead singer's squeals like a third-grader sawing away at an out-of-tune violin. There weren't words strong enough for how much I hated that kind of music.

"Was he the lead singer?" I asked.

"Yeah," Scruffy Hair said. "He really sucks."

I laughed. "Then why are you going?"

"Just to see our friends open for him," he said. "We're supposed to be on the guest list. We can probably get you in too."

"Sounds good," I said, and looked around for some more food I could pick off their plates, but there was nothing left.

CHAPTER 11
DECEMBER, 1983

By the time we got back to Austin, to the club, I'd cooked up a new plan for my life. I'd go stay with those boys for a while, get me a waitressing job in some little diner, save up enough money for a room in a house. I was close enough to eighteen by then that I felt confident lying about my age, and though I'd never worked a job before—not unless you counted busking on Guadalupe Street—I thought I could do it. And it probably would have turned out okay, if that's what my life was meant to be: fetching fries for college boys like the two I was with, maybe taking one of them home every now and again.

But, as Grandma would have said, the Lord had other plans for me.

The boys had some trouble at first talking my way into the club with them, but I saved the day by peeling off the sweater I was wearing and letting the bouncer see me in my tank top which I wore, as always, braless. I knew I didn't have much up there, but I stuck it out as far as I could and worked one of my smiles on the bouncer. He and the boys all laughed, but it got me in the club. Once inside, the friend in the opening band spotted the boys and brought us all backstage. That's where I met Ian Oliver.

He was somewhere in his forties, and although his clothes and haircut made him seem younger from a distance, even far away you could tell he was kind of soft in the middle, that his jeans were too tight and he was working hard to suck in his gut. Up close his face reminded me of a topographic map of the U.S. that Wendell and Guy had helped me make out of papier mâché for an eighth grade social studies project. It was all lumps and bumps and crags, his face, pale as Elmer's glue. Up close, he looked about fifty.

It became clear even before Ian Oliver played that he was taken with me. His English accent reminded me of the ones Guy used to do, though anymore I couldn't have distinguished between those different accents he'd taught me, not if you paid me. I just knew it was English. I asked him what part of England he was from, thinking this made me sound wise and well traveled. His answer would mean nothing to me, but I liked the sound of the question.

"Heart of London," he said. "Working class boy."

"Well, that's something you and me have in common," I said, turning the male-magic smile up to 10. By the way he was reacting it would have worked at about 7. "Being working class, I mean."

"You mustn't leave before my set's over," he said, snapping his fingers at one of the roadies. The roadie went off into a room and returned with two Heinekens without even asking, like he'd been able to read Ian's mind. I reached out to take the bottle Ian was offering me, and before he gave it over he took my hand and kissed it.

The whole time he was onstage—the music he played now wasn't loud, like Woolly Mammoth had been, but he still had that godawful grating voice—I sat there with the boys, wondering if I really wanted to work it this way. I'd gone from having nowhere to sleep to having two good options, and the night was still young, as Guy used to say. I felt like I'd lived a lifetime in that one day, which had started all the way back in the bus station in Beaumont at 6:30 A.M.

After the show Ian politely spent time talking to the boys, never taking his eyes off me. I was handed a fresh beer before I could even finish the one I had, but I stopped drinking them as soon as I started to feel dizzy. When the boys finally said they were getting ready to leave, Ian pulled me aside and whispered, "How old are you, my dear?"

"Nineteen," I said. I was starting to believe it myself.

"Nineteen, eh? And how much of the world have you seen?"

By now I knew what his pitch was going to be, and I looked him over good to see if I thought I'd mind being with him. His hair was kind of nice—too long for his age, but curly and thick, dark brown streaked with a bit of gray. I hated his pasty-looking skin, but I liked his accent a lot. Every time he spoke it reminded me of Guy, and Guy reminded me of Wendell, and thinking of them brought up fond memories that made me feel warm towards Ian.

"Not much," I answered truthfully, "beyond Texas."

"How would you like to see the world with me?" His hands were on my arms, and he was standing so close that I could feel his hard-on through his jeans. It was weird, the thought of having sex with someone besides Juan, especially someone I didn't love, barely even knew. I had a panicked thought that it would make me like Annmarie, having sex with someone I didn't love just for a place to sleep, a way out of Texas. But then I remembered that Annmarie had been in love with every one of those guys she'd been with, even the one-night stands. She'd come home with a guy she'd just met and then spend the next day crying because he'd slipped out early in the morning without so much as a goodbye kiss. In her red kimono she would pace around the living room, cigarette in hand, staring at the phone, and she'd be depressed for days until she scored some coke or picked up another guy, and the cycle would begin again. Confusing sex with love had been Annmarie's undoing. At least I was smart enough to know the difference.

"I'd love it," I answered, and pressed up closer against him.

Next thing I knew, we were saying goodbye to those college boys. They didn't seem to understand that I was going off with Ian, and they gave me the address and phone number of where they lived like they thought I was going to turn up later on that night. They were awful nice, those boys. Ian grabbed a bottle of champagne and steered me out back to a waiting car. Its leather upholstery reminded me of those seats of Mr. Clack's I'd thrown up all over. I politely accepted the glass of champagne Ian offered me, and, before I knew it, we were standing in front of the Carillon Hotel.

All the time I'd lived in Austin, believe you me I never thought I'd be spending a night at the Carillon. Even from the outside it looked like something in a movie, all glass and stone and whitewashed wood, a lit-up fountain smack in the middle of the driveway. Inside it was even better. The lobby was carpeted in a thick plush red, and there was furniture scattered around just past the front desk, sofas and overstuffed chairs covered in a silky material, a flowered pattern of deep greens and reds. I ran my hand over the back of one of the couches; the fabric was as soft and smooth as the nylon housecoats Grandma used to wear. I looked over my shoulder at Ian to see if it was okay for me to sit there, but he was already motioning me to the marble hallway, to the brass-plated elevators.

The room Ian brought me to was more like an apartment: there was a living room with a couch and coffee table, and a little dining area with a glass-topped table and two chairs, a sink, and a sweet little cube-sized refrigerator. Then there was the bathroom, with a sunken tub, a shower stall and not one but two sinks, side-by-side; and the bedroom, with its king-sized bed, sliding-glass doors leading to a balcony overlooking the city. I whirled around, taking it all in, looking from Ian to the room and back and thinking, shit, he's not so bad, I could get *used* to this. I resisted an impulse to jump up and down on the bed, thinking Ian would not take kindly to such antics.

The sex part wasn't so bad once I figured out to pretend it was Juan I was doing it with. Then it happened real easy, though I had to be careful not to take the fantasy too far. If I did, if I thought too long and too hard about Juan, it would hit me that it wasn't Juan, and I'd have to wonder how he'd feel if he could see me going off and doing this so soon after being with him. I'd picture how jealous he got just seeing me flirt with those boys at the Chili Palace, and then I'd imagine him breaking out of jail, storming the room and throwing Ian Oliver off the balcony, his puffy body making a splat like a big mashed cockroach when it hit the ground. Such thoughts did not make sex easy or enjoyable.

That first night, Ian fell asleep soon after he was finished, and I lay there too exhausted to really sleep, going in and out of scary dreams I couldn't quite remember. I got up a few hours later and locked myself in the bathroom, ran a bath in the big sunken tub. Once I slid into the warm water I began to shake as I had on the highway earlier that night; I just lay there and let my body shake and shake, and tried hard to cry softly enough that Ian wouldn't hear. After I got a grip on myself I dried off, wrapped my body in a fluffy white towel and went back out in the bedroom. Ian was awake, watching the sunrise on the balcony. I walked out and sat down next to him.

"Just how much of the world do you want to see, Miri?" he asked.

I shrugged and smiled at him, waiting to follow his lead.

"I was just wondering," he said, "if you'd be going home for the holidays."

With all I'd been through, I'd nearly forgotten that Christmas was just a little more than a week away. "No," I said. "I have no living kin I want any part of." I phrased it like this so he would think there were people who wanted me, that it had been my choice to leave.

"Indeed. That's something else we have in common," Ian said.

He only had three more shows—Dallas, Houston, and Baton Rouge—before his two-week break for Christmas and New Year's. Did I want to spend the holidays with him in the Keys? He asked it like there was actually a question, like I might say no. It made me understand, too, part of why he'd been so keen on me traveling with him: he didn't want to spend the holidays alone.

The Keys turned out to be some little scraps of land off the coast of Florida—I know because I looked at a map in the in-flight magazine of the airplane we took. The scrap we were going to was called Key Largo, and I asked Ian why they were called keys when they looked more like a flattened-out string of pearls, but he just laughed and asked the stewardess for another martini. I had never been on a plane before and was amazed at the view of the ocean, the land, the clouds rolling by in the blue blue sky.

The resort we went to depressed the hell out of me. All the guests were Anglos, and I thought at first that the staff was mostly Mexican but everyone I talked to turned out to be Cuban. One of the boys who ran room service reminded me of Juan and I'd fantasize about running off with him, starting a new life somewhere. I hid my feelings as best I could, for I was at work, and there was no place or time for moping around. My time-consuming and increasingly difficult job was to keep Ian happy; his happiness was what was putting me up in these digs.

The first thing that seemed to make him happy was making me over. He bought me dresses in the hotel stores, backless, strapless jobs that only covered what absolutely needed to be, and a gold bikini so tiny it would surely have given Grandma a heart attack were she not already dead. He sent me to the resort's spa to get my nails done, said they were not attractive, bit-down and raggedy as they were. When he wanted me to get my hair cut in a short, New Wave–do like Pat Benatar's, that was where I drew the line. I let the hairdresser trim off the split ends, but that was it. Nobody was messing with my long hair.

We'd lie on lounge chairs by the pool and sip margaritas or daiquiris, Ian dozing in the sun, me flipping through the pages of the magazines he bought me. They were fashion magazines, and the articles were mostly beauty tips: how to use tea bags to reduce puffy circles under the eyes; the dos and don'ts of cuticle care; how to tell if your hair is ready for another perm (quiz). Then for good measure they'd throw in a story on anorexia, or how a woman was beaten nearly to death by her husband. Some of the beauty articles would make me laugh out loud, what they considered problems being so beyond worry in my own life, and Ian took that as a sign that I enjoyed these magazines, and bought me more. I'd imagine Lolita Clack lying on her canopy bed in the big Clack house, taking a quiz to see if it was time to touch up her strawberry-blonde curls, and I'd laugh until tears rolled down my face.

Things were okay until right up to the end of our stay in Key Largo. The day before New Year's Eve I got bored sitting out by the pool, and went back in the room to see what I could find on the TV. There was nothing that interested me, so instead I picked up Juan's guitar and started strumming it, softly at first, then harder. I sat out on the balcony and sang Ma Rainey, Bessie Smith, every blues song I'd ever known. When I finally stopped, a couple on a lower balcony applauded and whistled up at me. I waved and felt pleased as punch until I heard Ian's angry voice behind me.

"You never told me you could sing like that," he said. His eyes were squinted up, all the sun he was getting exaggerating the lines on his face.

"It wasn't a secret," I said. "Just never came up."

"Don't think you're about to start singing in my band," he said, his voice as icy as the piña colada in his hand. "The last thing I need is another hanger-on. If you're here because you think I'll give you a singing job, pack your things and get out now."

I couldn't imagine why he was so upset about my singing a few little songs on the balcony. I said, "That's not why I came."

"Good. But do me a favor?"

"Sure," I said, leaning Juan's guitar in the frame of the balcony door.

"Don't ever let me hear you singing again." He turned and walked out, the ice clinking in his glass as he moved away.

I stood there for a few minutes staring down at the pool area, watching as Ian crossed in front of a potted hibiscus bush and laid his body, pink from sunburn, out on a lounge chair. A couple of older women a few chairs down from him were chatting about Palm Beach; I could hear little kids laughing and splashing in the kiddie pool, and the very faint sound of a Spanish radio station coming from the cabana where they passed out the towels. In the midst of those sounds I heard Grandma, her words as clear and strong as if she was on that balcony with me: *They're all jealous of your beautiful voice, Miri.* For a second I was so certain I had really heard her that I looked around to see if Grandma was standing somewhere—behind a potted palm, maybe—but she was nowhere I could see. I knew her words must have come from somewhere in the past, somewhere in my memory— the time when we were having trouble with Mrs. Clack, maybe—yet for the life of me I couldn't remember Grandma ever saying it just like that. Memory or no, I knew right off that it explained what had just happened with Ian; he was jealous, and rightly so. His own voice sounded like a dying cricket. I went back in the room, put Juan's guitar in its banged-up case, and wondered exactly how long I was going to have to keep myself quiet.

CHAPTER 12
DECEMBER, 1983–JANUARY, 1984

Things with Ian went straight down the chute after that. Didn't help that New Year's Eve, which we spent at a fancy party thrown in the resort's Crystal Ballroom—imagine, this place had more than one ballroom, and had to actually name them to tell them apart—we were approached by that young couple who had applauded me from the balcony. They introduced themselves, said they were from Michigan and on their honeymoon, and asked if I was somebody famous they might have heard of.

"Not yet," I said, laughing at how crazy a question it was.

"Well, you should be," the wife said, "with a voice like that."

Just then I caught sight of Ian's face, redder than I'd ever seen it. I thought of Grandma's warning about his jealousy, and tried to make it right by introducing him to the couple, saying he was a famous rock star.

"He was the lead singer of Woolly Mammoth," I said.

The couple's faces were blank as pool water. They were only a few years older than me, and obviously had not had parents like Annmarie. They'd never heard of Woolly Mammoth.

"They were real popular in the '60s," I said, and Ian steered me away by the arm before I could say anything else.

That night, Ian was much rougher in bed than he needed to be. Didn't bother me. I was on that blanket with Juan, in the moonlight at the Gulf's edge. Nothing Ian did could reach me there, and so I let him go on and do whatever made him happy. Just keep him happy, I thought, dancing with Juan on the sand. Just keep him happy.

It's a testimonial to my powers of patience that I kept the thing with Ian going as long as I did. After the holidays I continued along with him on the tour bus, heading north and then east on the last leg of his tour. Almost every night we were in a different city: Daytona Beach and Jacksonville;

Shreveport, which was way too close to Liberty County for my taste; Little Rock; Tulsa. As we headed through the Ozark Mountains the weather got cold, a freezing, bone-deadening cold like I'd never felt in Texas. In Kansas City Ian bought me a wool winter coat, since it was too cold for the only coat I had, my jeans jacket. The coat Ian bought me was black, with deep pockets and a notched collar, and if I do say so myself I looked like a movie star in it, what with the way it swung out like a cape when I walked and all. That coat was the only thing Ian bought me that I really liked.

As we headed east through St. Louis, Indianapolis, Cincinnati, Ian became more and more difficult to please, and I don't mean just in bed. He took to ordering me around like I was a roadie, snapping his fingers for me to fix him a drink, give him a blow job, a backrub. I hated the backrubs the most, because of the mole just below his left shoulder blade. It was big and chocolate brown and shaped like a little oil spill, but what really got me were the hairs: five of them, long as my fingers, growing out of that mole and hanging down his back like they belonged there. I did my best to avoid touching it, him constantly complaining I was missing his left side, me saying my hands were tired, how about a martini or a blow job instead?

The straw that broke the camel's back came in Pittsburgh, late one night after a show, when he started going on again about how I gave the worst backrubs in the Free World, maybe even on the entire planet, and I was tired and had had enough and told him if he'd do something about that fucking hairy mole maybe I *could* give him a satisfying backrub. He sputtered for a second, then pulled a pair of tiny little scissors from his shaving kit and told me it was now my job to keep his mole hairs properly trimmed. I told him he didn't want me anywhere near him with those scissors, what with the mood he'd just put me in, and he got so mad he slept on the couch that night. Best night's sleep I had since I'd run off with him.

The next day, I tried hard to make up for the way I'd behaved. As we drove east for hours and hours on the rutted Pennsylvania Turnpike, a bumpy ride past snow-covered barns, silos, mountains, through a tunnel, I did my damnedest to cheer him up. I joked with him, flattered him, tried all my wickedest smiles, but he just stared out the window, shrugging without interest even when I offered to take him to the back of the bus and give him a blow job.

Ian asked me to stay at the hotel when we got there; he said he didn't want me at the show. I could tell by his face not to argue, and so I strummed Juan's guitar while Ian was off performing and tried to think up ways to fix what I'd done.

He came back from the show late, more than a little drunk, but still we had sex that night, twice actually. I fell asleep soon after, what with how much effort it took to conjure sufficient fantasies to get through two times in a row, and slept real sound through the night, as I usually did in those fancy hotels.

I woke up the next morning to the sound of someone banging on the door. I figured Ian had ordered room service, like he oftentimes did, and I waited for him to get it. When the pounding continued, I finally stumbled to the door, asked who it was.

"Maid," came the answer.

"We'll be out in a little bit," I called through the door. The room was dark and quiet. I went back into the bedroom and pulled the thick curtains open, flooding the room with light. Ian's suitcases were gone; I checked the closet, the bathroom, but could find no trace of him. I called his name once or twice, half-heartedly, but I already knew what had happened. Ian had ditched me.

I paced around the room for a few minutes, trying to figure out what to do next, but my mind would not cooperate; all I could do was picture Ian, riding off somewhere without me, laughing and joking with Jess, his tour manager, about how he'd gotten rid of me. I got more and more steamed at him as I paced the room, and it wasn't until I stubbed my toe on the bed frame and had to sit down for a minute that I saw the white envelope, sitting on the nightstand, leaned up against a heavy brass lamp. The envelope had my name on it.

I opened it, and counted the money folded inside: 10 twenties, $200. I counted it over and over, 20, 40, 60, 80 . . . , must have counted it as many times as there were twenties before I finally read the note.

"Sorry to interrupt your life," it said. "It was great fun at first! This should get you back to Texas—Ian."

I had to laugh at that. Of all the things I could possibly do with $200, going back to Texas wasn't even on the list. I rubbed my throbbing toe and tried to remember where I was. Somewhere in Pennsylvania, I thought, and I opened up the nightstand drawer and pulled out a tourist booklet. It had a picture of the Liberty Bell on the front, that bell surrounded by tow-headed white children, dimple-faced black children, a girl with long ringlets of hair and skin the color of a Sugar Daddy. Above those impossibly beautiful children, above the big cracked bell, the pamphlet read, in fancy script, "Philadelphia, Pennsylvania: City of Brotherly Love." I read those words over and over, just to be sure I was getting it right, for somewhere in the course of my schooling I'd gotten the idea that Philadelphia was the capital city of New Jersey.

PART II

Chapter 13
January, 1984

First thing I did was to order Room Service: a cheese omelet, French toast, orange juice, coffee, and two muffins I would wrap up and take with me. I had a mind to order more but didn't want to arouse suspicion, seeing as I planned to charge it to the room, hoping they'd just add it on Ian's bill. My plan worked, for a half-hour later, a handsome boy in a waiter's uniform turned up with my food on a linen-covered table and allowed me to sign for it, no questions asked.

I sat down at the little table he'd rolled in and turned on the TV, leaving the sound off. It was a habit I'd developed as a kid from spending so much time alone when I lived with Annmarie; I liked having the picture to look at, made me feel like someone was there with me, but all that noise just made me anxious, especially the shows with sirens and gunshots and the like. Drove Grandma crazy when I lived with her; a waste of the Good Lord's electricity, she called it, like the juice came direct from God himself and not from Southeast Texas Power and Light.

I dug into my French toast, stared at an old *Starsky and Hutch* rerun, and considered my options. Ian's suggestion that I go back to Texas was not a possibility, unless I went to Austin and hooked back up with those nice college boys. But I couldn't quite picture it, me knocking on their door a little over a month since that night I met them in San Marcos, accepted their offer of hospitality and then ran off with Ian.

I racked my brain to remember Ian's tour schedule. I was pretty sure he was playing in New York City that night, and I considered taking a bus up there, tracking him down and begging his forgiveness, acting all sweetness and light so he'd take me back. But my pride would not allow me to do this. And, truth be told, I was glad to be rid of him despite the fix I was in. The thought of never seeing that mole again could get me through anything that waited for me out in the streets.

My only other option was to stay in Philadelphia, at least for a while. Now, I wasn't real keen on this idea either. I knew nothing about Philadelphia except that it was a big Northeastern city, and that itself was enough to scare me. Grandma used to say the Northeast was populated by radicals and communists and people let loose from loony bins; she'd been to Maryland once visiting kin, and felt that made her qualified to judge. Still, I figured every big city had to have a college in it, and maybe a street like Guadalupe, where I could busk and meet some other kids who might clue me in on getting by in these parts.

I finished my hot food, wrapped the muffins in a napkin, and got out my black bag, spilling its contents onto the bed. I'd take only what I absolutely needed so as to keep my burden as light as possible, and this meant I'd stick mostly with the stuff I'd brought from Texas: jeans, cutoffs, a couple of t-shirts, two tank tops, a sweater. The bright yellow sundress Juan had always liked me in, and the Huarache sandals that looked nice with it. For underwear I had just panties—there were times I was thankful for having no titties—and a couple pairs of socks. I kept all the clothes in a plastic sack that separated them from the other junk in my bag: a hairbrush, the stolen make-up, a toothbrush, and the Loteria cards Juan had given me; some little shampoos and soaps I'd been collecting along the road, a bottle opener I'd got from God knows where. Wendell's dog tags were in there, too. Mad as I was at him, I still couldn't see fit to throw them away. Of the clothes Ian gave me, I was keeping only the black leather boots he'd bought me after I complained across Ohio how cold my feet were in my worn-out tennis shoes, and a sweatshirt from his tour that I thought might come in handy in the dead of winter, and that gold bikini, seeing as there was so little of it to take up space and you never knew when it might come in handy. And, of course, I'd keep the black coat. The Barbie doll evening dresses he'd made me wear out to dinner, to his shows, I'd leave behind, along with the spike heels and hose he'd liked.

. . .

The first thing I noticed when I stepped outside was how much Philadelphia didn't look like Austin, or Corpus Christi, or, for that matter, any of the cities I'd passed through with Ian. The buildings looked older than anything I'd ever seen; they were made of stone, or brick, with marble steps and carved columns, black iron railings, and fancy cut-glass windows. Across the street from the hotel was a little park, and I cut through it, passing by a couple of old white ladies sitting on a bench, tossing peanuts to the squirrels; a middle-aged black lady who hurried past me in an ankle-length, cream-colored wool coat, a briefcase in her hand; and an old black man, dressed in rags, pushing a shopping cart. He stopped at a trash bin across the path from me, dug through it with his hands, and came up with a 7-Up can, which he tossed into his cart. I straightened my back a little as I passed him, so the ladies wouldn't mistake me for being as down on my luck as he was.

I came out the other side of the park and found a street sign. I was on the corner of Walnut and 18th streets. There was a big old stone building across the road, and what looked to be shops and banks and the like heading on down Walnut Street. Cars jammed the intersection, and people in long wool coats, puffy-looking bomber jackets, and thick nylon ski parkas hurried past me, scarves wrapped around their necks, their mouths. On their feet they wore hiking shoes, fleece-topped galoshes, or leather boots like mine. It wasn't until I crossed the street that I started to see the other people, the ones who weren't in a hurry to get anywhere.

To walk down Walnut Street I had to step over bodies: black, white, all shades between, there seemed to be a body every block. They laid out right on the sidewalk in broad daylight, nursing the heat from a steam grate like a calf at a teat. Street people in Austin tried to hide themselves more, especially when asleep—the grown-up ones, I mean, though us kids kept a low profile as well. The older guys who'd been on the streets for a while, like the Balloon Man, always had out-of-the-way places they slept, places that were as much theirs as a house somebody might own. For us kids, territory was not as clearly marked; it changed with the seasons, the closing of dorms, the boarding up of abandoned buildings.

I headed on down Walnut Street, past expensive-looking clothing stores, banks, a coffee shop, an art gallery. At the corner of 16th a not-so-old black guy was propped up against a bus shelter, holding a beat-up paper cup, lounging just as natural as you please. He was watching people walk by the way you might watch TV, lying on your living room couch. There was something about this guy's attitude that I liked. He was saying, this is me, this is how I live, look and see for your own self, rather than hiding away in a basement, trying to pass for normal like Juan and I had done. But while I could appreciate what he was doing, I still held myself somehow above him. I told myself that I personally would never be caught sleeping in public view atop a steam grate, made a promise to myself that it would never happen.

That first day and night it seemed I'd left all my luck back in Texas. I tried following the guide I'd taken from the hotel, to get a feel for the city. What I needed was to find a college, a place a girl like me could hang, but the guide only listed fine shopping and dining establishments. I swore that if I ever made it in life I was going to write my own guide, a runaway's guide to the best places to crash in major U.S. cities. I'd do it with a fat cash advance from a New York publisher, which would put me up in style while I went around to the Guadalupe Streets of America, so far removed from that world by then that I'd sound to myself like a social worker as I talked to the kids.

It was way too cold for my Texas bones, and so after walking down to City Hall and not finding much of anything there I headed back toward the park, ducking in at every diner and café along the way. I was trying to kill time and stay warm, sipping on cup after cup of coffee until the waitress or waiter started making eyes at me like I'd overshot my welcome. When the sun went down and I was no closer to finding a place to sleep, I asked a waitress if there was a college anywhere in these parts. She was a middle-aged white woman with bloodshot eyes and hair bleached the color of creamed corn. Her nose wrinkled with annoyance at my question.

"There's a bunch of colleges in Philly," she said. "Which one you looking for?"

"Not sure," I said, smiling a way I thought would encourage her to keep talking. "Where are the ones you know?"

"All over," she said, nodding and holding a finger up to a customer who was trying to get her attention. "West Philly. North Philly. Center City.

The suburbs. There's too many to remember them all." She rushed off then, returning only to toss my check on the table as she passed by with a tray full of food.

It was dark and I hit the streets again. My mind started roaming to the $200 tucked into my left boot, but I didn't want to touch it, not yet. If I spent it now on a place to sleep, I'd have nothing left for harder times. I decided to try to find one of those places the waitress had mentioned— West Philly, North Philly, or Center City—and I headed down the steps of a subway entrance, thinking maybe there'd be someone at a ticket booth to help me. A sharp, sour smell hit me as I got halfway down into the dimly lit tunnel. The smell got stronger with each step, and I felt a wave of sickness as it brought to mind the odor of the Clacks' slaughterhouse. At the bottom step I spotted a man peeing alongside a column; he looked right at me and just kept on without a break in his stream, the smile on his face more chilling than the cold air outside. I turned around and ran back up the stairs fast as I could.

I spent most of that night just as I'd spent the day, wandering from block to block, diner to diner, the walks between getting longer and more urgent as restaurants closed at 10:00, 11:00, midnight. There were only a couple that stayed open all night, and I went back and forth between them. Round about 2:00 in the morning I was so tired I dozed off sitting straight up in a booth, and woke to find the waitress staring at me like she was trying to figure out what to do with me. She was a kindly-looking black woman about Grandma's age.

"You can't sleep here, hon," she said quietly. "Night manager's gonna boot you out if he sees you." She poured more coffee in my cup and headed to another table.

I sipped the coffee and tried to come up with a plan, but my foggy brain just kept returning to the $200. I decided to give up on saving that money for a time when I might really need it; it looked to me like that time had already come.

I caught the waitress's eye and waved her over. "Do you know a good place to stay around here, a cheap place?" I asked. "Like, for a student passing through town?" I decided on the spot that I was a down-on-my-luck

University of Texas student. Maybe I'd come to visit a boyfriend and found him with another girl. I could add more details if I found I needed to.

The waitress tapped her pen on her order pad for a minute and stared out the window. "I know a place," she said, "cheap and real safe for a girl alone. But you got to follow some rules."

"What kind of rules?" I asked.

"They religious over there," she said. "They like for girls to wear a skirt. Nice people, though. Put you up in a nice room."

I was a little leery of anything religious after the Preacher Dad, but I figured it was worth a try. I went into the bathroom and put on my sundress, pulled the sweatshirt on over the top of it, and laced my boots back up.

By the time I found the bus line the waitress had told me to take, it was nearly 3 A.M., and I arrived at the Divine Tracy Hotel so tired from having walked the streets all day and half the night that I could barely speak to the woman at the desk. She was an older white lady with a hairdo from the 1950s and a dress even more shapeless and out-of-fashion than the ones the Blue Hairs in Prairie Rose used to wear. But unlike that gossip squad, this lady didn't ask me any questions; just told me that the smallest rooms were $49 a week, more if I paid per day, and so I decided to go for the bargain, figuring I could stay for a couple of weeks, if I had to, at that rate. She gave me a sheet that listed all the things I could and could not do, but I didn't care by then. I went to my room, took off my boots, climbed into bed with my clothes on and slept until noon.

According to a pamphlet I found in my room, the Divine Tracy Hotel was run by Father and Mother Divine, who, best as I could figure, had started their own religion. The hotel had its strange ways, to be sure. There were rules about men and women staying on separate floors; women weren't supposed to wear shorts or miniskirts or slacks, and no drinking or smoking or cussing were allowed. But overall, it was just as the waitress had said—they put me up in a nice little room.

I met all kinds of people passing through, students mostly, some from different countries—Germany, Denmark, Australia, places I couldn't even imagine. I told these folks my hard-luck story about coming out to

Philadelphia only to find my boyfriend with another girl, how all my money got stolen after I paid up for my room here at the Divine Tracy, and now I had to put enough cash together to get back to Texas. Sometimes they would buy me a meal or give me a few dollars, but they were all young, traveling on budgets, and didn't have much to spare. I didn't meet anyone there who actually lived in Philadelphia, who could put me up for a while. As my second week at the Divine Tracy came to an end, I knew I had to get out and start meeting the locals, and fast.

The hotel was near two colleges, Drexel and the University of Pennsylvania. These schools didn't have their own separate campuses like U.T.; their buildings were sprawled out through a small slice of the city, random as a river cutting a path through dry land. I never did find any center of student life at Drexel, but Penn, as everyone called it, had a little student restaurant place I found. I spent four days there, off and on, trying to cozy up to various groups of kids I thought might be friendly, but it didn't work. No one was interested in my hard-luck story, and more than once whole groups of students got up and left the table after I started telling my tale. I guessed they'd been scammed before and knew bullshit when they heard it.

My third week at the Divine Tracy came to an end without my being any closer to finding a place to stay. I had $23 left—not even enough for one more week. So I packed up my belongings, thanked the lady at the desk— who frowned at the jeans I was wearing—and headed back down to the other side of town.

I went to the diner where the nice waitress had been. I liked that diner— it had neon signs in the windows, old Citgo and Camel ads and a big flashing brown-and-white sundae with a bright red cherry on top. My nice waitress wasn't there, but I asked the one who waited on me if I could borrow a phone book and I sat flipping through it, not really knowing what I was looking for except maybe the address of some other college, one with friendlier students. Never found that, but I did see a listing for a runaways' shelter. I ripped that corner of the page off and stuck it in my coat pocket, just in case I got desperate, but it would take a lot more than what I'd been through so far to get me in a place like that. They'd just put me up for a night or two and then send me back to Liberty County, and I wasn't going back.

I camped out in a booth for hours, feeling my situation getting more and more hopeless, trying to remember that it could be worse: I could be crazy, like the Balloon Man, or in jail, like Juan. My waitress was young and appeared to be on some kind of drugs and so didn't seem to mind that I had only ordered coffee and then switched to water. I was staring at the cover of a free newspaper I'd picked up, too distracted to really read anything in it, when I heard talk behind me that perked me right up.

"We need beer for the party," a boy's voice said.

"I can get it at Colletta's Market," a girl answered. "They never card me there."

"That's 'cause you flash your tits at the checkout guy," a different boy said. His voice was loud and I didn't much care for his manners, but I got up and grabbed a sugar canister off an empty table so I could see what these three looked like.

The girl's hair was dyed purple; she had painted-on, jet black eyebrows that came to points, with black lipstick and an ear so full of rings it looked like it had a zipper up the side. Both boys had hair as black as Texas crude, cut in the same style with layers on top that stuck straight up and fanned over like little fountains. One boy wore a black leather jacket and a chain-link around his neck, like a dog that had just broke free from being tied up; the other had on a green army jacket and two silver clips in one ear. His eyes were rimmed with black liner. All three had their faces powdered to look even whiter than their natural skin color.

I sat back down and listened some more.

"You sure the R.A. won't be around?" the girl asked.

"Nah, he goes to Rutgers to see his girlfriend every weekend." The guy started coughing, his hacks so liquid they gave me chills.

"We should get going," the other boy said, and I knew I didn't have much time left. I turned all the way around, peeked over their booth and said, "Hi," smiling my friendliest smile. The girl glared; the boys just looked startled.

"I'm new in town and couldn't help but overhear," I said. "Would y'all mind telling me where that party is tonight?"

The girl and the guy in the leather jacket looked at each other and started laughing. "Y'all," the girl choked out, and the two laughed that much harder. But the boy in the eyeliner smiled a little bit at me.

"PCA," he said, and the girl stopped laughing long enough to punch him in the arm.

"Don't tell her, man," she said. "We'll have every little belle in the whole fucking South there."

The boy in the leather jacket was still chuckling at whatever it was that had struck them so funny, but now he was looking me over. Even though the only one I liked of the three was the eyeliner boy, I gave this other one my male-magic smile anyway.

"You go to PCA?" he asked me, and the girl let out a long, aggravated sigh.

"Yep, just starting up this term." I hoped the term was close to starting up.

"That's cool," he said, that smile of mine warming even his cold northern punk-rock bones. Sometimes I think my smiles could cure a rainy day. "Where you from?"

"Texas," I said, and the girl started laughing but nobody joined her so she stopped. "My name's Miri."

"I'm outta here," the girl said, pushing the eyeliner boy out of the booth so she could get up. "I'm not going to sit here and watch you pick up Little Miss Y'all." She stormed off in combat boots that looked like men's they were so big. The leather-jacket boy looked from me to her for a second, then started off after her.

"Suzette, wait up," he called out, and I thought, shit, a name like that and she's making fun of *me*? But I just continued to fix my smile on the other boy.

"I should go," he said, looking out the window where his friends were yelling at each other.

"You think it'd be all right if I showed up at that party?" I asked, resting my head on my hands and batting my eyes.

He smiled, lowering his eyes to the table. "I guess, if you stay out of Suzy's way."

"I sure will. Now where did you say the party was again?"

"Johnston Hall," he said, and with that the other boy called out from the doorway, "You coming or what?"

"I gotta go," he said, but he smiled at me on the way out.

"See you later," I said, and turned back around, telling myself, well, Miri, glad to see you got the touch even with these boys up North. I sipped at my water. Now all I had to do was find out what PCA stood for, and where Johnston Hall was.

CHAPTER 14
JANUARY, 1984

With the help of the druggy waitress, who seemed pretty good with directions despite the lag time it took for her brain to sort out my questions and come up with a response, at 10:00 that night I was standing at the corner of Pine and Broad streets, looking at the main building of the Philadelphia College of Art. It was an old stone building with deep steps and big columns in front, and reminded me more of the Capitol building in Austin than anything on the U.T. campus. The whole area, in fact, looked nothing like a college campus, which was probably why I'd walked right past it that first night I was in Philadelphia and not even known. My waitress friend hadn't known where Johnston Hall itself was, but she thought if I went into the main building there'd be a guard to tell me.

A group of punk rockers like the diner kids came down the steps as I headed up. Now, I'd seen punkers in Austin, but these ones up north were more extreme: they looked like the kinds of punks I'd seen only before on album covers. One of the boys coming down the stairs had his hair in an aqua-colored Mohawk, a good three inches of bright blue hair made to stick straight up from his head like a fish's fin. Through his nose he wore a thick gold ring, like the people I saw in a *National Geographic* I flipped through once in Doc Busbee's office.

I had a feeling these punkers were going to the same party I was looking for, so I turned back around and followed them. They veered down an alley off the back of Broad Street and wound up pounding on a steel door I would never in a million years have found on my own.

I could hear bass coming from behind the door. One of the boys hammered on it again, and yelled, "Hey, we're freezing our asses off!" Two of the girls noticed me hanging behind them, and they whispered something to each other and laughed.

The warehouse crowd in Austin hadn't seemed to care how people looked: punker, hippie, whatever, as long as you liked to dance it was all the same to them. I got the feeling these punks were only happy if you looked just like them, and I knew my clothes and my long hair didn't fit their standards. Didn't worry me much; I knew there'd be at least a few boys at that party old Miri's smile would work on, punk or not.

The door opened, and I filed in on the heels of those other kids. We were in either an apartment or some kind of dorm room. There looked to be a bunch of little bedrooms, all connected to a living room where most of the party seemed to be. The lights were turned down, the Ramones blaring from the stereo. I noticed a table with some food on it, and made my way over, setting my guitar and bag down on the floor.

I stood there nibbling on chips and pretzels for more than an hour. One boy who passed by me mumbled something about the keg being in the kitchen, and that was the friendliest anybody was to me. Like the kids I'd overheard in the diner, this crowd was white, for the most part; I scanned around for some lonely-looking boy I could work on but they all seemed to be with tough-faced girls like that Suzy, girls who looked ready to beat the shit out of anybody who approached their guys.

I was getting ready to leave my stuff by the table and work the crowd, see if there was somebody I'd overlooked, when out of nowhere came the eyeliner boy.

"Hey, you made it," he said, looking genuinely pleased.

I swallowed a mouthful of chips and worked my smile back up. "Hey yourself," I said. "What's your name? I don't believe I caught it before."

"David," he said, grabbing a handful of chips. As he moved, he kicked my guitar case, and the strings let out a burst of sound. I pushed it farther back, out of his way.

"That's yours?" he asked.

"Yeah."

"Are you in a band or something?"

"Not yet," I said, "being so new in town and all. I was in a band in Austin, where I came from." It wasn't entirely untrue.

"Austin, Texas?" he asked. "That's supposed to be a pretty cool place. Good music scene."

"Sure was." I thought of 6th Street, and all the bands Juan and I had seen.

"So you played guitar in your band?"

"Some guitar," I said. "Mostly I sang, lead vocals."

"Huh." He took a sip of beer. "You don't know how to play bass, do you?"

My mind clicked into auto-lie mode. "Sure," I said. "I've played a little bass in my day." Truth was, even the strumming I did when I busked was limited to three chords. Juan had been the real guitar player; I'd just covered up my lack of playing with my voice.

"Wow, this could really work out. The band I'm in, we just lost our bass player." His eyes darted around the room, scanning the crowd. "Stay here, okay? The other guys are here somewhere. Let me see if I can find them."

"Sure thing," I said, sending him off with a big grin. Looked like this party might turn lucky for me after all.

He came back a few minutes later with two other boys who he introduced as Bobby and Rick. Bobby was about as tall as David, the two of them standing like skyscrapers over me. His hair was light brown, cut short and spiky on top, and he had three earrings in one ear, two in the other. He wore jeans and a plain black sweater.

Rick was a whole different story. He looked so young, younger even than my real age, which I lied about so often I could barely remember but which I was pretty sure was currently fixed at seventeen. Rick was scrawny, much shorter than the other two boys, with a face full of pimples I suspected looked a lot worse in better light. He had curly dark brown hair that grew in a shapeless lump, like somebody'd stuck a wig on his head that didn't fit right. Underneath a worn-out flannel shirt, which he kept unbuttoned, he had on a t-shirt that said "Satan is my co-pilot," as if such words could make a boy like him appear tough.

"I think Miri should jam with us tomorrow," David said. "See how it goes."

"I don't know," Bobby said. "A chick on bass?"

I gave him the evil eye, and looked over at Rick, who was just staring at me like he was in some kind of stupor. I wondered if he was stoned or something.

"Yeah, man, like the Talking Heads. Like Tina Weymouth." David looked pleased with himself.

"I don't know," Bobby said. "We'd have to change the name and every-thing."

"What's the band's name?" I asked, directing the question at David, not Bobby.

"Catholic Boys Gone Bad," David said, and I heard Rick chuckle softly. It was the first sound he'd made.

"So I take it you're all Catholic boys?" I asked, batting my eyes at David again just so I could see him turn away shyly, which he did.

"No," he said. "I'm Jewish. I think Bobby's the only Catholic boy."

"But I'm really an atheist," Bobby added.

"Rick's . . . what are you, Rick? I don't even know."

Rick looked at us in a panic, like he'd just been called on in school and didn't know the answer. He swallowed hard, his Adam's apple jutting out from his skinny neck.

"Presbyterian." It took him four tries with the "P" sound and two with the rest of the word to get it all out. That was when I realized he had a stut-tering problem, probably talked very little because of it.

"Our old bass player was this Indian kid, raised Hindu. See, that's why we thought it was funny to call ourselves Catholic boys. You know, iron-ic." David smiled at me, more fearlessly than he had before.

"Well then, wouldn't it be even funnier if one of y'all was a Southern Baptist gal?" At least the Southern part of it was true. I laid my accent on thick, getting the feeling that David liked it.

"I think so," David said. "What do you guys think?"

Rick nodded yes, and I smiled at him. It was one of my lowest-watt smiles, just an encouragement smile, but he turned bright red and stuck his hands in his pockets. The redness in his face made his pimples stand out more.

Bobby sighed. "I guess it wouldn't hurt to try her out," he said. "No offense, Miri, I just think it would be weird to have a chick in the band."

"You're not having a chick in the band," I said, "you're having me." I turned away from him and smiled so hard at David I almost blew his head off.

. . .

After many more rounds of beer between the boys—I drank Coke, seeing as I had to stay sharp and on top of the situation—I went home with David. He was so drunk by the time the party broke up that I had to suggest it myself, but he seemed pleased with the idea. We went back to his dorm room, where he kissed me twice and then passed out cold on the bed. My immediate thought was: Thank you, Jesus. I'd wandered the city for hours earlier that night, killing time, and my feet were swollen and sore; all I really wanted was to sleep. I took my boots off, pushed David over and climbed into bed next to him, and lay there for a good hour listening to him snore.

His snoring was louder than Grandma's TV, louder even than the machinery at Wendell's Garage. It was that kind of wide-open snoring people do when they've been drinking too much. And the smell—I hated that smell, that sickening fruity-sour smell on David's breath that brought back all my worst memories of Annmarie's drinking. I got up, put my boots back on and wandered down the hall to see if there was a couch somewhere. All I wanted was a few hours' sleep.

The hall bent into an L-shape a few doors down from David's. I turned and saw an open doorway. I peered inside; it was some kind of common room, a space with tables and chairs. In the dark I could just make out two chairs pulled together in a corner, a body stretched out between them. I stepped inside to get a closer look.

In the darkness I could see only fuzzy brown hair and some sort of blanket. As I moved closer and my eyes adjusted to the dim light I saw it was a sleeping bag, a Snoopy and Woodstock pattern on a grimy background. It looked like it could get up and walk away by itself, that bag. Whoever was in there was clearly in the same kind of fix I was. I tried to tiptoe around and get a better look, but when I stepped closer the floor creaked and the body in the bag turned, sat up, and looked at me. It was Rick.

I didn't say a word, just pulled up two chairs next to him and stretched myself out between them. "Hope you don't mind a little company," I said. "David's passed out and snoring so loud I can't sleep, and it's too late to go home."

He looked at me then, not saying a word, just looking like a million individual thoughts were running through his head but he wasn't going to voice them, not a one. It was in his eyes. Despite his size and his pimples and how quiet he was, Rick's eyes, if you took a good look, had something deep about them. They were wise eyes.

He lay back down but before I could get myself settled he was propped on an elbow, looking at me.

"David said you were starting at PCA this semester," he said, only stuttering a little at the beginning of the sentence.

"That's right," I said. I wasn't sure I wanted to tell him the truth about me.

"You live in a dorm?" he asked, this time stumbling at the end of the question, at the word "dorm." It took him an ungodly long time to get that last word out.

I could have kept lying, but something about the effort it took him to ask me these questions just got to me. It seemed somebody who had to go to that much trouble to ask a question deserved a straight answer.

"No," I said.

"Apartment?" This word came out with only a little hitch.

"No. And I'm not really going to PCA." He looked me over for a good few seconds, and nodded.

I twisted around, trying to find a comfortable position on the chairs. Just when I found one and closed my eyes, he said, "You ran away? From Texas?"

"Yep," I answered. "From Texas. From foster homes. From a bunch of bullshit."

He didn't answer. I wasn't sure if he was out of questions or if he was just afraid he'd stutter too much getting them out.

"You too, right?" I asked.

"Yeah."

"From where?"

"Stepfather," he said, with a break between each syllable. Stepfather, like it was a place, not a person. I thought of Juan, the boyfriend of his Mom's who used to beat them all up, and realized as I sometimes did that my life wasn't as bad as some. None of Annmarie's boyfriends were ever as bad to me as she was herself, and some, like Tommy Clayton, were right nice. The only person who'd ever really beat me was that scary Preacher Dad; Annmarie had slapped me around a few times, but it was usually when she was drunk or stoned and so it was easy for me to duck away from her, lock myself in a bedroom or bathroom, and wait for her to sleep it off.

"How did you get here?" He whispered it so soft I barely heard him.

"Long story," I said. Not wanting to sound unfriendly, I added, "I'll tell you sometime. But you can only believe half of what I say."

He let out a quiet little laugh. "Me, too," he said.

I pulled my hands inside the sleeves of my sweater, trying to keep them warm. It was cold in that lounge, though nothing like how cold I would have been wandering around outside. I heard Rick sigh and move around a bit in his sleeping bag.

"Do David and Bobby know about you?" I asked. "Do they know you sleep here?"

"No. They think I go to the High School for the Performing Arts. I told them I was a junior this year." We both laughed a little at that. "When I sleep here I always clear out before anyone in the dorm wakes up."

"That was how we did it at the U of T—University of Texas," I said. "We'd sleep in the basement and leave before anybody in the dorms got up."

"There's other places I sleep sometimes," Rick said. "I could show you." He cleared his throat a little, and I was amazed at how his stuttering had just about fallen away. "I mean, if you want."

It was just the invitation I was hoping for. Rick was the type of kid who could show me the ropes here, and I knew he wouldn't expect me to sleep with him for it. He was too shy, too unsure around girls, I was able to see that right off.

"I'd appreciate that," I said, putting a little extra sweetness in my voice just to make the deal sound that much better to him.

We both fell quiet for a few minutes, but as I thought back over all that had happened I realized I had another problem.

"Rick," I whispered.

"Yeah?"

"Can you play bass?"

He propped himself on his elbow again. "You can't play bass," he said. It came out perfectly, without a stutter, and he laughed a little as he said it.

"Look," I said, "I'll tell you a few true things right now. One, I got stranded here three weeks ago, I don't know this city at all and I had to meet some people so I could find a place to sleep. Two, while I am musically inclined and have a truly good voice, I only play a little guitar and, no, I have never played bass. But I bet I could learn."

There was a long stretch of quiet while Rick digested all I'd just told him.

"I could teach you," he finally said. "Enough, anyway. We're all pretty bad."

"But I'm supposed to practice with y'all tomorrow."

Rick shook his head. "David and Bobby'll be too hung over tomorrow. We won't practice again for a few days, at least."

I expected him to say something more, but he fell silent again, and next thing I knew I heard the rise and fall of his breath. Not loud, nothing like snoring, just a steady rhythm of quiet little breaths. I fell asleep, too, curled in a ball to keep warm, my feet hot in my heavy boots but the rest of me freezing.

When I came half-awake the next morning, I wasn't sure where I was, thought for a second I was in a hotel room with Ian. I could feel a blanket on me, and I fought my way fully awake, opened my eyes and looked around. I was in that lounge, on those chairs, the dirty Snoopy and Woodstock sleeping bag unzipped and tucked around me. Now it was Rick who was in a ball, hugging himself on the chairs next to mine, his elbows peeking at me through the worn spots on his shirt.

CHAPTER 15
AUGUST, 1984

Catholic Boys Gone Bad played the Big Bang, a little club in a burned-out-looking block of South Street, on the night before my eighteenth birthday. The club was about five blocks from the fashionable part of South, and, as I'd found to be true all over Philly, five blocks could make a world of difference. The club itself was cinder block on the outside, with the name spray-painted graffiti-style in black over the entrance. Inside, it wasn't a whole lot prettier, but it had a reputation for attracting lots of different types of people—students who'd just turned of age, artists in their thirties and forties, gay men, and middle-aged guys from the neighborhood, who had an air of being down-on-their-luck and who sometimes started brawls when they drank too much.

Because no type of music could appeal to all these folks, and because the owner, Loretta—a woman in her forties who had a snake tattoo that stretched from her wrist up to her elbow and who seemed to have a soft spot for punk-looking boys like David and Bobby—couldn't afford to pay anyone to play there, it was an easy place in town for a band to get a gig. Loretta would pretty much let anyone play if they asked her nicely, which is the only reason that Catholic Boys Gone Bad—the band was, truly, so bad that Rick and I had taken to calling it Catholic Boys Just Plain Suck—had been allowed to play the club four times, on this particular night opening a triple bill. Neither of the other two bands were much better than we were.

Rick and I stuck with the band mainly because David and Bobby had taken to looking after us a bit. Although we never came out and told them we were on our own, somewhere down the line they seemed to have figured it out. We knew because they would pay when we went out for burritos after band practice, and because David often said things like, "If you ever need a place to stay, just call." They were nice boys, especially David, nice college boys with nice middle-class parents who paid their tuition and gave them extra money if they needed it and worried if they didn't get home on time. I would have sooner slept on a steam grate than asked either of them for help. I didn't want them to lose respect for me.

We were a team pretty much from that first night we met, Rick and me. It was a fair exchange; he knew the city inside out, and I had all kinds of scams and plans up my sleeves. We started busking on South Street right after we met, the first warm winter day we had; by the end of March we were playing pretty much every weekend. Throughout the winter and spring, up until the end of May when the colleges let out, we slept most nights in a variety of dorms, which were not hard to get into thanks to the carelessness of most students. They left doors propped open, first-floor windows unlocked, and were always willing to hold the door on their way in for a nice girl from Texas who'd traveled all the way to Philly to see her boyfriend.

On occasion we'd sleep in an apartment, thanks to some off-campus college boy I'd meet when our band played at a party or school event. On those nights, Rick would follow about half a block behind me and the boy, easily getting into the boy's building thanks to the chewing gum I would stick in the doorjamb. Rick would hang in the hallway until I finished up with the guy and he'd fallen asleep; then I'd tiptoe to the door and let Rick in the apartment. Usually those boys were drunk enough that Rick and I could get showers in the morning, eat whatever we could find, and leave, all long before they woke up.

I was usually pretty good at picking these boys; Rick and I could always find a place to sleep, and so I was never desperate. But one night earlier that summer, I'd made a huge mistake. A boy I went home with turned on me, started throwing me around and smacking at me, and had Rick not been out in the hall to hear me scream, Lord knows what might have happened. Rick pounded on and kicked at the door until it sounded like he was going to break it down and the guy let go of me and opened up, punching Rick in the face and then pulling him into the apartment by his shirt collar. I then jumped on the boy's back and ripped at his hair, digging my nails into his scalp and sinking my teeth in his shoulder until his screams brought the neighbors over; Rick and I ran off in the commotion that followed. We stuck to sleeping in the dorms for some time after that.

Given what our lives were like, the main interest Rick and I had in this gig at the Big Bang was simple: free food. Since Loretta had a habit of serving the musicians free beer—and since she'd made it clear to me and Rick that, since we were underage, we could only play there if we didn't even think about trying to get a drink—she gave me instead a Nacho platter, and all the Cokes I could get down; Rick had a cheesesteak, and the ginger ale he favored for his stomach. I liked Loretta; she had the tough-and-soft-at-the-same-time air of someone who's seen the other side of hell and lived to tell about it.

Catholic Boys Gone Bad played mostly covers of the Clash and the Ramones, which was a good thing considering how awful David and Bobby's original songs were. We had just added a new song to our playlist: a Blondie song, "Dreaming," which was David's idea after he realized I could really sing. The song was for my taste a little too New Wave and arty in the version David played for me on the expensive-looking turntable in his dorm room, but I convinced them to slow it down enough when we played it that I could sing it like a torch song.

I was wearing the same thing I'd worn the other times we played the Big Bang: jeans and a green army-type shirt I'd borrowed from David and never given back. Under the army shirt I wore the gold bikini top that Ian had bought me. Onstage, I kept the shirt buttoned up because I didn't want guys staring at me; but if I saw one in the crowd later that I might want to go home with, I'd unbutton the army shirt so that it became a jacket. And, despite what I lacked in the chest area, I can tell you that the bikini top had done well for me in the past.

We took the stage and played our godawful punk cover tunes, Bobby missing beats on the drums and wailing his lungs out like a cat in heat; David winding his arm around to hit the guitar strings in a way that somehow reminded me of the Sam Houston High School baton twirlers; Rick playing sloppy but not altogether awful rhythm guitar; and me, plunking a few notes out on the bass when the spirit moved me. Truth be told, I'd picked up bass well enough by then to play it passably, especially in a band like ours where no one could really play; but the instrument just bored me.

Because of this I sometimes skipped playing in whole sections of songs. No one seemed to especially care. And on this particular night at the Big Bang, no one in the bar was paying attention to us, anyway.

But that changed when I launched into the Blondie song. I sang the first verse *a capella*, and then the rest of the band was supposed to join in, but by then heads were turning, people were approaching the stage, smiling at me and nodding. David, Bobby, and Rick never kicked in, and when I looked over at David he just waved me on, leaning against his guitar. I slowed the song down even further and sang it as I saw fit, changing a word here or there when I felt like it. By the time I was done everyone in the club was applauding, with so many people calling out for another song that I thought, what the hell, and launched into "Stormy Weather," a song I knew from the Etta James version I'd heard Wendell play many times. I hadn't sung it since I'd lived in Prairie Rose, and if I'd had time to think about it I would have been afraid I'd forgotten all the words but somehow it came to me, all of it, and I belted out just about as fine a version as I could have hoped for, a version that would have done my old music teachers proud. Halfway through the song, Bobby walked off the stage, and by the look on his face I knew this would be my last performance with Catholic Boys Gone Bad so I just worked that much harder to make it worthwhile. When I was done, the whole bar applauded and whistled, the people at the front of the stage clapping their hands together especially hard. That was when I first saw Jamie.

He would have been tough to miss. For one thing, he was tall, and I don't just mean tall the way everyone looked to me at my height; he was well over six feet, taller than most of the men in the bar. For another thing, he was flat-out beautiful. He had sandy blond hair the color of Wendell's, only Jamie's was straight rather than curly; he wore it parted in the middle, just below chin-length, long enough to look hip in these parts but short enough to look respectable. He looked to be a little bit older than the college boys I'd become used to picking up. That silky hair framing his face wasn't the hair of a boy; it was man's hair.

So of course, after Rick and David and I had gotten our stuff off the little plywood stage—we had to take down Bobby's drum kit as well, since he seemed to have stormed out of the club entirely—and I was at the bar with Rick collecting my fifth free Coke and I saw the gorgeous guy with the silky hair approaching me, I unbuttoned the army shirt right away so he'd get a good look at the bikini top. Rick saw what I was doing and got this pained look on his face he always got in those situations. I was pretty sure Rick had never had sex, but it wasn't something we'd ever talked about.

"That's some voice you got there, kiddo," Loretta said as she flew past me with a tray full of beers, and the compliment threw off my timing so that I didn't even have a chance to run some gloss over my lips before Silky Hair was at my side. He was dressed simply, in new-looking blue jeans and a black cotton t-shirt so crisp it looked like it had been ironed; or maybe it was just that fabric wouldn't dare wrinkle on this man. His eyes were a sparkly hazel, flecked with green and brown and yellow, and he had the pinkest fullest lips I'd ever seen on a guy.

"You have a beautiful voice," he said.

"Thanks." I flashed him a medium-voltage smile and pushed my chest out as far as it would go. "I'm glad you liked it."

"You seem to have a pretty broad range. Have you trained formally?"

I almost lied and said I'd studied voice at the University of Texas, but something held me back. "Not really," I said. "But I soloed in the chorus in elementary school and high school, and in my Grandma's church choir."

He smiled sweetly. "Where are you from?"

"East Texas," I said, batting my eyes and taking a bite of one of Rick's cheese fries in what I thought was an alluring way. "I grew up singing blues and country, gospel too. To be honest that's what I really like to sing, more than the punk stuff."

He smiled and nodded like this made perfect sense to him. "The way you sang 'Dreaming,'" he said, and for a minute he looked off in the distance, like he was lost in some world of wonder, "this is going to sound nuts, but you reminded me of Patsy Cline. I was thinking, if Patsy Cline sang Blondie, this is what it would sound like."

I beamed at him. "I love Patsy," I said. "'Crazy' is one of my favorite songs to sing." I made sure to brush his arm with mine as I leaned in for my Coke.

"My name's Jamie," he said, holding out his hand to shake. Like everything else about him, his grip was just right—not too firm, not too weak.

"Miri," I said, "M-I-R-I." I'd found it was easier to just spell it out for people rather than have to explain that I hadn't said "Mary."

He looked at Rick, who was sitting on a stool next to me. "And what's your name?" he asked in a kind voice.

Rick was so surprised that his face turned red, and I just knew he was going to stutter like crazy. In these situations, Rick was usually ignored; the guys I chatted up either didn't notice him or pretended they didn't. It occurred to me that this Jamie was maybe one of the first people I'd met since Prairie Rose who had actual manners. But not the same kind of manners as, say, Grandma, or Wendell. What Jamie had, what drifted around him in a cloud like the humidity of that August night, was class. Jamie had actual, five-star class, the kind of class both the Clacks and Ian Oliver had pretended to but did not possess.

"Rick," he stammered out after a terribly long process of r-sounds, which he actually had to interrupt and then restart before he could finally get his name out.

"Rick is my little brother," I said, just to make sure Jamie didn't get the wrong idea. It didn't feel like a lie.

Jamie smiled. "I'd like to hear you sing again sometime," he said.

I decided Jamie was on my hook, so I cranked the male-magic smile up to 10, to reel him in. "Sure thing," I said. I took a sip of my Coke, waiting for him to suggest that we go back to his place.

"I play guitar," he went on, "and piano. Maybe we could get together and try out a few songs sometime."

It wasn't the kind of invitation I'd expected, but I thought maybe this was his way of working up to something else. Maybe, I thought, studying him, he's shy, though I couldn't imagine how a guy that gorgeous could truly be shy. He'd attract attention whether he wanted to or not.

Just then, David came up and said that he was going over to a party one of the PCA crowd was having.

"Write down where it is for me," I said to David, smiling at Jamie in a way that was meant to tell him I would much rather spend the night with him than at some PCA party. "Maybe I'll be over later."

Rick made a sound in the back of his throat like he was strangling. I ignored it, for oftentimes he got weird about me picking up guys, even though it meant he'd have a couch to sleep on and a shower in the morning.

"I don't really want to go to that party," I said to Jamie after David had left, working the smile hard and giving him what I thought was my best I-want-you look.

I saw a hint of pink begin to creep into Jamie's cheeks. It settled there, making him look like he'd just gone for a brisk walk in the cold. I thought at first that maybe this was some kind of flush he got when he was working up a hard-on, but after studying the way he was looking at the bar, no longer making eye contact with me, I realized he was simply embarrassed. This was how Jamie blushed, not bright red like Rick, just a hint of color in his smooth pale cheeks.

I was, to say the least, confused.

"I'm really interested in putting together a duo or a band," Jamie said, looking off in the distance. "I just moved here from Boston." He looked for a second like he was going to say something else, and then stopped himself.

Just then I noticed a guy, tall like Jamie, and handsome in a rugged way but not nearly as sweet-looking, boring his eyes into both me and Jamie. At first I thought he was jealous because Jamie had gotten to me first, but as I watched his face, the way his eyes settled on Jamie, I realized it wasn't me he was jealous over. It was Jamie. The whole thing made sudden sense to me.

"You're gay!" I blurted out, in a way that seemed to startle both Jamie and Rick.

Jamie looked around nervously, but no one else in the bar was paying any attention. "That's my partner, Clay," he said softly, motioning to the brooding guy across the bar.

"Well, thank the Lord," I said. "I was starting to think I was losing my touch."

This made both Jamie and Rick laugh.

"I really would like to get together and play sometime," Jamie said. "Try out a few songs. See how it feels."

"Sure thing," I said. Goddamn, I thought, this guy isn't even attracted to me. I wondered if he'd ever been with a girl, if he could be lured over to my side. If anyone could do it, I thought, my confidence returning, old Miri could. And if not, it might just be fun to sing for reasons other than spare change, or free cheese fries.

"Do you play any other instruments?" he asked. "I don't get the feeling you're all that interested in bass."

I had to laugh at that. "I'm not," I said. I was tempted to go on and exaggerate my strumming abilities, but I had a feeling this guy could see right through me. "I know a few chords, and I make up songs now and again, but mostly I'm a singer."

Rick then stunned me by saying, out of the blue, "Miri and I play on South Street, near 4th, every Saturday and Sunday. You should come down some time and listen." He somehow managed to get it out with only a few catches here and there. Rick was like that; he'd get nervous to the point of total silence when asked a direct question, but when he decided to offer something up he could get it out there real matter-of-fact. When he was able to, he spoke better than most street kids, sometimes using words that I had to ask him what they meant. It had started to dawn on me that summer that Rick was a very smart boy, and probably had once been the kind of nerdy kid who read all the time and got straight A's, and that something pretty bad must have driven him away from the New Jersey suburb he'd told me he was from.

"Thanks for the invitation, Rick," Jamie said, smiling real nice at him. I knew, gay or no, Jamie wasn't interested in Rick; he just knew he was a shy, awkward kid and was trying to encourage him. This made me like Jamie right off. "Will you be there tomorrow?" Jamie asked, directing the question at me.

"Yep, we'll be there," I said.

"Well, I should go," he said, looking over at Clay, who was now brooding by the door, motioning to Jamie. "Look, just in case I don't make it tomorrow, let me write this down for you." He scribbled two phone num-

bers on a cocktail napkin: one was his home, one was the Olde City guitar shop where he had just started giving lessons. "If you don't see me
tomorrow, please call me. We'll get together."

I tucked the napkin into the pocket of my jeans. I considered buttoning
the army shirt, but kept it open in case some other guy came along. "I sure
will," I said. "I hope y'all have a good night."

He smiled, and I was glad that even though he wasn't interested in girls,
I could at least charm him a little bit with my accent.

Rick and I never did make it to that PCA party; my mind was still too
much on Jamie, and Rick pretty much followed me wherever I wanted to
go. We headed instead for the abandoned rowhouse in West Philly where
we'd been crashing on and off since the dorms had closed in May. We'd
become true street kids that summer, sleeping sometimes in the rowhouse,
sometimes outside in a spot we'd found on the Penn campus, under a parking lot overhang at the foot of a set of stairs that led up to Walnut Street.
We slept outside on the hottest, most humid nights, when the heat inside
the squat would be at its most unbearable, not to mention the smell. There
were about fifteen other people squatting in the rowhouse; white and
black, young and old, desperate folks with nothing at all in common
except that we had nowhere to go. None of them made an effort to clean
themselves enough for Rick's or my taste.

Granted, they couldn't all go home with someone and grab a shower like
I could, but they could at least wash up in the bathrooms at the Free
Library. I'd done that, many times that summer. No way I was going to
turn into some smelly crazy bag lady.

Truth be told, Rick and I were creeped out by the people in that rowhouse, and not just for their smells. There was an old guy who leered at
both of us, like he couldn't make up his mind which one he wanted; and
there was a fourteen-year-old girl, a junkie, who was always trying to convince us to shoot up with her. She told us she'd been on the streets since
she was eleven, and believe you me, she looked it. There was another girl
who was pregnant, and who talked about how she loved her baby and how
motherhood was going to change her life, but who drank so much I could

only imagine that poor baby as a cocktail onion, floating around in a martini. When Rick and I slept at the rowhouse, we slept spooned together. Everyone there knew we were a team, and that if you messed with one of us, you were messing with us both; this gave us some protection.

On the way back to the squat, we stopped at 30th Street Station, at the locker where we'd stashed Rick's sleeping bag and the green quilted comforter I'd stolen from a guy I once picked up. Everything else we had, we carried with us; for me, this was my big black bag full of all my earthly possessions, and Juan's guitar. For Rick this was a beat-up-looking backpack he'd got from God knows where.

It wasn't until we'd gone into the squat, rolled out our bedding in the most private corner we could find, and laid down side-by-side that we started talking about what had happened that night.

"Do you think he's really a musician?" I asked Rick in the darkness.

"Well, he sure wasn't trying to pick you up." Rick let out a little laugh that told me he'd enjoyed that part of it a bit more than I personally thought was necessary. "I can't see why he'd lie."

"Yeah, but people in this city are full of crazy shit," I said.

We were both silent for a second.

"I hope he comes tomorrow," I said finally. "There was just something about him I really liked."

Rick didn't answer, and I figured he'd fallen asleep. But just as I settled myself and began to drift off, I heard him whisper, ever so faintly, "He'll come."

Chapter 16
August, 1984

But Jamie never did come that next day. Rick and I awoke early on that sticky August Saturday, the sun already melting through the slats of the boarded-up windows, cooking the various human smells into a godawful stew. Without a word we got up, grabbed our stuff, and headed for the Free Library, where we could wash up.

We got there just as the library was opening, the best time because it was unlikely anyone would need to use the bathroom right off. First I washed my hair in the sink, with the pink liquid hand soap they kept in dispensers, and dried it best as I could with armfuls of paper towels. Then I stripped off my top and washed my upper body, splashing water onto myself from the sink. When I'd finished with that I pulled a tank top from my bag and put it on, then took off my jeans and cleaned the rest of me. When I was done I took wads of paper towels and cleaned up the water I'd splashed onto the floor; if you weren't careful to clean up after yourself, the library people would catch on and stop letting you in. This had happened to more than one street person Rick and I had met.

Before I left I put on a little mascara from my bag, and some lip gloss I'd stolen from the Rite-Aid. I ran a comb through my damp hair, knowing with the humidity outside that even hours later it wouldn't feel completely dry. I looked at myself in the mirror and wondered if I now looked eighteen. I didn't feel any different.

Rick was the only person I'd told it was my birthday. The night before, I'd considered telling David, who I knew still had a lingering soft spot for me even though we hadn't had sex since late January, when his girlfriend came back from whatever tropical island she'd gone to with her Bryn Mawr friends. David's fondness for me was clearly visible to his girlfriend, who I'd seen at dorm parties where our band had played. She and her friends would stand in front of us, arms folded, giving me rich-girl dirty looks that reminded me of my cousin Mary Gay. Still, David was always complimenting me, telling me my hair was pretty or that my bass playing was improving. I knew if I'd told David it was my birthday he would have bought me a nice present, maybe even taken me out to dinner behind his girlfriend's back. But I was afraid that such an occasion would lead to a lot of questions I didn't want to answer. I'd rather leave the idea of how I got by unspoken between us.

We spent the day, Rick and me, as we'd spent most weekend days that summer, working the corner of South and 4th, Rick playing Juan's guitar and me singing. Given the right conditions—a warm but not-too-hot day with enough pickup-truck loads of Jersey tourists passing through—usually the most we could make was $20, but it seemed like my birthday was bringing us all kinds of luck. We started singing at 11:00, and by 4:00 in the afternoon we'd made $32. Still, I was feeling a little bit down, since not even my birthday luck had brought Jamie out to see us play. Maybe, I thought, he was just shitting me. I wondered if the phone numbers he'd given me were even real.

"We should go out to dinner tonight," Rick said after he'd finished counting the money. He left the change in the guitar case but folded the bills and tucked them in his pocket for safekeeping. "For your birthday."

I beamed at him, surprised and pleased that he'd remembered, since he hadn't mentioned it all day. I had told him weeks before and hadn't spoke of it again.

Rick shrugged, and blushed the way he always did when I smiled at him. It was a sad thing to see, for any redness in his face made his pimples stand out that much more. What with the summer heat and his not being able to wash his face as often as it really needed, his skin was even worse than it had been when I'd met him.

"You know," I said, "we shouldn't waste all this money on one dinner."

"But it's a big day," Rick said, a slight catch in his voice on the "but." "You're free now, Miri. They can't ever come after you."

Rick was right; turning eighteen was a very big deal. It meant I was no longer on the lam from the state of Texas, that I could do as I pleased without fear of being discovered, dragged back south and put into some crazy preacher's home. What it really meant, of course, was that I was now a homeless adult rather than a homeless minor, but I didn't look on it that way. I saw it as old Miri's Independence Day.

"I know," I said, smiling at a family that looked like they were waiting on us to start playing. "But I want to have my cake and eat it, too."

Rick smiled, catching my drift: I was cooking up a scam. "What's the plan?" he asked. No matter what kind of crazy idea I had, Rick was always willing to go along with it. I'd learned how to scam with Juan back in Austin, but on my own I'd developed it into a talent that was second only to my singing voice.

"We'll get a dinner out of somebody," I said, whispering to Rick so it looked like we were deciding on what song to play next. "Then you can buy me a piece of birthday cake."

We played for another hour as I looked for a likely target. A few coins were dropped in our guitar case, but nothing like the money we'd made earlier. It was too late in the day. Folks had already spent their money in the trendy shops that lined South Street from Front down to about 7th, where the road took a seedy turn as you headed on down to the Big Bang. South Street was a lot like Guadalupe in Austin, only it wasn't on a university campus and it was a hell of a lot colder in the winter.

Finally I saw our man. He was by himself, a balding, paunchy guy who wore a wedding band. Neglected by his wife, I figured, or separated. As I sang a Janis Joplin tune—Rick and I did pretty much the same songs Juan and I had performed in Austin, except for the Spanish ballads and one or two others that had chord progressions Rick couldn't quite master—I stared straight at Mr. Lonelyheart, which caused him at first to look away, embarrassed. He quickly recovered, and started to flirt back. Yes, Miri, you do have the touch, I thought. When we finished the song, I gave him my biggest smile, my 100-watt smile, making sure to turn it away from Rick, whose ears began to singe on just a flicker of one of my smiles. Mr. Lonelyheart cleared his throat to speak.

"You have the voice of an angel," he said. It sounded like he'd rehearsed the line in his mind over and over for the past five minutes.

"Thank you," I said, shining my light full-force on him. "What a kind thing to say."

"Do you kids perform at the clubs around here?" he asked.

I glanced over at Rick, and with one look told him what I wanted him to do. He put the guitar down and stuffed his hands into the pockets of his worn-out, sweat-soaked jeans, and looked up at Mr. Lonelyheart. I may have had the corner on the smile market, but Rick had me beat in the big, sad, brown eyes department. He could look more pitiful than the starving girl from Honduras that the Home Sweet Home Bible Church had sponsored for $10 a month. Truth be told, we weren't in much better a fix than that little gal was.

"Well, sir, we'd like to," I said, flashing my more modest, good-girl smile, "but we don't have enough money for equipment. Right now, my brother and I are staying in a shelter. Everything we make I try to save up so I can get us an apartment one day."

The story took on a life of its own from there. I told him how our parents had been killed in a car crash just after my eighteenth birthday, and how I'd dropped out of high school to take care of "little Ricky." After a year of struggling to make ends meet, the bank took the big old house where our folks had raised us in Virginia—why Virginia, I had no idea, but Rick and I liked it and started saying we were from Virginia a lot after that. I said we'd moved to Philly to live with an aging aunt who'd thought we could supplement her Social Security checks. She soon discovered we cost too much, and next thing we knew we were on the street.

"And you live on just what you make from street performances?" Mr. Lonelyheart asked, his eyes wide with the excitement of meeting actual poor people.

"Yessir," I answered in my best good-girl Southern voice. That, and the kindness of strangers, I thought.

I waited a minute for my story to sink in, then added, "Sometimes, folks who see us play are right kind to us. Once a nice man bought us both dinner."

Rick stretched in such a way as to exaggerate his sickly-thin frame.

"Would you . . . what was your name, dear?" he asked.

"Mary," I said. When I was scamming, I went by Mary. It didn't require explaining like Miri did, and I liked how it sounded so wholesome. Some of these guys got off on thinking I was some down-on-my-luck virgin.

"Mary," he said, "would you like me to buy you and your brother dinner tonight?"

This was the crucial point in the scam. It was important not to look too pleased or self-assured, or the whole deal could fall through.

"Oh gosh, I didn't mean to hint around like that," I said. "I'm really sorry, sir. It's just that it's been a while since we've had a hot meal."

Rick looked up at him with pathetic eyes.

"It's honestly no trouble," he said. "I was thinking of getting a bite to eat across the street at the Spaghetti Factory. I'd be happy to treat you both."

"Well, I don't know," I began, and Rick quickly cut me off.

"Please, Mary?" he said. "I know you don't like to take charity, but just this once?" He stuttered through the sentence, and I honestly couldn't tell if it was natural or if he was putting some of it on.

"Well," I said, smiling shyly at Mr. Lonelyheart, "I guess I'm in no position to be so proud. We would love to have dinner with you, if it's not too much trouble."

"No trouble at all," he said, and as I turned to head across the street he put his hand on the back of my neck, where my tank top scooped low.

Rick ordered spaghetti and meatballs, and I had fettucini alfredo. This was something I'd learned I liked when I was traveling with Ian. When Mr. Lonelyheart went to the bathroom, I dumped the basket of rolls into my black bag, and asked the waiter to bring more.

Mr. Lonelyheart, whose name was Fred, made it pretty clear that he was interested in a lot more than dinner. He kept trying to touch my hand as he talked about his stupid law firm, and the big case he'd just won. Like I cared. Of course, I looked clear at him while he talked and said things like, "Really? And then what happened?" while keeping my mind on other matters. The guy talked like no one had listened to him in months. I had to struggle to keep from shrinking back every time he exhaled; his breath stunk even before he dug into his shrimp scampi.

There was no way I would sleep with this guy; even the boys I'd picked up mainly for a place to crash were always boys I was attracted to. I was not about to have sex just for a roof over my head. I'd done that with Ian Oliver, and I'd learned my lesson there. This was a different type of scam I was running on Mr. Lonelyheart. It was a dine-and-dash scam.

After Rick and I had cleaned our plates, I announced that I had to go to the bathroom. I gave Rick a quick glance as I said it so he'd know what to do.

"Hurry back, hon," Mr. Lonelyheart said, grabbing my wrist as I got up. "I have a proposition for you."

"Sure thing," I said, pulling myself loose. About as sure as snow in Texas, I thought as I headed back toward the bathrooms.

The guy's back was to me. As Rick kept him involved in conversation—by simply nodding and listening, I was sure, it didn't take much with this guy—I slipped around the restaurant's bar and out the front door, where I would wait for Rick, ready to run when he came out.

Rick was supposed to pretend he saw someone he knew, and excuse himself to talk to this imaginary friend, then dash for the door. I hated the waiting part of a scam like this; you never knew what might happen, though there wasn't much the guy could do in a crowded restaurant. I figured Mr. Lonelyheart for a harmless type, just sex-starved.

Rick burst through the front door. "C'mon," he yelled, grabbing my hand as we bolted down South Street. We ran a block, turned left down Fifth and ran two more, then took a right on Fitzwater and dashed a few more blocks to a little park, where we threw ourselves in the scrubby grass behind a broken-down plastic fence. We sat in the grass and waited, but Mr. Lonelyheart was nowhere to be seen.

"He figured it out as soon as I tried to get out of my seat," Rick finally said after he'd caught his breath. "He started going, 'Where's your friend?'"

"Friend, huh?" I said. "So he never believed the brother and sister story."

"Guess not," Rick said.

"Was he mad?"

"Yeah. His face got real red. He knew we scammed him. He went after me when I ran for the door. Then the waiter started yelling for him to pay the check."

I had to laugh at this. "I bet they kept him from leaving."

"Probably," Rick said. "But I didn't want to stick around and find out."

I noticed something bright red in the grass next to me, and rolled closer to look. It was a man's bedroom slipper, a velvet one; the other slipper didn't seem to be anywhere nearby. I pulled it out of the grass, saw that some kind of slugs or beetles had made a home inside, and dropped it back where I'd found it. It seemed an odd place for someone to lose a slipper.

"Look at this," I said to Rick, pointing at the slipper.

He rolled over and took a look. "Ewww," he said, peering inside at the bugs.

"Don't you think it's weird?" I asked. "I mean, how does someone just lose a slipper in the middle of a park?"

Rick shrugged. "I've seen weirder stuff than that," he said, and closed his eyes.

But I couldn't stop my mind from wondering how that slipper had gotten there. I stared up at the sky and tried to imagine: a fight between two lovers, maybe, in the middle of the night, one storming out after the other.

Annmarie had a fight like that with Tommy Clayton once. I must have been nine then. He'd found out she was seeing someone else—a creepy older guy named Don who owned a used car lot and who eventually gave us the Oldsmobile we had when we made our escape from Corpus Christi, the night Annmarie dumped me at Grandma's—and he'd come over to confront her about it. There was screaming, and Annmarie pleading with him not to leave her, that she didn't really care about Don. Looking back on it, she was probably telling the truth; she was simply running a scam on Don, not all that different from what Rick and I had done to Mr. Lonelyheart. But of course Tommy didn't see it that way. He stormed out of the trailer, and Annmarie ran after him in her short kimono and scuffed-up slippers, and I watched from the window as she tugged on his car door, trying to keep him from leaving. He drove away, then turned around at the end of the road and came back, and they wound up sitting in his car for hours. I fell asleep in a chair I'd pulled up to the window. As far as I knew Annmarie didn't lose a slipper that night, but you could see how it might happen.

"Okay, Rick, I'm ready for dessert," I said, mostly to avoid the rush of thoughts now in my head. "Where are you taking me?"

"Jesus, Miri," he said, laying on his side in the grass. "Give my stomach a chance to settle, okay? I just ate a truckload of spaghetti and ran a half-mile dash."

I pulled a compact out of my bag and checked my face in the mirror. My nose and cheeks were shiny from sweat, and I applied more of the white face powder I'd taken to wearing. "Well, I wouldn't want you to lose that spaghetti we worked so hard for," I said, patting his stomach. He groaned and rolled away from me.

Truth be told, Rick was not cut out for life on the street the way I was. He would go along with any idea I had, but he didn't have the stomach for constant scamming. He always felt sick afterward. Some folks, I guess, just have a natural aversion to lying. For me, it comes pretty easy.

I painted my lips with a bright red lipstick I'd got from god knows where, blotting them on a napkin from the Spaghetti Factory. Rick rolled over and looked at me.

"Okay," he said, "I'm ready."

"For what?" I said it in a seductive voice that I knew was going to embarrass him, but sometimes I just couldn't keep down the devil in me.

"Brownie a la mode," he said, pulling a handful of grass out of the ground and throwing it at me. I was glad he took it as a joke and didn't get all flustered the way he sometimes did. You just never could tell how Rick would react.

We walked up to More Than Just Ice Cream, a place I liked because it had old-fashioned ice cream parlor chairs that reminded me of the Kountry Kitchen back in Prairie Rose. Rick ordered us a brownie with mint chocolate chip ice cream and two forks, and when it came, he pulled out of his pocket a candle that looked like it had seen better days on someone else's cake. I wondered where he'd found it, how long he'd been saving it for me. The handsome waiter frowned, but begrudgingly brought a book of matches, and Rick lit the candle and half-whispered, half-sung a version of "Happy Birthday" so soft that I was surely the only one in the restaurant who could hear it. He stuttered a little on the "b" in birthday each time he had to sing it, and I was touched as can be to see him put himself through that for me.

I blew out the candle with an exaggerated burst of air.

"What did you wish for?" he asked. He said it without a stumble, clear as you please.

Before Grandma died, my wishes had always revolved around my singing: to become the next Patsy Cline, or maybe the next Janis Joplin, but without the drug problems. Once Grandma was gone, though, my only wish was for a family: for Wendell to take me in, and later, for Juan and me to get married. After Juan went to prison and I was on my own, I stopped wishing for other people. My only wishes now were for what I could do for myself, and that seemed to bring me back to my voice.

"To get somewhere with my singing," I said. It seemed more possible after my performance at the Big Bang, after attracting the notice of someone like that Jamie.

"Where do you want to get?" he asked.

"Well, I do not want to be sleeping in dorm lounges or squatting in filthy run-down rowhouses the rest of my life, I can tell you that. I don't mean to become rich, but I'd like to make enough to have a nice little house like my Grandma had." I took another bite of the brownie. "And I want a German Shepherd."

Rick laughed. "What kind of music would you sing?"

I gulped my free refill of iced tea. "Blues and country, mostly, maybe with a little rock thrown in there too. Maybe a little folk."

Rick was quiet for a minute, poking his fork around in the melted ice cream. "You could make it, you know," he said. "I've never heard a voice as pretty as yours."

I was used to getting compliments about my voice, and usually they made me feel pleased as can be, but there was something about the way Rick had said it that made me feel a sadness so sharp and so sudden I couldn't even begin to understand it. Rather than think on it for too long, I turned the tables.

"What do you wish for, Rick?" I asked him. In all the time I'd spent with him—nearly twenty-four hours a day for the past six or seven months—I really knew very little about him. At first, I didn't ask him questions because I was afraid they'd make him stutter. Later, when he stuttered less and I was more used to it, it seemed he always found ways to change the subject, if the subject was him.

"Brownie a la mode," he said, spearing the last piece with his fork and sliding it into his mouth.

"I'm serious," I said, giving him a look that told him he would not get out of answering me. "I want to know what you wish for."

He was quiet, scratching his fork around on the plate. His face got red and he almost talked once, then stopped. Finally he said, "If you mean what do I want to do with my life, I want to go to college."

I started laughing until he gave me a look that told me to stop. "I'm sorry, Rick," I said. "It's just that you haven't even finished high school."

"I have my G.E.D."

This was news to me. "Where the hell'd you get a G.E.D.? You're only fifteen."

"I'm almost sixteen," he corrected, and I fought back the desire to smile. "I got it last year when I was working with a shelter on going back home. One of the things I had a problem with was going back to my old school, with everyone there knowing I'd been on the streets and all. So we worked out this deal where I would get my G.E.D. and then move back with my Mom, take classes at a community college."

I sat there for a second and stared at Rick. It shouldn't have surprised me that behind that scared shy pimply face was a boy smart enough to consider starting college at fourteen; I'd seen signs of how smart he was before. It was just that I wasn't sure I could pass a test like that. I had no idea what kinds of questions they would ask, but since I'd hardly ever paid attention in school once I left Prairie Rose, I figured my chances of doing well were pretty slim.

"So what happened?" I asked.

"The deal fell through." When I gave him a look that said to go on, he added, "My stepfather moved back in with my Mom, so I couldn't go there."

Rick had mentioned this stepfather before. I didn't know what had gone down between them, but I didn't want to press Rick with questions he didn't want to answer. Instead I asked him, "So what would you study in college?"

He smiled. "You're gonna laugh," he said.

"Rick," I said, squeezing the remains of a lemon slice into my final sip of iced tea, "nothing would surprise me at this point."

"Physics." He scanned my face for signs of amusement or disbelief.

Physics. I wrapped the word around my tongue. I myself had never had anything beyond Basic Science in the various high schools I'd attended; this was science for kids like me who weren't expected to go much of anywhere beyond high school. Even in Prairie Rose, where people had respected me because of Grandma and because of my voice, I was not exactly in what you'd call the college prep courses. Once, though, Mr. Duggan had asked me to run down to the senior Physics class to get two students out for a special chorus practice they seemed to have forgotten, and I remembered the strange feeling of that class, the numbers and arrows and equal signs on the blackboard, the pulsing of all those smart kids' brains grasping onto ideas I couldn't begin to reach.

"You must be really smart," I said softly, feeling for a minute like that little girl in the doorway of the Physics class, forgetting that this was Rick I was talking to.

Rick smiled in a pleased way, which was not a look I'd seen on his face too often. "If I'm so smart," he said, "what am I doing living like this?"

For some reason, this just struck me funny, and I started to laugh, and when I started, Rick started too. Pretty soon we were both laughing at everything and nothing in particular, and in the midst of it the waiter came over and slapped the check down on our table with an annoyed little sigh.

"Let's leave him all change," I said, "just to piss him off."

And that was what we did, with a good tip which he'd only realize once he finished counting out all the pennies, nickels, and dimes. I had made Rick save most of the quarters for laundry.

The next day, after hitting the laundromat, after doing our best washing-up job at the library, we headed for South Street again, ready to make more money. If we had another day like the one before, we could get a room in a cheap motel, where we could shower and watch TV and jump up and down on the beds. We were both hoping for this without even saying it out loud.

But the day was overcast, threatening to rain with little spits of water every so often. The clouds did nothing to cut the heat; instead the air was thick and hot and wet, and just walking felt like swimming in a dim boiling fog. Hardly anybody was on the street, and in two hours we only made $1.25. We were just about to pack it in when we saw, heading toward us about a block away on South, a tall man with sandy hair carrying a guitar case. As he got closer I saw it wasn't just wishful thinking; it was definitely Jamie.

Maybe, I thought, I'll get my birthday wish after all.

CHAPTER 17
APRIL, 1985

Jamie and I were sitting at his and Clay's kitchen table, talking about barre chords; he'd just started teaching me those. The last time we'd played together, two nights earlier, I'd had a terrible time of it, and I was now offering Jamie a variety of excuses: I hadn't had time to practice, I hadn't felt well, my nails were too long. Truth was, I felt like Jamie was throwing things at me too fast, like I was in way over my head, but of course I never let on.

Jamie waved my excuses away with a sweep of his hand in the air. "Everything's harder for you," he said, "because your hands are so small."

"It doesn't make a difference," I said, pushing a piece of parsley around with my fork on the plate in front of me. We'd just finished what had become our weekly dinner; at first, Jamie invited only me, but I'd managed to talk Rick's way into a standing invitation as well.

Rick and Clay had both been gone from the table for long enough that I had to wonder where they'd gotten to. Rick hardly talked to Jamie and Clay, seemed somehow fearful of them; and Clay was equally quiet and guarded around both me and Rick. I figured they'd retreated to opposite corners of the apartment, which was nearly as big inside as Grandma's whole house had been.

"I think I just need to practice a little more," I added.

Jamie shook his head. "No," he said, and he leaned across the table and picked up my hand, held it up to his. Mine was just about half his size, and looked like a child's hand in comparison.

"See?" he said. "You have to reach twice as far to get the same chords."

Jamie was kind like that about my limitations as a guitar player, had been ever since we'd started practicing together. It all started up pretty much from that day he brought his guitar down to South Street; Jamie

played and I sang and it sounded that very first time like we'd been playing together for months. Jamie seemed to know every song I did, and once
in a while he'd sing a little harmony and there was something about his
rough voice blended with mine that made my own sound that much sweet-
er, like the way Grandma would put a little salt in a batch of cookies to
bring out the flavor. After that first day we started getting together once a
week, then twice as Jamie began giving me guitar lessons and teaching me
new songs. Sometimes we'd meet at his apartment, if Clay was out; other
times we'd practice at the music shop where he worked, at night when the
store was closed.

My playing was improving; Jamie kept saying that, and I knew he was-
n't just bullshitting me, I could hear it myself. That spring he'd started
teaching me some songs he'd written, and we played around with them,
taking them apart and putting them back together in ways that showcased
my voice while downplaying my guitar limitations. We were becoming a
band, or maybe we already were one; but we never spoke of it, we just kept
playing.

It wasn't just the idea of a band or a free dinner that kept me practicing
with Jamie; it was Jamie himself. What I felt for him—it wasn't exactly
what you'd call a crush, or at least, it wasn't really sexual. Not that I would
have minded, but after a couple of months of getting to know him I figured out it was hopeless to try to seduce Jamie over to girls. He had eyes
only for Clay, and nothing was going to change that.

As time went by, it wasn't so much that I wanted to be *with* Jamie as I
wanted to *be* him. I liked the way he gestured in the air when he talked,
the odd facts about bad TV shows or Bruce Springsteen or Buddhism that
he could recite at will. I liked the way he touched his guitar when he lifted it out of its case: gently, like he was lifting a baby out of a cradle. He
even smelled good.

We didn't just talk about music when we got together. I told Jamie stories about Prairie Rose, about Grandma and Wendell and the Clacks and
the Easter play; Jamie told me about summers on Cape Cod, how his
father was a surgeon in a big hospital in Boston and how Jamie as a teenager had fainted dead away in the observation room once when he'd gone to
watch his father perform an operation; he'd fainted before the operation

had even started. How his mother did paintings that were sold in art galleries like the ones I'd seen on Walnut Street. Jamie's face lit up when he talked about his mother, but not so much when he mentioned his father.

There were things we didn't talk about, too. Jamie hardly ever mentioned Clay when he wasn't around, and never spoke about being gay or what that was like. And I never talked about the things that happened after Grandma died—the foster homes, how I'd got to Philly, how Rick and I lived. Jamie thought Rick was my brother, and I'd told him we lived with an aunt in South Philly; to explain the obvious differences in our accents, I said that Rick had been living here since he was ten, whereas I had just come up from Texas a year ago, when I'd finished high school, to take classes at PCA. I could never tell if Jamie really believed this story, or if he just chose not to question it.

"I want to start playing that mandolin you have," I said to Jamie, to break a little stretch of silence that had crept in.

"Mmm," Jamie said, "you can take it with you tonight if you want," and before he could say anything else Clay walked in with a chocolate-frosted cake full of lit candles, which he put in front of Jamie as he began singing "Happy Birthday." I had no idea it was Jamie's birthday, but I joined in and then Rick came in from the living room and just kind of watched, mouthing the words.

Jamie blew out all his candles, took them out of the cake in neat rows, and began cutting slices onto the small white plates Clay had just put down on the table. I asked Jamie how old he was.

"Twenty-five," he said, and I couldn't get over how grown-up it sounded, twenty-five, like he'd lived a whole lifetime before me.

"He's such a child," Clay said, and a sweet look passed between them. I didn't see them exchange such looks too often, and I wasn't sure if it was because they weren't open in front of other people or if they weren't all that happy together. I could tell Jamie was crazy in love with Clay but I wasn't so sure it went the other way around.

"How old are you, Clay?" I asked. It hit me that I knew very little about him; just that he was studying English, and that they'd moved to Philly that past summer for him to go to school at Penn.

"Thirty-one," he said. Almost as old as Annmarie, I thought, but I kept this to myself.

"He seduced me," Jamie said, cutting into a slice of cake with his fork. "Stole away my youth."

"How did you all meet?" I asked. Jamie smiled and exchanged a look with Clay. Rick was staring at his plate, shoveling forkfuls of cake into his mouth.

"Ah, the scandal," Jamie said, smiling broadly. "Miri doesn't know about the scandal."

"Jamie took advantage of me and nearly destroyed my career in academia," Clay said, wiping a bit of chocolate frosting from his lip.

"Excuse me, Mr. Robinson? I think it was the other way around." I'd never heard them talk like this before—their voices were different, their vowel sounds kind of exaggerated—and they sounded so happy that it made me feel glad just to be there.

"So what happened?" I asked. "Come on, I want all the dirt."

Jamie laughed. "Okay, Miri," he said. "It was 1978. There I was, a mere lad of eighteen, on my own in college in the big city—New York."

"He went to college in New York because he figured it would be easy to get laid there," Clay added. I'd never heard Clay say anything like this before, and it sent me into a fit of laughter. Rick had a funny look on his face and kept picking at his cake.

"No, I went to college in New York because my father wanted me to study piano at Juilliard," Jamie said, "only I'd secretly enrolled at NYU instead."

"What's Juilliard?" I asked.

"A music school," Jamie said.

"The best one in the country," Clay added. Given the way Jamie played, that didn't surprise me.

"Anyway," Jamie said, his cheeks flushing slightly, "there I was, the first day of my freshman English class at NYU, and who walks in to teach it but the man of my dreams."

I looked at Clay. "You were the teacher?" I asked. I could tell this was going to be a story to rival the juiciest of Prairie Rose gossip.

Clay sighed. "I was in my first semester of graduate school, teaching for the first time. They told us not to date the female students, but they never said anything about the boys." He and Jamie both laughed.

"Did anyone find out?" I asked, pouring a glass of milk to wash down my chocolate cake.

Jamie nodded. "That's how it became 'The Scandal,'" he said, hitting those two words like they were the title of a movie. "We were caught in a compromising position."

"In my office," Clay added, exchanging a grin with Jamie.

Rick got up and left the table, and I saw Jamie's smile fade as he watched him leave.

"So what happened then?" I asked.

"Let's see," Jamie said. "Clay was kicked out of his graduate program. My parents were called."

"Holy shit, Jamie, what did you tell your parents?" I asked, trying to imagine how something like that could be explained.

"Well, the first thing my Dad wanted to know was why the hell I was at NYU and not Juilliard," Jamie said, and he and Clay both laughed. "Eventually I told them the school had misunderstood, and that nothing had happened."

"Jamie thinks they believed him," Clay said. "He thinks his parents don't know he's gay." With that Jamie shot Clay a look that was not at all pleasant.

"Well, do they know you live together?" I asked.

"Jamie tells them I'm his roommate. They don't know I'm the lecherous teacher."

"I never said you were my roommate, Clay," Jamie said quietly.

"You never said I wasn't," Clay shot back.

I could tell I'd stepped into a fire-ant hill with that question.

"So what did you do after Clay was kicked out of school?" I asked, to change the subject.

"I dropped out," Jamie said, "and we lived in the Village for a couple of years."

"We worked as waiters," Clay sighed.

"And then Clay decided to apply to some schools that didn't know his reputation, he got accepted into a Master's program in Boston, and we moved up there," Jamie said. "And we were blissfully happy there, and Clay could have gone on for a Ph.D. at Harvard or B.U. but for some reason he chose Penn instead." Jamie clearly wasn't happy with the choice himself.

"Penn had the best program for me," Clay shot back. "I'm sorry if Philadelphia isn't glamorous enough for you."

"You don't like it here?" I asked Jamie. It was clear I couldn't side-step this stuff, so I figured I might as well dive right on in.

Jamie let out a long breath. "It's okay," he said. "I haven't really given it much of a chance, I guess. I just miss our friends in Boston. You're the only real friend I've made here, Miri."

I beamed at him, pleased as anything that he considered me a real friend.

"I'm not enough for him," Clay said.

"That," Jamie said, becoming very serious, "is not true." They looked at each other long and hard for a minute, and I decided to start carrying the plates over to the sink. Clay pushed his chair back with a noisy flourish and left the room, but Jamie just sat there, staring at the half-moon of birthday cake. After I'd cleared most of the table, Jamie got up and handed me the last few dishes.

"Sorry about that," he said. "We get into it a bit sometimes."

"That's okay," I said. I was thinking about some of the little fights Juan and I had gotten into when we were on the streets, and the bigger ones that came after he'd started dealing.

Jamie opened the dishwasher, and I helped him load the plates in, watching to see how he did it. I'd never actually used a dishwasher before.

"I'm glad I was here for your birthday," I said.

Jamie smiled. "Me too."

I wanted to say more—how nice it was to see him be himself, how much closer I felt to him at that moment than I ever had. But I couldn't figure a way to say it so I just kept quiet, handing Jamie dishes to put in the washer.

He turned to me, a plate still in his hand. "You're okay with this?" he asked, making a little sweeping motion with the plate that told me by "this" he meant his life, he meant Clay, he meant being gay.

"Yes," I said. "I mean, once I got over the fact that Clay beat me to seducing you." I batted my eyes at him, and he laughed.

"I'm serious, Miri," he said. "I just thought . . ." His voice trailed off.

"What?"

"Well," he said, "being from a small town in Texas and all . . ." He shook his head. "Forget it."

I smiled at him, knowing what he meant. "Nobody in Prairie Rose even talked about stuff like this," I said. "Nobody came out and said it was wrong or anything; it was like it just didn't exist." That wasn't entirely true; I remembered hearing something on the news once about gays, but when I'd asked Grandma what it meant she'd said they were just extremely happy people, and then she'd made sure we got to church extra early that Sunday. The only other person I'd ever met who I knew was gay was Robbie, back in Austin, but our conversations had never gone much beyond the warehouse parties, tips on working scams.

Jamie nodded. "I'm just glad you're okay with it," he said, "because I think we're going to be playing together for a long time."

I loved it that he felt we had a future together; it made me feel like I was a part of something, like I was somebody, not just this kid living on the streets. When I was with Jamie I could forget what my life was really like.

"I don't think Rick's so comfortable with it," Jamie added. He kept his voice low so Rick wouldn't hear in the next room.

"He's young," I said quickly, not knowing how else to excuse Rick's behavior. A sad little smile brushed Jamie's lips. "He gets weirded out if I talk about sex, too."

Jamie shook his head and laughed. "You talk about sex with your little brother? Miri, you really are something."

I had gotten so comfortable with Jamie that I'd forgotten the lies I'd told him. "Well," I said, going for a quick recovery, "I've never exactly been the shy type." Jamie threw his arms around me and kissed me atop my head, and I hoped for a sweet few seconds that he'd hold me forever.

Later on that night, after Rick and I had climbed up the fire escape to the squat we were now using on a side street off Fairmount, in what folks called the Art Museum area, I asked him why he'd left the table while we were all talking.

"No reason," Rick said as he finished lighting the candles we'd taken from one of the restaurants where we'd done a dine-and-dash. The squat was a small room above what had once been a hardware store, all of it now boarded up, though this little room at the top had been pretty easy to break into. We liked it because there were no other squatters we knew of in that block and because, miraculously, we'd never seen a cockroach, though the place had more than its share of spiders and waterbugs. I could handle slow-moving critters way better than fast ones.

"Jamie's really good to us," I said. "I mean, how many people would make us dinner every week like that?"

"He's good to you," Rick said. He sat cross-legged on the floor, frowning.

"Rick, he's always nice to you." I brushed the floor with my denim jacket just to make sure nothing was crawling there and then stretched out lengthwise next to him.

He started to say something and then stopped. This usually meant he was going to have a bad fit of stuttering. "He's nice to you because of your voice," he said, taking a terribly long time to get it out. "I'm just along for the ride."

"Well, I know he likes you, too," I said. Truth was, I'd always gotten the feeling Jamie felt kind of sorry for Rick, that he sympathized with his awkwardness, his bad skin, his stuttering.

"I don't want him to like me," Rick said. It came out quickly, without a hitch.

"What does that mean?"

"Nothing," he said, his stutter returning. He drew his knees up to his chest.

"Why don't you just say you have a problem with it, Rick?" I sat up and faced him square on.

He looked down at the floor. "'Cause you'll be mad at me."

I took a deep breath and reminded myself that he was just sixteen. "No I won't," I said finally. He looked up at me like he didn't believe me.

"I mean it," I said. "I won't be mad."

He continued hugging his knees, and we were both quiet for a while. Then he said, "Well, why doesn't it bother you?"

"I don't know," I said. "It just doesn't. I mean, I really like Jamie, and I figure what all goes on with him and Clay is their business."

Rick sighed, scratched his head. "I hate it," he said. "I hate all of it. Spending time with people like that just for a free dinner, watching you pick up guys. Sleeping in these dumps." He squished a waterbug with his foot, mainly for emphasis.

"Well, do you have a better idea?" I asked him. "I'm all ears."

"Why don't you get a job? You're eighteen now." He sounded like a nagging parent, and I would have laughed had I not been so pissed off.

"Why don't *you* get a job?" I shot back. "You're the one who's supposed to be so damn smart. What the hell kind of job am I going to get?"

"I bet Jamie could get you a job," he said, his voice as loud as mine now. "Jamie would do just about anything for you, except fuck you." He stuttered a couple of times on the word "fuck," long enough for my blood to start pounding in my ears as I realized what he was trying to get out. I put my jacket back on, gave the candles such a hard puff of air that I not only blew them out but nearly knocked them over, and headed for the window.

"Where are you going?" he asked. By his tone of voice I could tell he knew he'd gone too far.

"Away from you," I said, climbing down the fire escape. He followed me. "Get away," I yelled up to him.

He continued following me down. I hit the bottom and tried to push the last rung of the metal stairway up, so he couldn't go any further.

"Stop it," he yelled, but I wasn't really strong enough to collapse the steps, what with him standing on them and all. Still, I banged them around enough to knock him off, and he fell a few feet to the ground.

"Shit," he yelled. "That hurt."

"Good," I yelled back. "I wanted it to."

"Look, I'm sorry. I shouldn't have said that."

"Fuck you," I yelled. I was crying now, and I cut through an alley out to Fairmount Street to try to get away from him.

"Miri," he called out, following me to the street.

"You think I'll fuck anybody, right? You think I'm a whore. Why don't you just come out and say it?" I was standing on the curb of Fairmount Street, screaming at the top of my lungs. Cars slowed down as they passed by.

"I don't think that," he said. "I didn't mean that."

"Yes you did," I choked out. I was crying now, and felt like I wanted to break something, throw something—maybe even myself. I started pacing in a circle on the sidewalk, looking for something I could pitch across the street or put through a window, crying loud enough to draw the attention of everyone on the street and all the folks who lived within earshot. Lights went on in some of the nearby apartments.

Rick approached me carefully, the way a dog catcher goes after a stray. "I didn't mean it like that," he said. "I don't think that about you at all."

I was still crying and shaking but I let him put his arm around me, awkwardly, because I didn't know what else to do. He stood off to the side, afraid to really hug me.

"I'm sorry," he said again. "I didn't mean it."

"I do what I want," I said, still unable to stop crying. "I'm not like Annmarie."

"I know," he said, "I know." By then a few people had gathered on the street to watch us, and Rick walked me down the block, where we ducked onto a side street.

"Don't ever say anything like that to me again," I said. I was still crying, but softer now.

"I won't," he said, and we sat down on a patch of scrubby grass, beneath a power line from which a lone sneaker hung, dangling by its laces like a Christmas ornament. We held onto each other for so long that we finally just stretched out there and fell asleep, and woke up the next morning to the sound of the birds, an airplane flying overhead, and a city garbage truck clanging its way down Fairmount Street.

Chapter 18
July, 1985

By that summer, Jamie and I had decided our band would be a folk-punk duo. That was what we were calling the kind of music we made, but truth be told it was a little bit of everything: folk, rock, blues, country, you name it. Jamie said it was everything but classical, which was what he'd been forced to learn growing up and had rebelled against. I could hear that training sometimes in Jamie's guitar playing, in the precision of his timing and in how he put songs together, but of course I never let on that I thought so. Jamie loved alternative rock, the kind of music that had come after punk, and he thought our sound fell in that category. His favorite bands were R.E.M. and Hüsker Dü but he loved a whole slew of other bands, so many I could barely keep the names straight: Zeitgeist, who I'd once heard play in Austin; X, the Replacements, Mission of Burma, the Blasters, the Meat Puppets, the dBs, the Violent Femmes. And then there was the older stuff he listened to: Bob Dylan, Van Morrison, Joni Mitchell, Laura Nyro, the Byrds, the Velvet Underground, the Mamas and the Papas. He had some blues and jazz in his record collection, too, but just a little country and not much classical—it was rock music Jamie loved more than anything else.

I led Jamie to believe I was taking summer classes so he wouldn't wonder why my time was so flexible, why I was always free to practice with him whenever he wanted to. I'd told him that my aunt paid me a little to watch Rick, and that sometimes I made extra money by helping Loretta out at the Big Bang. None of this was true, of course, although I stopped in to see Loretta every now and again and she'd fix me a plate of nachos or cheese fries and I'd tell her about Jamie and the progress we were making. We had an open invitation to play there as soon as we were ready.

Jamie and I took to practicing every other day, and Rick grew more and more unhappy about it. We'd already told Rick that he could do our sound when we started playing out in clubs, but this did nothing to cheer him up. He'd mope around outside the music shop the nights Jamie and I practiced there, and whether he was upset that we hadn't invited him in for a listen or just because Jamie was taking up so much of my time, I couldn't really tell.

No one had heard any of our practices besides the two of us, and finally one night after our weekly dinner Jamie and I decided to play a short set for Rick and Clay. When we played, time seemed to disappear, like the laws of ordinary nature didn't apply to us, and so our five-song set felt like it was over before it began. When we were done, Jamie and I looked at each other and smiled and I knew we were feeling the same thing, a surge from the energy that went back and forth between us, like the sound waves that came from the guitar strings, from our voices; but Clay and Rick just sat there and stared at us, didn't say a word, didn't even clap their hands to be polite.

"Don't get too excited now," Jamie said to Clay. "We wouldn't want the adulation to go to our heads."

"I'm sure it's good for that type of music," Clay said. "You know I prefer classical."

"And I don't," Jamie said. His cheeks were getting red, and I knew in this particular case it was not embarrassment but anger.

"You're squandering your talent," Clay said. "I know you don't want to hear this, but it's the truth."

Jamie got up from the stool he'd been sitting on and flung his guitar case open so that the cover hit the floor hard. I took his guitar away from him so I could put it in the case; I knew he'd be mad at himself later if he did anything to it. He let me take it from him and stood there with his arms folded, just staring at Clay.

"You guys sounded like a whole band," Rick said, surprising all of us as he broke the silence. "It sounded like four guitars, not two." He swallowed hard, and gave me a look that broke my heart. "You'll make it," he said, with such a sadness that Jamie and I looked at each other and neither of us knew whether to thank him or apologize.

. . .

One night the following week, Rick was late meeting me at the diner, the neon one I liked so much. We'd made a few dollars on South Street the weekend before, and had taken to treating ourselves to milkshakes for dinner. It was too hot to eat anything that wasn't freezing cold; the milkshakes filled us up, made us feel like we'd had a full meal. Rick always got an upset stomach after, but that was normal for him.

I waited for an hour, drinking glass after glass of water until the waitress insisted I order something and so I finally had my milkshake, by myself. I was finishing the last few strawfuls when Rick finally walked in.

"Where were you?" I asked. "I tried to wait, but she made me order."

"It's okay," Rick said, sliding into the booth. He picked up a spoon and began twirling it around with his fingers. He let out a loud sigh but didn't say anything else.

"So where were you?" I asked.

He sighed again and looked at me. "I'm not sure how to tell you this." His eyes shifted back down to the table.

I felt a small pit trying to form in my stomach, and I fought to keep it from growing. "What?" I asked. I slurped the remains of my milkshake in a way that I hoped gave the impression I wasn't at all concerned.

"Okay." He let out another loud breath. "Remember I told you about that guy at the youth shelter who helped me get my G.E.D.?" He stuttered through the whole sentence.

"Yes," I said, my gaze fixed level on him. I knew I wasn't going to like whatever came next.

"I ran into him a few days ago. He said he'd heard from my mother, and that she wanted me to come home." He tapped the tabletop with the spoon he was holding. "I guess the guy had been looking for me for a while," he added.

"Don't tell me you're going back there," I said. "Don't even tell me that." I knew it was selfish, and kind of mean, but I couldn't imagine living on my own, without Rick.

"I told my Mom about you," he said quickly. "She said maybe if things worked out you could come stay with us for a while."

I snorted. "I doubt your Mom wants me to move in there. The way you've told it she was never so sure she wanted you."

I expected him to get real angry, but it seemed like he'd prepared himself for anything I could possibly say. "If you're gonna be mean, I'll just get up and leave," he said quietly.

I was fighting tears, and wiped my eyes in a way I hoped looked casual. "No. I don't want you to go." I turned my head and looked out the window.

"She said my stepfather's gone for good," he said. "She's in AA now, and she's facing up to everything she let happen. She wants to make it up to me."

I turned back and looked at Rick. "What did happen?" I asked. "You never told me."

He shifted uncomfortably in his seat. "He just beat me up a lot, and stuff."

"Just?" I asked. "Like, how bad?" I was thinking of that preacher, what might have happened to me if I hadn't got away.

He shook his head, shifted his eyes away from me. "Bad, okay? It was bad. But I think she's changed. I don't think she'd take him back again. She sounds totally different, like a different person." It sounded like he was trying to convince himself.

"As long as she doesn't start drinking again," I said.

"I have to try," he said. "I don't want this kind of life anymore."

I looked at him, sitting there in front of me, his face still full of pimples, so young-looking to have spent most of the last three years living the way we did. When I was his age I was still living with the Ramirezes, in love with Juan, coming home to hot meals, to stories of the day's events. To a family.

"I know," I said. "You can do better. I just don't know what I'll do without you, is all."

"Miri," Rick said, and he put his head in his hands, propped his elbows on the table.

The waitress came by and I ordered another milkshake, figuring, what the hell.

"You have Jamie now," Rick said after a while.

I looked at him in disbelief. "I have Jamie?" I asked. "No, I have a band with Jamie. We get together a few times a week to practice. He has no idea how I live, Rick. How we live." I twisted my straw in the empty milkshake glass. "He couldn't even imagine."

My second milkshake came, and I offered some to Rick but he waved it away. He watched me as I sucked it down.

"I'm leaving tomorrow morning," he said. "I'm taking a bus out at 10:00."

I finished my milkshake, said nothing.

"I'm sorry," he said.

I left six bucks on the table and headed out of the diner, Rick following me. "Are you just not going to talk to me?" he asked.

I shrugged. "As far as I'm concerned, you're already gone," I said, and he stared at me for a second, shook his head, and stamped off down 20th Street as I headed down Spruce.

Earlier that summer we'd lost our squat on Fairmount Street; we'd gone there one night to find the fire escape stairs gone, the whole building re-boarded up so tight that a waterbug surely couldn't have slipped in, let alone me and Rick. We'd been staying since then at an abandoned ware-house in West Philly that had been taken over by a group calling them-selves "The Collective": a mix of wacked-out college kids, wayward artists, aging hippies, and general down-on-their-luck folk. Rick and I had known about the place for some time, having played at a party there with Catholic Boys Gone Bad the year before, but as luck would have it we'd run into one of the hippies a few weeks before we lost our squat and he'd told us how it was now a place where people lived, like an old-style commune. Because some people hung out there who weren't truly homeless, the place was a little more fixed up than the squats we'd been in before; there were jugs of water for washing up and drinking, and one of the college kids had rigged it so we "borrowed" electricity from a neighboring building.

Rick never showed up at the warehouse that night. I'd always felt safe there, with him, but alone the place seemed more menacing. The college kids and artist-types cleared out by midnight, and then it was just the homeless folks left, rolling out their bedding. They were all men, all older than me, and if I'd noticed this before it hadn't made a difference until now. It was funny how I hadn't paid much attention to the fact that I was the only girl; Rick may have been skinny, but he'd grown taller over that past year, and there was a big difference between taking on two people and taking on one. I set my comforter up in a corner that got a little light from the street, curled myself around my bag and Juan's guitar, watched as the guys passed a bottle of whiskey around, and barely slept all night. I kept thinking about Rick, about how bad I'd treated him, how guilty I'd tried to make him feel.

Once the sun came up, sleep was a lost cause. I washed my face with water from one of the jugs near the sink, ran a brush through my hair, and decided to head on down to the Trailways terminal to see Rick off, to say goodbye.

I waited there for hours, so long that I began wondering if maybe there was another bus station he might be leaving from, but finally at 9:45 he showed up, carrying his backpack and his Snoopy and Woodstock sleeping bag, with a middle-aged black man in chinos and a sport shirt at his side. I figured him for the social worker.

When Rick spotted me sitting there in front of the terminal, he smiled. "Hey," he said, dumping his stuff on the ground next to me.

"Hey yourself," I said.

The social worker stood by his side, like he thought I might tuck Rick under my arm and kidnap him back out to the streets.

"This is Dave," he said, motioning to the social worker. "This is Miri."

"Miri," the guy said. "I've heard a lot about you."

I did not trust this guy one bit. "I'm eighteen," I said. "There's nowhere you can send me."

Dave the social worker laughed and went inside the building.

"I'm glad you came," Rick said to me.

"I wanted to say goodbye."

He nodded. "Maybe I could call you at Jamie's sometime. I know when you're usually there."

"Okay," I said, though I didn't believe he would call me. I felt certain I'd never see Rick again. He'd go back to the life he'd left in the suburbs, dive back into his studies like the last three years had been a dream. "You have the number?" I asked.

"Yeah," he said, though he didn't sound sure.

"You know his last name?"

Rick shook his head.

"Emerson," I said. "Jamie Emerson. Look him up if you ever need to get a hold of me."

"Okay," he said. By then people had lined up to get on the bus, and the driver was at the door, collecting tickets. Dave the social worker handed Rick the ticket he'd just bought him. I turned away, hoping neither one of them would see the tears in my eyes.

Rick moved around to my side. "Are you gonna be okay?" he asked me, and there was such a sound of concern in his voice that for a second I thought maybe if I said no, I wasn't going to be okay, that I was scared to stay at the warehouse by myself and that I didn't know where else to go, he would tell Dave the social worker to shove his bus ticket and he'd pick up his stuff and head on down the street with me. But I didn't want to do that to him.

"I'm fine," I said. "You know me, Rick. I always land on my feet."

Rick gave me a hug and shook hands with Dave the social worker and picked up his stuff and got on the bus. I was surprised to see he was still carrying his sleeping bag, like he wasn't sure he'd have a bed at his Mom's; or maybe it was just force of habit.

I stood next to Dave and watched the bus pull off down Arch Street.

"Do you have a place to sleep tonight?" Dave asked me in his best concerned-social-worker voice.

"I always have a place to sleep," I shot back.

He smiled. "Here's my card," he said, handing it to me. At the top of the card it read, "Philadelphia Emergency Youth Services."

"I really am eighteen," I said. "There's nothing you can do for me." Or to me, I thought, but kept that to myself.

"There might be," he said. "If you need help, stop by my office. The address is on the card."

I nodded and stuck the card in my bag just to shut him up. He offered me a ride into Center City, which I turned down, for I knew that was just his way of trying to get me back in the system. As soon as he drove away I tore his card in half and dropped it into a trash can outside the bus station.

CHAPTER 19
JULY–AUGUST, 1985

Without Rick, I felt as alone as the day Grandma died. My bones felt hollowed out, like the thin reeds I used to see growing in the marshes near the Gulf. It seemed I was made up of bird bones, and I came to believe that anyone who passed me on the street must surely hear the wind rushing through me. I felt like I was disappearing, like the hollowed-out parts of me were eating right through everything that was solid.

I continued playing on South Street by myself on weekends, but I didn't make as much money as I had with Rick. I wasn't sure if this was because he'd looked so pathetic, or because my heart wasn't really in those songs any longer. All the music I had in me I stored up for the nights I practiced with Jamie, but even he could tell that something was not right. I told him Rick had gone back to visit kin in Texas, and that I missed him. Jamie always seemed to accept my lies right off.

The Collective felt more and more unsafe; after two nights without Rick, one of the older guys there asked me what had happened to him. I told him and the others within earshot that Rick would be back in a day or two, but I got the feeling they didn't believe me; they started looking me up and down like I'd make a really good meal. I tried the old rowhouse, which I hadn't been back to in almost a year, and it was even worse than I remembered it; the smell had become unbearable, and the people who were living there were all either junkies or truly crazy, and I mean crazy in a dangerous way. I slept a couple of nights in the place Rick and I used to like by that parking lot under the Walnut Street bridge, but then one night I went there and it was all torn up for construction. I stretched my bedding out in the midst of the plastic traffic cones and left-out equipment, but just as I started to lay myself down I saw motion out of the corner of my eye. It was a rat; when I looked closer in the darkness, more than one.

I picked up the corner of my blanket and shook it out, hearing something heavy hit the ground, then a high-pitched squeal in the dark. I grabbed my stuff and ran up the stairs to the bridge.

I spent that night walking the streets around the Penn campus, occasionally resting on a bench or a set of stairs in front of an ivy-covered building. As the night wore on I passed groups of students, many of them clearly drunk, on their way home from some bar or band or fraternity party. Any one of those kids could be Lolita or Jimmy Clack, I'd think, looking them over good. Much later in the night, I saw a girl walking nervously by herself, her makeup smeared, her clothes not on quite right, and I decided, with an evil twinge of satisfaction, that she could be my cousin Mary Gay, though in reality it was more like something Annmarie would have done.

I remembered a story about a time Annmarie had gone to visit Aunt Melissa at college. I'd heard versions of the story from both Annmarie and Grandma, and could piece together everything else from knowing all parties involved. I was a baby then; Grandma had agreed to take me for the weekend, thinking, I guess, that it would be good for Annmarie to have a look at college life, that maybe she'd decide to go back to school herself. Aunt Melissa was, as you'd expect, in some uppity sorority, and she'd laid down all kinds of rules and regulations to Annmarie before she'd agree to let her visit. Annmarie had promised Melissa that she'd be on her best behavior; instead, she arrived three hours late, already stoned thanks to some guy she'd met on the bus ride, and that was just the beginning. After a party Melissa took her to that night, Annmarie went home with the boyfriend of one of Melissa's sorority sisters.

Aunt Melissa probably thought Annmarie had done it just to embarrass her, but I knew how Annmarie's mind worked. The girl whose boyfriend it was had probably given Annmarie some kind of attitude, had probably looked at her in a way that said she thought she was above her; and Annmarie's message back to her was clear: I'm good enough for your boyfriend to fuck. At the end of that weekend, Aunt Melissa told Annmarie they were no longer sisters, that she wanted nothing more to do with her. And by extension, I guess, she wanted nothing more to do with me.

Around dawn, I ran into a group of street kids, ones Rick and I had noticed in our travels. There were five of them that moved together in a pack, three boys and two girls; they sometimes slept in a park just below South Street. They were stoned night and day and sometimes shot smack, and I knew at least two of the boys got their money by either sleeping with or hustling the gays who cruised the corner around 17th and Lombard— you could never get a straight answer from these kids as to what they actually did—but they were all younger than me and I figured I could handle them. I asked them to wait up and told them I'd buy them breakfast but of course I didn't have enough money for all of us so we had to do a dine and dash, which they seemed to enjoy. I spent the next few nights in the park with them, and though they treated me fine I didn't like being right out on a bench like that. It was just one step away from sleeping on a steam grate, far as I was concerned.

One night, I got fed up with sleeping outdoors and decided the Collective had been mine once and I'd be damned if I'd let a few hard-luck drunks scare me away. I grabbed my stuff and headed over there around 10:00. They were having some sort of party that night for one of the artists—a guy who made sculptures of lumpy-faced, deformed creatures. Gargoyles, one of the college kids called them. They were everywhere in the warehouse—raised up on wooden planks, sitting high on makeshift tables, some of them dotting the floor. Each one was a foot or more high and as ugly as anything I'd ever seen, but I smiled sweetly while one of the college kids described them as "radical," and I shared a couple of beers with those kids before they headed home for the night. I knew I should have tried to pick up one of the boys, go home with him, but I hadn't slept much in days and was too tired and depressed over Rick to muster up the energy required.

By 1 A.M. it was just me and the older guys who had nowhere to sleep— bums, Grandma would have called them. On that particular night there were seven men, all of them old enough at least to be my long-lost father. I rolled out my comforter and laid down in a corner of the warehouse next to a couple of the sculptures, rolling over so I wouldn't have to look at them. I tried to give off my best air that said I shouldn't be messed with. I was awake for a long time, and I heard a couple of the men whispering but nothing seemed to happen, so finally I let myself doze off, glad to be off the street, to have a place where I could wash up in the morning without going to the library.

I had a dream that I couldn't breathe. In the dream I was fighting for air, I was clawing and punching out with my arms, desperate to ease the crushing weight that kept my lungs from filling up. It was like all the oxygen had been sucked out of the air, or the air itself was gone, like I was floating in outer space. I *was* in outer space; I was an astronaut, and I was fighting something that was trying to get into my spacesuit, something that seemed to be all tentacles, like an octopus. Something that seemed to be all arms.

I opened my eyes and saw, felt, that one of the men was on top of me— the biggest and drunkest one of the group. His smell was a heavy sour mash of body odor and whiskey. I was pinned down from his weight, crushed so completely that it took me a minute to realize he had my jeans unzipped, his fingers inside. His eyes were closed. I tried my best to move my body, to heave him off of me, but he didn't budge. His face was pressed up against my left cheek, the smell of alcohol invading me in waves, with each of his breaths. I felt pretty sure that he hadn't just fallen asleep but had passed out cold.

My right arm was the only part of me not held down under his weight. I remembered the sculptures, and slid my hand as far to the side as I could, groping around on the floor. His breaths gave way to snores but still he didn't stir, and I tried hard not to panic as I inched my fingers around on the floor, desperate to feel something solid. It seemed to take forever— minutes that felt like hours, I couldn't really tell how long—but finally I felt something rough and cool and firm and I eased it closer to me with the tip of my finger, almost losing it more than once but finally knocking it on its side and rolling it over towards me. It felt heavy in my hand as I lifted it up and, without a second's hesitation, smashed it over his head, hard as I could.

He moaned and rolled to one side and I had to slide his hand out of my pants and push him over. He landed on his back, like a tick. I couldn't tell if I'd really hurt him or not, but he didn't seem to be moving. The warehouse was silent; no snoring, no breathing, no sounds of any kind. If anyone else had heard all this commotion, they were pretending they hadn't. I wanted to take the sculpture and smash it over him again and again, until it dissolved to powder in my hands, his big filthy body just a pulp of blood and bone beneath me. The thought of this scared me almost as much as what had already happened, and I grabbed my bag and ran out the door, into the early morning light.

I dug some change out and took the first bus I could catch into Center City. I got off at 18th Street and walked up to Rittenhouse Square Park, and it wasn't until I'd sat down on a bench and had a minute to catch my breath that I realized I'd left Juan's guitar and my bedding back at the warehouse. They were both a lost cause; I could never go back there. I'd left behind either a dead body or a really pissed off guy with a terrible headache, and either way I had to keep my distance.

Over the next few days I became convinced I'd killed him. In diners I stole newspapers folks had left behind and scoured them for word of a homeless man murdered in a warehouse; but either I hadn't killed him, or nobody cared that I had. I took to dozing in parks during the day and walking the streets at night, afraid to sleep anywhere once the sun went down.

I was down to my last dollar, and without the guitar I had no way to make more money. I ran into the teenagers who slept in the park off South Street, and one night they treated me to pizza. One of the boys had a wad of money; how he'd gotten it I didn't know and didn't ask. I roamed the city with them for a few days, maybe a week, watching them shoot up, taking a swig of whiskey with one of the boys now and again. I hated drinking but it seemed to take the edge off my nerves. The energy required to go to the library and wash up became too much, and so I stopped.

I blew off a week's worth of rehearsals with Jamie. I knew what I looked like by then, as crazy and dirty as the street people I'd always sworn I'd never become. The thought of Jamie seeing me like that was more than I could stand; I decided I'd rather have him think I was dead. He had no way to contact me; I'd told him that the aunt Rick and I lived with didn't have a phone.

One of the boys in the pack seemed to like me. He was about seventeen, a white boy who'd grown his long hair into dreadlocks that reached below his shoulders. His idea of bathing was jumping into the Logan Square fountain fully clothed, then stretching out on a bench in the broiling sun to dry out. I encouraged his attention as a way of protecting myself from everyone else; but one night when he tried to kiss me I panicked, pushed him away so hard that he lost his balance and fell to the ground. He started laughing, maybe thinking I was kidding, and as he got up I didn't wait around to explain. I grabbed my bag and ran off, blocks and blocks down 17th Street, down little side streets whose names I never noticed, until I found an alley that looked safe to me, and ducked in. I spent the night there, crying and talking to myself, unable to think clearly enough to come up with any way out of the mess I was in.

I'm not sure how much longer I spent like that, wandering by myself, getting more and more crazy from the heat, the hunger, the lack of sleep. It was late July or early August by then, and felt even hotter than the summer before—it felt to me like Texas heat, the kind of searing hell I'd always thought didn't flare up in the north.

I wandered to the library one day, with a vague hope of cooling myself off inside, maybe even cleaning up a little, but I was so tired by the time I got there I had to sit down on a bench outside to rest and I fell asleep, sitting straight up in the roasting sun. I went in and out of dreams I couldn't quite grasp on to; shadow figures, they were, people from my past I couldn't make out. I felt something warm on my back. At first I thought it was just the sun, and tried to fall back asleep; but gradually the warmth increased, moved in circles, and I fought my way awake enough to figure out it was a hand, the hand of someone gently rubbing between my shoulder blades. I opened my eyes.

She was sitting on the bench with me, wearing the powder-blue dress she was buried in, the open-backed silver slippers I'd once given her for her birthday; her gray hair was fixed in bobby pin curls atop her head. She smelled like Ivory soap.

She patted the back of my neck, and I could feel the heat, the touch of her fingertips, their pressure and weight.

It wasn't a dream. Given the state I was in, it would have made more sense that way, to figure it as something I'd imagined, some hallucination. And maybe it was, but as I looked past her, at the traffic rushing down Ben

Franklin Parkway, out to the Logan Square fountain and the tall office buildings beyond, all of it shimmering in the haze of that white-hot sun, I was sure I wasn't dreaming. I was sitting in front of the library, and Grandma was there with me.

"Miri," she said to me, still patting the nape of my neck, "you go see Jamie."

I closed my eyes and opened them again, but she was still there. I wondered if I was supposed to answer her, or if my voice might break whatever kind of spell or state of being had sent her to me. I just sat there and looked at her, smelled her, felt her.

"Go see Jamie and tell him what happened," she went on.

"I don't want him to see me like this," I said. I hadn't expected to answer her; the words just floated out of me.

She shook her head, the sunlight reflecting off the shiny bobby pins. "You listen now, Miri," she said. "You go talk to him." She looked at me for a second—a piercing, intense look like nothing I'd seen before when she was alive, not even at her most agitated—and then she faded, the feel of her hand on my back, the smell of her soap, the blue of her dress all growing fainter until she was just a ghost image, a blur you think you see out of the corner of your eye, and then a wave of light in the thick humid air, and then nothing.

I reached my hand out to where she'd been sitting, felt the moist air, and looked around. I was looking for someone who might have seen her, but the only folks nearby were across the street at the fountain, not paying me any mind. It made no sense, Grandma coming back from the dead to tell me I should go see Jamie. I wasn't sure how she'd even have felt about him, her being so religious and all; and if she could come back like that, it seemed to me she wouldn't have let me wind up in the fix I was.

My mind wandered to the life I might have led if Grandma hadn't died, the life I was supposed to have: graduating from Sam Houston High School, maybe marrying one of the local boys like Troy Wilson or even Jimmy Clack, maybe leaving town to study voice at a university. Maybe even going on to Nashville. The only time in my life I'd ever felt truly good about myself was the three years I'd lived in Prairie Rose. I'd been cheated out of that life, and the thought of all I'd lost fed an anger that gave my ragged body a short burst of energy, just enough to drag myself off the bench, through the soupy air, across the expanse of weedy grass and into the library, past the stare of the lady at the information desk, into the bathroom where I stripped off the clothes I'd been wearing for a week or more, washed up as best I could, put on the least dirty thing in my bag—my old sundress—and checked myself in the mirror. My hair still looked a mess, dirty and full of knots; the circles under my eyes seemed to be permanent, etched in black; and my skin looked a sickly pale gray, the color of cigarette ashes. But it was the best I could do, and so I left the library and pushed myself through the liquid heat up to Chestnut Street, where by some miracle I found enough change in my bag to catch a bus to Olde City.

I had no idea what time it was, or even what day. Judging by the sun I figured it for late afternoon, and hoped Jamie would be at the music shop, giving his final lesson of the day. If he wasn't there I thought I might just sleep in the little lot behind the store and wait for him to show up in the morning. I couldn't imagine going to his apartment, facing Clay.

I got off the bus and walked the few blocks down to the shop. Heat rose from the asphalt streets in waves that I could actually see. I had no feeling in my feet; it was like they were dissolving beneath me. I made it up to the shop and stood off to the side, peeked in the window. Jamie was standing behind a girl, pushing her fingers into position for a C chord in the same manner he'd taught me. I had almost forgotten how beautiful he was; he just seemed to glow, the lines of his cheeks, his jaw in shadow, his smooth hair shining blonder than I'd remembered it. The girl was about my age, with dark, perfectly cut hair, a clean white t-shirt and a flowered skirt. A college girl, no doubt, one who probably had a crush on Jamie. I thought about how bad I'd looked in the light of the library bathroom, and lost my nerve. I stayed there by the side of the window, watching as the girl put her guitar in its case, handed Jamie some rolled-up bills, and headed for the door. As she passed me on the street she gave me a funny look, not realizing that she could be me, had her life's events taken a different turn. She smelled of patchouli; her hair bounced when she walked.

I stood there for a few more minutes, trying to get up my courage. Jamie was moving things around in the shop, putting instruments in their cases the way you'd tuck a child in to bed. He made a move toward the front of the store, a quick move I hadn't expected, and I whirled away from the window but he caught sight of me. I ran down the alley alongside the store. I heard the front door open and close, and footsteps behind me. "Miri," he called, uncertainly, like he wasn't sure it was me. He followed me into the lot behind the store.

I turned and faced him, not knowing what to say or how to explain myself.

"Miri," he said. "God, what happened?"

His voice was so soft it made me want to cry, and I think I did a little. I was all prepared to make up a story about my aunt and how she'd kicked me out, figuring I'd build on it as I went along like I always did, but before I could launch into my lies I felt a burst of warmth between my shoulder blades, spreading down my spine, and I fought it for a second but then gave in. I told Jamie everything I'd never told him, from Annmarie to Prairie Rose to the foster homes, to Juan and Austin and Ian Oliver, to Philly and Rick, how Rick had finally left, and most of what had happened since. When I got to the warehouse I couldn't get that part out, so I skipped over it and went on to my vision of Grandma, knowing it made me sound crazy but unable to stop all the truth that I was spitting out of my mouth like teeth. Jamie was quiet through all of it, standing in front of me, his expression changing with turns in the story, his eyes getting wide, his hand flying to his mouth once or twice. When I was all done, he stayed quiet for a minute—maybe just a few seconds, but it seemed so long that I had time to become afraid he was mad at me, for blowing him off those past few weeks, for all the lies I'd told.

"I'm sorry I told you so many stories," I said, finally.

Jamie shook his head and turned away from me. I thought for sure he was trying to come up with a way to tell me he didn't like the band idea any more—a nice, polite way, that would be how Jamie would do it—but instead he headed up the two back steps and into the music store, motioning me to follow. He kept his head turned away from me, so I couldn't begin to guess what he was thinking, what he was feeling.

He moved slowly, locking up the cash register, turning off the lights and putting his own guitar in its case, the silence as loud as the sun was bright.

I didn't know what to say or do, just stood there watching him. He straightened some pages of sheet music that were loose on the counter, moved them a few inches away, and straightened them again. Finally he picked up his guitar and nudged my elbow with his other hand.

"Come on," he said, but there was an uneasiness to his voice, like maybe that wasn't what he'd meant to say, or it had popped out of his mouth unexpected. "Let's go."

"Where?" I asked.

His eyes were fixed out the window, where rush-hour business people had begun to hurry by, briefcases clutched to their hips like weapons. I wondered what it was like, having enough places you had to be that you just ran from one to the next. Jamie moved toward the front door, opened it, motioned me through.

"Home," he said. "We're going home."

CHAPTER 20
AUGUST–SEPTEMBER, 1985

Jamie fixed me a bubble bath and brought me a cup of tea that smelled like flowers and tasted sweet as new-mown hay. Clay got home right after us, and so Jamie left me a fluffy white towel big enough to dry off the entire Home Sweet Home church choir, closed the door, and went on out there to talk to Clay. It was quiet for a while, and then the fighting started up in harsh whispers, bursts of angry words.

It was Jamie doing the whispering; Clay's words came through the bathroom walls clear as can be: "street urchin," "steal us out of house and home," and, my personal favorite, "It's already so cramped here." After having squatted with ten, sometimes twenty people on the floor of one room, it was hard for me to imagine a two-bedroom apartment not being big enough for three people. I couldn't hear what Jamie said in return, but he was obviously disagreeing because Clay kept up the insults. This went on for a good half-hour until Jamie's voice came through, loud, angrier than I'd ever heard him.

"Look, I've been supporting you for the past three years," he yelled. "If I want to support someone else, that's my decision." I heard the sound of breaking glass, and then a door slamming shut so hard I had to wonder if it had popped its hinges.

Miri, you sure know how to cause trouble for folks, I thought as I sat there soaping my hair up for the third time with Jamie's conditioning shampoo. I felt revived, though, like the hot water was soaking all the trouble right out of my bones.

Jamie came in a little while later, and asked me if I was hungry. I was, but I shook my head. I didn't want him to feel like he had to keep waiting on me.

"I don't want to cause a fight between you and Clay," I said. "I'll try to find a place as soon as possible."

Jamie shook his head, and waved his hand as if to dismiss Clay.

"We fight all the time anyway," he said.

"What about?"

Jamie sighed. "Everything. Nothing." He sat down on the commode, completely unselfconscious about me being naked in the tub. I sat up and poured more bubble bath in, just to see if the sight of my naked top half would do anything for him. It didn't.

"It wasn't always like this," he said, and it sounded like an apology.

"Well," I said, finishing up my last sip of tea, "I'll start looking into finding a place to stay tomorrow. I just need to get a good night's sleep, is all." There was nowhere for me to look, of course, but I felt like I had to say it.

Jamie shook his head. "Just stay, Miri."

I soaped my arms up for the fourth time. The tub water was turning a grimy brown, and I thought I might need a shower after I finished the bath. I poured more bubbles in so Jamie wouldn't see how dirty the water looked.

"Okay," I said, "until I figure something out."

"No," he said. "I mean, stay."

I looked at him and he nodded so I'd know he really meant it. I figured it was his guilt talking, guilt over how much he had and how much I didn't have. Nice as he was, much as I loved him, I didn't want to be his boy scout project.

"I can't live off you, Jamie," I said. "Wouldn't be right."

He examined his fingernails for a second, then stared off into the white-tiled distance.

"It'll be like a business arrangement," he said, and I could see the sparkles in his hazel-brown eyes working overtime. "It'll be for the good of the band." It sounded partly like he was rehearsing these words for Clay.

I looked him square in the eyes. "Do you really think we're that good?"

"Yes. I know we are." He picked up the empty tea cup from the side of the tub, set it atop the toilet tank. "Don't you think so, Miri?"

I wanted to be as honest with him as was possible for a natural-born liar like me, not keep playing him like I had oftentimes done before.

"When we're rehearsing, I think we sound as good as anything you could want to hear, but when I think on it later I wonder if I just exaggerate it in my mind." I swirled my feet around at the bottom of the tub. "You know, I always dreamed of making it in music, but it wasn't like I could dream about much else. Singing is the only talent I ever had." Aside from lying and picking up boys, I thought, but I didn't want to lay that much truth on Jamie in one night.

He smiled at me. "I've been in other bands. I told you about them, didn't I?"

I shook my head.

"I did the folk circuit with another guitar player in New York for a while," he said, "and then I was in a rock band in Boston." He kicked at the edge of the bathmat with his toe. "And I knew in both cases that we'd never go anywhere."

"And you think we can."

"I know we can." He was just about convincing me. "So here's the deal," he said. "We practice every day. We try to start playing out around town by early next year. And when we make a little money you can pay me back for staying here."

I smiled. "When we're famous I'll buy you the whole apartment building," I said.

"Deal," Jamie said, and he patted the back of my neck with his hand. Just then we heard the front door open and close.

"I'd better go deal with that," he sighed, and left me to finish my bath.

Somehow, Jamie worked it out with Clay, my staying there, though it was clear that Clay was not happy with the arrangement. If I was still asleep on the futon when Clay passed through the living room in the morning, he'd kick it just to wake me up; then he'd complain he'd stubbed his toe because there was no room to walk. I learned to wake up before Clay, get the futon pushed back together like a couch, and remove from the living room all traces that I'd slept there. It wasn't hard; I'd done the same thing in squats. When I heard Clay get in the shower I'd put a pot of coffee on so it'd be ready for him when he came out, and this helped to ease the tension a bit. Jamie slept through all of these morning doings; he was never up before 10:00, never scheduled a guitar lesson before noon. It was a good thing for Jamie that he was rich on his own, for it was clear he wouldn't have been too happy working nine-to-five.

We never talked about Jamie's money, where it came from, how much he had; it was just there, like the paintings on the walls, the floor-to-ceiling bookcases, the shelves full of record albums. I knew from their arguments that Jamie paid the rent, and since he only worked giving guitar lessons I figured it was some kind of family money. I imagined people like Jimmy and Lolita Clack could live the same way, just working every now and again, dipping into the family fortune when need be.

Those first few weeks I stayed with Jamie and Clay, the thing I found the most surprising was how much time I had on my hands. You'd think all I had was time, living on the streets, but it wasn't time you could use. Most of it was spent just figuring how to stay alive, and anything left over was time to kill.

But now, the hours stretched on endlessly. In the mornings, I'd sip coffee with Jamie and then watch as he did yoga for an hour before he went off to the music store. I'd never seen anyone sit with their legs crossed like that for so long, just doing nothing but breathing; he tried to teach it to me, but once he started talking about finding his third eye I knew the whole thing was too far out there for my personal taste. Jamie called himself an agnostic Buddhist; he said that meant he meditated but he didn't believe it would really help.

When Jamie was out giving guitar lessons and Clay was at school, I watched TV, catching up on celebrity gossip and game shows, hypnotized by the music videos on MTV, which I'd heard about but had never seen before. I picked books off Clay's shelves, skimmed the opening few lines, and put them back; I riffled through Jamie's albums, which filled shelf after shelf and which looked to number over a thousand. Sometimes I'd practice on his instruments: his mandolin, his dulcimer, his acoustic Martin and his Rickenbacker twelve-string, everything but the Gibson, which he usually took with him to the music shop. I even worked on songs of my own, and after I got a couple sounding good enough I surprised him with them at our next practice. I made sure the place looked clean and neat when Clay got home at night.

As I fell into a routine there—a routine with Jamie, that is, more like an uneasy truce with Clay—I started to really think about my life, more than I ever had in the past. Now that I had the luxury of time, I couldn't stop the thoughts and memories from flooding my mind. I'd picture Juan, sitting in a cell down in San Antonio, and feel full-blown guilt at my part in getting him in that mess; I'd imagine Wendell, fixing the Clacks' Lincoln Continental, and wonder why it was that he'd abandoned me. As much as I didn't want to go back to Texas, there were times I missed it more than I could say, especially Prairie Rose; at times it felt like a part of me had been cut out, and the pain was coming from this missing piece, like the pain they say people sometimes feel when they have an arm or leg cut off.

As the weeks went on, I started to come up with reasons to stay in the house all day; by that fall it had worked itself into a fear of going out. I was partly afraid of not being let back in, and partly afraid of what could happen to me outside—of what had happened to me in the warehouse. Where I used to walk down the street enjoying the way men looked at me, it now filled me with dread. I wanted to start busking again, so I could make enough money to buy groceries from time to time; but the day I finally got the nerve to walk down to South Street with one of Jamie's guitars I played one song and got so freaked out by having people look at me that I packed up and hurried off to the Big Bang to visit Loretta, and to get my courage up so I could head back to Jamie's.

It was only 11:00 in the morning; the Big Bang wasn't even open for lunch yet. I pounded on the door a couple of times, and was just about to give up when I heard Loretta scream, "Keep your pants on!" from somewhere inside. This made me laugh and I waited until she got to the front door and unlocked it for me.

"Hey, Miri," she said, motioning me to follow her through the bar. From the kitchen I could hear voices, chopping sounds, the whir of a blender. "I was just feeding the cats."

"The cats?" I asked, setting Jamie's guitar down against a wall as Loretta opened the back door that led to an alley behind the bar.

She picked up a box of Friskies, shook it, and the cats came running. There were three of them, three of the most ragged, beat-up looking cats I'd ever seen. I helped her pour the food onto paper plates and set them down in the alley.

"I've been feeding them since last spring," she said, "and they're still so skinny." She scratched her scalp, the snake's head tattooed on her wrist looking like it was striking out as she lifted her arm. "They probably have worms. I wish I could find them homes."

"Why don't you take them home, Loretta?" I asked her.

"I have two cats already. They wouldn't appreciate any company."

I watched as one of the cats, a little red-beige tabby, pushed a black-and-white tomcat twice her size away from a plate so she could get some food. The little cat was really just a bunch of bones with some skin and orange fur thrown on top, but I liked her nerve. The tip of her left ear was missing, either chewed off by insects or lost in some kind of fight; she had patches where her fur was missing, the skin beneath raw-looking. Because of all the places she was missing fur, you could easily see how full of fleas she was. I wished I could take her home, but I didn't want to wind up back out there, sharing the alley with her.

"So when are you and Jamie going to play here?" Loretta asked me as she closed the back door.

"I think he's hoping to start playing in front of people early next year," I said.

"Next year?" Loretta sniffed. "Miri, how long have you two been practicing?"

"About a year."

"Hell, I've had bands here that never played together before they hit my stage! You played here with those awful college kids—what were their names?"

"David and Bobby," I said.

"Yeah. Man, they were awful. Nice kids, but they sure couldn't play."

I nodded agreement. Loretta ducked behind the bar, pulled out a calendar.

"What are you and Jamie calling yourselves?" she asked me, poring over the month of October.

"We don't have a name yet."

She shook her head. "A whole year, and you don't even have a name yet," she muttered. "I'm putting you down as 'Jamie and Miri.'" She looked at me for a minute. "Nah, 'Miri and Jamie.' Why should the guys always get top billing?" She flipped forward to November, then looked back at October.

"I'm putting you down for October 30th," she said. "It's a Friday night."

"But Jamie doesn't think we're ready."

"Do you think you're ready?" she asked me.

"I don't know," I said. I didn't want to contradict Jamie or insult Loretta, but I couldn't see how we could not be ready for the Big Bang. Our first practice was better than any music I'd ever heard in that bar.

"You don't know? It's rock and roll, not Mozart. You've been playing together for a year. You're ready." She wrote our names in magic marker on the calendar. "October 30th," she said. "You tell Jamie."

"He might not go along with it."

"Men," she said, shaking her head. "Sometimes they just need a good kick in the ass. You remember that, Miri."

I laughed, told her I would.

Jamie went into a panic when I told him that night.

"That's only six weeks away," he said, pacing the living room. "We don't have the songs perfected yet. We'll never get it together by then."

"I think we can," I said. "We already have enough good songs to fill an hour."

"But Miri, we change the arrangements every time we play." What Jamie called change was actually a very slight variation here and there, usually of his own devising.

"I think we can do it," I said again.

"How could you agree to a date so soon?" he asked me. "October 30th. My God."

Clay looked at us over the top of the French newspaper he was reading. "For God's sake, Jamie, it's the Big Bang, not Carnegie Hall," he said.

That's pretty much what Loretta was saying, I thought. Jamie made a face in Clay's direction after Clay shifted his eyes back to the newspaper.

"Jamie, I think we should do it. It gives us something to shoot for," I said. Truth was, I thought it might help me, too, with the fears I'd suddenly developed; I was pretty sure I could face a crowd if I was with Jamie.

He continued pacing, making the little noises he made in his throat that I'd come to learn meant he was working on something in his mind.

"We'll have to practice every day," he said. "Twice a day."

With that, Clay got up, folded the newspaper, and tucked it into his backpack. He pulled his blazer jacket from the coat rack.

"Where are you going?" Jamie asked, an edge of annoyance in his voice.

"The library," Clay said.

"You've gone to the library every night this week," Jamie said.

Clay sighed. "In case you haven't noticed, it's fall. I'm teaching two classes and taking four. I'm going to be at the library a lot."

Jamie looked at him, his eyes softening. "Will you be late?" he asked. "I didn't even hear you come in last night."

I did. It was 3 A.M., and I doubted any library stayed open that late. But I was not about to let any of that on to Jamie. I did my best to stay out of their problems as much as I possibly could.

"Not too late," he said, pecked Jamie on the cheek, and headed out the door.

Jamie stood there for a second, looking bewildered. "Well, I guess that gives us more time to practice," he said, but there was something in the way he said it that made me think he had some doubts about where Clay was going, too.

CHAPTER 21
OCTOBER, 1985

By the day before the show, we both felt pretty good about the forty-five-minute set we'd come up with; we'd been practicing just about every night for the past six weeks.

Our only problem was that we still didn't have a name. We were getting desperate, reading aloud the brand names of appliances, shuffling through the titles of albums and books in the apartment.

"*Ulysses*," Jamie called out to me. "*Finnegans Wake. Tristram Shandy.*"

I made a face and shook my head.

"*Mrs. Dalloway*," Jamie went on. "*King Lear, Othello, The Merchant of Venice*—my God, Clay has a whole shelf of Shakespeare," he said.

"How about 'Whole Shelf of Shakespeare'?" I asked. I was kidding, but Jamie seemed to actually consider it for a minute.

"Too long, too hard to say," he finally answered. He flopped on the couch. "Why does this have to be so hard? I read somewhere that R.E.M. picked their name out of a dictionary. Maybe we should do that."

I shrugged, watched as he got up and went into the extra bedroom Clay used as his study. Jamie's instruments were in there, too, and even though it seemed to me it would make more sense for me to sleep in there, out of the way, since neither one of them suggested it I figured I'd better just stay put on the living room futon.

He came out with a huge dictionary, plopped down with it on the floor.

"Begone," he said. "Begonia. Begorra. Begot." He scratched his head. "There's a Grateful Dead song called 'Scarlet Begonias.'"

"I do not want to be named after a Grateful Dead song," I said. The Grateful Dead was one of the bands that Annmarie used to like.

"Chieftain, chiffchaff, chiffon," he continued, apparently having skipped ahead.

"Chiffonier, chigger, chignon, Chihuahua."

"I got chiggers once," I said. "They itch like hell." I'd been playing in a field with Mary Gay, behind Aunt Melissa's house one Christmas; my cousin was only two or three, not old enough yet to have started taunting me. The grown-ups had all let us wander off out back to play; I'm not sure how long we were out there. When our legs started itching, Mary Gay and I ran back to the house. Aunt Melissa should have known there could be chiggers in that field, but she put the blame on me; I was only four or five, but to hear her you'd have thought I'd lured my cousin out there just to get her infected.

Jamie sighed. "This isn't working," he said.

"I know." I walked over to the window, sat on the sill and looked outside. "Brownstone," I said. "BMW. Rusted Rabbit—oops, sorry, that's your car." Jamie laughed. "Kid on Bike. Wawa—Jamie, how about Wawa? It sounds kind of punk."

"It sounds like a baby crying," Jamie said. "And we're not taking the name of a convenience store. We might as well call ourselves 7-Eleven."

I continued surveying the street below. "Dorky Guy," I said. "Big Mean Dog. Kinda Cute Guy. Mmmm, Very Cute Guy." I still had my fears, but being two stories up in an apartment with Jamie filled me with all kinds of bravery. I opened the window as far as it would go and stuck my head out. The rush of cool fall air felt good on my face.

"Hey you," I called down. "What's your phone number?"

At this point Jamie ran up behind me to get a look at the guy. I got the feeling he liked seeing me do things he would never do himself.

"Sorry, honey," the guy shot back in a swishy voice he laid on thick to get his point across. "You're not my type."

I pulled Jamie in front of me. "What about him?" I called back.

"Oh my God, Miri, I'm so embarrassed," Jamie muttered to me, but he was smiling and made no move to leave the window.

The guy on the street stopped in his tracks. "Now that's more like it," he called up. "What's your name, gorgeous?"

Jamie turned bright red then, his whole face, even his ears. "Clay wouldn't like this," he mumbled, and moved away from the window.

"Don't go away," the guy called up, but I just shrugged my shoulders at him and closed the window. Jamie was sitting on the futon, picking at the stitching.

"Maybe we should just go on as Miri and Jamie, like Loretta has us down," I said, more to change the subject than for any other reason. I still wasn't quite sure then how much I could joke around with Jamie, or when I'd gone too far. "Or Jamie and Miri," I added quickly. "Whichever way."

"It sounds like a children's show," Jamie said. "God, why can't we come up with a name? All I ever wanted in life was a band I could be proud of, and I can't even think of a goddamn name." He sighed, heaved the dictionary off the ground and headed back to Clay's study. I went in the kitchen for another cup of coffee—Jamie and I were both completely addicted, and had the coffee pot going practically day and night—and a few minutes later he came running in, waving a binder full of papers in his hands.

"Look at this," he said. It was something Clay had written, and gotten an A-minus on. The fact that he got a minus gave me an evil burst of pleasure. "Read the title," Jamie added, pointing.

"Beyond 'Cloud . . .'" I looked at Jamie for help.

"Cloud Cuckoo Land," he said.

"Beyond 'Cloud Cuckoo Land'," I started again, "A Comparative Analysis of Animal Models As Societal Parodies in Literature from Classical Greece to Contemporary Britain." I gave Jamie a disbelieving look. "What is this shit about?" I asked him.

Jamie laughed. "Never mind," he said. "I thought 'Cloud Cuckoo Land' sounded interesting so I looked it up."

"And?"

"A fanciful or ideal place," he said. "It's from a Greek play where it was a kind of bird heaven, according to Clay's dictionary."

"Bird heaven," I said. I liked the idea of that; between my voice and my size, I'd often been compared to a bird, and had come to think of myself as one. Bird heaven seemed to describe well the recent upturn my life had taken. "Cloud Cuckoo Land," I repeated.

"It sounds kind of psychedelic," Jamie said. He'd been on a kick lately with something called the Paisley Underground, a bunch of bands that sounded like garage-rock psychedelia.

I wasn't sure it was the greatest band name, but Jamie seemed pleased with it, and I was happy not to have to keep trying to come up with something else. "Cloud Cuckoo Land," I said. "We're Cloud Cuckoo Land."

Jamie smiled. "So that's it?" he asked, reading my face carefully for signs of disapproval.

"That's it," I said, and he seemed so happy I didn't have the heart to tell him that no one would ever be able to pronounce it, remember it, or figure out what it meant.

Loretta had booked us as the second act on a triple bill. The headliners were the Primates, a band that Jamie said had gotten a decent write-up in the local alternative paper. The opening band was called Teddy and the Train Wreck, and they were—a train wreck, I mean. Teddy was about 5-foot-2 of stringy blonde hair and bone. There was something about him that didn't look put together right; one arm looked shorter than the other, he limped favoring his right side, and his left eyeball darted around wildly while the other one looked straight ahead. Jamie said he looked like Tom Petty, if Tom Petty had been in an accident and was reconstructed from spare parts by some alien scientist who'd never seen a human being before.

After we watched him for a while, Jamie said he felt bad about saying that, because it became clear there was something really wrong with Teddy. He sounded slow when he talked between songs. I don't mean he talked slowly; he sounded slow, like the kids in the special-ed class at Prairie Rose Elementary School. He also drooled a little bit. The other guys in the band pretended not to notice. Jamie went to the bathroom five times during their set, and kept looking around for Clay, who'd said he would meet us there but had not shown up yet.

It didn't take us long to set up once Teddy and his band had finished; it was just us, three guitars—Jamie's Gibson, his Rickenbacker, and that Martin of his I'd been using since I'd lost Juan's—and our amps, pickups, and mikes. When we rehearsed, we played around with more instruments, like the mandolin and dulcimer, and sometimes we experimented with percussion, tambourines and maracas and some weird little bells Jamie'd got from God knows where, but we'd both agreed to keep it simple our first time playing out.

We set two stools up on the stage, and as we sat down Jamie looked like he was going to puke. It struck me funny, because I'd been nervous about playing in front of people after the weird panic I'd gone through the last time I'd tried to busk, but once I got up on stage I felt fine, while Jamie looked about to slide off his stool. To move things along, I said into my microphone, "We're Cloud Cuckoo Land."

"What?" somebody called out from the crowd. The place looked nearly full that night, I guessed about 100 people. I figured most of them were there to see the Primates.

"Cloud Cuckoo Land," I said. "Don't ask me what it means."

Everybody laughed, including Jamie, and we tuned our guitars and went into the first song.

Just like the time we played for Clay and Rick, I had trouble remembering our set once it was over. I mean, I know what we played; we played eight of our own songs and ended with a crazy cover of "Philadelphia Freedom" that was almost unrecognizable from the Elton John version; we made it sound like a country song. I know exactly what we played, the places where Jamie's voice faltered once or twice, the couple of chords I messed up on; but I remember it like a dream, like I wasn't really there but only think I was. We played for a little over forty minutes, but it was like time had stopped and speeded up all at once, like the longest ten seconds of my life. We fell into some kind of zone, Jamie and me. At different points, I felt like I was in my body, or in Jamie's, or out in the crowd, watching; at one point I felt like I was my own voice, like I was made of pure sound.

I could tell the crowd liked us as we were singing, but neither one of us was prepared for the way people reacted when we left the stage; it seemed like everyone was screaming and stomping their feet and demanding that we come back on. We stood in the back of the club and stared at each other in a kind of shock; Loretta came around and told us to get back out there and do one more song, and since we hadn't planned on doing an encore as a middle act we got back on the stage and fussed around for a minute, Jamie shaking his head at every song title I whispered to him, so finally I started singing Bessie Smith's "Young Woman's Blues" *a capella*, and some people in the audience started clapping along with me, and then Jamie picked up his guitar and just strummed along lightly in the background. When we finished, some folks stood on their chairs and whistled.

As we took our instruments off the stage I saw Jamie's eyes focusing in the crowd, and I followed his gaze. Clay was sitting at a table with two other men, good-looking guys about Jamie's age. Jamie did not look happy. As we walked off the stage I brushed past a tall, thin guy with thick brown hair that reached nearly to his waist. He put down the huge amp he was carrying, then caught up with me and took my amp out of my hand, carried it to the back of the bar for me. Jamie caught sight of this and shook his head, smiling.

"You guys were awesome," he said. "I don't think I've ever seen you play before."

"That's because this was our first show," I said, batting my eyes up at him.

"Wow," he said. "Our first show we sounded like something dying."

It turned out his name was Bill and he was the lead guitarist for the Primates. He described their music as "alternative heavy metal," and, after chatting with him for a minute, I decided I might like heavy metal a little more than I had in the past. After he left to finish helping his band set up, I noticed Jamie over in the corner talking to Clay. Jamie's arms were folded across his chest, his chin hanging as low as a hound dog's.

"Miri!" Loretta screamed my name and threw her arms around me. I'd never seen her so excited before. "You guys were amazing. I'm putting you down for a couple of dates in November. Hey, where the hell is Jamie?"

"I'll get him," I said, but as I walked toward Clay's table Jamie was already headed in my direction.

"What's going on over there?" I asked, motioning toward Clay.

"That's what I'd like to know," Jamie said.

"Well, what did he say?"

Jamie grabbed my elbow, steered me over to a quieter corner of the bar. "He's drunk," he said. "He claims he went out for drinks after class. Those guys are in his program."

"Do you believe him?" It was a bold question; Jamie and I had never talked about Clay, or their problems.

He looked over at the table. The three of them were talking and laughing, slurping down the tall blue margaritas that the Big Bang was known for.

"I think everything he said was true," Jamie said, "but I also think there's more to it."

"Fuck him," I said. "This is our night." It just sort of popped out of me, and I bit my lip a little after I said it.

Jamie glanced back at the table, then looked at me and smiled, though his eyes still looked sad. "You're right. Fuck him." And he steered me over toward the bar, where Loretta leaned over and kissed him with such exaggerated force that his cheeks turned red; where men tried to buy me drinks, which I had to refuse for fear of Loretta losing her license; and where Jamie had to fend off nearly every woman in the bar, also receiving up-and-down looks from a few of the men. Halfway through the Primates set, I looked back and noticed that Clay and his friends had left.

I thought about going home with that guy from the Primates, but I wasn't sure I was up for it yet. He was cute, and I got a kick out of flirting again; it had been a while, but I felt like I wanted a little more time to myself. Still, I knew that sooner rather than later I'd be going home with boys again. I felt that night like nothing that had happened to me could keep me down for too long; all the compliments we'd gotten had given me a kind of crazy optimism.

Clay didn't get home until 5:00 the next morning. I heard him stagger through the living room, and then I really heard it when he got to the bedroom. I wrapped my pillow around my head to try and drown it out; it was like fights Annmarie'd had with her boyfriends. There was a pain in Jamie's voice that I couldn't bear to hear, and after a half-hour of this I pulled on some clothes, ran a brush through my hair and stumbled in the darkness down to the neon diner, where I ordered up some French toast and coffee. I had $40 in my jeans pocket, money Jamie had given me to buy groceries.

I felt guilty about always taking his money; I was going to have to figure out some way to get a job.

There were only two other booths of people in the diner. One was an old couple, both dressed in sweats, who looked to have stopped in after an early morning jog; the other booth held three girls, maybe a couple of years older than me, who looked like they'd been out all night. They all had their hair cut at strange geometric angles, like a Spirograph had gone crazy on their heads. One of them kept looking over at me, and I slunk low in my booth and sipped my coffee. I was tired, and just wanted a little quiet.

After my French toast arrived, the girl who'd been looking at me walked over and sat down in the booth across from me. I gave her a look, annoyed at her nerve. Her hair was dyed a dark purple color, cut so that one side was short, one was long. She was wearing a big black sweater, and a skin-tight stretch skirt the color of a traffic cone. The skirt made her hips look huge, but I couldn't imagine fluorescent orange spandex looking good on too many people. Black eyeliner was smudged beneath her lower lashes.

"You're in that duo that played the Big Bang last night, aren't you?" she asked me.

Well, Miri, I thought, taking a bite of my French toast, you're famous already.

"Yes." I was too tired to say anything else.

"You were fantastic," she said, with the overly enthusiastic voice of a Sam Houston High School cheerleader. "I've never heard a band in this city like you guys. You have more of an Athens sound."

I'd been around Jamie long enough to know that she meant Athens, Georgia, a town whose music scene had been written up in the likes of *Rolling Stone* and *Spin*.

I smiled and kept eating my French toast, not really knowing what to say. She stuck her hand across the table for me to shake, but I ignored it for long enough that she took it back. Miri, you really have been in Philly for a while, I thought. I knew I never would have been so rude back in Texas, but I just couldn't help myself. There was something about this girl's chirpy voice that grated on my last nerve.

"I'm Kirsten," she finally said, "Kirsten Wood. I cover music for the *RealPaper*."

I knew I was in trouble. The *RealPaper* was the free alternative paper that you could get in a big yellow box on just about every street corner in Center City. It wasn't much to get excited about, but they covered the rock scene pretty thoroughly, and I knew Jamie would be mad at me if I screwed up a chance for some publicity.

I put my fork down and tried out a smile I hoped looked charming and apologetic. "I'm sorry," I said. "My name's Miri. I didn't mean to be rude before, I just had kind of a rough night."

She smiled back at me, seeming grateful for any opening. "That's okay," she said, "it's really late—or early, I guess." She laughed like a seal barking. "I wanted to talk to you guys at the club last night, but I had to watch the Primates' show, too, and I couldn't find you after." She took a sip of my water without asking; I held back an urge to smack it out of her hand. "I was going to call Loretta to get your numbers, but now I don't have to."

I wrote down Jamie's phone number on a card she gave me; above the number I wrote our names, Miri Ortiz and Jamie Emerson. The corners of her mouth drooped when she read it.

"You live together?" she asked, and I knew then that part of her interest in the band had to do with Jamie, and I just couldn't resist giving her the wrong idea.

"Yes," I said, "over on 21st and Spruce."

"Oh." It came out as a small sad sound.

"Give us a call," I said. "Jamie loves to talk about music. He'll go on and on."

The thought of this brightened her face a little. "Okay," she said, and I thanked the Lord as she got up. She looked at the card as she stood next to the booth.

"Miri," she said. "That's an interesting name."

I smiled at her and thanked her for introducing herself, and as she moved back over to her friends I had a feeling that girl was going to be trouble in my life.

Chapter 22
November, 1985

Kirsten's column was called "Zen Arcade," and the one she wrote the week after our first show was almost entirely about us; the Primates only got a couple of short paragraphs at the bottom. She started the column with a quote—not from a rock song, like you might expect, but from the Greek play that gave us our name:

> *My City is Cloud Cuckoo Land,*
> *And men of every nation*
> *Confer on us, I understand,*
> *Ecstatic approbation.*

I wondered if she'd gone to the library, looked up the kind of books and articles that Clay had used for his A-minus paper.

"What the hell is 'ecstatic approbation'?" I asked Jamie. We were standing at the *RealPaper* box on 21st and Pine; Jamie hadn't been able to wait until we got back to his place, and he'd opened the paper up right on the street, reading parts of it aloud.

"It means she liked us," he said, and then went on reading from the column.

"'Imagine two musicians sounding like a full band,'" he read. "'Sounds impossible, but Cloud Cuckoo Land manages this feat, and then some. The sound this duo gets out of just two guitars is truly amazing.'"

Kirsten then went on and on about Jamie's guitar playing—"prowess," she called it. Jamie's cheeks flushed and he stopped reading aloud, so I grabbed my own paper out of the box and read it myself, a whole section about how he was a piano prodigy, but had taken up the guitar at fourteen. This was stuff he'd told her over the phone. Jamie had a pleased look on his face that I'd come to recognize, a look he got when he was getting just the right amount of attention, and the right kind. I flicked the paper with my fingers, motioned toward my mouth and made retching noises.

"Miri, she's saying we're great. Why are you acting like that?"

"I don't like her," I said.

"Why not?"

"I think she's fake. She's laying it on thick because she has a crush on you."

"She's never even met me. She saw us play and talked to me on the phone once."

"Trust me, Jamie. She wants to sleep with you."

I could tell by the look on his face he was getting tired of me. He just wanted to enjoy the good review, and instead here I was sticking a pin in his balloon.

"Face it, Jamie," I added, going for a save. "Everyone wants to sleep with you. Men, women, even the statues in the park."

Jamie's eyes sparkled. I knew he loved to be flattered, though he'd always deny it. "Stop it," he said, weakly.

"You're just going to have to get used to the fact that you're a sex god, Jamie."

He shook his head at me the way he did sometimes, but he was smiling, his eyes still scanning the article.

"Hey," he said, "maybe she wants to sleep with you, too. And I quote: 'Miri Ortiz has an amazing vocal range, like a cross between Janis Joplin, Bessie Smith, and Maria McKee of Lone Justice.'"

I shrugged and rolled my eyes at him. The column was five paragraphs about Jamie's guitar playing and that one line about my voice.

"She didn't mention Patsy Cline," I said.

Jamie ignored my comment. "We should call her and thank her for the article."

The thought of thanking that girl was more than I could stomach.

"You do it," I said. "I bet you dinner at the diner that she asks you out." This was a joke, since Jamie always bought me dinner.

He took a stack of newspapers from the box, tucked them under his arm. "You're on," he said.

We went back to the apartment, and I picked up the phone in the living room, held it out to him. He dialed the *RealPaper* office, and as I sat there listening to his end of the conversation, I knew I was right. He turned away from me, his cheeks pink as anything, a funny half-smile on his face.

"Okay," he said after he'd hung up the phone. "I guess I owe you dinner."

I laughed. "Told you so. What'd she say?"

"Well, she told me again how much she liked the band, and then she asked me out for coffee."

"What'd you say to that?"

"Well, I didn't know what to say, so I said okay."

"Jamie!"

"It's just coffee. Maybe she didn't even mean it like a date."

"We're still eating dinner at the diner tonight," I said. "And yes, she does mean it as a date." And, I thought, considering the fact that I'd led her to believe Jamie was my boyfriend, it said a lot about Kirsten that she'd ask him out anyway. It said that she had more guts than I would have guessed.

Jamie did set Kirsten straight about himself at that coffee date, but she continued showing up at our shows, in one bad fluorescent skirt after another. We played two gigs at the Big Bang in November; Loretta charged a $2 cover, which she'd started doing for bands she thought were good enough, so she could pay us. While the first night only sixteen people showed up, by the second show we had an audience of almost fifty as word about us spread. We made $64 each—not a fortune and certainly nothing to Jamie, but we were both thrilled with the money anyway. I spent mine on groceries, including a few boxes of Friskies for the cats out back of the club.

We dropped the cat food off one night on our way to see Hüsker Dü, a band whose loud guitars Jamie loved. I had brought earplugs, figuring it might be good for one of us to keep our hearing.

Loretta started laughing when I handed her the boxes of cat food. "You guys are too much," she said, and Jamie and I watched as she opened the back door and shook the boxes, summoning the cats.

"Look at that little red one," I said to Jamie. "She's got spunk." I was getting bold, feeling more confident now that we were really a band, now that I wasn't the only one who had something to lose if we parted ways.

Jamie watched the cat pull the paper plate toward her with her paws. "I don't think Clay likes cats," he said, in a way that made me think Jamie himself did.

"They're tamer than you'd expect," Loretta said, bending down and scooping up the little one I liked so much, who had finished her food and begun devouring the paper plate. Loretta had figured out exactly what I was up to, and knew just how to play along. The cat knew her role, too—she made a sound that was a cross between a purr and a meow, and rubbed her head on the inky scales of Loretta's tattoo.

I reached out to take her, but Jamie stopped me. "This isn't a good idea," he said. "Things are difficult enough with Clay right now." He walked away from us, and Loretta looked at me, the cat still in her hands.

"I'll keep working on him," I whispered, and followed Jamie out of the bar.

Jamie and Clay seemed to have made some sort of peace, but it felt shaky to me, like a house of cards about to collapse with one false move. Clay was home by 11:00 most nights, but every now and again he'd stumble in at 2:00 or 3:00 A.M., banging into the futon I slept on and cursing under his breath. I didn't hear them fighting the way I used to when Clay came in late, but the next day Jamie would look miserable, his eyes red like he hadn't slept all night.

There was a park a few blocks over from Jamie's building. It had a real name I could never remember, but everybody knew it as Judy Garland Park; it had a reputation as a gay pick-up place. One night when Clay was supposed to be studying at the library and Jamie was home listening to the Camper Van Beethoven album he'd just bought, I ducked down the street to pick up a couple of things we'd run out of: milk for the morning coffee, bread for toast, a few bottles of the bubbly water that Jamie liked to drink. Half a block into my walk back, I realized I'd picked up too many bottles of water; the heavy bags were killing my arms. I stopped in front of the park to put the bags down for a second, shift them around, and that was where I saw a man in the shadows who looked an awful lot like Clay. He was leaning against a tree, whispering to a handsome young guy who stood close to him, smiling and nodding. The young guy was nearer to the streetlight outside the park's entrance, and so I could see him clearly, but the older guy, the guy who looked like Clay, hung back just enough that I couldn't tell it was him for sure. After a minute the two of them walked away together, deeper into the park. I picked my bags back up and hurried home, trying my best to convince myself it wasn't Clay, to forget what I'd just seen.

Loretta asked us to play another show a few days before Thanksgiving. Clay didn't go, as he hadn't to the other two that month; he always said he had to study, and I don't know if Jamie believed him but I sure didn't. Because of this I was surprised when we got home from the gig at 2:30 A.M. to see a light coming from Clay's study, at the end of the hall. Maybe he really was here working all night, I thought, making pot after pot of coffee as I'd seen him sometimes do. Or maybe he'd just got home fifteen minutes ago and was putting on a show for us.

Jamie and I put our equipment down in the living room and headed for the kitchen. We'd developed the habit, after our shows, of sitting at the little table in there, munching on whatever we could find and discussing the night's set, how we thought we'd played. We were laughing about the number of people who'd come up to us and quoted Kirsten's column without even realizing it: "The sound you get from two guitars is truly amazing." Jamie was still laughing as he flicked on the kitchen light, and surprised a small rat that was standing at the foot of the dishwasher. It ran behind the refrigerator as Jamie and I both let out startled little screams.

"Please tell me that was a mouse," Jamie said.

"It looked like a rat to me," I said. It hadn't been so big, but I was sure I'd seen a thick rubbery tail on it, not that little wisp of gray velvet you found on most mice.

Clay came in to see what the commotion was about, and just as he entered the room the rat scurried out from behind the refrigerator and across the kitchen, where it tried to hide behind the microwave stand next to the back door. It looked naked, like an armadillo without its armor.

Clay screamed loud enough to bring Grandma back from the dead.

"Oh my God," he wailed, "that wasn't a mouse." He was wearing a plush red robe with gold piping at the edges, and matching slippers. With his dark brown curls he reminded me of the Cowardly Lion.

"It's a rat all right," I said.

"What'll we do?" Clay asked, now standing well behind Jamie.

"I'll get a broom," I said, thinking I could shoo it out the back door, down the fire escape stairs.

"God," Clay said, "she's going to beat it to a bloody pulp! Jamie, do something."

Clay had some kind of idea that my time on the streets had made me part-Amazon, which was pretty funny given my size.

"What do you expect me to do?" Jamie asked.

I could see it was up to old Miri to take charge here, so I went and got a broom and opened up the back door and, with Jamie and Clay watching, shooed that rat from under the microwave stand and straight outside. I was relieved it went right out and I didn't have to chase it. I wasn't too crazy about rats myself, but Clay and Jamie made me feel brave in comparison.

"We need to get rat poison," Clay said, inspecting the spot where the critter had been hiding as if another rat might spring up in its place.

I saw this right off as a chance for that little orange-red cat; in fact, if I'd thought of it I would have put the rat there myself. "What y'all need," I said, "is a cat."

"I like cats," Jamie said. I was sure he knew what I was up to. "Let's get a cat."

Clay shook his head. "It'll pee on the carpet. It'll ruin the furniture."

"We'll teach it not to," Jamie said, his voice sounding tired and irritated.

Clay sighed in a dramatic way. "And what if we fail? Jamie, think about my Oriental rugs."

Jamie laughed. "Your Oriental rugs? Clay, you bought them at the Carpet Warehouse for $79 apiece."

It looked to me like they were headed for a fight. I tried to sneak out of the kitchen, but Jamie caught my arm.

"Miri, didn't Loretta have some cats she was trying to find a home for?" He winked at me when Clay couldn't see. Clay stood there silent, brooding.

"I think you're right," I said, playing along. "I'm pretty sure she's been feeding some cats in her back alley. I can stop over there and ask her tomorrow."

Clay snorted. "Just what we need around here," he muttered. "Another flea-bitten ragamuffin."

I knew before Jamie even said a word that Clay had gone too far. His hostile glances, the way he sometimes rolled his eyes when I spoke, the put-down tone of voice he oftentimes used with me; Jamie noticed all of this, and didn't like it, barely tolerated it. I knew a direct insult would put Jamie over the edge, and I stood back to watch the battle, just as I had watched Grandma take on the Clacks, years ago.

Jamie got that blush in his cheeks, but in his anger it spread to other parts of his face as well.

"At least the people I bring home," he said, "I don't sleep with."

"Well," Clay said, "it always comes back to that, doesn't it?"

"Yes. It does." Jamie folded his arms and fixed Clay with an angry stare. "Miri, would you leave us alone, please?"

"Oh—sure," I said. I hustled off to the living room, where I pulled out the futon and tried to listen in—since, after all, this fight did concern me—but I couldn't make out anything beyond harsh whispers.

The next day I decided to bring that little cat home. I knew it was a gamble, but I thought if I went about it the right way I could get both her and me in good. I was going to try to make her a present for Clay.

I went down to the Big Bang a little after 11:00 that morning, when I knew Loretta would already be in but wouldn't have opened the bar yet. On my way there I found a box on the street that I thought would work for taking the cat home in, a sturdy cardboard box with a lid I could close. Loretta helped me poke some air holes in it and used a dishrag from behind the bar to line the bottom. We went out back, shook the Friskies box and the little orange cat came quickly. My plan was to let Clay name her, but in my mind I thought of her as Mittens, a cat I'd had when I was nine or ten.

Tommy Clayton had given me that cat, a striped orangey tabby kitten in a basket with a ribbon around the handle, and though Annmarie had protested that she couldn't handle one more thing to take care of, I'd talked her into letting me keep it, promising to take care of it myself. And I did a pretty good job, always feeding Mittens when she meowed and playing with her when she looked lonely. But after Tommy left Annmarie, she said the cat reminded her too much of him and she started talking about wanting to get rid of it. Once when she got mad at me, she threatened to take Mittens to the SPCA, where she said they killed cats in big gas ovens. Looking back on it, Annmarie would never have done it; she was attached to that cat herself. But I was little, and Annmarie's behavior was unpredictable back then and so I believed her.

As soon as Annmarie left for her waitress job that night I put Mittens in her basket, which she by then barely fit into, and left her on the doorstep of a teacher in my school who everyone knew was partial to cats. I left a little note in the basket that said her name was Mittens and that she was a good cat and it was no fault of hers that she was being left, just her own bad luck at having gone to the wrong people as a kitten. I rang the bell and watched from the bushes to be sure Miss Mercer found her and took her in. When Annmarie asked me the next morning where Mittens had got to, I told her I gave her to a good home. She'd looked surprised for a second, but then she'd shrugged and said, "Well, that's one less thing to worry about." For me, it was one less thing she could use against me.

Loretta helped me get this new Mittens into her box—she was struggling against us something fierce—and we closed the lid. The cat meowed miserably inside. I looked into the holes and made whisper sounds I thought might calm her, but she continued her sad wailing.

The cat cried the whole bus ride back, and the driver finally booted me off at 18th Street, telling me that he wasn't allowed to transport animals. I wanted to tell him I'd ridden those buses with people a lot less civilized than the cat I had in that box, worse-smelling too, but thought better of it and just got off the bus quietly. It was only three more blocks to Jamie's, not far enough to be worth a fight.

Once I let her out of the box she calmed right down, prancing around the living room and rubbing on all the furniture, seeming to know right off that she'd landed in cat heaven. I ran down to the corner market and bought some flea shampoo so I could have her all bathed and fixed up when Clay got home from school. It was a Thursday, a day when Clay got done early and sometimes came home in the afternoon.

I was in the bathroom still washing the cat when Clay came in. Mittens's soapy fur clung even more sadly to her bones wet than it had dry, and she dug her nails into my forearms, her eyes as big as saucers of milk. She had started up meowing again, worse than she had on the bus. I knew this was not the best time for an introduction.

"Oh my God," Clay said in that high-and-mighty voice of his, "where *did* you find that poor little bag of bones?"

"Behind the Big Bang," I said, rinsing her off with the sprinkler attachment. Dead fleas floated in the soapy water. I turned my body so Clay wouldn't see them.

To my surprise, he handed me a towel and scratched the cat atop her head as I dried her off. "Poor little ragamuffin kitty," he said, in a voice that was more sweet than normal for him.

Once her fur dried, Mittens looked better than she'd ever looked in her life. She still needed to put on some weight, but she was clean and fluffy and after we gave her a saucer of milk she purred louder than the old refrigerator in the kitchen. Clay looked at her skeptically as she finished the milk.

"She looks too weak to tangle with a rat," he said, kneeling down next to her.

Before I could say anything, the cat looked up at him and began rubbing on his leg, purring as loud as when she'd been drinking the milk.

"Well, look at this," Clay said, genuine surprise in his voice. "She likes me."

I thought to myself, Miri, you sure know how to pick a smart cat. That little gal was sucking up to Clay like nobody's business. Keep at it, honey, I thought, you'll be eating out of a crystal bowl in a week's time.

I picked up the empty saucer and washed it out in the sink while Clay cooed at the cat. "We need a name for you, little ragamuffin," he was saying.

"Why don't you name her, Clay?" I said it like the idea had just occurred to me.

"She's your cat," he said, in a downhearted voice.

"Not really. She's for you and Jamie, and I think you should name her. I bet you can come up with a real good name." Giving him a compliment was more painful than a scorpion's bite, but I had to do it for Mittens's sake.

"Hmmm," he said, standing up and scratching his chin in what I guess he thought was the way a professor might. "Let me think about it." He started out of the kitchen, then turned back around at the doorway and called, "Thanks," in a small, uncertain voice. I wasn't sure what he was thanking me for and so I just kind of smiled at him and watched him walk away.

Later on that night I was alone with Mittens and the TV, watching Madonna roll around on her belly in what looked to be a foreign country, a lion prancing behind her. I had the sound turned off because I couldn't stand the music, but I was fascinated by the images. I watched these little films on MTV like I was from another planet studying life on Earth. I couldn't get over it, all this crazy stuff going on in the background of a song, like the music itself wasn't enough. Jamie and I both swore we hated videos, and yet neither of us could stop watching them. Given the right amount of popcorn and time on our hands, we could sometimes watch them for hours, laughing at some of the stupid stuff that went on, joking about how if we had a video we'd set each other's hair on fire or perform our song in ripped clothes and warpaint or put on fingerless lace gloves and hump the microphone stand.

It was never as much fun to watch videos without Jamie making cracks about them, though, and I was getting ready to turn the TV off when the phone rang. I thought maybe it was Jamie calling to tell me to meet him down at the shop for an extra practice, or one of Clay's friends from school—there was one who sounded so high-falutin' on the phone that Jamie called him "Dr. Pooh-Pooh Ph.D.," but only to me. This particular person on the phone turned out to be Jamie's mother.

"Oh, this must be Miri," she said, actually pronouncing my name right. I had never talked to her before; in fact, I didn't even know that Jamie had told her anything about me.

"Yes, Ma'am," I said, trying to picture what she might look like. Jamie once said his mother had looked like Grace Kelly when she was young, and I tried to call to mind some of the old movies I'd watched with Grandma.

"How are you?"

"Fine, Ma'am," I said, and too much quiet went by as I searched hard for something else to say. Finally I offered up, "We just got a cat."

"Really? What does it look like?" She sounded so nice, no airs at all about her.

"Orange tiger-striped with white paws and white under her chin. She's real skinny but I think she'll fill out." I considered telling her how she used to live in the alley behind the Big Bang, or about the first Mittens, but decided I'd be better off not saying too much.

"Was it a stray?"

"Yes."

"I like strays," she said.

I didn't know what to say after that, and there was silence again for a minute. Finally she asked, "Dear, is Jamie there?"

I felt like an idiot; I didn't even know how to handle phone calls anymore.

"I'm sorry, Ma'am," I said. "He and Clay are both out right now. Can I take a message?"

It hit me then that I had no idea whether Jamie's mother knew he lived with Clay; or, for that matter, if she knew he was gay. That's right, Miri, I thought, just keep putting your little old foot in your mouth.

If she was surprised by what I'd said, she didn't act it. "I just wanted to make sure you were all coming up for Thanksgiving."

Thanksgiving. I hadn't celebrated a one since Texas, and when I thought of it now, I had a picture of Juan being led out the front door of our apartment building in Austin, in handcuffs. Jamie hadn't said anything about the holiday to me, and I didn't know if this meant he'd just forgotten or he didn't want me to go.

"I don't really know," I said, "but I'll sure ask him to call you when he gets home."

"Did he forget to invite you?" This lady was a mind-reader.

"Well, he didn't say anything about it."

"He meant to, dear. He asked me if he could bring you." She laughed. "My son is a little spacey sometimes."

Hearing her use the word "spacey" made me laugh too. "He sure is," I said. "He went off to give a guitar lesson one day in his bedroom slippers, and had to come back in to put shoes on." This was a true story; actually, I'd seen Jamie do it twice.

She laughed. "Oh, I could tell you stories. Maybe I will, when you come up here. Tell him to call me when he gets in, will you?"

"Yes, Ma'am," I said, and as we said goodbye and I hung up the phone I started trying to imagine Jamie's mother, looking like a movie actress whose face I couldn't quite picture, in some New England mansion I hadn't yet seen.

CHAPTER 23
NOVEMBER, 1985

After many phone calls back and forth between Clay and his friends from
school, Jamie finally took matters into his own hands and got Kirsten to
watch the cat while we were away. That girl was so crazy for Jamie she'd do
anything he asked; it was embarrassing to watch, but I had to admit it was
serving us well. Clay had named the cat Artemis, which he said was the
goddess of hunting. I could tell Jamie thought it was as dumb a name as I
did. When no one was around, I called the cat Mittens. When Jamie
thought no one was around, I heard him call her Red.

It was six hours in Jamie's car—a gray-green Volkswagen Rabbit that was
rusted and dented in spots, and that Jamie told me he had bought after a
nicer car was stolen the first week he and Clay had lived in Philly—to
Newton, Massachusetts, where his parents lived. I had never been this far
north before; the air outside was a little bit colder each time we made a rest
stop. We stopped often because of Clay, who was fidgety and grumbly in
the car and who claimed every fifteen minutes that he was about to go out
of his mind from being cooped up; I finally switched seats with him so he'd
have the whole back of the car to stretch out in. I hadn't been on a trip like
this since my tour with Ian Oliver, and I was just enjoying looking out the
window, watching the scenery go by. Jamie played with the radio for a
while as he drove, then shut it off and we started singing songs. We sang
mostly old pop songs—"American Pie," "Heart of Gold," "Goodbye
Yellow Brick Road." After every song we finished, Clay would ask us if it
was one of ours. It was like he'd never listened to a radio his whole life.
After we did "King of the Road" and Clay again asked if we'd written it, I
could see Jamie getting irritated.

"If you ever came to our shows," he said, "you'd know which songs were
ours."

"I went to your first show," Clay said.

"Halfway through our set," Jamie said, "with company."

Clay sighed. "I was only asking if the songs were yours because they sounded good."

"If they sounded good, they mustn't be ours." Jamie stared out at the highway, his eyes narrowed.

"I didn't say that," Clay said. "But come on, Jamie. A folk-punk duo? How am I supposed to take something like that seriously?"

"If you believed in me, you would take it seriously." Jamie sounded hurt.

"Well, it's hard," Clay said. "If you had gone to Juilliard you'd be playing with a symphony right now."

"If I had gone to Juilliard, I never would have met you," Jamie said, and then he muttered something that I couldn't make out. I peeked in the mirror on my sun visor and saw that Clay had his arms folded, a pouty look on his face.

We passed a sign that said "Hartford 64 miles." I wondered how far Hartford was from Boston. I had the sorry feeling that they had plenty of time left to fight.

"Jamie," Clay finally said. "I'm sure you can make it in rock music. Your voices are harmonious. It's just that I think you could do much more."

Clay was some kind of master at back-door compliments.

"You're such a snob," Jamie said. I expected this to rile Clay up all over again, but he just laughed.

"I pride myself on it," he said.

I just never could predict how these fights would come out. Times when I thought it would take a real ugly turn, they'd wind up laughing; other times a comment that seemed little and unimportant to me would set one or both of them off. It was an education, living with those two.

Jamie put a Mahler tape in to keep Clay happy, and I wound up dozing off to the sound of a symphony crashing around me, just enough sun coming in the window to keep me warm. Next thing I knew, we were at a rest stop on the Massachusetts Turnpike and then, about an hour later, we were off the highway and pulling up in front of a big white house on a street so full of trees that you had to look carefully to find the houses behind all those branches. Leaves had been raked to the sides of the road in neat piles, and no cars sat on the street.

In my mind, I'd pictured Jamie's house as a cross between the Clack home and Tara from *Gone With the Wind*, set up on a breezy hill overlooking the sea. But this house was neither on a hill nor on the water, though Jamie said the ocean wasn't too far away and that he'd take me to the harbor before we left. It was a nice, big, freshly painted house in what looked to be a nice neighborhood, but it wasn't exactly the mansion I'd expected. Inside, though, was evidence of all the money I'd imagined Jamie's parents must have.

Jamie's Mom—she told me to call her Kathleen—greeted us at the doorway. She looked like a female version of Jamie: the same blonde hair, straight and thick, only hers was long and pulled into a loose bun at the base of her neck. She had blue eyes where Jamie's were hazel, but she had the same pale delicate skin, even the same fine hands. She hugged all of us, including me. I could tell right off I'd like her.

Now Jamie's Dad was another story entirely. He was always there, but just there. What I mean is, he gave off a presence, an air of being there, but it was almost ghostly. He rarely spoke, and the few times he did say something, it was almost always negative. He and Jamie barely greeted one another; they treated each other like spirits that could be seen but not heard. I had talked to Grandma's ghost more than these two living people talked to each other.

I mentioned this to Jamie the first night we were there, the night before Thanksgiving. Jamie's parents had already gone to bed, and Clay had gone to visit some friend of his from graduate school. Jamie and I were sitting in the living room, which was done in shades of blue. Every room in the house seemed to be fixed up like this; someone had picked out the furniture, the rugs, even the nicknacks, with time and care, not just thrown together a hodgepodge of junk. I knew that someone had to be Jamie's Mom.

"Jamie," I said, as we both sipped tea, "is your Dad able to talk?"

I didn't mean this to come out as flip as it sounded, but it made Jamie laugh so hard he spit his tea back into the mug he was holding.

"Oh my God," he said, still laughing. "That's a good question."

I waited for the answer.

"I'm a bitter disappointment to him," he finally said.

"Because you're gay?"

"Oh God, no. I'm not sure he's even aware of that."

I gave Jamie a disbelieving look over my tea.

"Well, my parents and I never talk about it. For all I know they think Clay's my roommate."

I thought back on a fight they'd had a long time ago, before I'd even lived with them, when Clay had complained that Jamie led his parents to believe they were roommates. Even though I mostly always took Jamie's side of things, I could see that Clay had a point here and there.

"Jamie," I said, " maybe your father is lost enough in his own world to believe that, but your Mom surely isn't." I fingered the rim of my mug, which was some kind of special pottery—black with tan designs, a Chinese letter on the bottom.

He stared into his cup as he thought about this for a minute. "But we always stay in separate bedrooms," he said finally. "Do you really think they know?"

I laughed because I'd started to think he was pulling my leg—it was so obvious to me that I couldn't imagine him thinking his parents didn't know. I couldn't imagine them not knowing—they were educated people, sophisticated in a way I'd only read about. I didn't yet understand the kinds of things that went unsaid in Jamie's family.

"Miri, don't laugh at me," he said.

"I'm sorry. I didn't mean to. I just can't imagine them not getting it."

"Well, if they have, no one's ever said so."

An uncomfortable quiet followed until I thought up something else to say. "So why are you a disappointment, Jamie? What did you mean by that?"

Jamie rolled his eyes. "I didn't become a concert pianist."

Seemed to me that was a disappointment Clay shared as well.

"So what made you hate the piano so much?" I asked. "I know how you took up the guitar and all, but you never told me why."

"Oh, I didn't hate piano itself," Jamie said. "I hated classical piano. I hated the way all of us at the conservatory were taught to mimic the masters. I remember walking down the hall one day and hearing Beethoven spilling out the doorways of a dozen different rooms. It was being practiced by kids who were considered the most talented in New England, but not one of them was playing it with any passion. They mimicked the notes, but they had no feeling."

Jamie leaned forward, put his cup down on the table.

"At first, I thought I wanted to be like Glenn Gould—someone who puts a new spin on the classics." I didn't know who he was talking about, but didn't want to interrupt the flow of his story. "Later, I realized I felt more when I listened to rock than I did when I heard the pieces I was forced to perform. Maybe it was just a case of teenage rebellion. It's all Bruce Springsteen's fault."

I laughed. "How come?"

"Once I heard *Born to Run* I was wrecked for classical music. I listened to it so many times I knew every note—I bet I could play every song right now, in order, from memory." He looked for a second like he was going to get up and get his guitar.

"That's okay," I said, "I believe you." Jamie could get really obsessive about music, but there was a sweetness to it, like he was still a teenager, discovering rock and roll for the first time.

"I wanted to *be* Bruce," he said. "Don't tell Clay, he'll laugh at me."

I thought about this for a minute. "I never really wanted to be anybody else," I said. "I wanted to be *like* Patsy Cline, I mean, I wanted to sing like her and be successful and all. But I always wanted to be me, just me in a better situation than what all I was in."

Jamie smiled and tapped his mug for a minute, as if keeping time to some song I couldn't hear. "That's one of the things I like about you," he said. "You have a strong sense of self."

I wasn't sure exactly what he meant—how could anyone not have a strong sense of themselves?—but I knew it was a compliment and so I took it as such.

. . .

After Thanksgiving dinner, I was supposed to go with Jamie and Clay to meet their friends; but first I helped Jamie's Mom clean up. I scraped the dishes into the garbage disposal while she loaded them in the dishwasher.

"So, Miri," she said, "Jamie tells me you're from Texas."

"Yes, Ma'am," I said, trying not to make a face as I pushed the turkey bones to the side of the sink.

She smiled. "You know, you don't have to keep calling me Ma'am. We're not that formal around here."

I wondered if by trying to be polite, I'd come off sounding like a hick. Even though I liked Jamie's Mom I had no idea how to act around her.

"It's just my Grandma always said to call anybody older 'Sir' or 'Ma'am,' to show respect," I said.

She smiled at me. "That's nice," she said. "I like that."

For a minute all I could hear was the sound of the scraping I was doing, then the clank of the dishes as she put them in the washer. Finally she said, "Did your grandmother raise you, Miri?"

"Pretty much," I said. I almost added more, but decided against it.

"What happened to your mother?"

She said it real kind, like she thought my mother was dead or something. I didn't know what to say; I couldn't imagine how to explain someone like Annmarie to Mrs. Emerson.

"My mother," I said finally, "wasn't exactly the motherly type."

She nodded like she was waiting for me to go on.

"She was real young when she had me, and we didn't have a lot of money, and she kind of blamed me for it," I said, leaving out the fact that she was a no-account tramp. I thought such information might reflect bad on me. "So I went to live with my Grandma." The sound of all I'd left out was roaring in my ears.

Mrs. Emerson poured detergent into the dishwasher. "I didn't have much money growing up," she said.

I looked at her in disbelief.

"I didn't. I married into this."

I had always thought things like that happened only on TV, or in the movies.

"Wow," was all I could think of to say.

She shut the door of the dishwasher and turned it on. The sound of water spraying started up right away. Once it was going, she whispered to me, "I was Jamie's father's receptionist. Our marriage caused a family scandal."

This made me smile, because "scandal" was the same word Jamie and Clay had used about their affair. Seemed like any real-life stuff that wasn't neat and orderly was a scandal to these people.

"His parents wouldn't talk to either of us until after Jamie was born," she went on. "We named him James after his grandfather to bring the old man around." I smiled when she said "old man"; it just sounded so funny coming from her.

"But Jamie's grandfather adored him," she added. "Jamie thought he was a saint."

Jamie had once described his grandfather to me as "the crankiest old man in New England," and told me he'd dreaded his visits. But I just smiled at Mrs. Emerson and nodded in agreement.

We walked into the living room to wait for Jamie and Clay. Jamie's Dad had got off to somewhere, some quiet lonely place where he could be the ghost he seemed to want to be. I looked at some of the pictures on the mantel while Mrs. Emerson talked about her cats. I felt like I was starting to understand why she liked strays—not just the cats, but a stray like me. I was getting the idea that Mrs. Emerson had been a stray herself.

Lots of the pictures on the mantel were of Jamie: Jamie at about age two, hugging a spotted dog that stood higher than he did; a few years later, dressed as a cowboy for Halloween; and a teenaged Jamie in what must have been his high school yearbook photo, with a bowl haircut and a striped wool sweater. There were other pictures, too, some of Mr. and Mrs. Emerson, or folks I didn't recognize. But there was one in particular that caught my eye.

It had to be from the '60s—not the hippie '60s, but earlier than that. Mr. Emerson had a full head of brown hair, and brown thick-rimmed glasses. Mrs. Emerson had a blonde bouffant, but not a big one like the ladies in Prairie Rose used to get. This was a small, dignified Northern bouffant, like those pictures of Jackie Kennedy you see in old magazines. She looked beautiful enough to be a model, Mrs. Emerson did. Jamie was in the picture, and he looked about five years old; his hair was white-blonde, and his big smile showed that one of his teeth was missing. But what really got my attention was the little brown-haired girl he had his arm around.

She looked to be about three. Her hair was more the color of Mr. Emerson's, shoulder-length with a little ribbon bow at the top of her head. She had the same exact eyes as Jamie.

"Who's this?" I asked Mrs. Emerson, holding up the picture and pointing to the girl. From the look of shock on her face I realized I'd stumbled onto another thing the Emersons didn't talk about.

She sat down on the sofa. "That's Victoria," she said, the words coming out with great effort. "My daughter."

I had no idea Jamie had a sister, and I couldn't believe he hadn't told me. Mrs. Emerson picked up on my look of surprise.

"Jamie didn't tell you he had a sister," she said, and I nodded. After a long stretch of quiet, she added, "She died."

From the way she said it, I knew better than to ask any more questions. I started talking about the weather, and places Jamie had promised to take me sightseeing before we left, and she seemed grateful for the change of subject. Jamie and Clay finally came back downstairs, ready to go, and I knew this was not something I could bring up until sometime later, sometime when Jamie and I would be alone.

We pulled up outside a brownstone building in a part of Boston that Jamie said was called Back Bay. It reminded me of his neighborhood in Philly, except it was a lot cleaner, and colder. I shivered in my coat as Jamie rang the bell, and we waited for the door to open.

The man who opened it had a red feather boa wrapped around his neck. He was about Clay's age and was not quite as good-looking but seemed much friendlier. He let out a little scream as he hugged both Jamie and Clay, and then when he looked at me he let out the same short scream and said, "You must be Miri! Look at you, you're cute as a button!" Then he steered me in the living room and walked me around, introducing me to people and making me talk so he could say, "Listen to that accent! So cute." His name was Paul and Jamie tried to rescue me from him twice but truth be told I was getting off on all the attention, even if it was from men who'd never sleep with me. There was something more real about compliments from boys who weren't after something.

The whole party was me and nine gay men, including Jamie and Clay, and I was completely entertained the whole time. One young guy started complaining to me about his boyfriend, telling me how cheap the boyfriend was despite all the money he had, and as I talked to him more I got the feeling that he wasn't much different from me—he was only a year or two older than I was, he had nothing but had hooked up with this wealthy guy who was taking care of him. The only real difference between us was that I wasn't sleeping with Jamie, and I wasn't sure if that put me in a better or worse position.

Another one of the men there, an older guy named Roger, took me aside and told me how much happier Jamie had seemed to him since we'd started the band.

"Really?" I asked. This was news to me.

"I talked to him right after he met you, and he was so full of hope. He told me, 'I met this girl with the most wonderful voice.' When you started practicing together he updated me every week."

I smiled, sipped at the spiced cider Paul had given me. It felt strange that these people had heard so much about me and that Jamie had told me so little of them.

"I wonder if he told you how much trouble I had learning barre chords," I laughed.

Roger shook his head. "Jamie's very hopeful about the band," he said. "We—Mark and me—" he motioned toward one of the other men in the room, "want to come down to Philly and hear you next time you play."

"You should," I said. "I think we might play one or two more shows in December."

Roger nodded. "You know, Jamie really needed this. He gave up an awful lot for Clay."

I'd never thought about it like that before, but I knew Roger was right. Jamie had given up college for Clay, and maybe even would have done more with the music he loved if Clay had not always discouraged him so.

I started thinking about how warmly everyone there had greeted me, and looked around at all the conversations going on. Everyone was chatting and laughing except Clay, who was standing behind Jamie, looking off in the distance, brooding. It hit me then that this Roger didn't much care for Clay; that in fact, these were all Jamie's friends, not Clay's.

"Jamie's . . ." I stopped for a minute, not really knowing how to describe it. "Jamie's my best friend, I guess." He felt like so much more to me, but I knew of no words to explain it. "I just really love him," I said. It was unusual for me to say so much to a stranger.

Roger smiled at me. "I'm glad," he said.

Before I could offer up or ask anything else, I was being steered into the living room by Paul, where they'd already forced Jamie onto a bench in front of a piano.

"We want Christmas songs!" Paul said, and Jamie looked at me and laughed and we went instead into the few songs we'd played around with on the keyboards at the music shop, songs Jamie and I had written, and then we did Brenda Lee's "Rockin' Around the Christmas Tree," which we'd been planning to do at the Big Bang in December but had only practiced on guitar. I was amazed at how Jamie could just switch over like that, just apply the same notes to a completely different instrument. I figured that was the difference between a true musician and someone like me, just born with a good voice.

When we were done with the song Jamie's fingers began gliding along the keys; he went into some music that was grand and dramatic and which I figured was some classical piece he had learned long ago. He closed his eyes and the sound flowed out of his fingertips like it was part of him. I had never heard him play like that before, and for a brief second I thought maybe Clay had a point about Jamie squandering his talent—until I saw the look on his face. When Jamie played guitar, even when he'd played our own songs on piano just then, he always had a look of pure joy, like he was in some land no one else could reach; I felt that too, sometimes, and was starting to think of it as Cloud Cuckoo Land, our own private bird heaven. But the look on his face as he played this piano piece was not joy, it was pain. His forehead was furrowed like a heavy weight was bearing down on him; the weight of his father's expectations, maybe, or some other kind of weight. When he was done, everyone was silent for a minute, then burst into applause, myself included.

"I want Miri to sing something *a capella* now," Jamie said, and so I sang "Silent Night," since they'd wanted Christmas songs and I'd done it in so many grade school Christmas pageants I could practically sing it in my sleep. When I was done everyone applauded me and Paul draped the feather boa around my neck and said that I should be sure to dress like a diva with the voice I had, and everyone laughed except Clay, who just kind of stood in the corner and watched.

Later, as we were getting ready to leave, I heard Jamie ask Roger about some guy named Tom who wasn't at the party.

"He's sick again," Roger said, "in the hospital."

"How sick?" Jamie asked.

"You should go see him before you go back to Philly," Roger said.

"What's wrong with him?" I asked, and by the looks on their faces I could tell it was a question I should have kept to myself.

"He has AIDS," Roger said, and Jamie kind of winced at the sound of it.

At that point, I'd only heard of AIDS in brief mentions here and there on the TV news. I knew what it was, but I hadn't really paid much mind, and just then it hit me that everyone at this party was gay, that this was something they had to worry about, a real threat.

"Is he a good friend of yours?" I asked, and they both nodded and looked so sad that I was sorry I'd even gotten into the conversation in the first place.

It was later in the weekend—the last night we were at his parents'— before I got the nerve to ask Jamie about his sister. When I brought up her name he got the same weird, far-off look that his mother had gotten. He said, "My sister," like he was trying out the idea to see how it felt, like a little kid whose baby sister has just been born. He stared past me.

Finally I said, "Jamie, never mind. I just wondered, is all, because you never mentioned her."

He looked at me then, coming slowly back into himself. "Tory died," he said. "She was seventeen. She got sick, and she died." It had the well-rehearsed sound of something a family says when they don't want folks to know the whole story.

I knew right off this was something I would have to back off from asking. It was like Rick not talking about his stepfather. Whatever had happened had been the end of the world, had divided their lives into before and after.

Me, I'd had so many worlds end, so many befores and afters, I couldn't keep them all straight. I'd told so many stories over the years that I got confused sometimes between what was real and what I'd made up to impress someone, for a free meal, a place to crash. But even with the stories I told, or the parts of stories I left out, I couldn't imagine not being able to tell a story at all. I couldn't imagine having that much of myself closed off.

"I'm sorry, Jamie," I said, not knowing what else to say.

He nodded, and I got up to leave the room. On my way out the door, he said, "She would have liked you, Miri," in a voice that sounded not like words but notes of music, a sad melody that didn't quite work, that just didn't have the strength to bridge the gap between the before and the after.

CHAPTER 24
FEBRUARY, 1986

I was half-asleep, and couldn't quite make out what I was hearing. Loud thumps, the sound of something dragging along the floor. It had to be early morning—it was already early morning when I'd got home the night before—but it was still dark, and I lay stiff on the futon, pretending to be asleep. I figured what I was hearing had to be a burglar, and I was not about to risk death for the TV or the stereo, not even for the guitars.

I heard a few more thumps and then, "Shit," whispered under someone's breath. My heart sped up but I kept my eyes shut tight, hoping they'd just take some of Jamie and Clay's stuff and be on their way. It was quiet for a minute, and then Artemis meowed and I heard "Shhhh, kitty." I recognized Clay's voice, and opened my eyes.

By the time I sat up, I just saw a glimpse of him, pulling the front door closed. Artemis was standing there, rubbing on the door hinge; when she saw I was up she bounded over to me, let out a series of the meow-purr noises she made when she wanted to eat. I pushed her aside and walked over to the window.

The streetlights were still on, reflecting off the grimy ice and snow at the sides of the road, but the sky had just started to turn, from black to a very dark gray. There was a taxicab in front of our building, a man loading suitcases into the trunk. I saw Clay get into the backseat; the driver closed the trunk, stepped inside the car, and drove away.

It all happened so fast that for a minute I wasn't sure I'd really seen it. I rubbed my eyes and looked down Spruce Street for the taxi. It was gone, and I began to wonder if I'd dreamed the whole thing. I'd been out late, had a few drinks and not much sleep.

The night before, Jamie and I had played at a club called Ground Zero, opening for the band Chutes and Ladders. We had seen them once before

and liked them a lot; they were your typical four-piece rock band, three guitars and drums, all guys, but their songs were good, and the lead singer and
guitarist, Peter Fenster, played well enough to impress even Jamie. None of
the guys in Chutes and Ladders were what you'd call cute, exactly, but Peter
seemed to take a shine to me, telling me how much he'd liked us and buying me a drink. Peter and I had a fine time until his girlfriend showed up
right before their set; still, I hung around and chatted with both of them
after the show, out of some perverse desire to make trouble, I guess.

Clay had shocked both me and Jamie by turning up at the club just
before we started our set. When Jamie saw him standing near the edge of
the stage, he got so nervous his hands were shaking as he tuned his guitar.
But we played one of our best sets ever—they almost always seemed like
that, like we just kept getting better and better. Clay and Jamie took a table
in the back of the club after we finished playing and sat together, talking
in hushed tones, Jamie looking pleased as can be. Clay's face was an expres-
sionless mask I just couldn't read. They left together halfway through
Chutes and Ladders' set, and I'd figured it meant things were on the
upswing with those two.

After Peter's girlfriend practically dragged him out of the club, I headed
down to the Big Bang, where Loretta's bouncers all knew to let me in. Even
though I could drink at Ground Zero—where the owners didn't realize I
wasn't twenty-one—I much preferred the Big Bang. I liked how it was a
crossroads, how old black men in plaid sportcoats and tattooed white guys
in leather jackets and punk girls in miniskirts and big-haired women from
the Jersey suburbs and gay men with every hair in place all sat side-by-side
on barstools and got along, more or less. Loretta once told me that when
she'd bought the place it was a neighborhood bar, and how even though
South Street was changing and she made most of her money off the
tourists and the college kids, she tried to keep it friendly for the guys in the
neighborhood.

At the Big Bang, I found what I was looking for: Bill, the long-haired
guy from the Primates who I'd become friendly with. More than friendly,
actually. I liked the way Bill was in bed, both tender and kind of wild at
the same time; but it was pretty hard to have a conversation with him that
went beyond what he'd eaten for breakfast, or the new Megadeth album.

And I knew he wasn't looking for much more than a friendly face, a warm body, somebody he didn't mind waking up next to on occasion.

It was twenty minutes before closing, and I walked up to Bill, who was halfheartedly chatting up a woman with bleached blonde hair and big hoop earrings. She looked to be in her thirties, and had a strong Philly accent. I leaned against the bar and stared at him until he turned and saw me. A slow smile crept up his face. He had a handsome face, Bill did, all dark and sharp lines, and that long long hair.

"Miri," he said, and winked at me. "I've been waiting for you."

"Thought so," I said. "Let's go."

He said goodbye to the blonde, who looked so disappointed that I almost felt sorry for a minute, but not enough to tell him to stay. Between Peter and his girlfriend and then Jamie and Clay, it had felt like happy couples night, and I thought I deserved a little affection myself.

When I got back to Jamie's at 4:30 that morning—I hardly ever spent the night at Bill's, thanks to a lingering fear that if I wasn't on the futon each morning when Jamie and Clay woke up, it would somehow no longer be mine—I had just assumed that the two of them were fast asleep, after a good night of togetherness. Now it hit me that Clay may already have been packing when I pulled out the futon and climbed into bed.

It was starting to get lighter out; I stumbled into the kitchen and looked at the clock. 6:10 A.M. I thought about letting Jamie sleep, waiting to tell him until he finally woke up on his own, and wondered if there was any possibility Jamie knew Clay was leaving. Maybe they'd had a fight and Clay was just taking off in a huff, to make a point, and would be back. But from the way Clay had snuck out, from all the suitcases, I doubted it. He wasn't making a grand dramatic gesture to catch Jamie's attention; he had taken off the way Annmarie had always liked to, late at night or early in the morning, when folks are too tired to know what's happening around them, too tired to ask the hard questions.

It was awful, trying to think of what to say to Jamie. I stood outside his bedroom for a good fifteen minutes before I finally got my courage up and opened the door.

In his sleep, Jamie looked like a little boy. The blankets were tangled around him, his knees pulled up toward his chest. His hair had fallen over his face. It was darker in the winter, his hair—a light brown that turned gold as soon as we got a few days' sun, and something about the brownness of it reminded me of the picture of Jamie's sister. I wondered how she'd died, and how Jamie had found out, if his mother had gone into his room one morning, found him asleep just as I did now, and had to wake him up to tell him his sister, her daughter, was dead. He might have cried, might have fallen into her arms. Or they might have sat there and looked at each other, just looked, quiet in their way.

I knew from experience that being left was being left, whether the person died or just took off. But it seemed to me that being left by the person's own choice hurt even more than having someone die. I had nothing but warm feelings for both Grandma and Juan, neither of who had had a say in being parted from me; but I was full of anger at all the people who'd left me of their own free will—Annmarie, Wendell, even Aunt Melissa, who was never really there for me in the first place. Clay's leaving, of course, fell in the same category.

I touched Jamie's shoulder lightly. He didn't move, so I shook it, him, until he opened his eyes. I wished I could undo whatever had happened, rewind time like a tape and bring Clay back from the street, up the stairs, pop him into bed.

He smiled at me. "Hey," he said, "what's up?" He rolled over toward the clock. "What time is it?"

"Jamie," I said, sitting on the edge of the bed, "Clay just left."

"Huh?" He sat up and yawned.

"He's gone, Jamie."

He looked at me for a minute, as if trying to get what I was saying.

"What do you mean, he's gone?" He didn't look upset, just truly confused. I wasn't sure he was fully awake yet.

"I mean, I saw him leave. He's gone."

He closed his eyes and stretched, as if thinking on the idea. "No, Miri, he probably just went out to pick up croissants or something," he said.

"I saw him get in a taxicab with a bunch of suitcases."

Now a look of panic took over his face. He ran to the closet and flung open the door; one side of it was empty, just a row of naked wire hangers dangling from the rod. Jamie looked at me. "How long ago?" he asked. "Why didn't you wake me up?"

"I just did wake you up," I said. "Jamie, it all happened so fast. I was asleep, and I thought I heard something, and I looked out the window and Clay was taking off. There was no time to do anything."

He walked over to the window, opened the blinds and peered through them, as if Clay might still be out there. "Are you sure?" he asked, his eyes fixed outside.

"Yes," I said. I didn't know what else to say. Sunlight was starting to filter through the blinds, and as I followed the stripes of light with my eyes I noticed the envelope, with Jamie's name on it, propped up on the nightstand. Just like Ian Oliver, I thought—that's how these assholes leave.

"Jamie," I said, and pointed to the envelope. He looked at it, put his hand to his mouth but made no move to pick it up. I squeezed his arm and left the bedroom, to give him a chance to be alone.

I sat in the kitchen for about a half-hour, hoping he would come out and tell me what was in the note. He didn't. I was falling asleep sitting up, having only slept for about an hour that night, and so I made a pot of coffee and paced the kitchen, hoping the smell of it would draw Jamie from the bedroom, but all I heard was the sound of my own footsteps. After two cups of coffee I knocked on Jamie's door and asked him if he wanted me to bring him in a cup. He said "No," and his voice was so flat and emotionless coming through the door that I couldn't tell what was going on in there. I waited a half-hour and asked him if he wanted me to make him some toast, one of the few things I knew how to cook. Again, he said no.

I sat in the kitchen and drank my third cup of coffee and put a saucer of milk on the table for Artemis—I'd gotten used to calling her Artemis by then—and ran my hand along her back as I tried to figure what to do for Jamie. Artemis arched her back as I moved my fingers along her spine, her attention still on the milk. She'd developed airs, Artemis had; she seemed to have forgotten she'd ever been on the streets. She rubbed on the furniture in the apartment like she'd bought it all herself. I'd come to think her high-and-mighty attitude was from spending too much time with Clay; of course, I didn't help, letting her drink off the table and all.

I poured my fourth cup of coffee and my mind started racing. I became convinced that Jamie was mad at me, that he thought it was my fault Clay had left. He'd never really accepted my living there, and even though I'd gone out of my way to remove all traces of myself when I got up each morning—even putting the throw pillows back in the exact arrangement he favored—just the very thought that I had slept there seemed to annoy Clay. I'd tried my best to give him space, hanging out in the diner or the park on the afternoons he had off; but still, Clay had always found ways to let me know he didn't want me around.

I kept listening for some sound from the bedroom: sobbing, or the smashing of something breakable. That would have seemed more normal to me than the silence I was hearing. It was the same sad silence of the Emerson house, which I'd visited twice by then, both Thanksgiving and Christmas. They turned themselves off like faucets, those people. I had no idea what to do for someone like that.

I got dressed, put on my coat, and wandered down to the diner, though I really didn't want anything to eat. It was 9:30 A.M. on a Sunday and there was a line for tables and so I walked on, past the park where I would have sat for a while had it not been so cold, past the beautiful old stone and brick buildings I had come to love, down Spruce Street with the numbered cross streets getting lower. I could see my breath in front of me and I shivered in my coat, but kept going past Broad until I wound up in the neighborhood where Bill lived. Even though it was early and I thought he might be pissed that I'd left so quickly and then come back a few hours later, I rang his bell anyway, three times before he opened the door. I just needed a place to go.

I told Bill my roommates were having a fight. He didn't know Jamie was gay, and I didn't think it was his or anybody else's business, unless Jamie himself decided to tell. Bill let me in, on the condition that I let him go back to bed, and I got undressed and crawled in with him, finally getting a few hours' sleep that I desperately needed.

We woke up about 1:30 that afternoon. I called the apartment to see how Jamie was doing, but he didn't answer; the machine picked up. It was new, the answering machine; his mother had given it to him for Christmas. I left a message saying that I was at Bill's, and I'd bring him a sandwich or anything he wanted if he'd just pick up the phone, but he didn't. I left Bill's phone number and hung up.

I tried Jamie twice more that afternoon but still he didn't answer. Finally it was 5:00 and Bill had to leave for work—he was a bartender at the Khyber Pass—and so I walked back across the city in the cold, stopping at Jamie's favorite Middle Eastern restaurant to get him a sandwich. It was dark by the time I got back to Jamie's; I felt like my hands and feet were frozen.

Artemis ran to greet me, but I heard nothing from Jamie. The door to his bedroom was still closed. I hung up my coat, fed the cat, hesitated for a second and then knocked on his door. He didn't answer.

"Jamie, I have a sandwich for you," I called through the door. "From Sabra." I thought the mention of the restaurant might perk him up, but there was no response.

"Jamie?"

"Just put it in the fridge," he said, the words choked out like he was dying.

"Can I come in for a second?" I felt like I needed to see him, to see how he was.

"Miri, I'm okay," he said, in a voice that was meant to dismiss me.

I tried the door handle and found that it was locked.

"Please," he said. "I just need to be left alone."

I waited an hour to see if Jamie would change his mind, then ate the sandwich myself. I went into the study, which was still full of books and notes of Clay's, and a word processor that he wrote his papers on, and picked up my new Martin, the guitar Jamie had given me for Christmas. It was beautiful, the curves of the glossy wood, the sharpness of the steel strings. I'd felt embarrassed, taking such a present when I had so little to give him, and Clay. Everything I gave them I'd found on the street, on trash day: a small bookshelf for Clay that didn't look so beat-up after I painted it white; for Jamie, a pair of high-top sneakers that looked almost brand-new, and a little embroidered box I filled up with guitar picks. It was unbelievable, the things people threw away in that neighborhood.

I played my guitar for a while, practicing a few of our new songs. I sang along, loud, hoping my voice would draw Jamie out of the bedroom, but once I put the guitar down the apartment was as quiet as the Emerson house. It hit me that with Clay gone, it *was* the Emerson house. At one point I heard Jamie get up and go to the bathroom, quickly moving back to his room when he was finished, shutting the door. About 10:00 that night I couldn't stand it anymore and I knocked lightly on the bedroom door. When I didn't hear anything, I tried the knob. This time he had left it unlocked.

Jamie was asleep under a pile of blankets, about twice as many as had been there before. I couldn't make out his face in the darkness, but I could tell he was tossing a bit. Nothing else in the room looked like it had been disturbed. I put Artemis in there with him so he'd have some company, closed the door, and finally just went to bed myself, since there was nothing else to do.

When I got up the next morning, Jamie's door was still closed, and I felt I couldn't take much more of hanging around, worrying about him. I went outside and walked down the block, hoping for some kind of inspiration. It was Monday, trash day. There had to be something out there that could cheer Jamie up.

I headed straight for Delancey Street, the wealthiest street in the neighborhood and the place where I'd found both the high-tops and the little embroidered box. The air that day was colder than the freezer section of the corner market, with a little wind that nipped through flesh like a paper cut. I wrapped Jamie's scarf tight around my neck as I walked up 21st Street, eyeing the rows of trash bags and boxes. So far I wasn't seeing anything good in the trash. What I kept noticing, though, were the shoes.

People had taken to abandoning shoes in the streets like children. Ever since I'd arrived in Philly I'd noticed the odd shoe here and there: a velvety slipper, a cheap plastic sandal, a workboot with duct tape wrapped around from sole to top and back again. Wandering the streets with Rick, I'd seen sneakers, single and in pairs, dangling by their laces from trees or power lines, but I was too busy hustling back then to give it more than a passing thought, to really wonder why people were leaving shoes strewn about the city. Now that I had more time to think, it seemed the shoes were everywhere, and I couldn't for the life of me figure out where they came from, what they meant.

I saw two of them just on the walk from Jamie's place to Delancey. One was a bedroom slipper, the open-back kind that Grandma used to wear but in a silky green fabric that looked expensive. It was just sitting in the middle of the Pine Street sidewalk like it had a reason to be there. I held my foot against it and saw that it was about three sizes bigger than what I wore. The other one I saw was a black leather basketball shoe, men's, this one hanging from the top of a utility pole. It was getting out of control, like the shoes were multiplying. I just had to shake my head.

The high-tops I'd given Jamie that Christmas weren't the first shoes I'd ever given him. Back when I was on the streets with Rick, when Jamie would have us over for dinner every week, I'd once brought him a present as a thank-you for the meal: a pair of flip-flop sandals I'd found on one of my trash expeditions. They were the kind we used to wear at the Liberty County pool, rubbery thongs with a sole about a half-inch thick. They were in pretty good shape and they looked to be about Jamie's size, and so I'd picked them up and brought them to him despite the fact that it was March, not exactly sandal weather.

I'd wrapped them in a brown paper bag and tied it with some ribbon Rick had found. Rick had a talent for finding things like that, birthday candles and ribbons and little glitter star stickers, things he would give me because he thought, I guess, that I would like them. Jamie looked a bit confused when he unwrapped the sandals, and then Clay started up before Jamie could say anything.

"My God," Clay said, "where did you find those things? In the trash?"

Of course, it was true, and I was embarrassed then, my great find of a gift now seeming like an insult, like I'd picked rotten vegetables out of a dumpster and handed them to Jamie. Before I could come up with a response, an explanation, Jamie had taken his shoes and socks off, without a word, and slipped on the sandals.

"Hey, they fit," he said, wiggling his toes, smiling. "Thanks, Miri." And he'd worn them the rest of that night, despite the faces Clay kept making at his feet.

I walked the length of Delancey Street looking for something that would make Jamie smile again, but on that particular day it seemed no one had thrown away anything worth having, or else it had all been picked over the night before. I gave up and was heading back home when I thought I saw some motion behind a pile of trash bags. I ducked my head around, and there it was: a little black kitten, so tiny its eyes were the dark milky-blue of a cloudy night sky. It seemed to look through me like a blind person might. When I picked it up it let out a tiny high-pitched sound that was too young to even call a "meow." It had a tiny spot of white under its chin but was otherwise pure black, even its paw pads.

It didn't look dirty like Artemis had when I'd found her, and it didn't seem to have fleas. It must have gotten lost from one of those fancy homes, I thought, where its mother and the other kittens lived inside. Surely no one would put a baby cat like this out with the trash on a cold day in February.

I saw a man come out of a big brownstone at the end of the block, and I ran up to him, kitten in hand, and asked him about it. He shook his head, said he didn't know anyone on the block who had kittens, and walked away with an air like I'd wasted a few valuable moments of his time. The kitten seemed to be shivering, and I tucked her in my coat, holding her up with one arm. She curled in a ball and purred faintly.

At first I hadn't thought of her as a present for Jamie; all I knew was that I couldn't leave her out there. I was halfway home before it hit me that she and Jamie needed each other, that maybe she could help bring him out of his funk. That if I couldn't get Jamie to do anything directly for himself, I could trick him into it by letting him think he was doing for this cat.

There was still no sound in the apartment when I got home, just pale unhappy silence coming from Jamie's room. Artemis came up and rubbed on my feet, and I took the kitten out of my coat and held her out to the bigger cat, afraid Artemis might think it was a mouse and pounce on it if I set the kitten on the floor. But Artemis took a few sniffs of the kitten and rubbed on her and I could tell right off she liked her, so I put the kitten down and watched as Artemis continued to sniff her, then began licking her from head to tail, the kitten letting out little sounds that sounded more happy than sad. I hung my coat up on the rack and took off Jamie's scarf.

I carried the kitten down the hall, and stood at the door a minute to listen. Nothing but quiet. I knocked hard, and walked in before Jamie could protest.

He was still in bed, rolled up in the covers, curled in a ball like he'd been when I woke him the morning before to tell him Clay was gone; but instead of looking like a little boy, as he had just a day ago, his face now sagged like an old man's. It was like he'd aged fifty years in one day. He looked at me but seemed to look right past me, blind as the kitten.

I didn't say anything, just put the kitten down on the bed next to him. For a minute he ignored her, but then I saw his eyes follow the kitten's motion as she tried to climb up the mountain that was his body, huddled under the blankets. Finally he reached a finger out from under the covers and touched the top of her head.

"Miri, this kitten's too young to be away from its mother," he said. It came out as a croaky whisper.

"I found her on Delancey Street," I said. "She doesn't have a mother."

By now he had a whole hand out, and was running his fingers along the kitten's back. "But it'll die without its mother."

"She'll do just fine without her mother," I said, thinking that I always had. The kitten's mother was probably a furry version of Annmarie, I thought, running off with a tomcat, leaving her baby to take care of itself. "Artemis has already took to her."

Jamie propped one arm on a pillow. "Miri," he said, "we can't feed her. She's too little to eat cat food." He had the hollow look of someone who's dying.

I hadn't thought about that. "I could give her milk," I said.

Jamie shook his head. "Replacement formula."

"What?"

"My Mom had to do this when I was in grade school, with a litter of kittens whose mother had died. Tory and I took turns feeding them with a baby bottle."

It was the first time I'd heard him mention his sister since I'd found out about her.

"That must have been fun," I said.

He shook his head. "They didn't live, Miri. When they're this little it's hard to save them." He got up, and I saw he was still wearing the same undershorts he'd had on yesterday.

He looked out the window, stretched and sighed. I was starting to think maybe I'd made a mistake, that this kitten might die and he'd wind up feeling even worse than he had before. But then he reached for his jeans, and stepped into them. "We have to take it to the vet," he said, and I knew my plan had worked.

CHAPTER 25
FEBRUARY–MAY, 1986

Pulling that cat through was a team effort. When Jamie and I were both home, we took turns feeding her every couple of hours; when he had guitar lessons scheduled, I took over. For about a month our lives revolved around that kitten, and when it became clear that she would pull through, Jamie named her Nico, and took to singing "Femme Fatale" whenever he fed her. I thought it was a pretty silly name for a kitten, but I just bit my tongue. At least it was a better name than Artemis.

Pulling Jamie through was another story. As winter gave way to spring, Jamie began to talk about Clay a little, just kind of easing around it, the way you might touch the edge of a stove to see how hot it is. He would tell me little details about Clay, small things, like how Clay would cut all the crusts off every piece of bread he ate, like a child; or this certain smile he had that always took Jamie by surprise, how it had made Clay look like an angel. I myself had never seen this smile, and I sure couldn't picture Clay—who seemed mostly to sneer and look down his nose at everything—as an angel, but I smiled and nodded as Jamie told me these things, since it seemed he needed to say them, and hearing him say anything was better than that awful silence.

Since Jamie was too depressed to cook and I didn't really know how, we took to eating dinner at the diner almost every night. It was one of those nights, early April, before Jamie's birthday, that I finally got the nerve to ask him outright what Clay had written in the note.

A look of sadness that I, by then, knew well took over his face, and he looked miserable as he chewed a bite of his hamburger. He didn't answer for a minute, and I thought maybe I shouldn't have asked.

"Forget it," I said. "It's none of my business."

Jamie shook his head. "It's okay," he said finally. "He didn't say much, really. Just that he'd been trying to leave for a long time, and that I hadn't let him. He said he was sorry." He took a sip of water, stared down at his plate.

"Had he?" I asked. "Been trying to leave, I mean?" I said it real quiet, hoping I wasn't pushing Jamie too far.

Jamie raised his eyebrows and sighed. "I guess," he said. "I think he decided to go to Penn because he thought I wouldn't want to move to Philly. He tried to discourage me from moving with him. We almost broke up before we got here." He stared out the window for a second. "Yes, I guess he was trying to leave."

I was glad to hear about this other near-breakup, for it meant that maybe I really wasn't the reason Clay had taken off. I thought about the fights they'd had, the night I thought I saw Clay in the park.

"Did he . . . fool around a lot?" I was afraid it was too blunt a question, but Jamie nodded.

"Not at first," he said. "Well, not the first year, anyway."

"Did you?" I was pretty sure I already knew the answer.

"No." He poked at the food on his plate with his fork. "I thought one person was enough. Clay didn't."

I felt like I could understand both lines of thinking. I liked knowing that I could go home with whoever I wanted after a show, and didn't really want someone to answer to; but still, when I was with Juan, I'd had no desire for anyone else.

"So how did you deal with it?" I asked.

Jamie shrugged. "As best I could." He took a small bite of a french fry, swallowed like it was going down hard. "I guess not very well. We tried to compromise on it, but it was never what I wanted."

I tried to imagine what it might have been like for Jamie. I sure couldn't have stood it if Juan had slept with other girls. But it was also hard for me, now, to imagine being so wrapped up in one guy. It seemed like a childish fantasy, putting that much hope and feeling in one person.

"Tell me about your other boyfriends," I said, thinking it might be time to change the subject. "I want to hear about the guys before Clay."

Jamie smiled, his cheeks blushing pink. "Oh, there were so many. I can't count them all." He rolled his eyes and took a bite of a pickle.

"Come on, Jamie," I said. "Who was your first love?"

He smiled. "Christopher," he said.

"How old were you?"

"Eight when we met. Thirteen when we drifted apart."

The thought of two little boys having a love affair surprised even shock-proof me, but I did my best to hide it. "So you were eight when you had your first boyfriend?" I asked, as matter-of-factly as I could.

Jamie laughed. "Oh, God, no," he said. "Nothing ever happened with Christopher, Miri. He never knew I loved him."

I laughed, too. It struck me funny how different we looked at things, me and Jamie, that by "first love" he could mean "first crush."

"Okay," I said, finishing the last bite of my grilled cheese sandwich, "so how old were you when you had your first real boyfriend?"

Jamie shook his head. "Hey, what's in that sandwich, anyway? You sure are full of questions tonight."

"Sorry," I said, but I wasn't worried because he didn't look upset, really, just surprised. "I just wondered."

"It's okay." The waitress stopped and took our plates, and Jamie ordered us two coffees. After she left, he said, "I was eighteen when I had my first real boyfriend. In college."

I looked at him in disbelief. "You don't mean Clay," I said.

He nodded.

"You're kidding me."

"No."

"But you've been with other guys, right? Like, when you and Clay weren't getting along?"

Jamie's cheeks got more intensely red. He didn't say anything.

"You're almost twenty-six years old and you've only slept with one guy in your whole life?" I hadn't meant to blurt it out like that, but I was in a state of shock.

"Shhh, Miri," Jamie said, looking around nervously. "Don't broadcast it to the whole diner, okay?"

"Sorry." I looked at him for a minute. "Wow."

"Pretty weird, huh?" He was looking out the window again. A Dalmatian puppy was taking a leak against a mailbox; the girl holding the end of the dog's leash was chatting with a guy. She was wearing a short dress in a wild paisley print, a bright purple band pushing back her dark brown hair.

"No," I said. "It's not weird."

He looked at me like he didn't believe me. "You think it's weird."

I shook my head. "I think it's sweet."

He rolled his eyes. "Sweet," he said. "Yuck."

I smiled, sipped the coffee the waitress put down in front of me.

"Have you been with a lot of guys, Miri?" he asked.

"Well," I said, "it depends on what you mean by a lot."

He tapped his fingers on the table for a few seconds. "More than ten?"

More than ten—I was about to say "no," thinking just of Juan and Ian Oliver, those few times with David, Bill, and one or two other guys I'd gone home with after Cloud Cuckoo Land shows. But then I thought of all the boys I'd picked up when Rick and I were on the streets—at least one a week, over the course of a year and a half.

"Yes," I said, "more than ten."

"How many?" he asked.

I squirmed around in my seat. "I'm not sure," I said.

"Come on, Miri. Tell me."

I didn't know how to explain it to him, picking up guys just for a place to sleep. It was so far out of his world. I put another spoon of sugar in my coffee, stirred it good.

"I really don't know, Jamie," I said softly. "Things were kind of crazy when I was on the streets." After he took me in, we'd never really talked about that time; it was one of those subjects we'd always stepped around, like his sister, or even his being gay.

He reached across the table and squeezed my hand. I let him for a minute, but I wasn't comfortable with his pity and so I pulled my hand back, waving him away. "It's no big deal," I said. "I just really don't know." I gulped my coffee, hoping to push down the thought that maybe I *had* become Annmarie, at least for a while.

He was quiet for a time. "Have you ever been tested?" he finally asked.

"Tested?"

"You know," he said. "For HIV." He whispered the last part like we were planning a bank robbery.

I shook my head. I'd been hearing more about it on the news lately, but I had never thought about it having anything to do with me.

"I was tested," he said, "last year."

I looked at him, waiting for him to go on, but he was staring back at me.

"You're okay, right?" I finally said.

He nodded. "Yeah, I'm fine."

"That's a relief." I'd seen pictures on TV, men shrunken down as if by voodoo. It had never occurred to me before, the thought of Jamie getting sick like that.

"Miri, you really should go. Get tested, I mean."

It struck me funny, how I was sitting there worrying about him, and here he was thinking about me.

"Jamie, I'm fine," I said, though suddenly I wasn't so sure.

He shook his head. "Just like Clay. He never wanted to get tested, either."

"He didn't?"

"No," Jamie said. "He figured anything he had he'd gotten long ago and he didn't want to know about." He drank another sip of coffee.

I smiled at the waitress as she refilled my cup, and we both were quiet until she walked away from our table.

"You really think I should do that?" I asked.

"Yes," he said. "I'll look up the number for you when we get home."

I looked out the window again, where the girl with the Dalmatian was still chatting with that guy. They were both about Jamie's age, mid-twenties, flirting with each other, enjoying the beginning of spring. There was something about her dress, the way her hair was swept back, that made her look so carefree, and I wished for a second that I could be her: just a pretty girl walking my dog in the spring, having a job and an apartment and a life that was mine, not borrowed from somebody else. It was like I'd just moved into Jamie's life and taken it over for my own, the way I took from everyone. I might not have driven Clay out, but I sure hadn't helped matters any.

. . .

Jamie gave me the phone number of the clinic when we got back that night but never said anything else about it, getting tested or being sick, yet over the next few weeks I became obsessed with the idea that I was going to die. I thought about all the boys I'd had sex with, most of them boys I hadn't really known, hadn't seen past the one night I'd crashed with them. I tried to come up with a number. Before Philly, it had been just Juan and Ian Oliver; but once I got here, I'd taken the idea of brotherly love a little different than it was meant to be. I did sexual math in the margins of newspapers; 1 boy a week (give or take a boy), times 4 weeks a month, times 18 months I was on the streets, minus a few weeks here or there when Rick and I had crashed only at the warehouse, plus David and Bill and the 2 other boys I'd picked up at Cloud Cuckoo Land shows. I decided I'd slept with about 70 boys. Any one of them could have had just about anything, but all I'd ever worried about was staying on the Pill so I wouldn't get pregnant like Annmarie. I'd hit up Planned Parenthood in Philly just like I had in Texas, going back when I needed more pills and taking the antibiotics they gave me when I got infections now and again; they'd lectured me about diseases but I'd never really listened. A few of the boys had used rubbers, but not many. It seemed clear to me that I had little time left on this earth.

I didn't tell Jamie any of this. I walked around worrying on it through that spring, pouring the feeling into songs I wrote about old women on the verge of death, claiming to Jamie that they were about my Grandma. The best of these songs Jamie and I worked on until we both felt they were right, and put them in our shows. By May, we were playing just about every week, and I felt like each show would be my last. I alternated between turning guys away in fear, and going home with them anyway, thinking that I might as well have fun with my short time left on earth. When I stopped sleeping entirely, I decided it was time to call the number Jamie had given me.

I chickened out twice and canceled appointments, but finally I made it to the clinic. As I sat in the waiting room flipping through magazines I imagined Jamie sitting there by himself the year before, looking through the very same pages. I waited long enough to almost leave before they finally took me in.

The lady who went over my form asked what I thought put me "at risk," and I said, "About seventy boys." She didn't even crack a smile, just tapped my arm for a vein, then slipped the needle in. I watched as my blood filled up a vial. When that was done, she gave me some rubbers, a lecture about safe sex, and told me to come back in a week for my results.

I went home that night and practiced a new song we were working on. Jamie had come up with a tricky guitar part, some quick chord changes I was having trouble with, and I just practiced and practiced and tried hard not to think. I spent the week avoiding Jamie as much as I could, for I hadn't told him about my worries and didn't want to concern him, depressed as he still was over Clay. I got up early in the mornings, before he was awake, and walked down to the diner, or the park. It was May, and Rittenhouse Square Park was green as you please, planted with flowers here and there. I didn't mind hanging in the park during the day so long as I had a place to sleep at night.

Finally the day came, and I walked over to the clinic in a fog of late-spring air, heavy and wet. I was so sure my life was nearly over that when the lady came in and told me the result was negative, I didn't believe her.

"Are you sure?" I asked.

She smiled. "You'd rather be positive?" she asked, in a kindly way. She had a slight Spanish accent that made me think of Juan, of the Ramirezes.

"No, Ma'am," I said, and listened to her instructions that I should be retested in six months, accepted another handful of free rubbers as I headed out the door.

Later on that night, after we'd finished practicing and were heading to the diner for some dinner, I told Jamie what all had been going on. He laughed at how worried I was, but looked relieved when I told him I was negative.

"I didn't mean to put you through all that, by bringing it up," he said.

"It's okay," I said. We were walking down Spruce Street, toward the diner, and the night was so warm and clear I felt as full of possibilities as that girl with the Dalmatian I'd seen. "You know, they said I should get retested in six months."

"Yeah, I think they told me that too," Jamie said.

"Did you go back?"

"No, I forgot about it. I guess I should." He grimaced, and whether it was at the thought of the needle or of Clay I couldn't tell.

"Maybe we can both go back together," I said. "It wouldn't be as scary."

Jamie agreed. As we headed the last block toward the diner we came upon an old black man who was wearing a crown made out of tin foil, coloring on the sidewalk with pastel chalk. He was wearing two different shoes, one a grimy yellowed high-top, the other a dark blue rubber rain boot that had seen better days. He was seated with his legs tucked in a way that reminded me of yoga positions I'd seen Jamie do, humming as he colored on the sidewalk, and if he felt uncomfortable in those mismatched shoes he gave no sign of it.

We walked past him, but then Jamie stopped, turned back around and tried to give the man a dollar. He shook his head no. When Jamie tried to tuck it under his box of colored chalk, the man stood up and went into a little rant about how he didn't take that fake money, he only took real money but nobody used it anymore, and he wished people would just keep their play money to themselves. When I finally tugged Jamie away from the man, he seemed shaken, looked at me uncertainly.

"Was that wrong of me?" Jamie asked. "Should I not have done that?"

I shrugged. "He was just crazy," I said. "Probably if you caught him on a different day he would have taken it."

He nodded, and even though I knew he saw me as the expert on such matters I was already starting to feel removed from all that, like my life, my place in Jamie's life grew stronger with each passing day. Like I was finally getting a foothold in the world.

CHAPTER 26
AUGUST, 1986

I came awake slowly, uncertain of where I was. Nothing in the room seemed like it was in the right place, and at first I thought I was at Bill's, or maybe the apartment of some other boy I'd picked up; I couldn't yet remember what had happened the night before. I heard a throaty noise, and came aware that there was someone in the bed with me; rolled over and realized, with a start, that it was Jamie. In the minute or so it took my foggy brain to piece together the night's events, I was very confused.

There had been a party. There had been a lot of drinking.

I looked at Jamie, who was on his back, asleep. There was a sheet pulled up to his waist; his chest was bare. I was afraid to look under those covers and see if he was wearing anything else.

Jamie and I had kissed, once, earlier that summer. It had been after a Cloud Cuckoo Land show at Dobbs, where we'd opened for a band called Molly Bloom, a band from California that had an album out on an indie label. They'd liked us enough to tell us to send a demo tape to their label; of course, we didn't tell them we didn't even have a demo.

We'd gotten home at 5:00 that morning, and Jamie was about as drunk as I'd ever seen him, although he'd been drinking a lot, in those months after Clay left. I flopped myself on the couch, put my feet up on the coffee table and clicked on the TV, with the sound off the way I liked. Jamie sat down next to me and, next thing I knew, he was kissing me. He kissed me the way a starving man might devour the first edible thing he found; I mean, he *inhaled* me. I was confused and surprised but I certainly wasn't going to stop him; I wanted to see where it would lead. After kissing me like that for thirty seconds, maybe a minute, he pulled away suddenly, and looked at me.

"I," he said, and then he was quiet for a few seconds, moving further still away from me on the couch. "I shouldn't have done that."

"I don't mind," I said. He had a look of panic and horror on his face, and I figured in this situation, the less I said, the better.

"Miri," he said, and put his hand to his forehead, the gesture exaggerated in his drunken state. I touched his sleeve.

"I miss him so much," he muttered, then headed off to his bedroom. He never mentioned it the next morning; I wasn't even sure he remembered.

But I knew if anything had happened this time, it wouldn't be as easy to dismiss; at least, not for Jamie. I got up as quietly as I could and headed into the bathroom. My head was throbbing. I splashed water on my face and cupped my hands, drinking from the faucet; my mouth felt dried out, coated in dust, and I brushed my teeth to get rid of the taste. When I was done I stumbled into the kitchen, slumped onto a chair, and began to piece together what had happened.

The party had been for me, for my birthday. Jamie had surprised me, thinking it was my twenty-first birthday, and I couldn't remember if I'd actually told him it was only my twentieth or if I'd let him continue thinking it was my big leap into adulthood. He'd invited a mix of people he knew I'd want to be there, like Loretta and Bill, and all of Chutes and Ladders because he knew I had designs on Peter Fenster; and then he threw in people he thought he should invite, like Kirsten and some people from local bands, the Johnsons and Scram! and the Electric Love Muffin. He told me that he'd even called PCA and tried, without success, to locate David, who I hadn't seen much since Catholic Boys Gone Bad had broken up; Rick and I had run into him once or twice last year, but without the band we really had nothing in common. He'd wanted to invite Rick, of course, but neither of us had any idea where to find him. I wondered how he was doing, if he'd finished his first year of college like he'd planned.

I put on a pot of coffee, filled a glass with the cold spring water that Jamie kept in the fridge and drank it down. The big disappointment of the night had been Peter Fenster, who'd showed up with his girlfriend, Annie. Annie turned out to be good friends with Kirsten, and though the two of them talking and laughing together did help give me a little more access to Peter, the fact that they were friends just drove home how much I disliked them both. Annie was dressed in thrift store chic: a wide-skirted 1950s dress the color of fresh blueberries, with a matching beaded hat and purse. Kirsten had moved on from her fluorescent stretch skirts to a retro-hippie look: she wore '60s minidresses with wild geometric prints, big plastic earrings, and a suede fringe jacket. She was so attached to this jacket that she wore it even in August. The way their outfits were put together so carefully, the way they whispered and laughed in that chummy way girls sometimes have, just put me off of them both. They may have thought they were hip and artsy but as far as I was concerned they were just slightly off-center versions of my cousin Mary Gay and her friends. It was funny to me how many of the different people I'd met were all just variations of a few basic types.

But Peter was different. He seemed to like me, but didn't flirt the way most guys did; if that was because of Annie or for some other reason, I wasn't sure. He talked more like Jamie than the other people I knew from bands; they were both smart, and equally obsessed with rock music. They hit it off right away, and I hung around pretending I knew what they were talking about when Jamie described the Meat Puppets as a cross between the Clash and the Grateful Dead, and when Peter called the band's lead singer a "punk Johnny Cash." They went on like that, one trying to top the other with obscure band references until they both realized they were evenly matched and just started enjoying it. Jamie knew I was faking it as I stood there, smiling and nodding, but Peter didn't and so he included me in the conversation like he thought I could offer up some amazing insight about Big Star or Sonic Youth that they hadn't yet explored.

When Jamie had finally left us I managed to shift the subject to Peter, pumping him for information on himself, but then Annie came over and by the way Peter touched her arm, by the glances they exchanged, I knew there was no hope with him, at least not that particular night. I moved off and chatted with Bill and watched them from afar—the way their eyes met when they spoke, the gentle way he touched her hair. It had been a long time since anyone had touched me with that much feeling, and I started thinking maybe I wanted something like that again.

There were a few guys at the party I could have left with or invited to stay, but in the end I let them all go; it was Peter I really wanted. As the party wound down and I saw him and Annie getting ready to leave, I waited for a moment when he was alone and then asked him if he wanted to see the new mandolin Jamie had just bought for me. To show Peter the mandolin I had to take him into my bedroom.

It was the room at the end of the hall, the one that had been Clay's study. For months after Clay left I remained sleeping on the futon in the living room; Jamie alternated between extreme depression and flashes of hope that Clay might return, and I didn't want to upset him by suggesting I take over the other room. I thought it smarter to wait for it to be his idea, and sure enough, one day I came home to find Clay's stuff boxed up in the living room, Jamie's instruments moved to his own bedroom. He'd fixed up Clay's study for me, with my guitar, the futon, and a few other pieces of furniture; I didn't say a word, just helped him move the boxes to the basement. Eventually we found a couch for the living room one trash day, which Jamie reupholstered as his summer project.

Peter followed me into the bedroom, uncertainly, like he was sure he shouldn't be doing this, but we both stopped in the doorway. The bass player for the Primates was passed out cold in my bed, a potato chip pressed like a feather between his lips. Peter and I had looked at each other and started laughing, and I just gave up; I knew I'd run out of chances for seducing him that night.

I realized then, sitting at the kitchen table, sipping the coffee that seemed like it had taken forever to brew, that this was why I'd crawled in bed with Jamie. Bill and the rest of the Primates were already gone by then, and no one else knew this bass player very well; he was new, and none of us could even remember his name. When Peter and I came out of the room, he and Annie and Kirsten were the only people left at the party, and after a minute it was down to just Kirsten and the passed-out bass player, who Jamie was checking out with some amusement. I found Kirsten in the kitchen, putting glasses in the dishwasher.

"You don't have to do that," I said. "We'll clean up in the morning."

She shrugged, and poured detergent into the little cup on the dishwasher door. It bothered me, seeing her move around in our kitchen like she lived there.

"I just thought I'd give you a head start," she said, and turned the washer on. She moved past me without another word, her lacy stockings snagging for a second on a rough spot in the kitchen doorway.

By the time I'd locked up behind her, Jamie had already gone to bed. I tried to roll the bass player off my futon, but he was heavy and I couldn't budge him. I gave up and went into Jamie's room, crawled into the bed next to him. He seemed to be asleep, so I didn't say anything, but as I started to doze off I heard him say, "Happy birthday, Miri," and then his breathing was soft and even and I knew not to answer.

I drank a whole pot of coffee before I got the energy to look in my room and see if the bass player was still there. He was gone, a few potato chip crumbs the only reminder that he'd slept in my bed. I staggered back to the kitchen and was at the table, starting another pot of coffee, when I heard Jamie shuffle out.

"Shit," he said, collapsing into a chair across from me. "I need water."

"There's some in the fridge," I said, closing the top of the coffee maker and slumping over the table.

"That's too far to walk," Jamie said.

"I know."

We sat there for a good five minutes, both of us staring at the coffee maker, waiting for the rich brown liquid to begin dripping down, before Jamie said, "Shit" again, and started laughing. He leaned across the table and flicked the switch on.

"I guess that would help," I said.

He made his way to the refrigerator and pulled the bottle of spring water out, gulped it down straight from the jug. The coffee had just begun to drip down; I'd been so out of it for the first pot that I hadn't even noticed its strong earthy smell, how it seeped into my nostrils and cleared my mind a bit before I even started drinking it. I was sitting there with my empty mug waiting for the coffee to finish brewing when the phone rang. It seemed unnaturally loud, and Jamie put his arms around his head and made a face.

"I'll get it," he moaned, shuffling over to the phone, which seemed to be visibly vibrating.

He picked it up, and I didn't pay much mind at first, figuring it would be for him. Soon, though, I noticed a confused look on his face, and then I heard him say, "Hold on a second, she's right here."

Jamie held his hand over the receiver. "It's Rick," he said.

I was so hung over that at first I couldn't place the name. I started to go through a mental list of guys in bands I knew, until it hit me: Rick. It had been more than a year since he'd gone back to his Mom's.

I took the phone from Jamie. "Rick?" I asked.

"Yeah, it's me," he said, his stutter as bad as I'd ever heard it. There was a lot of noise in the background, and I got the feeling he was at a pay phone.

"Where are you?" I asked.

"Bus station. Mount Laurel." It was something I'd heard him do before to control his stutter, reducing his sentences down to only the words he absolutely needed.

"What's going on?" I asked. Jamie poured me a mug of coffee, handed it to me. I took a grateful sip.

"I thought I had enough money to get to Philly, but I don't." It took him so long to get it out that I had to fight an urge to finish the sentence. I remembered this urge well from all the time we'd spent together. "I don't know what to do," he added. He sounded like he was going to cry.

"Hold on," I said. I put my hand over the receiver and told Jamie what he'd said.

"What does he want us to do?" Jamie asked. He'd poured too much milk into his coffee and was mopping up the spill.

"I guess he wants us to come get him," I said. "Jamie, he sounds real bad off."

"Damn," Jamie said, slurping coffee from the top of the cup. "Miri, I can't deal with this right now. My head is pounding."

"I know." I took my hand off the phone. "Rick?"

The operator was asking for more change, and I could hear coins going down.

"Rick?"

"Gonna get cut off soon," he said. "Don't have enough change."

"Is there a train I can take there?" I asked him. "Maybe the High Speed Line?"

"I don't know," he said, and I heard muffled sounds I couldn't quite make out. "Miri, I need help." There was something in his voice I'd never heard before, a hopelessness that frightened me.

"Just stay there," I said. "I'll find it. Might take me some time, though. Can you hang for a while?"

"I think so," he said, and it sounded like he started to say something else but the phone clicked off.

I sat down at the table. Jamie was watching me intently over his coffee.

"I'll just take the High Speed Line out there," I said.

"Does it go to the bus station?" he asked.

"I don't know. I'll figure it out."

Jamie ran a finger over the rim of his coffee mug. "Are you bringing him here?" he asked. His face was a mask; I couldn't tell what he was thinking.

Truth was, I hadn't thought that far ahead. I was as tired and hung over as Jamie was, and the whole thing had taken me by surprise. I had no right to bring Rick there; barely had a right to be there myself.

"'Course not," I said.

"Then where will you take him?"

He was looking right at me, and it was almost as if he wanted to force me to ask him if Rick could stay. I was really too tired to play games with him.

"Jamie, I don't know," I said. "Believe me, this is the last thing I want to deal with right now. All I know is I can't leave him there."

He nodded, took a sip of his coffee.

"But it's not your problem," I added. "I'll figure something out." I picked up my coffee and went in my bedroom to get dressed. When I came out, Jamie was tucking a t-shirt into his jeans. He picked up his keys.

"Come on," he said. "I'll drive you." I gave him a hug that nearly made him lose his balance.

Neither one of us knew anything about the Jersey suburbs. Because of this, and because my map-reading skills were not exactly as good as I'd hoped, we went over the wrong bridge—by the end of the trip we'd learned that there are at least three different bridges that go from Philly into New

Jersey—and wound up on an interstate headed for Delaware. It took us almost two hours of stops for directions, wrong turns off divided highways, and puzzled attempts at studying the map before we finally pulled up in front of the Mount Laurel Bus Station. Jamie was quiet most of the way; a combination, I figured, of hangover, not knowing where he was going, and getting involved in something he wasn't at all sure he wanted to be mixed up in.

I knew I might be trying Jamie's patience, getting him into this. Just a few months ago I was sleeping on the couch myself, and I still wondered from time to time if Jamie held any blame for me in Clay's leaving. Sure, I'd pushed my luck with the cats, but this was different, bringing home a stray boy. I'd have to find a place Rick could stay right away. I was fretting over this as we approached the bus station, a tiny little building surrounded by a huge empty parking lot gridded with white lines, like a spider in an oversized web.

"This must be all for commuters," Jamie said. From the isolated feeling I got there, the scrubby brush surrounding the huge expanse of blacktop, the August heat, it could easily have been a little bus station somewhere in Texas. It looked like the end of the Earth.

I noticed a slight figure seated forward on the curb, shoulders slumped, arms around his legs. As we got closer, I could tell from the mass of curly hair that it was Rick; as we got closer still, I wondered if I could have been wrong.

What I could see of his face looked swollen and distorted. There was a black eye, cuts, raised purple bruises. He was holding one of his arms at an odd-looking angle.

"Oh my god," Jamie whispered. He looked at me, and I could tell from the look that whatever reservations he'd had were gone, at least for now. Jamie wasn't the kind of person who could leave someone in a state like that. He said nothing else, just pulled the car up next to Rick, jumped out and lifted up the back seat. Rick climbed in without a word, turned his face to the window, away from us.

We drove in silence for a few minutes, until I was sure Jamie was on the right highway, headed back into Philly. Then I turned around and tried to talk to Rick—not about what had happened, but about anything else I could think of. I told him we'd named the band Cloud Cuckoo Land, and how much folks seemed to like us. Rick just kept his head turned away, staring out the window.

"Miri," Jamie said, glancing at me sideways. He gave me a look that said he thought I should stop talking. I folded my arms and looked out the window myself. I know him better than you do, I wanted to say, but I wasn't about to get in an argument with Jamie.

After we'd crossed the Ben Franklin Bridge, Jamie looked in the rearview mirror.

"Rick," he said, "I think we should stop at a hospital."

"No," Rick said, so quickly that I got the feeling he'd been expecting the suggestion.

"Do you think your arm is broken?" Jamie asked it in a quiet, calm voice, like a doctor might. I turned around and looked at Rick, at the unnatural way he was holding his arm out.

"I shouldn't have called you," Rick said, in the stop-start way he had when he was trying not to stutter.

"Rick, we just want to make sure you're okay," I said.

"I'm fine," Rick said. "Just drop me off anywhere."

"That's bullshit," I said. "You know we're not dropping you off on the fucking street. So just shut up and let us take you to the hospital." Jamie looked at me in horror, but I knew how to handle Rick better than Jamie did. And I was right; he stopped arguing after that and, when Jamie pulled up at the emergency room entrance of Graduate Hospital, Rick walked in with us quietly, without protest.

CHAPTER 27
AUGUST–SEPTEMBER, 1986

After four hours and several arguments between Jamie and the desk nurse, we were back at the apartment with Rick, his arm in a sling, parts of his face bandaged, a bag of prescriptions in his free hand. "Do you want to sleep?" I asked, and he nodded, letting me steer him into my bedroom, and I knew I was back on the couch for a while.

I never did get the full story of what had happened, though bits and pieces came out. Most of it I had already guessed; his Mom started drinking again, his stepfather came back. Rick would never tell me much in the way of details, like why his stepfather hit him, what set him off. I guessed it didn't much matter.

As the weeks went on, things got tense in the apartment. Most of the time when Jamie was home, Rick stayed in his room—my room—or went out; when he did run into Jamie he would barely speak to him. And Jamie seemed uncomfortable around Rick, too, like he wasn't sure of what he'd brought home. I knew that once Rick was all healed up we'd have to find a place for him to live; it was like when Clay had been there, living in constant tension.

One night in September I was walking down South Street with Rick. We'd stopped by the Big Bang to say hi to Loretta; Rick's face was all healed by then, and he told a story about being in a car accident to explain his arm, the sling. As we walked back to the apartment we passed a group of boys, college boys from the looks of them, headed out for the night. I asked Rick if he'd gone to college in New Jersey.

"Yeah, I finished a year," he said. "I was planning to do another year there and then transfer to a better school."

"Well, maybe you could go to school here," I said.

"I don't have any money." He was talking real plain just then, no stutter at all.

"Can't you get loans and stuff?" I asked. I'd heard kids like David and Bobby talk about loans.

"I guess, but I think I have to wait 'til I turn eighteen to keep my Mom out of it," he said. "I'm not sure what's involved, legally."

"How much longer until you turn eighteen?" I felt bad for not remembering his birthday.

"November," he said, and I nodded like I all of a sudden remembered.

"You should talk to Jamie," I said. "I bet he knows about that kind of stuff. I bet he'd help you." I was sure he'd help him, as sure as I was that he'd like for Rick to find another place to live.

Rick didn't say anything.

"Really," I said. "He's like talking to the information desk at the library." I thought this would make him laugh, seeing as how we used to have to sneak past the information desk to get into the bathrooms and wash up, but Rick was looking at the sidewalk, his lips pushed out in a pout.

"I don't want to talk to Jamie," he finally said, quietly but firmly, without a stutter.

"Why not?"

"Just don't feel comfortable."

"Why not?" I stepped on a ginkgo berry and it let out the puke-like smell that hangs through Center City in the fall. I dragged my feet on the sidewalk, hoping to get the remains of the stinkball off the bottom of my tennis shoe.

"Because," he said under his breath, "it's disgusting."

"Huh?" I sidestepped another ginkgo ball, not really taking in what he was saying.

"It makes me sick," he said, "what he does."

I didn't get it at first; "what he does" didn't mean anything to me. Next to me, Jamie was downright boring, and I couldn't imagine what Rick was talking about. Then it hit me.

"I really hope," I said, "that I'm not getting your meaning."

"Miri, did you ever think about it? It's just disgusting." It amazed me that this kind of ugliness could pour out of him, without a stutter. "He's always looking at me," he added.

I'd seen Jamie look at Rick, too, the same kind of look he'd given Artemis and Nico when we'd first taken them in. If I was honest with myself, I'd probably gotten that look at first, though I was sure there was more to how Jamie felt about me than that. I looked at Rick, his pimply, angry-looking skin, his misshapen hair, his scrawny body. It was almost laughable for him to think what he was thinking; I knew what Jamie's type was, not just from Clay but from the rare few guys Jamie would point out to me when we were at clubs. They were always tall, broad-shouldered, at least Jamie's age or older, with the handsome faces I'd come to expect on gay men. I could never get Jamie to approach any of these men; he claimed he was afraid they were straight, but really it was that he wasn't over Clay yet. One time at Ground Zero he picked out a guy I thought was cute as well, and I marched right up to the guy and asked if he was straight or gay; I pointed out Jamie and told him he could have whichever one of us he wanted. He made a bee-line over to Jamie and the two of them talked for a long time that night, but in the end, Jamie still went home alone. When I really thought about what Rick was hinting at, anger flashed through me like a grease fire.

"Rick, Jamie feels nothing but sorry for you," I said. "Do you really think he's interested in some ungrateful pimple-faced street kid? Believe you me, he's had better offers."

Rick had a look on his face like I'd just slapped him. I knew it was harsh, but I couldn't help myself. I wanted to say even more. I wanted to say everything I felt about Jamie, his kindness, his talent, his beauty, but I didn't know where to begin. I expected Rick to run off, maybe never come back, and at that point I almost didn't care if he did. I was surprised to see him just keep walking, apart from but alongside me, that just-struck look settling into his features. We walked for three blocks like that, the silence as thick as the South Street crowds on a Saturday night in August.

"I know you're right," he said, taking nearly half a block to get the words out. "I just can't help the way I feel."

. . .

The next morning, Rick was up and out before me. I didn't know where he went and didn't care, I was still so mad at him.

I went out to pick up croissants for breakfast, the kind that Jamie liked. When I came back in, he was on the phone, in the kitchen. He had music on, Muddy Waters at medium volume, and so didn't seem to hear me.

"I know," I heard him say. "Really."

I hung my jacket on the rack—it was an old blazer of Jamie's that I'd pretty much taken over—and was just about to bring the croissants in to him when I heard him say: "It's crazy, I know. It's like I'm running a homeless shelter or something."

I stopped in my tracks, trying to think of a way I could have misunderstood the comment, a different meaning than what it appeared to be. It was possible he'd been talking about Rick, that he'd meant it more toward Rick than me, but I was sure I was in there somewhere. I figured he was talking to one of his Boston friends, and decided just then that I'd been wrong about everything; none of his friends had liked me, they'd all looked down on me just as Clay had. Even Jamie didn't care about me, just took me on like a social work project, like the cats. The band was his way of amusing himself by slumming, I decided. I'd been crazy to think that Jamie really cared about me, loved me even. Why would he? I was nothing to him, not even someone he could sleep with.

My whole body started feeling twitchy, like I needed to get out of there and run as fast as I could the twenty city blocks to Front Street, then onward to the pier, the waterfront, to take flight and soar across the river, across land, to the Atlantic Ocean and beyond. It was a feeling I'd had before, the day that Wendell told me he couldn't adopt me, the day I knew I had to leave that house where the scary preacher lived. I wondered if Annmarie had felt something like this, all the times she ran off; but I wasn't like her, I was nothing like her, I was simply running from people who had already made it clear they didn't want me. I would never leave behind someone who really needed me, and I convinced myself that this was what made me different from her.

I went into my room, pushed Rick's backpack aside and gathered up some of my stuff, fighting tears. When I'd crammed my bag full I stomped past the kitchen and out the front door and slammed it, loud, so Jamie would know I'd heard him.

I wandered down to Bill's. I knew it was only about 11:00, and that Bill worked nights and rarely got up before noon, but I rang the buzzer anyway, four times until he came to the door. He opened it, shaking his head when he saw me. His long hair was matted in clumps on his head, pieces of it sticking out at odd angles. Flecks of yellow crust clung to his eyelashes. He was wearing a Metallica t-shirt and a pair of boxer shorts.

"Miri," he said, and it sounded like a moan. "Why can't you ever come over here when I'm awake?"

I walked in past him and put my bag down near the bed. It was a studio apartment, and reminded me of some of the dorm rooms I'd seen at PCA. There wasn't much space, and I'd seen a good number of cockroaches there at night, but I figured I could make do for a while.

"If you want to go back to sleep, it's okay," I said. "I'm sorry I woke you."

He stretched, scratched his side. "What's up?" he said.

I knew better than to tell him right off that I needed to stay there for a while. I sighed and gave him a sad smile that I thought made me look younger than my age and deserving of sympathy. "I guess I'm just having a bad day," I said, making sure to drawl it out the way I would have back in Texas. I'd been hearing bits of Philly creep in to the way I said things; I knew I talked faster, cut my words off more quickly.

He shook his head and climbed back into bed. "I'm going to sleep," he said, and I knew this was my invitation to crawl in beside him. I lay awake for an hour while he slept, and when he started to wake up again I gave him a blow job, figuring it would be a good idea to make myself useful. When we were done he propped himself on an elbow and looked at me, without saying anything.

"What?" I asked, feeling a bit unnerved.

"Tell me what's going on," he said.

We'd never really talked much before. Our relationship had always been about sex, with a little chatter thrown in here or there. The times I had tried to talk to him I hadn't got the feeling he was much of a conversationalist, and so I'd stopped. Now he was offering up an opening, and I wasn't so sure I wanted to take it.

"Nothing," I said.

He kept looking at me. "Come on."

I thought about it for a minute, and decided to tell him some bits of truth, but to shape the story as I saw fit. So I told him how I'd been between places to live—that was how I put it—before I moved in with Jamie, and how now we were putting up a friend of mine, Rick, and it had caused some strain between us.

"Is that the kid you used to play with on South Street?" he asked.

I had no idea he'd seen me before the night Cloud Cuckoo Land opened for the Primates at the Big Bang, and my surprise must have been on my face.

"I'd seen you around," he said. "People wondered about you."

"Wondered what?"

"Well," he said, shifting around so he was lying on his back, "you sounded like a professional singer but you looked like you were living on the streets. A lot of people wondered whether you were a rich kid from PCA or the performing arts high school, slumming or something, or if you were really a street kid."

It was just this kind of confusion I'd always tried to create, and I was glad it hadn't been clear that I was on the streets, that people had noticed me for my voice and not just seen me as some kind of panhandler.

"What did you think?" I asked him.

He shrugged. "I didn't know."

I told him a little bit more, more than I expected to tell him; how Rick and I had lived, how he'd gone home to try again, how Jamie had finally let me live with him. I didn't tell him about the Collective. I never told anyone about the Collective. He just listened, Bill did, with an expression on his face I couldn't read.

"So you've been living there for, like, a year, without paying any rent or anything?" he asked. It sounded awful, put like that.

"Yeah," I said.

Bill sighed, wiggled around in the bed. "Maybe you should get a job."

It seemed like such an obvious thing; that was what regular people did, they got jobs, paid for their places to live, their utility bills, their cars. But it felt like something unreachable to me, a world I was not a part of. I didn't know how to explain this.

"It's not that I'm lazy," I said finally. "It's just that I have no idea how to do that."

"How to work?"

I wanted to tell him how much work it was to live from day to day, always looking for a place to sleep, but I held my tongue. "How to actually get a job," I said. "I mean, they ask you questions and make you fill out forms and stuff. I just wouldn't know what to do." I knew it must have sounded ridiculous to him; I didn't know how to explain how different my mindset was, how removed I felt from the real world. Even the last year, living with Jamie, had not been living in the real world, not truly; it was still crashing at someone else's place, even if he tried to make it feel like home.

"I could get you a job," he said.

I looked at him to see if he was serious. "Where?"

"You know that used record store over on 5th Street?"

I nodded. I knew it because Jamie spent a few hours a week in there, and always came home with an armful of albums that he didn't have shelf space for.

"They're looking for somebody to work a couple of nights a week. Everybody who works there is in a band, and they have trouble finding enough people to cover nights." He propped himself up on a pillow. "John works there," he said. John, it hit me then, was the name of the bass player who'd passed out in my bed the night of my birthday party.

"You really think they'd let me work there?" I asked.

He nodded. "Why not?"

"I've never had a job before."

"Well, don't tell the owner that," he said. "Miri, it's totally mindless. If John can do it, anybody can."

He was right about that; John was dumber than tacks, far as I'd been able to tell.

Bill called the shop for me and, an hour later, we were down at the Whirling Dervish, where in the first five minutes of conversation I had so charmed the owner—a gray-bearded old hippie guy named Paul—that I thought he might not just give me a job but the whole damn store by the time I left. I told him honestly that I had never worked in a record store, but my smile and the fact that I was in a band he'd heard talk of seemed to be the only experience I needed. I would start the following Monday, 5:00 to 11:00 three nights a week, rotating my schedule around gigs like the other people in bands did.

I was happy about the job and thought it would help the situation with Jamie, but still I didn't want to go back there, not right away. Jamie's comment had hurt me and I couldn't let him off the hook for it that easy. I knew that Bill's getting me the job meant it was the end of the line with him, and so later on that afternoon I took my bag and headed down to the Big Bang, where Loretta was getting things ready for the night. There were only three people in the bar, older guys from the neighborhood. They huddled on their stools, nursing small glasses of liquor that smelled to me like rubbing alcohol. I hung around talking to Loretta for long enough that she finally asked me what was up.

"I had a fight with Jamie," I said.

"Men," she said, shaking her head. I didn't know if she thought, as many people did, that Jamie was my boyfriend. I wasn't about to say that he wasn't.

"You think there's any way I could stay with you, Loretta?" I asked. "Just for one night?"

She looked me in the eyes. "He didn't kick you out, did he?" There was something about the way she said it that made me think somehow she knew the whole true story, but I couldn't imagine how. Only a few people in the music scene knew bits and pieces of it: Kirsten knew Jamie was gay, and I had told Peter once in a moment of drunken weakness that I'd run away from home when I was young. As far as I was aware that was all anybody knew, besides what I'd told Bill that morning; but he had remembered me from my busking days, and I wondered how many others did. It hit me in that moment that maybe Loretta did know, that maybe everyone had put the bits and pieces together; that maybe the Philly music scene was not unlike Prairie Rose in its clannishness, its talent for the spread of gossip.

"No," I said. "We just had a fight. But I don't want to go back there straight off." I could have asked her what she knew, but I wasn't sure I wanted the answer.

She nodded. "You can stay with me, Miri. No problem."

I hung out with Loretta at the bar for a couple of hours, fetching food from the back for her, cleaning off the tables, chatting with some of the regulars. As the night wore on the day's events started catching up with me; it had been some time since I'd been without a place to sleep, and the whole thing had exhausted me. I'd gotten soft, living with Jamie. Loretta saw me yawning, and seemed to understand; she tossed me a set of keys, pointed up the back steps. Her apartment was above the bar.

I played with her cats, watched a little TV, and then dozed on the couch for a spell, but I was awake by the time Loretta came up the steps. It was nearly 3 A.M. She asked me if I wanted to have a cup of tea with her, and I followed her into the kitchen.

"Jamie called the bar," she said, putting a teakettle on the stove. "He wanted to know if I'd seen you."

"Did you tell him I was staying here?" I asked. I was glad to hear that Jamie was worried enough to call around town looking for me. Maybe this was all I'd really wanted, to know he cared.

She nodded.

"What did he say?"

"He said to tell you to come home."

I shrugged. The teakettle began making sizzling noises.

"He doesn't sound like he's mad at you, Miri."

"He shouldn't be," I said. "I'm the one who's mad."

"Oh." Loretta pulled two cups from a cabinet, tossed a tea bag into each one.

I knew she wanted more of an explanation, that maybe I even owed her that for letting me stay there, but I wasn't ready to go into it with her. What I'd heard Jamie say on the phone reflected bad on me, and I didn't want Loretta to know the details just yet.

"It's a long story," I said.

The teakettle began to whistle, and Loretta poured the water into the cups. "It's okay," she said. She reached up to get a box of sugar out of the cabinet, and her sleeve fell down, exposing the full length of her tattoo.

"How long have you had that tattoo, Loretta?" I asked, mostly to change the subject, though I did wonder about it.

She turned and looked at me. "The snake?"

I nodded.

"Oh, man—1969. I had a boyfriend then who did them. Tattoos, I mean."

"Why did you want a snake?" I asked. She put the cups of tea on the table, with the box of sugar and a carton of milk from the refrigerator.

She smiled, but it wasn't a happy smile. "I didn't want a snake," she said. "I was passed out when he did it."

"He gave you a tattoo when you were passed out?"

Loretta stirred sugar into her tea. "It was a pretty crazy time in my life," she said.

I blew on my tea to cool it down, waited for her to go on.

"I mean, I did a lot of stuff then that I don't do now."

"Like what?" I asked. I could guess, of course, but I wanted to hear her tell it.

"Well, I tripped a lot. I did a lot of speed. I'm really lucky I didn't turn out half brain-dead. Some of the people I hung out with back then, you talk to them now and it's like you're phoning your comments in to Venus and waiting for a satellite reply." She laughed a little. "The truth is, I was afraid of snakes. My boyfriend gave me the tattoo because he was mad at me."

"Really? Why was he mad?"

She shrugged. "I don't even remember. We were both pretty fucked up, hitchhiking cross-country, camping wherever we felt like, and doing so many drugs we had no idea where we were. We had camped somewhere out west and woke up one morning to find our tent full of rattlesnakes. I mean, like a dozen." She stopped talking for a few seconds, took a sip of her tea. "Of course, we could have been hallucinating. Maybe there was only one. Or none at all. Anyway, it freaked me out and I started having nightmares about snakes. Jay—that was my boyfriend's name—knew how scared I was. So when he got mad at me, he gave me a snake I couldn't escape."

"Wow," I said, stirring another spoon of sugar into my tea.

"Yeah." She looked at her arm and gently ran the tips of her fingers over the tattoo.

"Did you ever try to get it removed?" I asked.

"I thought about it," she said, "but after a while it started to grow on me. It's like a scar, I guess, a scar that you become proud of. I can't imagine not having this old snake with me now."

"Annmarie had a butterfly tattooed on her ankle," I offered. "She said it hurt like hell." The tattoo had been Tommy Clayton's idea; he had them up and down his arms, hula girls and palm trees and an anchor from when he'd been in the Navy. When he played guitar for me and taught me those blues songs, I loved watching his arms, looking at all the different designs and how they moved with his muscles.

"Who's Annmarie?" Loretta asked.

"My mother." The word had no meaning to me; it was like it was from another language.

Loretta was quiet for a minute, looking at me over her tea.

"What year were you born, Miri?" she asked. It seemed an odd question to me, out of the blue like that.

"In 1966," I said. "Why?"

"Just wondered." After a little stretch of quiet, she added, "I had my daughter in '68."

It wasn't something she'd ever talked about before. "You have a daughter?" I asked.

"Had," she corrected. "I gave her up for adoption."

"Oh," I said, not knowing what else to say. I drank a few sips of tea and watched Loretta; the sadness that was settling into her face reminded me of Jamie, how he looked when Clay's name was mentioned.

"Annmarie should have done that," I said. "Given me up for adoption, I mean." I tried to imagine it, the life I might have led, adopted by someone like the Emersons, maybe, or the parents of college kids like David and Bobby. I'd have turned out like the girls who took guitar lessons from

Jamie; or, worse, like Kirsten or Annie. I didn't want to be those people, but I wanted the ease of their lives.

"You'd rather not have known your mother at all?" Loretta asked.

I considered trying to change the subject, but I felt bad to shut Loretta down just then, her looking so sad and all. Instead I told her about Annmarie, about what living with her had been like, how she'd finally left for good. I didn't go into anything about my running away, but Loretta was smart; I could tell she got the picture.

"That's what it would have been like," Loretta said. "That's exactly what it would have been like, if I'd kept her."

I shook my head. "Not you. You loved your daughter."

She smiled, a thin, sad little smile. "Miri, your mother loves you," she said. "A mother can't help but love her child."

I couldn't believe, after all I'd told her, that Loretta would side with Annmarie. "Loretta," I said, trying to keep the anger out of my voice, "you don't know the particular mother involved here."

"I know she might not have acted like she loved you," she said. "She could be a bad mother and still love you."

I would never have expected all this from someone as no-bullshit as Loretta.

"I don't really see how that's possible," I said.

Loretta looked away for a minute. "Do you think you'll ever see her again?"

"Not if I can help it."

She shook her head, and looked for a moment like she was going to say something else but then knew enough to back off. "Are you going back to patch things up with Jamie tomorrow?" she asked.

I thought about Loretta's life, all she'd been through in the past but now owning her own bar, with a nice place to live upstairs, and I wished, for a second, that I had something of my own like that. Even my singing was no longer my own, but was part of a collaboration with Jamie. "Yeah, I'm going back tomorrow," I said.

. . .

I made my way over to Jamie's around 11:30 the next morning, walking as slowly as I could, not in any hurry to get there. I felt embarrassed, both by what Jamie had said about me and by the fact that I'd stormed out the way I did. And I had no idea what I'd find there, having left Jamie and Rick alone for twenty-four hours.

I was pretty surprised, then, to walk in to the smell of coffee brewing, the BoDeans playing low on the stereo, and Jamie and Rick sitting on the couch with some official-looking forms spread all over the coffee table. I threw my bag down by the door, walked over and picked up one of the papers. "Financial Aid Form, 1986–1987," it said at the top. Jamie and Rick both looked up at me like they were waiting for me to say something.

"Huh," I said, and put the form back on the table.

Jamie cleared his throat. "Rick's applying to colleges for next semester," he said. "He's going to stay here until then."

"On the couch," Rick added. "My stuff is out of your room, Miri."

I wondered if they had any idea what I was upset about, if Jamie even realized I'd overheard him on the phone. I shrugged at them and went into the kitchen to pour myself a cup of coffee. Jamie followed me in.

"Miri," he said, keeping his voice low so Rick wouldn't hear. "I don't know what you heard, but I never meant to say anything to hurt you. I'm glad you're here."

"I got a job," I said. "Part-time, at the Whirling Dervish."

"Bill told me," Jamie said.

"You talked to Bill?" I asked, remembering that Loretta had said he'd called her as well. "What did you do, call everyone I know in Philly?"

"Pretty much. And you'll be happy to know that Peter Fenster sounded very worried about you."

"He didn't," I said, and I couldn't help but smile.

"He did. He made me promise to have you call him when you got home."

I took a sip of coffee and sat down at the table, leaned back against the chair.

"You didn't have to get a job, Miri," Jamie said. He pulled the other chair out and sat down across from me.

"Yes, I did," I said, "and you know it."

He was quiet for a minute. "I guess I did start to feel a little taken advantage of."

"I should have done something sooner," I said. "I just never really thought I could get a job. I know that must sound stupid."

Jamie shook his head. "It doesn't." He rubbed at a spot on the table with his finger. "It's not that I care about money, Miri," he said, "but what I have isn't bottomless, you know? I can't really afford to support two other people forever. That's the only reason I got upset about it."

"Well, it's not like Rick was being too appreciative, either," I said.

He glanced out toward the living room. "We have that all worked out," he whispered.

"Really?"

"Yeah," he said, "at least I think so."

With that the phone rang, and Jamie got up to answer it. As he said, "Hello," I could hear Rick in the next room, shuffling papers around and muttering to himself. I had a weird feeling just then; it was like they were my brothers, like we all belonged living there together. The feeling passed over me as Jamie covered the receiver with his hand and raised his eyebrows at me.

"It's for you," he said, in a whispery-seductive voice. "It's Peter. I bet he didn't sleep all night, worrying about you."

I laughed and poured more coffee, cleared my throat, and took the phone out of his hands.

CHAPTER 28
OCTOBER, 1987

It was 3:25 A.M., according to the little clock on the dashboard of Jamie's car, and we'd been riding around parts of Cambridge and Somerville, Massachusetts, for the past hour. I knew because every now and then we'd pass a sign that said "Welcome to Cambridge"; and then, ten minutes and half a dozen wrong turns later, we'd pass a sign that said "Welcome to Somerville." I was supposed to be navigating, but the map wasn't helping me much; every street I suggested would turn out to be one-way in the wrong direction, closed for construction, or would mysteriously dead-end, forcing us to turn onto yet another street whose name Jamie didn't recognize.

"I thought you knew Cambridge like the back of your hand," I said, crumpling the map into a heap and tossing it on the floor of the car. I'd heard him tell Clay this once when we'd gotten lost visiting Jamie's friends, on one of our holiday trips up here. I knew by now, of course, that Jamie had no sense of direction whatsoever; it didn't matter how many times he went somewhere, he could get lost coming home from the corner market. At least in Philly I could tell him which way to go, but here, I was as clueless as he was.

"I didn't drive a lot when I lived here," he muttered. "I took the T when I went into the city."

We'd played in Cambridge that night, at a place called T.T. the Bear's, opening a triple bill. The second act that night was a Boston band called the Pixies; Jamie thought they were incredible and predicted that they'd be famous. He had a weakness for bands that made a lot of noise—dissonance, Jamie called it—but which had strong melodies at the cores of their songs. A lot of the music he liked was nothing like our sound, and I had to wonder sometimes if Cloud Cuckoo Land was what Jamie really wanted, or if he sometimes wished he was in a real rock band, with a bunch of sweaty guys and loud guitars. Of course, I was not about to ask him; didn't want to plant ideas in his head that might not already be there.

We'd played T.T. the Bear's before, a couple of times that year. Jamie and I had started to play gigs outside of Philly, places within driving distance: Boston and Cambridge, New York, Baltimore, Washington, D.C. I could navigate our way out of the other cities with a good map, but we were always in trouble up around Boston, with its triangular intersections like a geometry lesson gone wrong, its traffic rotaries that the locals raced around like they thought they were contenders in the Indy 500.

Just about every bar or store or diner we passed looked to be closed, the streets darkened and deserted; but up ahead I saw a sign lit up, a big convenience store. I told Jamie to pull in the parking lot so we could ask directions to Newton, where we were spending the night with his parents.

"Give me the map," he grumbled. "I can figure it out."

"Jamie," I said through clenched teeth, "we've been driving around for an hour."

"I just have to find Storrow Drive on the map."

"We should stop and call your Mom," I said. "She's gonna be worried that we're not back yet."

Jamie shrugged. "She knew we'd be late. She'll get over it." When Jamie stayed with his parents, even for a night, he had this habit of turning into the sulky teenager he must have once been. I felt glad we didn't know each other back then.

"Jamie, let me just run into the store, okay?"

"No."

I sighed, loud and drawn out enough to annoy him. This was a stubborn side of Jamie I only saw when we were trapped in a car together. I'd always thought the bickering he and Clay had done on long trips was mostly Clay's fault; and maybe it was, but I could now see that Jamie had his hand in it, too.

Jamie stopped at a red light, and I opened my door. "I'm going into that store and asking directions," I said. "You can pull in the parking lot when the light changes or you can leave me here." I knew exactly what he'd do:

circle around the block once or twice to make me think he'd left me, then pull into the parking lot. We'd been through this once or twice before.

There was a nice boy behind the counter who gave me my cherry slush for free, along with directions to Storrow Drive. He wrote them down for me and offered to take me to Newton himself when his shift ended if my friend didn't come back, but of course Jamie pulled into the parking lot soon enough. I got in the car and told him I had directions if he wanted them.

He stared over the steering wheel for a minute. "I really hate it when you act like I don't know what I'm doing," he said.

"Jamie, it's not that I think you don't know what you're doing. Everybody gets lost. Your problem is you won't admit you don't know where you are."

"My Dad always said they should never have given me a license," he said, under his breath.

"Why did he say that?" I asked. "You're a good driver." Just one with no sense of direction, I thought, but I held my tongue.

Jamie sniffed. "When I got my learner's permit, he'd take me out in, like, the worst rush hour traffic to test me. He'd take me on Storrow Drive at 6:00 at night, or make me maneuver through Harvard Square on a Saturday. I'd get freaked out and confused by the traffic, to the point where if he told me to turn right I'd turn left. He told my mother I was too stupid to drive. She had to finish teaching me."

It hit me then that we only got into these fights about directions up around Boston, hardly ever in other cities. "Jamie," I said, "you know you're not stupid."

"I just feel like if I get lost somewhere, it proves him right."

I shook my head. "From what I can tell nobody's good enough for your Dad. It's not you, it's him."

"If it weren't for Mom, I'd never stay in his house," Jamie said. "When Clay and I lived up here Mom used to come visit me. I hardly ever went there."

The clock on the dashboard clicked over to 4 A.M. I was tired, from the all-day ride up there, from playing, from hanging out at the club so Jamie could meet the people in the Pixies and so we could shmooze the headlining band, another band with a record deal who seemed to like our sound. We gave them the demo tape we'd made earlier that year, on a four-track Peter Fenster had lent us; Kirsten had been sending it out to basically everyone she met in the music business through her job at the *RealPaper*, and we'd been handing it to the people in bands we met, selling it to fans for $3 at our shows.

We were playing so much by then that I had trouble working out my schedule at the record store, and I personally would have been happy to play a little less but Jamie was convinced it was the only way we would get a record deal. I liked my life just the way it was, and it was the first time in a long time—since Prairie Rose, really—that I'd felt that way. I figured we'd make it eventually, but I couldn't see what Jamie's hurry was. I would have been happy to just sit back and enjoy it all for a while. But it mattered to Jamie—getting a record out, getting good reviews, getting known. Maybe he had some secret fantasy that Clay would see his face on the cover of *Rolling Stone*, come running back and say what a foolish mistake he'd made. Or maybe it was his father he wanted to impress, to be seen as Jamie the successful musician rather than the son that dropped out of college and lived off the family money. I figured that all had to be a problem with them, too.

"Jamie," I said, "fuck your Dad. You know? You're twenty-seven years old. Just—fuck him."

Jamie looked at me, his eyes crinkling the way they did just before he smiled. "I don't think he even does that with Mom."

I laughed. "Well, he did at least once," I said, realizing the mistake I'd made as soon as it was out of my mouth. "Umm, I mean, twice," I added in a soft voice.

Jamie was quiet for a minute, and I was afraid I'd put him in such a mood that we'd be parked at that convenience store all night. After a time, he said, "I never told you how she died, did I?"

"No."

He ran his hand around the rim of the steering wheel. Inside the store, a couple of what looked to be stoned college kids were buying out the place—bag after bag of chips, popcorn, frozen burritos, liters of Coke.

"Did I ever tell you that she was a violin prodigy?"

"No," I said. He'd never told me much of anything about his sister.

"She was. Piano, too, but she was amazing with the violin. At twelve she performed pieces most adults couldn't play. I mean, she performed with symphonies."

"Wow," I said. I thought of my successes at twelve, singing solos in the church choir, and it seemed so rinky-dink in comparison.

"She was twice the musician I ever was," Jamie said. He said it without a trace of jealousy, but with something like awe.

"Were you close?" I asked.

He smiled. "Yes. She was only sixteen months younger than me. We went everywhere together. We both—well, we just understood each other." He pushed his hair behind his ear. "She started getting sick when she was fourteen, but it didn't get bad until after I went away to college."

"What did she have?" I asked.

He was quiet for a minute. "She was anorexic," he said. "She starved herself."

I'd heard of anorexia, mostly from the daytime talk shows I had to admit I sometimes watched. I'd seen a disease-of-the-week movie about it when I'd lived with Grandma; the girl in the movie had hidden spoons under her hospital gown, I remembered, to make it look like she weighed more than she actually did. "Lord, the things people think up to do to themselves," Grandma had said. I have to admit I agreed with her; it seemed ridiculous to me, starving yourself on purpose like that.

"She seemed to be getting better, but then I went away to college," Jamie said. "And the whole thing with Clay happened, and my parents were so upset with me that I didn't go home for a long time. By the time my mother called and told me I'd better come home, Tory was almost dead." With the way the lights from the store were hitting Jamie's face, the distant look in his eyes, I got the eerie feeling, as I had once or twice before, that I was seeing exactly what he would look like as an old man.

"I'm sorry," I said. I squeezed his hand.

"She would have liked you," he said. "She admired people who didn't take shit from anyone."

I was quiet, still holding his hand. Would I have liked her, a girl with everything, talent and a great mother and brother and a beautiful house, who decided she had to starve herself to death? When I was living on the streets, eating out of dumpsters or scamming people for free dinners, I would have thought she was ridiculous. Now, it just made me sad. I knew Jamie's Dad had fucked them all up, but I didn't really understand how or why. The things Jamie would tell me his father had said to him never seemed any worse than things Annmarie had said to me growing up. Maybe Jamie and his sister were more sensitive than I was, I thought. Maybe they were soft, tender people, and I was hard as cement. Maybe I'd had to be. Still, I knew the things Jamie felt were real; he'd been through something with his Dad, even if I couldn't fully understand it. And losing his sister, that was something real. Being gay was real.

"You know," I said, "we could just drive back to Philly tonight. We could get a couple of jumbo coffees and get on the turnpike and just drive."

Jamie laughed, but he looked pleased by the idea. "It's a six-hour drive, Miri," he said. "I'll never be able to stay awake."

"Sure you will. You'll drink a lot of coffee and we'll sing songs and I'll poke you in the ribs if you fall asleep."

He looked at the clock—it was 4:20 A.M. now. "We wouldn't get home until after 10:00," he said.

I shrugged. "Let's do it. We can call your mother from a rest stop."

He thought this over for a minute. "I can find the Mass Pike from Storrow Drive," he said. "You want to go back in that store and get us some coffee?"

And that was exactly what I did, though I got us more directions, too, just in case.

When we got back to Jamie's later that morning, there was a message from Kirsten on the answering machine. "I have huge news," she said. "Call me."

I figured it was something about some guy she liked, or maybe she'd lost another pound at Weight Watchers. Kirsten had been going there for the past few weeks, and she loved to show Jamie the little gold stars and sneakers they pasted on a card when she lost a pound. While Jamie called her back I went in my bedroom to get undressed, to finally get a little sleep, but before I could crawl between the covers he let out a scream and called my name. I pulled on a t-shirt and went out in the living room to see what all the fuss was about. If it was something like Kirsten getting laid, I was going to be pissed.

"Kirsten heard from Sean Hunter," Jamie said, the phone balanced on his shoulder. "He liked our demo tape. Oh my god." Now he was talking to Kirsten. "What? Oh—my—god." Jamie looked like he was about to crumple to the floor.

Sean Hunter was the lead singer of the Lost Generation, a band that had five albums out and a reputation for helping other bands get started. Jamie had all their albums; they were one of his favorites. Me, I just thought Sean Hunter was cute.

"How did he even get a copy of our demo tape?" I asked. Kirsten had been helping us get bookings and some airplay on radio stations no one had ever heard of, but I couldn't imagine how she could get a tape to someone like Sean Hunter. It seemed to me he was out of her league.

Jamie put his hand over the phone. "She went to a music seminar in New York over the summer, and passed it to him there," he said. "Miri, I know I told you about this."

It was possible; Jamie and Kirsten were always plotting the road to fame, and I only listened about half the time. It's not that I wasn't interested, exactly; but I didn't feel like our making it was something that could be plotted. You could plan and plan your life, and it could turn out totally different from what you expected; or you could have no plan, and it could still turn out pretty good. I was living proof of that.

"Oh yeah, now I remember," I said, and I could tell Jamie knew I was lying. "So he really liked the tape?"

"Here," Jamie said, and he held out the phone to me. It was like taking medicine, talking to Kirsten.

"Hi," I said.

"Miri!" she screamed, so loud that I had to pull the phone away from my ear. "He *loved* the demo. He wants to come hear you guys play."

Now that part perked my interest a little, what with Sean being so cute and all.

"Really?" I asked. "When did he call you?"

"He left a message on my voice mail at work—at 2:30 Saturday morning. Rock stars," she said, like we all knew lots of rock stars and their wild antics. "I'll play it for you when I get to work tomorrow. Basically, he loved the demo and wants me to give him a list of your upcoming shows. He wants catch one next time he's in New York."

"Where does he live?" I asked.

"Minneapolis," she said, and as she said it I remembered Jamie talking about the bands from Minneapolis, Hüsker Dü and the Replacements and the Lost Generation.

"Okay, I'm putting Jamie back on," I said. "Uh, thanks, Kirsten." The words seized up in my throat, but I choked them out somehow. I handed the phone back over to Jamie before she could answer.

When Jamie finally got off the phone, he crumpled in a chair. "Oh my god," he said. He repeated it several times.

"Jamie," I said, "we shouldn't get our hopes up too much." What I meant was that he shouldn't get *his* hopes up too much.

"I know. But—he likes us! He really likes us!" Jamie laughed. "God, I sound like Sally Field."

The first person we called was Rick, since he'd been helping us some, setting up and taking care of sound at our shows nights when he didn't have to study. He was living in a dorm, going to school at Drexel; he and Jamie were getting along fine, seemed to have worked out whatever their problem was. After we talked to him, we called Peter Fenster, since it was his four-track we'd used to record our demo, and besides, I used any excuse I could to call him. He was still with Annie, but word on the street was that they were having trouble. Peter wanted to take us out to celebrate, which meant that we would both accept and Jamie would not show up. We'd already played this game several times by then. Nothing had happened with Peter, yet, but I was always hopeful.

Peter and I met for dinner that night at a Mexican restaurant. He didn't look surprised that Jamie wasn't with me.

"So, Sean Hunter," Peter said, after the waitress had taken our order. "I've never met him. He's supposed to be a good guy."

"What do you think of the Lost Generation?" I asked him.

"Technically, they're really good. They all play their instruments well, they write good songs, they have their own sound."

"But you don't like them," I said. Peter was as into indie rock as Jamie was, but his taste was sometimes different, and I enjoyed hearing how his ideas about certain bands varied from Jamie's.

Peter nodded at the waitress as she put two margaritas down in front of us. "They don't have enough of an edge for me," he said. "It's dreamy and melodic and all of that, but it doesn't have a backbone."

I shrugged. "I like them," I said, "but I don't think Sean's voice is all that good. He really hits some off notes."

"Well, I hit some pretty off notes, too," Peter said. "Not too many people have your kind of pitch, Miri."

This was the kind of thinking that tended to irritate both me and Jamie: that rock shouldn't be held to any musical standards, that it was asking too much to sing on-key or play instruments well. Peter, on the other hand, had only learned guitar so he could join Chutes and Ladders, and he was proud of his lack of musical schooling. Jamie thought that Peter played too well to have picked it up as recently as he said, but I believed the story. Peter wasn't the type to make something like that up.

"I've never noticed you hitting any off notes, Peter," I said, batting my eyes in a way that usually served me well.

He looked away and took a long sip of his drink. "Annie wants me to go back to school," he said.

He always brought up Annie when I flirted with him. "To college?" I asked. I had no idea how much school Peter had been through, but even in the club scene I rarely met anyone who had as little education as I did. This would have made me feel insecure were it not for that fact that so many of the people I met who'd graduated from college were dumber than doorknobs.

"Graduate school," he said. "In philosophy."

"Is that what you studied before?" I asked. "You know, undergrad?"

"Yeah," he said. "But I don't see the point."

"You don't like it?" I tilted my head to the side, put on my good-listener face.

"Oh, I like studying it. I mean, I read all the time. But the only reason to go to grad school in it would be to become a professor."

"And you don't want to be a professor?" I pictured Peter onstage, when he tossed his head back and screamed, threw himself on the floor and played the guitar upside down. I tried to imagine him in a turtleneck, teaching a class in the haughty tone of voice Clay had always used. I just couldn't see it.

"No. I mean, maybe I'm not ambitious, but I'm happy with my life. I have a great girlfriend, an apartment without roaches, and people actually pay to hear me play. I know it's not high art, but I'm having fun. Why would I want to change anything?"

It was then that I knew Peter and I were more alike than I'd ever imagined.

"I know how you feel," I said. "Jamie's always worrying about us making it, always thinking on the future, and I'm just having a good time now."

Peter nodded. "But it's good that he takes it seriously," he said. "You need someone like that in a band. None of us really takes Chutes and Ladders seriously, and I'm proud to say it shows."

I laughed and rubbed some salt from the rim of my margarita glass, licked it off my finger. I watched Peter watch me do this. Before I could think up my next move, two girls came up to us, looking slightly nervous. I was sure they were after Peter, and thought I'd enjoy watching this.

"We love your music," one of them said, looking at me instead of Peter in her nerve-wracked state. She was clearly an amateur.

I was surprised when Peter didn't answer, and I glanced at him, but he was looking at me.

"We saw you last week at the Khyber," the girl went on. I didn't know if Chutes and Ladders had played the Khyber Pass last week, but I knew that Jamie and I had.

"Oh," I said, my surprise registering in my voice. "Thank you! I didn't know you were talking to me."

"The sound you get from two guitars is amazing," the second girl said. We were still hearing variations on that phrase, two years after Kirsten's first column about us had come out.

"You have such a great voice," the first girl said.

"Thanks," I said. I'd been taking compliments on my voice since I was little, but still never knew quite how to answer.

"That guy you play with is gorgeous," the second girl said. "Is he your boyfriend?" This caused Peter to nearly snort a mouthful of margarita back into his glass, but he didn't say anything. The first girl gave her friend a dirty look.

"We just wanted you to know how much we like you," she said, and started off, pulling her friend by the arm.

"Thank you," I called after them.

Peter looked at me. "Where is your gorgeous boyfriend tonight, Miri?" he asked in a high-pitched voice similar to the girl's.

"I don't know why people always assume that," I said.

Peter tapped his fingers on the table. I loved watching his fingers move. "It's because you guys are so intense onstage," he said. "You have a real rapport. Most people assume you have to be sleeping with someone to have that."

I was thinking right then that Peter and I could have a real rapport. "I don't seem to be able to find both in the same person," I said. "And when I do, the person is attached."

Peter's face reddened a bit, but whether it was from the margarita or what I'd said, I couldn't really tell. I chewed on the lime slice they'd attached to the glass.

"Did it bother you," I asked, "that those girls were talking to me and not you? I mean, you guys are bigger than we are." Chutes and Ladders had just released an album on a small, local label. They'd even had a tiny write-up with their picture in *Spin*, the four of them standing on Locust Walk with their arms folded and serious rock-star looks on their faces. They'd gotten teased for that picture by just about everyone in Philly who saw it. People told them they needed to do a cross-country tour, but rumor had it that Peter didn't want to leave Annie for that long.

He smiled. "Nah," he said. "Like I told you, I don't take any of this too seriously."

There was something about the way the light hit his face just then, his expression when he smiled, how his eyes took me in, that made me certain he was thinking about me too. I'd have to be patient; he was not like most guys, not the kind I could get with a glance or a 100-watt smile or by sticking my chest out. I'd have to work on him little by little, piece by piece, like a song that won't quite come together. Eventually, I knew, I'd stumble upon the right combination of notes, and Annie would stumble upon the wrong ones, and Peter would be mine.

Chapter 29
December, 1987

Sean Hunter gave us the runaround for more than a month, saying he'd show up at gigs and then canceling at the last minute. Jamie became such a nervous wreck thinking Sean might turn up unannounced one night that he was sometimes barely able to play; he made sloppy mistakes I'd never heard from him before. Finally Sean called Kirsten and said he would be in New York the first week in December, that he would definitely come down to Philly for a show at the Big Bang.

Jamie made us get to the club so early that nobody was there except for a couple of the regulars. I spent the next hour sipping coffee and flirting with Loretta's new bartender, who had an armful of blue tattoos and played upright bass in a rockabilly band, while Jamie went to pee about fifteen times. Rick finally showed up, with two guys he knew from school, all of them getting in on fake IDs. I looked at the photo on Rick's ID, and the age it said he was—twenty-two—and had to laugh. He had just turned nineteen. I took a good look at him and realized that he did look a bit older. His skin was finally starting to clear up, and he'd taken my advice and begun to let his hair grow. It was still in an awkward in-between stage, but had gotten to the point where it was more Peter Frampton than Greg Brady. In a few years, I thought, Rick might actually be good-looking.

Kirsten showed up, and got Jamie in a corner where she wouldn't let him go.

"Maybe I should go rescue Jamie," I said to Rick. One of his friends was smiling at me, but seemed too shy to say anything. I gave him a little look out of the corner of my eye, and he blushed and turned away.

"From what?" Rick took a sip of beer.

"From Kirsten."

Rick glanced over to where they were sitting. "Actually, I think she's calmed him down."

Sometimes I felt like people took Kirsten's side just to piss me off. "I doubt it," I said.

"Miri, I don't know why you don't like her. If it weren't for her, Sean Hunter wouldn't even be coming tonight."

That was exactly why I didn't like her; she did things like that, helped us out with coverage, got us a gig here or there, gave our tape to someone who might "discover" us, but she didn't do it out of the goodness of her heart. She did it because she liked Jamie, she liked hanging around bands. If she'd been prettier, she would have been a groupie. I didn't like being forced to feel gratitude toward someone like that.

"Yeah, it's all Kirsten's doing," I said. "It's not like me and Jamie actually play good music or anything."

Rick gave me a hard look. "You know you do. I don't have to tell you that."

It used to be that Rick looked up to me, seemed to hang on my every word. But after that fight about Jamie last fall, the spell was somehow broken; now Rick enjoyed disagreeing with me whenever he could, and Jamie, who had once freaked him out, was the person he most admired. I didn't like this turn of events one bit.

Before I could think up something to say back to Rick, Peter walked in, which pleased me no end until I saw Annie behind him. This night was not going at all the way I wanted. I got up and walked out the door without saying a word to anyone.

I wandered down South Street, wondering how I could feel so alone in a bar full of people who were supposed to be my friends. Hadn't I just been telling Peter how much I liked my life, how much fun I was having? We were about to play for a well-known musician who might help our career, and there was a barful of boys ripe for the picking. But the only one there who I really wanted was with his girlfriend, and the ones who were supposed to be my best friends were slipping out of my reach. I crossed the street and sat down on some concrete stairs, and was surprised to feel tears stinging my eyes.

It hit me, as it sometimes did, that maybe this wasn't supposed to be my life at all. I'd wound up in Philly purely by accident; Ian could have ditched me anywhere along the road. If we'd fought days earlier, I could have ended up in Cincinnati, or Pittsburgh. I wondered if the life I was supposed to live was really in one of those cities, or if it was back in Texas—in Austin, or Prairie Rose. I pictured Juan, eating dinner in the prison cafeteria; and Wendell, out for a night with Guy at the Silver Moon Inn. And Annmarie, wherever she might be in that big pink car, driving away.

I sat there for a good while, knowing I should go back in but unable to move my legs. After a time I looked up and saw Jamie crossing the street, heading over to me.

He sat down on the steps, poked me with his elbow.

"What's going on?" he asked.

"Everything's changing," was all I could get out, and I started to cry again.

He put an arm around me, kissed the top of my head. "Are you scared?"

"I guess so." I knew he was talking about the show, about Sean Hunter; but I didn't know how to begin to explain the things I was really afraid of.

He rubbed my back with his hand. "Me too," he said. "I'm afraid I won't be able to get through our set without having to pee."

"I want things to always be the same with us," I said, choking out the words. Jamie laid his head on my shoulder. "Nothing stays the same," he said after a long pause. "But we'll always be there for each other. I know that."

"You sure?" I asked.

"Yeah. Even when we're famous." He laughed, a high nervous chuckle.

"I'm sorry," I said. "I just kind of freaked out for a minute." I wiped my eyes with the back of my wrist. Jamie handed me a tissue.

"Come on," he said. "We'd better get in there."

We walked down the street, arm-in-arm like we sometimes did, and I started to feel better with each step we took toward the club. From half a block away we could hear Laura McMartin, the opening act. She managed to sing an entire Joni Mitchell song off-key. We stood outside and marveled at how bad she sounded, and I wondered aloud to Jamie if Loretta had put her opening for us just to make us sound that much better in comparison. As we were getting ready to head inside, two men turned the corner. One of them was Sean Hunter.

He looked even better than he had on his album covers. He was wearing jeans and a black t-shirt, black shoes, and a leather jacket that was both hip and respectable at the same time. His brown hair was pulled back into a messy ponytail, a few strands falling around his face. His eyes were dark and mysterious. Someone like him could make me forget all about Peter, I thought.

Jamie and I both just stared as he came up to us. Whether Jamie was starstruck, or as taken with Sean's looks as I was, or a combination of both I couldn't tell. Sean had no idea who we were, and smiled at us, then started into the bar.

"Sean," I finally said, regaining my voice. "I'm Miri. This is Jamie." When he continued to smile with a blank look on his face, I added, "We're Cloud Cuckoo Land."

He relaxed then, shook both our hands, and introduced us to the other guy, a producer who he was working with on a record in New York. We talked outside for a while, none of us anxious to go in and hear Laura McMartin face-to-face. I had to do most of the talking, as Jamie remained unable to speak.

"So how long have you two been playing together?" Sean asked us both.

I waited a second to see if Jamie would respond. He didn't.

"About three years," I said, and Jamie managed to nod in agreement, his eyes still fixed on Sean. "We got together toward the end of '84, and played our first gig a year later."

Sean smiled. "And you write together?"

Once again I waited for Jamie to answer, but he seemed to have left his body for a spell. "Pretty much," I said. "Sometimes we write songs separately, but when we play them for each other we wind up working on them together."

I kept waiting for Jamie to jump in the conversation; normally he liked nothing more than to talk about the band, but he was unable to pull himself together. Finally it was time for us to go in and get ready, and we left Sean and the other guy, whose name I forgot as soon as Sean said it, at a table near the stage that Kirsten and Rick had saved for him.

Rick was handling the sound. He'd turned out to be a whiz at anything mechanical, and had started working with us out of gratitude to Jamie, I think, for helping him get his college forms together. He certainly wasn't doing it for the money, since we didn't make enough ourselves to pay him much of anything. He came backstage—which was really an area next to the stage that Loretta had curtained off—to check some wiring, and told us how excited everyone in the club was. Jamie looked as green as Mrs. Sprague had the day she fainted during that Easter play way back when.

"Jamie," I asked, "are you gonna be okay?"

He nodded.

"You want a beer?" Rick asked.

Jamie shook his head.

"Are you gonna be able to play?" I asked him after Rick had left.

Jamie looked at me. "I think so," he said. I decided the longer we delayed, the worse it would get, so I handed him his guitar, picked up mine, and guided Jamie onto the stage.

Kirsten's column the next week claimed it was not only the best show of ours she had ever seen, it was one of the three best rock concerts she'd seen in her lifetime. The other two were a Talking Heads show she'd snuck her way into when she was in high school in 1979, and R.E.M. opening for U2 in London in 1985. She even compared us to McCartney and Lennon as songwriters. It made me laugh, reading that stuff, but the funny thing was that other people actually seemed to believe it.

One of the converted was none other than Sean Hunter. He'd looked mesmerized during our whole performance; I tried to catch his eye a couple of times during the show, but he seemed transported, the same dreamy look on his face that Jamie had on his. This should have told me something right then and there, but I was too busy playing to really think on it. It wasn't until after the show, when I was turning my best smiles on Sean and getting no response, draping myself across the bar in the tight-fitting dress I'd bought for the occasion and attracting every other guy in the club except Sean, that it finally hit me.

Jamie and Sean were looking at each other.

325

They were sitting at two corner stools, talking, the right amount of distance between them for two men having a casual conversation, two musicians talking about the club scene, recording contracts, favorite types of guitars. It would have been easy to miss the way their hands moved, in subtle refined gestures that spoke the same language; or the glances and sparks moving back and forth between them. Finally, I thought, Jamie's getting lucky.

I might have been disappointed for myself, had it not been for the fact that my efforts to attract Sean really had caught the eye of just about every other guy in the bar. Five men stood around me trying to buy me drinks, and Bill was giving me the signal that he wanted me to go home with him. Peter paid enough notice that Annie's face became pinched and red. It was shaping up to be a good night in Cloud Cuckoo Land.

I didn't get back to Jamie's until 10:00 the next morning. He was in the kitchen, in his bathrobe, starting a pot of coffee.

"Are we alone?" I asked.

"No," he said, a sly little smile on his face.

"You dog," I said. "Hot damn."

Jamie laughed.

"Was he good?"

"Miri," he said, his cheeks getting pink. He pulled two mugs from the cabinet.

"You've asked me that before," I said.

"I don't have to ask, you volunteer."

"True." I slumped in a chair and kicked my shoes off. "Are you happy, Jamie?"

"Yes." He was beaming. I hadn't seen him look like that in a long, long time.

The coffee began to drip into the pot. "Were you terribly disappointed, Miri?" he asked softly. "I know you kind of liked him too."

"It's okay," I said. "I had my pick of the rest of the bar."

"So I noticed." Jamie laughed. "Who'd you end up going home with, anyway?"

"The bartender."

"Really? I wouldn't have guessed him." Jamie put milk and sugar on the table.

"I wanted to see the rest of his tattoos," I said.

Jamie smiled and poured the coffee, handed me a mug. We sat and sipped in silence for a minute.

"Does Sean have any tattoos?" I asked. "Dimples? Special freckles?" Jamie threw a dish towel at me.

Sean and Jamie spent that day together. I had to work in the afternoon, just a few hours, and we'd all agreed to meet for dinner. Sean wanted to talk to us both before he left, and he had to catch a train back to New York that night.

I walked into the restaurant and found the two of them there, looking so happy gazing at each other across the table that I hated interrupting. I stood back for a minute and just watched, and it hit me then how different Jamie and Clay had been, what different types of people they were. Jamie and Sean were the same kind; they liked the same music, dressed in the same calculatedly casual way, had the same shy sweet smiles. They were made for each other.

I headed over to the table; Jamie grinned at me and scooted over in the booth.

"How was work?" Sean asked.

"Boring as usual," I said, unwinding my scarf from my neck as I plopped down next to Jamie.

"It's a great used record store," Jamie said. "They have a good selection of both indie stuff and blues."

"It's mostly twelve-year-old skatepunks who hang out there," I said. "They all want to be Henry Rollins."

Sean laughed. "I bet you keep them in line, Miri," he said. His fingers brushed Jamie's on the tabletop.

"I do my best," I said, "but it's not an easy job."

"They're all in love with her," Jamie said. "She has a cult following among young boys."

"I'm not the only one," I said, and Jamie and Sean both smiled.

During the course of dinner, Sean made two proposals that nearly knocked me under the table: he wanted to help us cut a better-quality demo that we could shop around to record labels, and he wanted us to open on part of the Lost Generation's tour the following spring.

"You're kidding," Jamie said.

"We usually give the opening slot to a few different bands we like, changing from region to region," Sean said. "We already have bands for the West and the Midwest, and the band I'm helping produce in New York is opening in the Northeast. But we don't have anyone for the Southeast leg." He took a sip of water. "It'll be about a month, from Maryland down the coast over to Louisiana and Texas."

Jamie and I were both in too much shock to say anything.

"Can you do it?" he asked.

We looked at each other in amazement. "You bet," Jamie said.

After we finished dinner, I told them I was heading over to Rick's, to let him in on the good news; it was partly an excuse to give Jamie and Sean some privacy, so they could say goodbye, though I expected Rick would be excited for us.

He was living in a dorm for international students that was open year-round, even summers and holidays. One of his campus jobs—he had two—involved taking care of this dorm. It had worked out well for him, the whole college thing. I found him in his room, books and papers and a T-square and pencils spread out on his desk.

"Hey," I said, leaning in the doorway. "Whatcha doin'?"

Rick looked up, and smiled when he saw me. "Miri," he said. He got up and pulled a chair over for me to sit down.

"Are you busy?" I asked.

"Well, finals are coming up, and I have six classes this semester. I'm trying to finish school in two and a half years—did I tell you that?"

I shook my head.

"But I think I can talk for a few minutes," he added. I expected him to laugh and say he was kidding, but he didn't. Rick had become so serious, so driven, I felt I hardly knew him. He took a Coke from a little cube-sized refrigerator, offered me one. I waved it away.

"You could graduate that fast?" I asked.

"Well, they took most of my credits from the community college," he said. "So it would be more like finishing in three years." He spoke with hardly a stutter these days. I wondered if this could even be the same boy I'd scammed with on South Street, washed up with in the library, crashed with in that horrible rowhouse.

"What are you drawing?" I asked, looking at the papers.

"It's for an architecture class," he said.

I looked at the building he was drawing; it was an apartment complex, from what I could tell. There were numbers and symbols written here and there, as meaningless to me as the French newspapers Clay used to sometimes read.

"I thought you were gonna study physics," I said.

Rick shook his head. "I changed my mind. Physics was too abstract. I'd rather make something concrete, something people can use, you know?"

"I think so," I said. I studied the drawing, the detailed lines. "This is really good, Rick. I never even knew you could draw."

"Thanks." He smiled then, and gave me the kind of look he used to give me; a look that said we were the same, that we'd come from the same place. I hadn't seen that look from him in a long time. Nothing had been the same since we'd had that fight last year.

"Rick," I said, "I'm sorry about what I said last fall. You know, the whole thing about Jamie. I just couldn't believe you'd feel that way, was all."

He got a pained look on his face. "I don't feel that way anymore."

"So what changed your mind?" I was still curious about how he and Jamie had worked things out.

Rick put his Coke down on a piece of scrap paper. He looked uncomfortable.

"I just figured some stuff out," he said softly.

"About Jamie?"

"No," he said. "About me."

I pulled my hair behind my head, tied it in a loose knot. "What kind of stuff?"

"Just stuff." He stood up and started shuffling papers around.

It hit me that I'd never seen Rick with a girl. He'd always been so young that I hadn't given it much thought before; but I realized just then that he was nineteen, and had never seemed to have a girlfriend.

"Are you gay?" I asked. It just sort of popped out.

He had a look on his face like I'd slapped him. "Jesus Christ, Miri," he said. "No. I'm not gay." He paced over to the sink, glared at me. "Fuck," he said.

"Well, it's not an insult," I said. "I thought you said you were okay with it now."

Rick simmered from across the room, like a teakettle about to boil.

"Look, I'm sorry," I said. "I was just asking, that's all. I mean, I don't care if you are or aren't." I thought this would relax him, but he just looked more angry.

"What did you come here for?" he asked, his stutter starting up a bit.

I'd forgotten, in all this, the big news. I gave him the lowdown on what Sean had offered us, leaving out the part about how he and Jamie had hit it off. I wasn't sure but that it might make Rick fly off the handle again.

"That's great," he said. "Congratulations." He said it without feeling, like you might say it to someone who just beat you out for a part in the school play.

"Rick, I didn't come over here to fight with you. I don't know why we can't talk anymore." I walked across the room, stood in front of him. "I miss you," I said. "I miss the way we used to be."

He got a soft look in his eyes like he felt the same way, but he folded his arms across his chest and stood there silent for a good long while.

"I just think we're real different people now," he said. His lower lip was trembling. I tried to think of something to say, and when I couldn't I turned around and saw myself out.

Jamie came home from the train station with a bottle of champagne. I took a glass but was no longer in the mood for a celebration. When he asked me what was wrong, I told him about my talk with Rick.

He closed his eyes as he listened to me, sipped at the champagne.

"Go easy on him," he said.

I stretched out on the couch, my feet touching Jamie's thighs. "Why should I?"

Jamie looked like he was about to say something, then stopped. He took another sip of champagne. "How would you feel," he said finally, "if Peter Fenster asked you if you were gay?"

I laughed at the idea; it took a few seconds for Jamie's meaning to sink in.

"Don't tell me you're thinking Rick is in love with me?" I asked.

"Miri," he said, refilling my glass, "all the boys are in love with you. You should know that by now."

"Come on," I said. "Did he tell you he was in love with me?"

He sighed. "Not in so many words. But it's obvious."

I drew my legs toward me, sat up straight. "I think I'd know if Rick was in love with me. In case you hadn't noticed, I'm pretty good at picking up on things like that."

He smiled. "Not always."

"Come on, Jamie. Rick and I were like brother and sister."

He shrugged. "But you're not," he said.

I had no idea what was making Jamie think this, but the topic was starting to grate on my nerves. "How did you leave things with Sean?" I asked.

Jamie laughed. "Ah, changing the subject." He settled back against the couch. "We're getting together in New York this week. Tomorrow, actually."

"Really? Jamie, that's so great." I kicked his side lightly with my foot. "I think he's right for you."

Jamie smiled. "You know," he said, "I do, too." He sipped his champagne, still smiling.

I finished what was in my glass. "I never thought you'd be the one to help us sleep our way to the top," I said. "I always thought it would be me."

He threw a pillow at me. "That's not what I'm doing." He was quiet for a minute. "God, you don't think Sean thinks that, do you?"

I was just a little bit sick of everyone misunderstanding me that night. "Jamie," I said, "I was kidding." I got up and put my glass in the sink.

"I know," he called out to the kitchen. "I'm just wired because we may be about to be discovered, and I may be in love."

I walked back in and messed up his hair, which I loved doing. Jamie's hair was so soft and thick. "Last night was maybe the best night of my whole life," he said, looking up at me, and, after looking like an old man for so much of the past two years, he startled me by how much, at that moment, he looked like a child.

CHAPTER 30
JUNE–JULY, 1988

I was shuffling around the apartment in my bathrobe, waiting for Jamie to come back from the corner store. It was a Saturday morning, and our ritual was to watch *Pee Wee's Playhouse* and drink our endless pots of coffee on Saturday mornings, but we'd awakened to find no coffee in the house. After a brief argument over who had made the coffee yesterday and who had gone to the store the last time we were out of something, Jamie finally pulled on some clothes and went out, grumbling to himself as he slammed the door. I figured he'd be over it by the time he got back.

I passed a mirror, and caught a sight that could have raised Grandma from her grave: my hair, matted and dirty and sticking in five different directions; my face, pale as paper, mascara from the night before still caked beneath my eyes. A picture of me on an album cover looking the way I did first thing in the morning would surely scare off anyone thinking on buying our record; of course, the way things were going it didn't look like we'd ever get our record out at all.

We had recorded an album that winter, for Spin This! Records, a small independent label who signed us thanks to Sean's urging. After Jamie went around with the legal aspects of it—one of his Boston friends, Roger, was a lawyer, and after reading the papers he told Jamie to rebargain for some kind of change of royalties—we'd gone up to Minneapolis in February to record, with Sean producing.

Any illusions I might have had about recording an album being glamorous were nipped in the bud when we made ours. The studio itself was in about as seedy an area as I'd seen since I'd lived on the streets; on top of that, we had to record at night to keep the studio costs low. We were then so tired during the day that we did nothing but sleep. Not that I would have wanted to go outside other than to head over to the studio, anyway; Minneapolis in February was so cold it made Philly feel like Texas.

And then there were the endless takes, pieces of the same song done over and over, while Jamie and Sean argued about whether we'd gotten it right on the third or fourth or fifteenth try. Some of their arguments seemed to be true differences about the music, while others, I decided, were just extensions of their relationship. It was the first big chunk of time they'd been able to spend together since they'd met, and Jamie was nervous and insecure about the whole thing; I got the feeling he came across to Sean as a little too needy. Sean was a busy guy; he was remixing the Lost Generation's new album, and had produced another band before we went up there to work on our record. Jamie knew all this, but still he was often sulky and moody in the studio, his state of mind dependent on how the day had gone with Sean. To relieve the stress, I took to sleeping with the Lost Generation's keyboard player, Doug, who came in to work on a couple of tracks for us.

Despite all of these doings we got the album recorded, a mix of the best songs from our demo, stuff we'd written since then, and a new song we came up with right in the studio. Sean was going to mix it and was trying to hurry the record through so it might be out by the time we went on the Lost Generation's tour, which had been pushed back to the summer because Sean was remixing their album and because the band's drummer, Doug had told me, was in rehab.

Two months after we finished recording, we got word that the label was in some kind of financial trouble. There were legal terms thrown around that I didn't understand, but the upshot was that our album was caught in a stranglehold, and it wasn't clear if it would ever come out. Sean was mad as hell; he remixed our demo so we'd have something, at least, to send out to radio stations in the cities we were hitting on our tour. I was disappointed, but not as bad as Jamie was. The whole thing sent him into a funk, the likes of which I hadn't seen since Clay left. He seemed to blame Sean, too, for not knowing that the label was about to go under, and this put an added strain on their relationship, which was strained enough being long-distance and all.

It was now June, the tour just a few weeks away, and I wasn't looking forward to it, though I had reasons beyond what all was happening between Jamie and Sean. I'd put out of mind, at first, what Sean had said about our leg of the tour ending in Texas; but when we got the list of cities we'd be playing and I saw those names in black and white—Houston, Austin—I was filled with a kind of dread I hadn't felt in years. Try as I might I could not imagine setting foot in Texas, and I fantasized about bailing out on the tour somewhere in Louisiana, letting Jamie play the Texas dates by himself and then hooking back up with him later. But I never told Jamie about my fears.

The cats broke me out of my thoughts with their cries for food; they were so spoiled by then they expected breakfast the second either Jamie or I got up, and would sometimes swat us in the ankles if we didn't obey. I was pouring the little yellow pellets into their bowls, wondering how a couple of raggedy street cats could get to be so full of themselves, when the sharp howl of the door buzzer nearly knocked me out of my slippers. I figured Jamie had forgotten his keys, so I buzzed him in without asking who it was.

I was none too pleased, then, to hear a knock on the door, and to see Kirsten's face bloated in the peephole.

I opened the door and motioned with a tilt of my head for her to come in.

"Sorry," she said, just to remind me of how bad I looked. She was wearing jeans and a Keith Haring t-shirt. I figured she bought this shirt just for Jamie's benefit.

"Jamie went out to get coffee," I said. "He'll be back in a minute."

She sat on the couch without being invited. "I have some news," she said.

"Yeah?" I thought it might be about the tour, since Kirsten had become, more or less, our publicist. She worked every connection she had, sending out press kits she'd put together to anyone who showed a flicker of interest. She did this all for free, and it just added more layers of gratitude I was supposed to feel for her, which for me translated into greater waves of resentment.

"Chutes and Ladders broke up," she said.

Now this was news that caught my attention. I perched on the arm of the sofa, facing her. "Are you sure?" I asked. "I thought they were still on the road." They'd had a new album come out in February, and had left in May for a cross-country tour of small clubs. From what we'd been hearing they were getting good airplay on college stations all over, and had a major label interested in signing them. Jamie had been hoping we'd be in the same position after our album came out, though he'd stopped talking about it after the legal hassles began.

"I ran into Peter's brother at the diner this morning," she said. "He said Peter called Annie from a bus station in Lawrence, Kansas, a couple of days ago and said he'd quit the band, and was on his way home."

I slid from the arm to the couch itself, and took a minute to digest this news. "Shit," I said. "Why would he quit now?"

Kirsten shook her head. "I don't know. They were really close to getting signed. Their video even got played on MTV a couple of times. I mean, at like 3:00 in the morning, but still."

With that Jamie walked in, and we filled him in while he made the coffee.

"Maybe Peter just got sick of being on the road," he said. "Maybe they'll get back together once they all come home."

"I don't know," Kirsten said. "If what his brother said is right, he just walked out on the tour. The other guys are going to have a hard time forgiving that."

Jamie got out three mugs and poured Kirsten a cup without asking if she wanted one. Damn, I thought, we'll never get rid of her now. I was dying to call Peter's house and see if he was there, but I didn't want to talk if Annie answered.

"So how are things with the new man?" Jamie asked Kirsten. She tossed her head in a way designed to make her hair fall over her face. She was doing a better job with the red dye these days, I noticed. She had also lost weight. I wondered if this had happened before or after the new man.

"Great," she said, sounding for all the world like Tony the Tiger from the old Frosted Flakes commercials. "You have to meet him. He's wonderful."

Jamie smiled. "I'm so glad you finally met someone nice, Kirsten."

"What else did Peter's brother say?" I shot in. I had no desire to hear about Kirsten's sex life, but I did want to get all the scoop on Chutes and Ladders.

Jamie scowled at me.

"Peter's supposed to be home sometime tonight," Kirsten said. "That's all I know."

"So tell me more about the man—what's his name again?" Jamie asked her.

I sighed, poured myself more coffee, and, realizing we would not be watching *Pee-Wee's Playhouse* that morning, headed for the shower.

That night, I went on a mission. After calling Peter's house, hearing Annie's voice and hanging up without saying anything, I decided to go for a little walk in the West Philly neighborhood where I knew they lived. Since I needed a cover, I would take Rick with me.

Things had finally improved between us, me and Rick. He still didn't have a girlfriend, and I certainly didn't believe what Jamie had said about him being in love with me; I was sure he thought of me as an older sister, and this was why I irritated him at times. Jamie and I had convinced him to skip the second summer session at school so he could tour with us; though he did help out with equipment and sound, what we really needed him for was to split the driving with Jamie. I'd never gotten my license, and even though Jamie had vowed to teach me before we went on the road, the few attempts we'd made that spring were near disastrous. We'd gone to a cemetery in Chestnut Hill, Jamie thinking that this would be a way for me to practice turning and stopping without any traffic. I nearly took out two headstones, and once almost mowed down an elderly man who dropped the flowers he'd been carrying as he scurried out of my path.

Rick was in his room, studying as always. He had turned into a total egghead, and needed me around to loosen him up.

"Let's go to LeBus for coffee," I said. It was close to where Rick lived; more importantly, I'd run into Peter there before.

Rick shook his head without looking away from his book. "I have a bunch of exams coming up."

"But don't you need a break? Wouldn't coffee help?" I reached in front of him and closed the book.

"Miri," he grumbled, "now I've lost my place."

"Just an hour," I said. "A break'll be good for you." I gave him my "pretty-please" smile.

He closed his eyes and tried to frown, but the corners of his mouth turned upward a bit. "Okay," he said. "But just one hour. I have a lot more work to do."

I kept Rick out for three hours that night, but we never did find Peter. Two weeks later, Jamie ran into Brian, Chutes and Ladders' drummer. He told Jamie they were planning on auditioning a new lead singer and guitarist, and Jamie said it was pretty clear from his tone of voice that not a one of them was speaking to Peter. I got Jamie to leave a message at Peter and Annie's telling him to call either one of us if he felt like talking, but we didn't hear from him, not a word.

In mid-July, three days before Jamie and Rick and I were to leave on the tour, I saw Peter sitting in Rittenhouse Square park, feeding the pigeons. It had been my last day of work at the Whirling Dervish; Paul, the owner, had thrown a party for me, complete with a fake Cloud Cuckoo Land album cover and a big record-shaped cake. I kept telling people that our album was never coming out, but no one seemed to believe me. A couple of the skatepunk boys came in and asked me if they could kiss me goodbye. I reminded everyone that I was only going for a month, but they all acted like they were never going to see me again. I asked Paul to hold my job for me, and he shook his head and said I wouldn't need it; I didn't know if this was hippie optimism, or his way of telling me he'd already hired someone else.

I was still buzzing from the sugary cake when I stumbled onto Peter. I could tell he saw me, but he didn't look up. I sat down next to him, took a handful of popcorn from his bag and threw it out to the birds.

"Hey," I said. "Everybody's missed seeing you around town."

Peter shook his head. "More like everybody's sorry I came back to town."

"Well, I've missed you."

"You may be the only one." His voice sounded flat and distant, like something in him had broken.

"What happened, Peter?" I asked.

He sighed, his eyes following a pretty girl who was walking a big Dalmatian. The girl was wearing a short flowered sundress, strappy leather sandals on her feet, her long dark hair pulled back in a ponytail, and I knew I had seen her and that dog around town before. Peter actually seemed to be looking at the dog and not the girl.

"I just couldn't be trapped in that van with those guys for another minute," he said.

"You got sick of being on the road."

He turned and looked at me. "No, Miri, it was more than that. Somewhere in Ohio I looked around at those guys and realized I didn't like any of them. We have nothing in common. I hated their jokes, I hated their stories, I hated the way they drove." He threw some more popcorn out. "I hated smelling their farts." This made me laugh out loud, but Peter didn't look amused, and so I stopped myself.

"I started hating being onstage with them," he went on. "I got to where I just couldn't imagine being trapped with them on another tour, trapped by a record deal." He sighed. "Plus, I missed Annie. So I quit."

I thought over all of what he'd said. "I don't think I could picture doing all of this with Jamie," I said, "if I didn't love him like I do."

Peter nodded. "You'd hate touring with a bunch of asshole guys, Miri," he said, and a brief smile played across his face. "Even though you might think you wouldn't."

I wondered then what Peter thought of me, if he'd seen me go home with too many people and saw me as easy, cheap, not the kind of girl he'd want. The thought churned the sugary cake in my stomach.

"I've met enough assholes to know who I like and who I don't," I said.

Peter nodded. "How old are you now, Miri?"

"Twenty-two in a couple of weeks," I said, and flashed him a devilish grin. "I've been legal for almost a year."

He laughed, but it came out weak and hollow, closer to a cough. "You're so young," he said. "You've got it all in front of you."

He was sounding like an old man of about seventy. "Peter, you know, you're not so old yourself," I said, playfully kicking his foot.

He shook his head. "I'm twenty-nine," he said. "I didn't even start playing guitar until I was older than you." He looked out at the pigeons, who were competing for the popcorn he had thrown into the grass. "I waited too long."

"Well, Jamie's twenty-eight, and he's not old," I said. Peter shrugged, and I added, "You're not old, Peter."

He dumped the rest of the popcorn onto the ground, wadded the bag up in a ball and stuck it in his pocket.

"Do me a favor, Miri," he said.

"Anything."

"Stick with it. If there's anybody I want to see make it, it's you." He got up, gave me a sad half-smile, and shuffled off down Walnut Street.

CHAPTER 31
JULY–AUGUST, 1988

We were headed east on I-64 in Virginia, somewhere between Charlottesville and Richmond. Jamie was driving the van—he'd borrowed it from the remaining members of Chutes and Ladders, who'd lent it gladly since it was pretty clear they weren't going to be using it for some time—and I was in the front seat while Rick napped in the back. The van had 90,000 miles on it, all the hubcaps missing, and so much rust that we were afraid to wash it before we left. Every time we hit a bump, it sounded like the whole bottom might fall out, like we might find ourselves sitting atop a set of moving wheels with nothing around us. I had my doubts about whether this van would make it all the way to Texas; secretly, I hoped it would give out just before the border.

"I'm not sure how things are with Sean," Jamie said. "It feels awkward. Maybe I should stay with you and Rick tonight."

We'd been having this same conversation every day of the past four days since the tour had started. Jamie had been spending the nights with Sean—in the hotels the Lost Generation stayed in, which were much nicer than the places where we usually crashed—but he was constantly in a neurotic frenzy about the whole thing.

"Maybe you should," I said. "You keep saying you feel awkward, but you keep staying with him and then you feel more awkward. It's just gonna get worse and worse." I took a sip of the iced tea I'd bought at the last rest stop.

"But if I tell him I don't want to spend the night, he'll think I'm mad at him." Jamie sighed, glanced in the rear-view mirror. "I never should have gotten involved with someone I'd be working with."

"You didn't know you'd be working with him, at the time," I said.

"But I knew it was a possibility. I should have been more cautious." Jamie took a hand off the steering wheel and rubbed his stomach. "I think I'm getting an ulcer."

"Can't you do some of that Buddhist stuff to calm down?" I asked. "Like, breathe deep or something?" Truth was, aside from the yoga he did every day, Jamie didn't seem like much of a Buddhist to me. Every so often he'd tell me he was going to his room to meditate, but after a few minutes I'd hear him strumming his guitar.

"No," he said. "Nothing works. I have no center. I'm—I'm, I don't even know what I am." He sighed, reached over for the sip of iced tea I'd offered him.

"You're in love," I said.

He looked out at the road for a good long while. "I'm not sure," he said. "When I'm with him, I think I am, but I'm not sure how he feels. When we're apart, I'm not sure how I feel, and then I'm afraid the whole thing's on the verge of a nuclear meltdown."

I rolled down the window to get some air. In the distance above the highway the green hills were dotted with houses and barns, fences, horses. I felt a wave of longing I couldn't quite pin down.

"There's no way you can just put all this out of your mind and enjoy getting laid, is there?" I asked.

Jamie gave me a quick glance.

"I didn't think so," I said.

That night's show in Richmond went well for us, as the shows before it had. The Lost Generation was playing clubs and small theaters in the 1,000- to 3,000-seat range, much bigger places than the bars Jamie and I were used to performing in. We weren't sure at first how our sound would go over in a place that size, but we did our more electric stuff and just sang and played as loud as we could, throwing in cover songs that seemed totally out of character, like Kiss's "Rock and Roll All Night," or our gospel-punk version of the theme song from "The Jeffersons." People would often still be filing in to their seats during our set, but the ones who were there seemed riveted. It probably helped that Sean came out before we played each night and introduced us to the crowd. People would go wild when-ever they'd see Sean, especially the girls. I myself got a real kick out of this, but it seemed to aggravate Jamie. At first, I thought it was jealousy over Sean, but eventually I came to realize Jamie's jealousy was *of* Sean. Jamie hated being the grateful up-and-comer, dependent on Sean's kindness; he wanted to be the one in charge, the guy who could get a band a record deal with a couple of phone calls.

After the show, Jamie and Sean got into an argument backstage, but then, as usual, went to Sean's hotel together, leaving me and Rick to spend the night in a run-down motel. In Baltimore, we'd crashed with friends of Kirsten's, and we had stays with friends of Loretta, Peter, and Bill set up further down the road; but here in Richmond, the cheap motel was our only option. Personally, I didn't mind that Jamie was leaving us there; if we'd been splitting the room three ways, somebody would have had to sleep on a foldaway bed. Jamie was paying most of our expenses for this trip, so I couldn't rightly complain.

The next morning, while I was drying my hair, Jamie and Sean showed up to take us out to breakfast, seeming as happy together as the first night they'd met. There was just no telling what was what with those two, up and down as they were. We found a little diner down the road from the motel; Jamie and Sean sat pasted together in the booth. I watched Rick closely to see if it bothered him, but I couldn't pick up any reaction. Maybe he real-ly had outgrown that foolishness.

"I think I'll ride with you guys down to Virginia Beach," Sean said after we'd finished eating. "If you don't mind." It was clear to look at Jamie that he didn't mind.

"'Course not," I said, and started to bat my eyes at Sean but realized what I was doing and stopped. It was hard, not flirting with Sean. I had to keep reminding myself that he was gay, and he was Jamie's.

"You want to do some of the driving?" Rick asked. He said it kiddingly, Rick did, but I could tell he was already sick of driving, and we hadn't even gotten to the long stretches yet.

Sean smiled. "Well, maybe I will," he said.

The best thing about hanging out with Sean was that he told great sto-ries. He seemed to know just about everyone who'd ever been in a rock band, and to have at least one really funny story about them. I thought once or twice about asking him if he'd ever met Ian Oliver, but I didn't want to open that can of worms. And I was sure I knew better stories about that creep than Sean did.

By Tallahassee, Florida, we were all pretty much ready to kill each other. Jamie was grumbling about the heat, the redneck drivers, and my not having a license; Rick was wondering aloud how we ever talked him into doing this for no money when he could have been two classes closer to graduating. Sean quietly stopped riding with us, even for short stretches, though he and Jamie still spent each night together.

For my part, I was fed up as well. I felt bad about not being able to share the driving, and tried to compensate by entertaining Jamie and Rick. I told funny stories about Prairie Rose, like the time Grandma took me to the Liberty County Fair and very nearly beat the operator of the teacup ride to death with her purse when she saw me about to get sick and he refused to stop the ride; or the time Grandma and I saw Wendell's truck ahead of us in traffic, what looked to be a girl cozying up to him; when we got closer, we saw it was just Duke, his head flopped over on Wendell's shoulder. Grandma thought it was so funny she took to calling Duke "Mrs. Hewlitt" for a spell.

My stories were pretty good through Virginia and the Carolinas, but by Georgia they were sounding forced, and by Florida I'd pretty much given up trying. I'd offer to do something for Jamie or Rick, like pop open a Coke or stick another tape in the cassette deck, and whichever one was driving would complain that my offer wasn't quite what they'd wanted. We drove on Interstate 10 west across the Florida panhandle with hardly a word passing any of our lips. When I looked on the map, I saw the Texas border looming down the highway. I imagined the state could swallow that ribbon of highway like a shish kabob, the smaller states of the Southeast popping down its throat like chunks of the Clacks' beef. I felt vaguely sick with each passing mile.

The only thing still going well was the music. As we made our way along the tour, word seemed to have spread that the Lost Generation's opening act was worth seeing. In Tallahassee, we performed a couple of songs in the studio of a college radio station that had been playing our demo regularly; at that night's Lost Generation show the theater was nearly full when we took the stage. Jamie and I came out and sang on a Lost Generation song during their encore. People in the audience seemed beside themselves— "transported" was the word Jamie used.

After the show that night, Jamie and Sean went right back to the hotel, and Rick went off in our van with the college deejay who'd told us we could crash at his place. I sat by myself backstage, pulling the label off a bottle of beer and feeling like I finally understood exactly why Peter had quit Chutes and Ladders. This touring stuff was fun for about a week, and after that it went right down the hopper. I didn't care where I ended up sleeping that night; at that point, the street seemed as good a place as some college kid's apartment.

One of my big disappointments of the tour had been that Doug, the keyboard player I'd had that thing with when we recorded our album, had a new girlfriend, and she had come along with him. After wasting the first couple of weeks on the hopeless mission of trying to get him away from her, I'd given up and taken to flirting with Chris, the drummer who'd been in rehab last winter. He tended to wander around backstage with a ginger ale and a glum expression; some nights he went back to the hotel by himself immediately after the show. He wasn't cute, exactly, but he had a quality about him that reminded me of Peter.

I was glad to see, on this particular night, that he was still around, and waved him over to where I was sitting.

"Hey, Miri," he said. I made myself look as small and pathetic as possible to gain his sympathy, for I badly needed some. "What's wrong?" he asked, in a kindly way.

I looked him square in the eye. "I'm tired," I said. "I'm tired of Jamie, I'm tired of Rick, I'm tired."

He laughed and sat down next to me. "All four of us toured in a van smaller than yours when we first started," he said. "It's amazing we're all still alive."

"Being on the road wouldn't be so bad if the two of them wouldn't complain about it so damn much," I said. "All they do is complain, and Jamie has this new thing where he likes to buy really bad tapes and force us to listen to them. I mean, he had us listening to the Average White Band yesterday." What I didn't tell Chris was that I had started the whole thing by shoplifting Styx and Foghat from the bargain bin of a music store in South Carolina; I had wanted to give them to Jamie as a joke, but I wasn't going to *pay* for music that bad. I hadn't expected that Jamie would actually make us listen to them, and then start buying more of the worst of the '70s.

Chris laughed. "On one of our first tours, Sean was on this kick with the Clash," he said. "He played 'London Calling' so much we finally had to hide it from him. I mean, it's a great album, but not thirty times in a row."

I laughed and flashed him a medium-watt smile; I didn't have the energy for full voltage, and besides, I didn't think I would need it. Chris was on the shy side, used to Sean and Doug getting most of the attention, and all nerves because he was no longer able to drink or do drugs. I figured this would be pretty easy, and a few hours from now I'd be snoring away in a nice big bed in the Lost Generation's fancy hotel.

"You know," he said, moving closer to me so his leg was almost touching mine, "you could hang out on our bus for a while, if you like." He took a sip of his ginger ale. "I could use the company. I'm not looking forward to our next stop."

"Mobile?" I asked. I was pretty sure that was our next show.

He shook his head. "I guess it's the one after that," he said. "New Orleans. The last time I was there . . . well, it's kind of how I wound up in rehab." He laughed a little, trying to make it a joke.

For my part, I'd been focusing so much on not crossing the border into Texas that I hadn't even thought about New Orleans. Chances were good that Annmarie had gone back there after she'd left me in Sugar Land, all those years ago. I wondered if there was any way I might run into her; I imagined Jamie and I ducking down some seedy alley and seeing her, standing on the street in one of her hooker get-ups.

"Now that you mention it," I said, "I'm not too keen on going there either."

"Yeah? How come?" Chris's face was all open and eager, ready to listen, but I wasn't about to tell him the story of Annmarie.

"It's a long story," I said. "Why don't we go back to the hotel and talk about it?"

He smiled. "Well, okay then," he said, and we both knew there would-n't be much more talking that night.

Chris was sweet and the bed was big and comfortable, but still I slept badly. I dreamed that Annmarie came to our show in New Orleans; she was right in front of the stage, in a tube top and cutoffs two sizes too small, blowing smoke rings into my face. She made me forget what I was playing and Jamie and I had to stop the song; people in the audience shook their heads, saw me for the fraud I was, and began filing out. When I screamed at Annmarie and asked her why she always came back into my life to ruin it when it was going well, she laughed and blew more smoke in my face. I picked up my guitar by its neck and smashed it over her head; she dissolved into wispy fragments that blew away like ashes. I woke up drenched in my own sweat.

But as it turned out, nothing much happened in New Orleans. Annmarie did not turn up at the show, as she had in my dream; and I spent the night with Chris again, as moral support for us both. The next day, Jamie and Rick and I were back in the van, on I-10 West, passing through Metairie, Baton Rouge, and Lafayette as we headed for Texas, for our last two shows on the tour. After Austin, a different band would be opening for the Lost Generation from Dallas westward. We were to drive home through states we hadn't hit on the way down—Oklahoma, Arkansas, Tennessee, Kentucky, Ohio—where we would play clubs Kirsten had booked for us, on the strength of our demo and our having opened for the Lost Generation elsewhere. I hated to admit it but she was good at that kind of stuff, Kirsten was.

To avoid thoughts about where we were headed I dozed off for a spell, and when I woke up I saw a sign for Lake Charles, which made me think of Wendell's cousin, Guy. I wondered if he was still teaching high school, still going out to the Silver Moon with Wendell. They'd both be married by now, I figured. Around these parts folks tended not to wait too long for something better to come along.

Already there were signs for Houston, where we were playing that night. The biscuits and orange juice I'd had for breakfast were turning into a sour ball of dough in my stomach. I saw a sign that said "Last Exit in Louisiana," and a wildfire panic raced through my insides.

"Jamie, take the exit," I said.

"Huh?"

"Please, Jamie, I need to stop." I felt like I was going to be sick.

"It's just about another hour to Houston, I think. Can't you wait?"

"Jamie, goddamit, get us off the fucking highway." I felt sweat dripping down my neck and back.

He glanced over at me. "Are you sick?"

"Yeah."

He cut across two lanes to take the exit. Several cars honked at us, loud.

"Damn," Rick muttered.

We pulled into a truckstop crowded with semis that made our van look like a Matchbox car. I got out and walked around the side of the building, sat on the stoop outside. I felt light-headed, and tried to find something to focus on in the distance, but the bright sun made it near impossible to see. I wondered if I could see Texas from where I was sitting. I wasn't ready to go back there.

When I saw that sign, "Last Exit," I saw my whole life in Texas play out like some say happens in the moments before death: Annmarie, tucking me in bed in a trailer where we lived when I was little; a few years later, me trying to put her to bed when she was drunk; the Clack ranch; the night I found Grandma dead; Wendell, telling me he couldn't take me in; the foster homes, the Ramirezes, and Juan and Austin and all that happened there. I wondered if Juan was still in prison in San Antonio; ten years, he'd been sentenced to, but Ramon had said he might get out sooner.

When I left Texas with Ian Oliver, I hardly noticed crossing the border, and I never looked back. Now I didn't think I could possibly stand returning. I wanted to turn the van around and drive all the way back to Philadelphia, like that night in Boston when Jamie didn't want to go to his parents' house.

"What's up?" I expected it to be Jamie, and was surprised to hear Rick's voice.

"Not much," I said, squinting up at him.

"Not ready to go back to Texas, huh," he said.

I looked at him. "You understand that?"

"Yeah."

Of course he would. Rick was like me in that respect. He knew what running meant, and what it felt like to go back home.

"I don't think I can go," I said. "I mean, I really don't think I can cross the border."

Rick nodded. "That's why you should."

I sat back a bit, gave him a suspicious look.

"Sometimes you need to see what you left," he said, "to put it behind you."

"Have you done that, Rick?" I asked. "Have you put it behind you?"

"I'm trying," he said. "It's not easy."

I bit my lower lip. "What happened to you?" I asked softly. "You never told me."

He was quiet, looking off in the distance. It was so hot everything looked liquid, like the sun was dripping a pale clear yellow. Rick seemed to be bathed in lemony heat.

"Miri," he said finally. "Don't." He kicked at a pebble. "Don't ask me that." He sounded like he was struggling not to stutter.

I figured then that it was time to stop asking, that I would never know the whole story of what had happened to Rick. That maybe it wasn't my place to know.

"I'm sorry I asked you," I said. "I won't ask again."

He nodded, still looking off in the distance.

I got up and took his arm.

"I've missed you, you know," I said. "How close we used to be, I've missed that."

He looked at me out the corner of his eyes.

"Me too," he said. He looked for a second like he was going to say something else, but stopped short.

I saw Jamie walking toward us, a cardboard tray full of cold drinks in his hands.

Impulsively I gave Rick a quick kiss on the cheek, and led him by the arm through the heat and the dust over toward Jamie.

We had two days off between our shows in Houston and Austin. After the Houston show, Jamie and Rick and Sean and I were all talking about what we'd do those two days. The rest of Sean's band was heading for Austin—Chris had already told me this, and asked me to ride with them—and Sean thought it would be a good idea for us to head out there as well.

"We could hit the clubs on 6th Street," Sean said. "There's a lot going on there."

I thought of Juan, and the nights we'd hung out on that street. I thought of busking on Guadalupe Street, the warehouse parties, the basement of the UT dorm. Except for the end, when Juan got busted, most of my memories of Austin were happy ones. My time on the streets there hadn't been nearly as hard as what Rick and I had gone through in Philly, though I wondered if it had just seemed easier because I'd had Juan to rely on.

Jamie startled me by saying, "I think we should go to the town where Miri grew up. It's not that far from here, is it, Miri?"

Sean and Rick both looked at me. Sean looked curious; Rick looked concerned.

"I don't want to go there," I said.

"Why not?" Sean asked. Unless Jamie had told him things about me, far as I knew Sean had no idea of my personal history.

"Bad memories," I said.

"No good ones?" Sean asked.

Good ones. I thought of Guy, coaching me in my singing; Grandma, taking me shopping, telling me stories about when she was little, asking me about school; and Wendell, taking me out for a milkshake, to the beach with him and Duke, taking me in until the day he decided he couldn't raise me by himself. He couldn't have been much older then than Jamie was now. It hit me, for the first time, how much I had been asking of Wendell. Too much, it was.

"Some good ones," I said.

"Let's go tomorrow," Jamie said. "We can just ride through it without stopping, if you want. I just want to see it, after hearing all your stories." What he really meant was that he wanted me to see it.

I was quiet for a few minutes, thinking it all over.

"I have an idea," I finally said. "There's someone I'd like to visit."

PART III

CHAPTER 32
AUGUST, 1988

Prairie Rose is so small that it wasn't even on the map we had. I did find the nearby towns of Liberty and Vidor, and so we just followed the main roads along, hoping I would see something that looked familiar. Rick was driving, Jamie was backseat driving, and Sean had decided to come along with us, too. The rest of the Lost Generation was on the road to Austin.

I was trying to find Sour Lake Road, Grandma's house. I wanted to start there, since I *had* started there—Annmarie and I had lived with Grandma until I was two, when Annmarie turned eighteen and decided she could live her own life with no high school diploma, no skills, and a toddler in tow. We passed streets that looked familiar, but the names didn't register. I was wondering if we were in Prairie Rose or some town on the outskirts, and was ready to tell Rick to give up and point the van toward Austin when I saw something up in the distance, something big and yellow and somehow familiar.

It was a school bus; when we got closer, there was a line of them, three buses in a row on the right-hand side of the street. Behind them was a weed-choked green lawn, and a school that looked like it had seen better days. I recognized it even before I saw the sign: "Sam Houston High School, home of the Fighting Armadillos."

"Holy shit," I said. "That's my high school."

Jamie and Sean turned their heads with interest, like the tourists I'd seen at Independence Park, waiting to take a look at the Liberty Bell.

Rick glanced at the school, and slowed down. "Should I keep going?"

"Yes," I said. I knew I could find everything from the high school: Grandma's house, the Kountry Kitchen on Main Street, the Home Sweet Home Bible Church, and yes—I was sure I could find it—even Wendell's garage.

. . .

The house didn't look so different: still tiny, still weatherbeaten, with spent-looking brown-green grass and two big cactuses in pots beside the front door. Rick asked me if I wanted to stop, but I shook my head no.

The Kountry Kitchen was out of business, the building boarded-up and empty; a McDonald's stood across the street. But the Home Sweet Home Bible Church was there, with a fresh coat of paint and a new sign out front. I wondered if Mrs. Higgins was still directing the chorus, if they were still putting on that ridiculous Easter play with the Christmas song thrown in at the end.

Finally, we came up on Wendell's Garage. I was relieved to see the sign, to know that it was still Wendell's. The building looked greasy and in need of a paint job, as most garages do. We pulled up on the side of the building. Everyone got out, but I told them I wanted to go in first, and they all waited by the van.

I saw two men, one white, one Mexican, working on the underside of a car that was up on a lift. I asked for Wendell, and they both turned and looked at me, then smiled, their eyes moving up and down my body.

"He'll be back in a minute," the Mexican guy said. "You got an appointment?"

"She don't need no appointment," the white guy said, and they both snorted.

I glanced down at the tank top and army cutoffs I was wearing. I couldn't remember getting that kind of treatment in Prairie Rose before; it was the sort of thing I'd expect in Philly. I had to remind myself that I was a girl when I'd lived here, a child.

"I'll wait for him in his office," I said. The men looked surprised but said nothing.

I pushed open the door to Wendell's office. It was just as I'd remembered it: framed auto-course certificates, Wendell's high school baseball trophies, plaques with sayings that were supposed to be funny, but weren't, and clippings from old newspapers pinned to the wall. There was a calendar of antique cars behind the messy desk. I heard a noise under the desk, and felt something brush against my leg.

I jumped back and saw a dog, a German Shepherd whose black patches had faded to a dark gray, crawl out from under the desk. His eyes were cloudy from age, but I could tell right off it was old Duke. I put my hand out for him to sniff. He smelled my fingers for a minute, his eyes far away. He moved out closer to me with obvious effort, his back legs stiff and uncooperative. I sat down on the floor next to him and tried hard not to cry.

I heard the door open behind me. "Can I help you, Ma'am?" I was afraid to look, afraid Wendell would be in as bad shape as the dog.

"I'm just enjoying your dog's company here," I said.

"I'm surprised he's letting you get so friendly," Wendell said. "Old Duke doesn't like too many people."

I got up, turned and looked him square on. He hadn't aged badly at all; in fact, he didn't really look all that much older. He'd lost a little hair around his forehead, his middle section looked a bit thicker than it had before, but basically, he was Wendell.

I noticed something else. I'd heard it in his voice, something light and almost unidentifiable, a vibration or an idea of a sound more than a sound itself. And the way he was looking at me—he was looking the way a man is supposed to look at a pretty girl, without the desire itself actually being in the look.

Wendell was gay. I knew it in an instant, and I thought about him, and Guy, and about twenty puzzle pieces of my life snapped into place at once.

"Wendell," I said, my voice cracking a bit. "It's Miri."

He looked for a second like he didn't understand what I was talking about; then, all at once, a look so full of different emotions that I couldn't begin to pick them all out took over his face. He stared at me with those shifting feelings playing over his face for a good long while.

"Well, look at you," he finally said. "You're all grown up."

We both stood there for a moment, unsure of what to do. Finally I reached out and kind of squeezed his arm, and he reacted by moving closer and patting my back, so lightly I could barely feel it. The awkwardness hung between us like diesel fumes.

"I got some friends outside," I said. "They've heard all about you."

Wendell walked over to the window and looked out at the van, where Sean and Jamie and Rick were all shading their eyes and squinting at the building, trying to figure out what was going down. I had to laugh when I saw that.

"I didn't do right by you, Miri," Wendell said quietly, still looking out the window. "I know I didn't do right by you."

I wasn't sure how to answer that. "You did the best you could," I said, and for the first time in my life I believed it might be true.

After I introduced Wendell to the boys, he insisted that we all come over to his house for dinner later that night. We agreed, but first I had another mission for the afternoon: I wanted to find out what had happened to Juan. Wendell didn't know anything about Juan, of course; I told him all about the band, but he knew very little about my life after I left Prairie Rose, my time on the streets, and, now that I had him right there in front of me, I didn't want to make him feel bad. His regret over not taking me in was written all over his face. I just told him Juan was an old boyfriend I wanted to look up, and Wendell said I could use his office to make calls. He took Jamie, Sean, and Rick on a tour of the garage while I sat down with the phone book.

I started by looking up Ramon, but he was no longer listed anywhere in Liberty County. Jamie had suggested I try calling the prison, but the phone numbers in the book either didn't answer or gave me recordings that didn't help at all. Finally I decided to try the Ramirezes, to see if maybe they had heard anything about Juan.

Mrs. Ramirez answered the phone, and, when she didn't understand what I was saying, I heard another voice, one that sounded like a teenage girl. I guessed they were still taking in foster kids, all these years.

"Hi," I said. I wasn't sure where to begin. I peered out the office window, looking for Jamie; I wanted to put him on the phone and have him ask for me. He was good at things like that, Jamie was. But he was all the way across the garage, pretending to be interested in some greasy gear Wendell was showing them all.

"I lived with Mr. and Mrs. Ramirez a long time ago," I started. "My name is Miri Ortiz."

"Miri?" The girl's voice went up in pitch. "This is Rosa."

I hadn't thought about Rosa or Lupita in years. I remembered Rosa sitting at the dinner table, a girl of about twelve, flicking a forkful of peas at Juan; I could clearly picture the silly faces she'd made at both of us, when it became clear to her that Juan and I were in love. She had to be eighteen or nineteen by now, I figured.

"Rosa!" I said. "Wow. You still living with the Ramirezes?"

"Yes," she said. There was an iciness in her tone, and she made a noise like she was going to say something else, but stopped herself. "They adopted me a few years ago," she added.

"That's great," I said. "They were the best foster home I ever had." Rosa didn't say anything to that, so I cleared my throat and went on. "Listen," I said. "I'm in town just for today, and I really wanted to find out what happened to Juan Quinones. You remember Juan, don't you? He lived with the Ramirezes the same time I did."

Rosa made a small sound, something like a sigh. I waited for her to speak, but she didn't say anything.

"If you could maybe just ask Mrs. Ramirez for me," I said, "ask her if she's heard from Juan . . ."

"Juan's living here now," Rosa cut in.

"What? He's living . . . with the Ramirezes?" I'd thought he'd still be in prison; maybe, with luck, on the verge of getting out.

"He lives nearby," Rosa said. "He works with Papa."

Papa, I remembered, was what Rosa had always called Mr. Ramirez. "Wow," I said. "I—" Rosa cut me off before I could finish.

"Miri, there's something you should know." She was quiet for a second; I heard her breathe in and out. "Juan and I are engaged."

I nearly dropped the phone. "Engaged?"

"Yes." She was quiet again, but now I understood the edge in her voice. She didn't know what I wanted, why I was calling after all this time. She was afraid I wanted Juan back.

"I'm happy for you, Rosa," I said, though it was tough to get out and I could tell myself it didn't sound sincere. I didn't like the thought of Juan engaged to someone else when he'd promised, years before, to marry me. "I really just wanted to find out what happened to him, how he was."

"It took you a while," Rosa snapped, and the anger in her voice took me by surprise. If she was engaged to Juan, he'd probably told her a lot, if not all, about our time in Austin. I wondered if she'd picked up this anger from Juan, if he felt I'd abandoned him or helped get him sent to jail.

"Rosa, the last time I saw Juan, he told me never to come back," I said.

She was quiet for a minute. "Juan was in jail for about a year," she said. "Ramon's lawyer got the conviction overturned. Some legal thing." She took a breath. "When Juan got out, he called Papa, and came back here to apprentice. He's a carpenter now."

Like he was supposed to be, I thought, before he got sidetracked with me. I was sure this was what Rosa and the Ramirezes thought as well.

"That's great," I said. "I'm glad he's doing so good."

"He's at work with Papa," she said, "or I'd put him on the phone." I had a feeling that even if he was there, she wasn't about to hand the phone over.

"When are you getting married?" I asked.

"May 10, 1990," she said, a date two years in the future that she recited proudly. "Juan wants to save up enough money to buy a house before we get married."

This was the life I'd thought, once, that I'd have: a little house in an East Texas town, Juan coming home at night with sawdust on the cuffs of his jeans, sitting down to a meal I'd cooked for him. It wasn't a life I wanted anymore, but I also didn't want to give that life away to someone else, to Rosa. I wanted that life to exist only in my imagination.

"Would you tell the Ramirezes I'm grateful for how nice they were to me?" I asked, knowing there was a good chance she wouldn't tell them I'd called at all.

"Sure," Rosa said.

"And tell Juan—tell him I'm happy for you both." I could hear the sadness in my own voice.

"Do you . . . do you want to come here?" Rosa asked. It wasn't an invitation; she was simply trying to size up the threat.

Part of me wanted to say yes, to force her hand. I wanted to see Juan, see what I felt when I saw him now, years after we'd been in love. But I just couldn't picture it, me going over there with Juan engaged to Rosa now, she and the Ramirezes looking at me as the girl who dragged Juan off and ruined his life.

"No," I finally said. "I just wanted to know he was okay. Goodbye, Rosa."

She mumbled her goodbye in a bewildered voice, and hung up quickly.

I sat there for a good few minutes, trying to digest all that I'd just learned. Duke had flopped by my side, and I scratched his stomach absently, a reflex from years gone by. Finally I got up and walked across the garage to where Wendell was trying his best to entertain my friends with talk of car parts.

"Did you find out anything?" Jamie asked.

"Juan is engaged to a twelve-year-old," I said. "Wendell, any bars around here open this time of day? I need a drink."

Wendell laughed. "The Silver Moon is still downtown," he said, "and it's always open."

CHAPTER 33
AUGUST, 1988

The Silver Moon Inn was your standard honky-tonk, a lot seedier inside than I'd imagined it as a child. Just like you'd find at the Big Bang, there were a couple of regulars at the bar when we turned up; it seemed to me there were a few folks in every town who actually lived on their barstools. Sean and Rick played a game of pool while I filled Jamie in on the conversation I'd had with Rosa.

"I think they all blame me for Juan going to jail," I said, taking a pull on my beer.

"I doubt Juan blames you," Jamie said. "It was his decision to run off with you, to start dealing."

"I know," I said. "It's just that I have this knack for screwing up people's lives."

Jamie laughed. "Well, you haven't screwed up my life. Except maybe for the hour I had to spend today listening to talk about carburetors."

"Sorry 'bout that," I said, and finished off my beer. The bartender put another one in front of me without my asking. I must have looked like I needed it.

"Oh, it's okay," Jamie said. "Wendell's a nice guy." He ran his fingers over the surface of his beer bottle for a minute. "You know, there's something I think maybe I should tell you about him."

"What's that?" I heard the pool balls crack against each other on the table.

"Sean and I think Wendell's gay," Jamie said.

"You think?" I snorted. "I figured that out after talking to him for thirty seconds."

Jamie smiled, shook his head. Before we could say anything else, Sean and Rick came up to us. Sean didn't know much about my past, and I wanted to keep it that way; I didn't like too many people knowing how I'd lived. Jamie sensed this without my having to tell him. He asked Sean and Rick about their pool game, and we listened for a while, ordered another round, finished our drinks, and then headed over to Wendell's for dinner.

I expected Wendell would eat like me and Jamie: mostly at diners or cheap restaurants, once in a while boiling up some spaghetti. I was surprised when we got there to see his refrigerator and cabinets were stocked with food, too much to believe he'd just stopped at Chappy's Market and picked it all up after seeing us earlier. It turned out Wendell could actually cook. He had the fixings for tacos, and I helped him in the kitchen while Jamie, Sean, and Rick sat out in the living room.

"You still not eating meat, Miri?" he asked, chopping lettuce up with a knife.

I nodded, grating cheddar cheese into a bowl. Duke was lying in a corner of the kitchen, not quite asleep, just in his own little world of old age.

"Figured as much," he said. "I picked up some red beans in case. You ever tell them all about the Clack ranch?"

"Jamie and Rick," I said. "I haven't talked to Sean that much."

Wendell chopped the lettuce in silence for a minute. "So what are they all to you, exactly?"

We'd told Wendell about the band, but I knew what he meant. "Jamie's my best friend," I said. "But more than that—he's family. Like a brother, I guess."

Wendell nodded.

"And Sean—" Even though I felt certain Wendell was gay, I wasn't sure how much I should say, especially on the off chance I was wrong. This was, after all, Texas. "Sean is helping us get our start. We're opening for his band."

Wendell put the taco shells on a pan, slid them into the oven.

"And Rick is another friend," I said. "He's helping us out on the road."

I finished grating the cheese and set it down on the counter by the rest of the taco stuff.

Wendell dug a couple of tomatoes and an onion out of the refrigerator. "So he's not your boyfriend," he said after a spell. I figured he was talking about Jamie, and thought maybe it was time to just get it all out in the open, Texas or no.

"Wendell," I said, in as gentle a voice as I could muster up, "Jamie's gay."

He smiled and closed his eyes. "I was talking about Rick," he said.

This took me by surprise. "Why would you think he was my boyfriend, Wendell?" I asked. I couldn't imagine anyone looking less my type than Rick did.

He laughed. "Well, how he feels about you is as plain as the nose on your face. I just couldn't tell how you felt, was all."

I glanced through the kitchen doorway at Rick, who was flipping through an auto mechanics magazine he had found on Wendell's coffee table, while Jamie and Sean talked about how they wanted to see a live armadillo before we left Texas. All we'd seen were dead ones, on the side of the road. It was true that Rick was looking better these days; his hair had finally reached a length where he could pull it back in a ponytail, his face was not as broken out as it once had been, and he seemed a little bit taller every time I turned around. But when I looked at him, all I could see was a kid, a little brother who you love despite how much he bugs you at times. And I couldn't see any evidence that he didn't feel the same way about me.

"Boy, you and Jamie," I said to Wendell. "Two peas in a pod. He's got some idea Rick's in love with me, too. I don't know where y'all are coming up with that."

Wendell opened the canned beans and put them in a pot to heat. "You always was a stubborn one, Miri," he said, and winked at me.

I stirred the beans while Wendell started chopping up the onion.

"Wendell," I finally said, my curiosity overcoming my caution, "whatever happened to Guy?" He looked at me like he didn't know how to answer. I got bolder. "You were a couple, right?"

Wendell had a look of shock on his face, and for a second I thought that maybe I'd made a mistake like I had with Rick that time; though with Rick, I'd never really gotten the feeling he was gay. I was just looking for an explanation for the way he lived. I was half-afraid Wendell was going to explode and kick us all out of the house, and I stood paralyzed next to the kitchen counter for a minute until I heard him say, "You knew that, Miri? You could tell back then?" He sounded like he was in pain.

"No, not then," I said, and he relaxed a bit. "I just figured it out, talking to you now."

He nodded. "People knew. The rumors went around. Still do, once in a while."

"But nobody cared," I said. "I mean, everybody in Prairie Rose loved you, Wendell. Still do, I bet."

He shook his head. "Long as you don't rub their face in it, long as the part of your life that they can see is lived the way they believe it should be, folks around these parts will let you be," he said. "But there's a lot of pretending that goes along with that."

I felt like I knew something about that. Jamie and Sean may have been open around us, their bandmates, their friends, but they weren't exactly out in public. Sean had once been rumored to date a young movie actress, and he'd done nothing to discourage those rumors. In interviews he didn't talk about his personal life.

"So where is he, Wendell?" I asked. "Guy, I mean. Still over in Lake Charles?"

Wendell shook his head. "San Francisco," he said, and I remembered Guy talking about going there, years before. I thought of Clay, too, for San Francisco was where Jamie thought he'd run off to. I imagined the two of them meeting up somewhere, some little bar not unlike the Big Bang: Clay, his nose up in the air, throwing out all his big words to impress everyone; and Guy, using one of his accents to imitate Clay, calling him on his bullshit. The idea of it made me smile.

"He wanted me to go with him," Wendell added.

"Why didn't you?"

He shrugged. "It's hard to understand, I know," he said. He worked his hand over his hair, a gesture that felt both familiar and nostalgic. "That garage is all I have, Miri. Fixing cars is all I know to do. I couldn't see going to a big city and working for someone else, and I never could have made enough selling my garage here to buy one in California. Land's just too expensive out there." He paused. "It may not be a perfect life here, but folks know me. When I came back from Vietnam and soldiers out in California were getting spit on, folks here welcomed me back, told me to hold my head high." He swallowed hard, and I could see his eyes were watery. "Maybe people here aren't as accepting as they could be, but there are other kinds of meanness that go on in cities. I'd rather be somewhere that folks know me."

I had never thought before about what it must be like for someone like Wendell, growing up in a small town. Cities like Philly and Boston, and, by all accounts, San Francisco, were full of gay men—women, too, I guessed. What had I thought, that they were all just automatically born within easy distance of a big city? Most of these people had moved from some little town just like Prairie Rose, a town where they'd felt they had to pretend to be something they weren't. But there had to be lots of others, like Wendell, who were afraid of the unknown, and so they stayed.

"God, Wendell," I said. "I'm sorry."

He smiled. "You sounded like your Momma when you said that just now."

I couldn't believe, knowing how I felt about her, that he would pull something like that out after all these years. "Annmarie never apologized for anything in her life," I said sharply.

He looked like he wanted to say something, then changed his mind. Instead, he picked up two bowls of the taco fixings, set them on the table, and poked his head into the living room. "Supper's ready," he called.

We talked a lot about the band during dinner, Jamie and I trying to explain what our music was like, promising Wendell we'd play him a song after we ate. Sean told a story about an actor he'd met once and had us all nearly crying with laughter; Rick spit part of his taco out, which made us laugh even harder. After dinner Wendell made coffee and we all went out in the living room, which was when the trouble began.

"Miri, I got something I need to tell you," Wendell said. "I don't know if you want to hear this in private, or with your friends around. It's some bad news."

I couldn't imagine what Wendell would have to tell me that could affect my life at this point, and so I just shrugged and told him to go ahead.

"Honey, your Momma's passed on," he said. "She died last year."

It was a surprise, maybe even a shock, but I felt nothing for her; I was dead inside when it came to Annmarie. I glanced around the room; Sean had a sad look of sympathy on his face, while Jamie and Rick both just looked worried, like they had no idea how I'd react. The clock in Wendell's kitchen ticked loudly; the smell of beans and taco meat lingered in the air. I closed my eyes and tried to stir up some kind of emotion, but there was nothing there, just the strangeness of hearing she was gone.

"I didn't know how to tell you, honey," he said. "I'm real sorry."

"I'm not upset," I said, but my voice sounded shakier than I'd expected. "Annmarie's been dead to me for a long time."

Wendell shook his head. "You don't mean that."

I chose to ignore the comment. After the way Annmarie had treated me, neglecting me the whole time she had me and then dumping me on other folks every chance she got, I was expected to feel sadness at her passing. It just wasn't in me. I wondered if people went to hell for not taking care of their kids. I wondered if there even was a hell.

"What did she die from?" I asked.

"Hard living, mostly," Wendell said, then looked off in the distance like he was reflecting on something. "She wound up with some kind of cancer. Some female thing," he muttered.

"That's not too surprising," I said. "The hard living part, I mean."

"I guess she had it for a while before she got sick," Wendell said.

"How'd you hear about it?"

"Oh, I saw her a lot. She came back to Prairie Rose for a spell. Finally she moved in with your Aunt Melissa."

"You've gotta be kidding," I said. I could not imagine Melissa letting Annmarie in her house under the best of circumstances, let alone a dying—and probably raging—Annmarie.

Wendell smiled. "She just moved herself right in there," he said, "and you know how your Aunt Melissa is. She didn't want her there, but she couldn't let the neighbors see her kicking a dying woman out." Wendell shook his head. "She told all her society friends that your Momma was a charity case from her church, then hired a nurse to stay at the big house and moved her whole family out to their vacation place on the Peninsula."

The thought of Annmarie kicking snooty Melissa and my rotten cousins out of their own house made me smile a bit.

"That sounds like such a lonely way to die," Jamie said. Leave it to Jamie to feel sympathy for someone who didn't deserve it.

"I asked her if she wanted me to try to find you," Wendell said. "I thought since you were over eighteen, Child Services might give me some information. But she told me not to look."

"Course not," I said. "She spent her whole life trying to get rid of me. Why would she want you to look for me?"

Wendell shook his head. "She did want to see you," he said. "But she knew she hadn't done right by you, as a mother, and she didn't think it was fair to ask you to forgive her."

"Good thing," I said, "'cause there'd be a snowball's chance in hell of that ever happening." I felt my face getting hot.

"Now, Miri—"

"Goddammit, Wendell!" All at once, I was full of emotion, but not the sorrow Wendell expected of me. Just like the last day I saw Annmarie— that day on Mr. Ortiz's front steps, when I realized the whole thing was just another poorly thought-out scam of hers and not the meeting with my long-lost father I'd been hoping for—anger bubbled up inside me, an anger that turned to rage somewhere deep within my pounding head. It had to burst out of me; there was no way to stop it.

"All her life everybody made excuses for her," I said, aware that I was shouting but unable to quiet my voice down. "She left me over and over and didn't care what happened to me, and I'm supposed to feel sorry for her? I'm supposed to forgive her?" I could feel my whole body shaking.

Wendell remained calm, which infuriated me all the more. "I'm not try-ing to say your Momma did right by you, Miri," he said. "She didn't. But she did love you, even if she didn't know how to show it."

"If you love someone, you don't leave them on a stranger's doorstep, to fend for themselves," I said. Tears stung my eyes. "I wouldn't do that to a cat."

Wendell just looked at me. Everybody in the room just looked at me, like they'd all been paralyzed.

"When somebody has a kid, they're not supposed to expect their mother or their friend or anyone else to take care of that kid," I went on, my words sounding choked, my voice deep but shaky. "It's up to them. It's like a contract, and she didn't live up to her part."

Wendell looked pained, and was quiet for a minute. "Should be that way, Miri," he said. "But when a young girl goes off with some boy and does what he wants, does she know she's signing a contract? I wonder."

I was starting to think that I should have stayed mad at Wendell, as mad as I was when he first told me he couldn't adopt me. He would always take Annmarie's side.

"Wendell, I slept on the fucking streets," I said. "For years." Sean had a look of shock on his face, and I saw him glance at Jamie for confirmation; but Jamie kept his eyes fixed on me, and would not look away. Rick had found something very interesting to examine in the fabric of the armchair where he was sitting.

The expression on Wendell's face was one of horror.

"But you went to a foster home," he said.

"I went to a bunch of foster homes. I had to run away from the last one to save my own life. I lived on the streets in Austin, and then I wound up in Philly and I lived on the streets there until I moved in with Jamie." I was crying so hard I couldn't see. "So don't tell me how poor innocent Annmarie got knocked up and didn't know what she was getting into. I just don't want to hear it."

I barreled out the front door, slamming the screen as hard as I could. I got in the driver's seat of the van and sat there, crying into the steering wheel.

After a few minutes, Jamie came out and sat in the passenger's side, next to me. He put his arm around me, and I buried my head in his shoulder and continued to cry for a few more minutes.

"We can leave, if you want," he whispered in my ear.

I pulled my head away from him. "You think Wendell's right, don't you? Poor Annmarie is dead, and Miri's a horrible person for not feeling sorry."

"Nobody thinks that, Miri." He pulled a tissue from his pocket, handed it to me.

"Wendell does." I wiped my eyes, my nose.

"He doesn't think that," he said. "He's just trying to see Annmarie's side, I guess." He tapped his fingers on the dashboard. "But he's expecting way too much of you. You have a right to feel the way you do." He looked me in the eyes. "I would."

"You would?" I asked, still crying a bit.

"Anybody would. There are some things that can't be forgiven." A thin smile flashed across his face. "That's the agnostic part of my Buddhism."

"Like you can't forgive Clay."

"I wasn't thinking of Clay," Jamie said. "I was thinking of my father."

We hadn't really talked about his father since that night in the van, when we'd rode around Cambridge and Somerville, lost. Whenever Jamie talked about his family, he only mentioned his mother, like she was the only one still alive.

"You mean, for how he made you feel bad about yourself," I said.

Jamie looked out the windshield, into the hot Texas night. "No," he said. "I can't forgive him for letting my sister die."

I looked over at him, a bit confused by what he'd just said. It seemed to me that if his sister wanted to starve herself, there wasn't a whole lot his father could have done about it. "You mean you think he could have done more?" I asked.

"Miri," Jamie said, exasperation clear in his voice, "he's a fucking doctor! And he couldn't see that she was dying until it was too late. My Mom wanted to put her in the hospital months before they did, but he insisted Tory was fine." He pulled another tissue from his pocket, wiped at his own eyes.

I thought about Jamie's father, the silent ghostly presence he'd become, and it hit me that maybe he hadn't always been that way; that maybe Jamie and Mrs. Emerson had made him into that, blaming him for what had happened. That maybe Jamie had rejected his father before he had been rejected himself.

Jamie lay his arm across the dashboard, leaned his head against it, facing me.

"Shit," he said, "where did that come from? I came out here to cheer you up."

I put my hand on his wrist. "You kind of did, in a weird way."

"I guess what I was trying to say was that I understand how you feel."
He let out a bitter little laugh. "God, I'm turning into Clay," he said.
"Everything's about ME!"

This got me to laughing, and Jamie did a little bit, too, before we fell
into silence. We sat there in the van, both of us facing out the windshield,
too devastated even to cry. Crickets and grasshoppers chirped in the distance; a half-moon lighted the star-filled sky. This is where I started, I
thought, this town, this land. I was born an orphan here, without a father
or, really, any kind of mother, and the news about Annmarie did nothing
more than to make it official. But I had become someone other than the
raggedy girl who'd been left on her grandmother's doorstep, someone who
played music and traveled around the country and who knew things I
couldn't possibly have known if Grandma had lived and I'd remained in
Prairie Rose. I wasn't sure where I was headed, exactly, but I looked over at
Jamie and thought that as long as we ended up together, wherever it turned
out to be would be okay.

CHAPTER 34
AUGUST, 1988

Later, after we were home and had time to sort through it all, Jamie said he couldn't decide whether to call the final leg of our tour "Deliverance" or "Miri's Boys '88." The first choice was because Kirsten had managed to book us in a variety of shit-kicker bars, places that no one who listened to our kind of music would ever set foot in; the second was self-explanatory. After we left Chris and the rest of the Lost Generation in Austin, well, I guess I did get a bit out of hand. As we went from one hole-in-the-wall to another, through Oklahoma, Arkansas, and Tennessee, I managed to find some boy to sleep with almost every night—and it wasn't easy, the pickings being slim as they were in the dives Kirsten had found for us. Our audiences were generally fifteen to twenty good old boys sitting at a bar, glancing uneasily over at the makeshift stage where we were playing. It wasn't that I wanted to sleep with any of these guys, exactly; but it was easier than spending my nights thinking on all I'd found out about in Texas. The long drives during the day were bad enough. I'd doze off in the back of the van to a series of nightmare visions—Juan, touching Rosa in exactly the way he used to touch me; the Ramirezes, shaking their heads at me in disapproval; Annmarie, wasting away from cancer, lying in a bed alone in Aunt Melissa's house. I needed at least to have a way to stop my brain from thinking at night.

The low point came in Memphis—or, I should say, outside of Memphis. The bar where Kirsten had booked us was so far on the outskirts that the locals didn't even consider it to be part of the city. It took us two hours just to find the place, and we knew we were in trouble as soon as we pulled up. It was a cinder block building called The Dump, which it definitely was, located in a gravel lot on a back road to nowhere. The parking lot was filled with pickup trucks that sported gun racks and NRA decals. Jamie wondered aloud if we should skip the gig and head on to Nashville.

But we decided to be professionals. We went in and set up in the corner of the bar the owner referred to as "the stage," though there was no stage at all. About twenty-five people were seated at the bar, all of them men, with a sameness that Jamie joked was a result of "inbred cloning." They all had long, scraggly, mid-'70s-looking hair, which they wore with grimy-looking porkpie caps atop their heads.

Two songs into our set, a couple of the burliest guys in the bar came over and stood about a foot away from us, staring me up and down but good. Jamie kept glancing over at me nervously, but I just ignored them and kept on playing. When we finished the song, I thought it might be best to show them some appreciation.

"Thanks for coming over and giving us a listen," I said, flashing my lowest-wattage smile, a polite smile that was purposely lacking in sex appeal. "Shut up and show us your tits!" one of the guys yelled at me, and his friend roared with laughter.

We'd been purposely playing our more countrified songs in these bars, which tended to be the ones I'd written. But Jamie started into one of our louder songs just then, smashing into the chords and sending out an ear-splitting wail of feedback. I knew he'd done this on purpose, and I played along with him. Neither of us sang, we just wailed on the guitars.

"Show us your tits!" the guy yelled again, taking a long swig of beer, the foam catching on his bristly beard for a moment before it evaporated.

"She ain't got none," his friend called out. "That's why she won't show 'em."

Jamie broke two strings and kept on playing, sending out more feedback. His face was getting red.

The two assholes got the others in the bar to chime in so that it became a chant: "Show us your tits! Show us your tits!" By then about half the bar was standing there, chanting.

Jamie let off one more loud wail of feedback and stopped playing. His face was so red I thought his whole head might just blow off his shoulders. I strummed for another few bars of the song and then stopped, too. I looked over to Jamie to see what he thought we should do. The chanting was louder now that we'd stopped playing: "SHOW US YOUR TITS! SHOW US YOUR TITS!" Jamie unstrapped his guitar and, before I could figure out what he was up to, pulled his t-shirt up and off.

"You wanna see tits?" he yelled, holding the t-shirt over his head like a banner. "Look at my tits!"

I laughed so hard I nearly peed myself; there was a good fifteen or twenty seconds of lag time while the fact that Jamie was making fun of them registered in their brains, and then the beer bottles began sailing toward us. We ducked a few, and, as the bottles continued to come in numbers that suggested some were being taken from behind the bar and that, in fact, all hell had broken loose, we grabbed our guitars and ran for the back door. Rick was right behind us, with as much of the rest of our equipment as he could carry.

We locked ourselves in the van and looked at what all we'd escaped with. We'd left behind an amp, a pick-up and a couple of cords, and Jamie had, for a minute, the demented idea of going back in and telling the bar owner off. I told him he was crazy, that we had to get out of there, and while we were arguing Rick jumped behind the wheel and started the van up. He was not a moment too soon, as the crowd from the bar started to spill out into the parking lot.

"Fuck you!" Jamie screamed out the window as we peeled away.

"Jamie, what the hell is wrong with you?" I yelled. "They could follow us. Do you want to get us killed?"

Rick glanced nervously in the rearview mirror, but it didn't look like we were being followed. He was flooring it, barely making the bends in the road.

Jamie closed his eyes and took a few deep breaths, loud ones. It was something I'd seen him do with his yoga.

"Okay," he finally said. "I'm centered."

"You're centered?" I threw an empty Coke can at him. "You're not centered, you're out of your fucking mind."

"I just lost it for a minute," he said. "Man, I don't think I've ever been so angry." He said it with a sense of wonder, like a tourist who's just visited a new city.

"Jamie," I said, "a redneck bar on a dirt road in Tennessee is not the best place to get in touch with your anger."

Rick started laughing. Jamie and I sat in the back of the van and stared at each other, arms folded.

"Did you see the looks on those guys' faces when you took your shirt off, Jamie?" Rick asked. I imagined he said it to break the tension more than anything else. "You actually shocked them."

"It was pretty funny," I had to admit, and I poked Jamie in the ribs. He pushed my hand away, but he was smiling.

Rick took the entrance ramp to the interstate, a sight that relieved me greatly. "Man," he said, as he maneuvered onto the highway. "I thought we were all dead."

We drove all the way to Nashville that night and decided, in the course of the ride, that we'd bag the rest of the trip. We'd take a fleabag motel in Nashville, get some sleep and then drive back to Philly. Jamie thought if we pushed it we could do the drive in about sixteen hours.

But the next morning, when Jamie called Kirsten to tell her about our change in plans, she convinced him we had to play both Nashville and Louisville.

"She said we're getting college radio airplay both places, and a reporter in Louisville wants to talk to us," he called to me through the bathroom door, where I'd just finished taking a shower. I'd felt relieved at the thought of making it back to Philly in time for my birthday; the idea of turning twenty-two on the road had seemed romantic before we left, but by then I just wanted it to happen back where I knew folks.

I didn't answer him, and I heard Jamie sigh. "If we're going to do those shows, we might as well hit the others we have scheduled," he said.

I opened the door, a thin white bath towel wrapped around me. Rick, who was sitting on the bed, looked at me for a few seconds, then looked away. "How many other shows do we have?" I asked, allowing my irritation to register in my voice.

Jamie looked at the schedule. "Columbus, Pittsburgh, and then home."

I shook my head. "I want to go back to Philly," I said. "I've had it, Jamie."

He stared at the schedule for a minute. "Let's just do the Nashville show tonight. If it turns out like the others, then we'll blow off the rest of them and go home."

"If it turns out like last night," I said, "we might be dead."

But Kirsten was right, at least about those shows. We heard one of our songs played on the college radio station on our way to the gig in Nashville; this we took as a good sign, and it was. There was enough of a crowd that we made about $120, and some boys from a local band invited us to stay at their house. I hooked up with their lead guitarist, and in the morning I got the evil eye from Rick, which I chose to ignore.

The club we played in Louisville the next night was packed, thanks to that reporter who'd listened to our demo and had written us up as the concert pick of the week; I had many nice-looking boys flirting with me, and after all, it was my birthday. My goal was to forget all about Texas and have a good time that night. I picked out the boy I liked best and asked him if we could all crash at his place, a plan to which he eagerly agreed. This was fine with Jamie but not so fine with Rick, who'd stood in a corner and sulked as he watched me flirt with this boy.

Rick was still not speaking as we got in the van to follow the boy and his friends back to their place. He sat on the floor in the back, his arms folded.

"Rick, what's the problem?" I asked.

He didn't say anything, just stared straight ahead.

"Come on, tell me," I said, putting some sweetness in my voice. I didn't want to have another big blowout with him.

"I just thought we'd all go out and do something for your birthday," he said.

"Well, we are."

"I meant, just us," he said. He added quickly: "The three of us."

Jamie backed the van out of the parking lot. "Well, I guess it's Miri's call, since it is her birthday."

I smiled at Jamie. "Come on, Rick, we'll just go hang with these guys tonight. We can all celebrate when we get back to Philly."

"Fine," Rick said, in a way that told me it was not fine at all.

"I hope some of that guy's housemates are cute," Jamie said.

"Great," Rick said. "You guys both hook up, and I listen to everyone grunt and groan all night." He blew air out of his nostrils. "No thanks. I'll sleep in the van."

"Rick, I was kidding," Jamie said. "I'm sure they're all straight. It was a joke."

Rick said nothing. Jamie looked at me, and I shook my head at him, figuring we'd best just leave it alone for then. We rode the rest of the way in silence, finally pulling up behind the boys in front of a gothic-looking house on a tree-lined street.

We got out of the van, and Rick stomped ahead of us in silence.

"Should we talk to him?" Jamie asked me.

I shook my head. "He'll get over it. He needs to learn to live a little."

"He needs a girlfriend," Jamie said.

"Don't I know it," I agreed. With that, Derek—the boy I'd flirted with—came over and led us all inside.

When we got there, three guys were sitting on the living room floor, doing bong hits; but within an hour, about thirty more people had shown up, making it a full-blown party. There were some girls there, and I looked around to see if there was one I might be able to interest Rick in, but none of them were really his type. They all had that pancake-make-upped, rouged and contoured look that many girls in the South tended to favor. This trip was the first time I'd realized I was far apart from these girls. They all reminded me of Miss Staples, and my cousin Mary Gay, who by now was probably a miniature version of Aunt Melissa.

Far as I was concerned, it was as fine a birthday party as any, even if I hardly knew anyone there. I spent the night being chatted up by most of the boys, except the ones who were too stoned to talk; Jamie was pursued openly by the girls, and in a sneaky disinterested way by one of the boys.

Rick sat in a corner with the stoners and watched MTV, hunched forward in his chair, clearly miserable.

As the night got later and later, some of the stoned guys passed out on couches, or the floor. This left beds free for us, and Jamie eventually disappeared into a bedroom, followed by two of the girls. I couldn't wait to hear about that in the morning.

I woke up naked, in bed with Derek, my throat as dry as clay dirt. I stumbled out of the bedroom in nothing but the t-shirt Derek had worn the night before—it said "Derby Day '88" on the front, and "University of Louisville" on the back—and went to find the bathroom, the kitchen, any room with a water faucet.

On my way, I nearly fell over Rick, who was lying on the floor in all his clothes, just a pillow from the couch under his head. He pretended to be asleep; I could tell he wasn't, but I went along with him anyway. My head hurt, and I needed water. I made it to the bathroom and opened the door without knocking. Jamie was in there, shirtless, splashing water on his face.

"We have to get out of here," he said. "I can't face any of these people." He motioned toward the bedroom where he'd slept. "Those two women tried to *rape* me."

"What happened?" I asked, cupping my hands under the faucet and drinking as much as I could that way.

"I'll tell you in the van. Wake Rick up and let's get out of here."

"You wake him. I want to take a quick shower."

"Miri," Jamie said, "I don't feel like dealing with these people."

"They won't wake up," I said. "I used to do this all the time. You get Rick up and head out for the van. I'll meet you there in five minutes."

Jamie looked skeptical, but he left the bathroom, muttering to himself.

True to my word, I was in and out of that shower with no one in the house noticing; I dressed quickly without waking up Derek and met Jamie and Rick out at the van, a yellow towel from the bathroom wrapped around my wet hair.

"Miri," Jamie said as I got in the back of the van, "you can't take their towel. That's stealing."

I shrugged. "It's a souvenir," I said. This made Jamie, in the driver's seat, laugh. Rick stared out the passenger's window, said nothing.

As we headed for Ohio, Jamie told us about the two girls. They'd followed him into the bedroom, and each had crawled in bed with him, one on either side. He'd told them he had a girlfriend, and they'd said they didn't care, and started trying to kiss him.

"I'm sure this would be a straight man's fantasy," he said. "All I could think about was how to get them off me."

Rick snorted, continued staring sulkily out the window.

Jamie finally got the girls to stop kissing him by saying he was too drunk to get it up, but they both stayed in the bed with him anyway. He said they kept snuggling so close to him that he started sweating buckets, soaking through his t-shirt. Finally, he said, one of them gave up and went into the other room, and he crawled as far away on the bed as he could from the other one and slept curled in a sweaty ball.

"I didn't get much sleep, either," I said.

"I'll bet," Jamie said.

"That's really something to be proud of, Miri," Rick said. He turned around and looked at me, his face red, eyes flashing.

"What's your problem?" I asked. "You're no fun anymore, Rick. You used to be cool with anything. I swear, that college has turned you into an egghead." I said it all jokingly, hoping to coax him out of the mood he was in.

"I've just grown up," Rick said. "It's time you did, too."

"What's that supposed to mean?" I asked.

"Kids, let's not fight," Jamie said. He meant it as a joke, and I giggled, but Rick just continued looking steamed.

"Do you really think guys like that care about you?" Rick asked. "They don't care about you."

"Good thing," I shot back, "since I don't care a lick about them."

"How do you think they see you, Miri?"

"Oh, God," Jamie murmured.

"I don't know, Rick," I said. I could hear my own voice starting to sound angry. I unwrapped the towel from my head and fluffed my damp hair with my hands. "Why don't you tell me how they see me, Rick? Why don't you tell me how you see me?"

I was waiting for him to say one of those words—slut, or whore, something like that. I knew it was what he was thinking. He sat there stunned, seemingly unable to speak, and as I waited for him to say one of those words I began to feel like he'd already said it, and the anger welled up in me to the point where I felt it'd surely blow the roof off the van.

"You know what, Rick," I said through clenched teeth, "I don't need to take advice on my sex life from a fucking virgin."

Jamie choked down a gasp; it came out as a little wheezing noise in the back of his throat. I took a look at Rick and knew right away I'd gone too far. His face turned redder than any pimple he'd ever had in his life. I started to try to say something, to apologize or maybe take it back, but Rick cut me off.

"F-f-f-f-f-f-f-f-f-f-f," he said, with interruptions and restarts. "F-f-f-f-f-f-f-f." I was sure he was trying to say "Fuck you," but he couldn't even get beyond the first letter. It was painful to listen to, and I put my hand on his arm but he smacked it away and turned his face to the window. I could see his eyes tear up as he turned away from me.

After twenty minutes of bleak quiet, Jamie took an exit ramp and headed for a diner. "I can't deal with this without coffee," he said, and left the two of us in the van together.

We sat there in silence, watching Jamie head into the restaurant.

"If you want to go in, I'll stay here," I finally said, and Rick opened the door without looking at me, slammed it shut behind him. I watched him enter the diner, then did the only thing I could think of: I rolled out a sleeping bag in the back of the van and slid inside, hoping I'd wake up from a nap and find out I'd dreamed the whole thing.

CHAPTER 35
AUGUST, 1988

But it was no dream. Rick wouldn't talk to me for the rest of the way to Columbus, or at the show that night. He wouldn't talk to me in the living room where a college deejay had set us up to sleep, or on the ride to Pittsburgh the next day, or at that night's gig. He was completely silent along the Pennsylvania Turnpike as we headed back to Philly the following day. It occurred to me that I did not have good luck traveling this particular stretch of roadway, for this was exactly where the thing with Ian Oliver had gone down the chute. When we stopped at a rest area halfway between Pittsburgh and Philly, Rick got out of the van quickly and went in ahead of us. I asked Jamie what I could do to make it better.

"Miri, just let it rest," he said. "You'll only make it worse if you bring it up again."

The way he said it made me think Jamie was mad at me, too. Nobody understood that what Rick had been doing was comparing me to Annmarie, saying I was like her, I was like a woman who'd slept with most every guy she laid eyes on and died alone in a house where she wasn't even wanted. I couldn't just sit and take that; it wasn't in my nature not to defend myself. But still, if I could have taken back that last thing I'd said to Rick, I would have.

We got back to Philly around dinnertime, and dropped Rick back at his dorm. Jamie got out and walked to the door with him, and I watched the two of them talk for a few minutes, unable to hear what they were saying. When Jamie got back in the van and headed for our apartment, he was as silent as his own father.

"You're mad at me," I said.

He shook his head.

"Yes you are. I can tell."

He didn't say anything.

"See," I said. "You're not even speaking to me. I hate it when you do that, Jamie. I'd rather have you tell me I'm an asshole than not speak to me."

"You shouldn't have said what you said to Rick," Jamie said. "It was cruel."

Gay or straight, leave it to guys to take up for each other. "What about what he said to me?" I asked. "He called me a slut."

Jamie shot a puzzled look at me. "No, he didn't."

"Well, he was thinking it. He was about to say it."

Jamie sighed. "Oh, Miri." He looked like he was going to say something else, but he spotted a parking place and pulled the van in quickly. "All I want is to go to sleep," he said.

"That's just fine. I'll let you have your place back all to yourself." I slammed the door of the van and stormed off, wanting Jamie to call after me to stop. He didn't.

I walked down to the park, sat on a bench and cried. I hated how Jamie and I could be so close, so totally understanding of each other like we were outside Wendell's house that night, and then move so far outside of each other's feelings. When Rick had said something bad about Jamie, years back, I stood up for Jamie, and I would again; but I felt like when it came to me, nobody defended me, not even Jamie. I was always fending for myself, and though I was twenty-two, technically a grownup, I still felt sometimes that it was too much for me. These were the times I wished I still had Grandma; or a real mother, one who was nothing like Annmarie.

I sat in the park until it went from twilight to pitch dark, and then I remembered the cats; we'd left them at Kirsten's. I thought I might feel better if I could get Nico and Artemis, go back to the apartment and lock myself in a room with them, and so I walked to a pay phone and called Kirsten.

"Jamie already called," she said. "He said he'd pick them up tomorrow. Didn't he tell you he talked to me?"

"No," I said. I didn't want to tell Kirsten that Jamie and Rick were both mad at me; I just wanted the cats, but the thought of carrying the two of them across the city without a car suddenly seemed exhausting.

"I got you guys continuing gigs in Boston and New York for September and October," she said. "I wanted to talk to both of you about it tomorrow."

"What did Jamie say?" I asked.

"He said he needed to sleep for about twenty hours, and then he'd stop over."

"Did he say what time he'd be there?" I asked.

"Are you guys, like, not talking or something?" When I didn't answer, she added, "He said he'd be over about 6:00 tomorrow night."

"I'll meet y'all there," I said, and hung up the phone.

The first place I headed was Bill's. I figured he'd be glad to see me for once at night instead of in the morning. But I rang his buzzer five times, and there was no answer. I walked to the nearest pay phone and tried to call him, but only got his machine. He was either at work or out with someone else. I didn't leave a message.

I didn't know where to go next. The one person in all of Philly who could help me make sense of this trip was Peter; I wanted more than anything to talk to him, but I didn't want to deal with Annie if she answered the phone. She had to be on to the fact that I was after her boyfriend. It occurred to me that I didn't have a single female friend to my name; really, I never had. Jamie and Rick were my only true friends, and they were both mad at me. I put my hands in my pockets; I had four dollars and some change. I felt as homeless as I had been years ago. Jamie's apartment wasn't really mine; I couldn't pay the rent there, not with my part-time job at the record store. And I didn't even know if the job was still mine. I wandered down South Street, wondering where to go, when I saw the Big Bang and remembered the one female friend I did have: Loretta.

The bouncer greeted me with a hug, and I chatted with him for a few minutes before I walked in and looked around for Loretta. I didn't see her right off, and so I scanned the bar for an empty seat. I saw one, and I also saw the person sitting by himself the next seat over: Peter Fenster.

I fluffed my hair and pressed my lips together, hard, then headed over to him.

"Hi," I said, sliding onto the stool next to his.

"Miri," he said, looking at me through heavy-lidded eyes. "You're back." He motioned to the bartender, a guy I didn't recognize.

"Sure am," I said to Peter, and then I ordered a Rolling Rock from the bartender. It was barely 10:00, but it seemed like Peter had been drinking a good long while. "How've you been, Peter?" I asked.

"Annie and I broke up," he said, throwing a couple of bills down on the bar to cover my drink.

Finally, I thought, I have a chance, thank you Lord, amen. "Shit," I said, my mind racing. "I'm sorry, Peter."

"I lost my girlfriend and my band," he said, taking a long gulp from his mug. He was drinking stout, that thick dark stuff I personally couldn't stomach.

"That's awful," I said, sipping the beer the bartender had put down in front of me.

"They both dumped me," he said, slurring his words. "My girlfriend, my band."

"I thought you dumped the band, Peter."

"A technicality," he said. He held his finger up in the air as if he planned to say something else, but the idea must have left him, for his finger hovered in the air as he took another gulp from his beer.

Just then Loretta came out from the back of the bar. "Miri!" she screamed. She threw her arms out and we hugged across the bar. "How was the tour?" she asked.

"Exhausting," I said. I didn't know what else to say.

"That's how tours are," Peter agreed, "exhausting." Loretta gave him a sideways look.

"So did the crowds like you guys? What was Sean Hunter like? Come on, girl, dish it out, I want some dirt." Loretta washed and dried glasses as she spoke.

"People really did seem to like us," I said, figuring I'd leave out the part about the shows in Arkansas and Tennessee. "It was weird playing in such big places, with the Lost Generation and all."

"I remember when Chutes and Ladders opened for the Replacements at the Tower," Peter said. "And then the time in New York, when we opened for . . ."

"Peter," Loretta said, "we're talking about Cloud Cuckoo Land now, okay? Miri's band." She said it in the kind-but-stern voice of a schoolteacher who's trying to keep an unruly child in line.

"Sorry," Peter muttered, looking into his beer.

"That's okay," I said, nudging him, "we'll have to trade on-the-road horror stories later on, Peter." This seemed to perk him up. Loretta fixed a watchful eye on me.

"Any word on what's happening with the record, Miri?" she asked.

I shook my head. "Sean told Jamie there was a chance another label might buy the one that has our record, but there's nothing definite."

"It'll get settled," she said. "Your album will be out by this time next year."

"What makes you say that, Loretta?"

She winked at me. "My Tarot cards," she said, and laughed, and I couldn't tell if she was kidding or not. Loretta was always full of surprises.

"When you guys are famous," she added, "I'm gonna put a big sign in the window: 'Cloud Cuckoo Land played their first show here.'"

"Its," Peter muttered.

"What?" I asked him.

"Its," he said. "'Cloud Cuckoo Land played *its* first show here.' The name of the band is singular, not plural." He did an awful lot of slurring as he got it all out.

This made me laugh, but Loretta looked steamed. "Guess what, Peter? You're cut off after you finish that drink."

Peter muttered something I couldn't make out, picked up his beer mug, and moved off to a table in the back of the bar.

"How long's he been like that?" I asked Loretta.

"Couple of weeks," she said. "Don't fall for it, Miri. I see that look in your eyes."

"Me?" I gave her my mock-innocent look, and she rolled her eyes.

"One woman to another," Loretta said. "He'll just drag you down."

I understood what she was saying, but I also knew what Peter was like before he left the band, before Annie dumped him. This might be my only chance to get to him while he was single. He was the kind of guy who needed a girlfriend, and I was sure I could fit the bill. Once he got over the shock of all the losses he'd gone through, he'd be back to being the same sweet Peter he'd been before, and I wanted to be on the receiving end.

"I hear what you're saying," I said to Loretta.

"But you'll make your own mistakes," she said. "You're too young to listen to anyone else. I know, believe me, I was there once." She looked at my beer and frowned. "Hey, are you old enough to drink here yet?"

"Have been for over a year," I said. "I'm twenty-two now."

"Really? Let me see your ID." I couldn't tell if she was kidding or not, so I pulled out the state alcoholic beverage ID I'd gotten the year before.

"You don't have a driver's license?" she asked.

"No," I said, "I never learned how. Jamie tried to teach me before we left on tour, but I didn't do too well and he gave up."

Loretta shook her head. "You don't want to learn to drive from a man. And someone from Boston! Those people drive like a nuclear missile is on their tail."

I giggled.

"I'll teach you to drive," she said.

"You serious?" I liked the thought of Loretta, with her arm-length tattoo and her messy dark hair, teaching me to drive on her Galaxie 500.

"Hell, yeah. A woman's got to know how to drive."

I smiled at her. Loretta could easily have been my mother instead of Annmarie, and I wondered why I couldn't have ended up with someone like her, someone sassy and tough and good and kind all at the same time, instead of the sorry excuse for a mother I got. It was hard for me to believe that Annmarie was really dead, hard to believe someone that ornery could just up and die.

"You meet me here next Sunday, around noon," she said. "We'll have our first lesson."

"Thanks, Loretta. I'll be here."

She filled two beer mugs and slid them down to the bartender. "I gotta get back to work," she said. "I'll see you 'round." She disappeared in the back of the bar.

I looked at Peter. He was hunched over his stout, staring into the foam. I got the eerie feeling, as I had that time I'd seen him feeding the pigeons, that he was an old man trapped in a young body.

I walked over and stood next to him. He didn't look up.

"Come on," I said. "I'm taking you home."

Home, for Peter, turned out to be the Society Hill apartment of an old college friend of his. I had to help Peter unlock the door after he dropped the key twice, unable to get it in the slot. Inside, a sleeping bag was spread out on the living room couch; two open duffel bags sat in a corner, shirt sleeves and socks spilling down their sides. He's homeless now, I thought, as he stretched out on top of the sleeping bag. He reached up to me for a second, like he was going to grab me by the wrist and pull me down on top of him; but in midair his hand wavered and his arm went down, like the final plunge of a drowning man. His breathing soon became loud and even.

I'd cooled off enough by then to head back to Jamie's, and I decided to walk rather than catching the bus. I was in one of those moods where I noticed everything on the street: the black iron horsehead hitching posts that Jamie said had probably been there since Colonial times; the concrete lions outside some of the nicer homes, shiny pebbles fixed here and there in the cement; and, every block or two, a grimy-looking man or woman, curled up in a doorway. On Walnut Street I passed the Tin Man, as I'd come to call him, his foil crown slipped down over his forehead, his body curled around his pastel chalks and a garbage bag full of his possessions. I took two dollars out of my pocket and tucked the bills carefully in his shoe, in such a way that they wouldn't be visible to anyone else who passed by.

I expected Jamie to be asleep, but found him in his t-shirt and underwear on the living room couch, clicking the remote control from station to station, the only light in the room coming from the TV. He'd picked up my habit of watching with the sound off.

I sat down next to him, scanning his face to try and get a fix on what he was feeling. As was often the case with Jamie, it wasn't easy to tell just by looking.

"You still mad at me?" I asked softly.

"No," he said, quickly enough that I knew he meant it. "You?"

"Nah," I said, moving closer to him on the couch so our sides were touching. "I was never really mad at you. I don't know what happens with us sometimes."

"I think we just spent way too much time confined in small places together. It'd be hard not to get on each other's nerves after a while."

"Yeah," I said. "Rick didn't help, either."

Jamie sighed, stared at the video on the TV screen. It was The Cure, "Just Like Heaven."

"Miri," he said slowly, like he was picking his words with care, "if you and Rick can't sort things out, we'll have to stop working with him. I don't want to referee between you two anymore."

"I know," I said. "I don't know how to fix it. I miss the way Rick used to be."

"He says he misses the way you used to be."

I looked at him. "He's the one who's a pain in the ass all the time."

Jamie shook his head. "You know what I think about the situation. Just do something to work it out, or we're going to have to find someone else to help us out when we travel." He tapped the remote control against his knee.

"So what happens now?" I asked, in part to change the subject. "I mean, we did the big tour we'd always imagined. We're back. So what do we do now?"

Jamie shrugged. "I guess we do the gigs Kirsten's lined up for us," he said, "and we wait." He sighed. "It's weird, huh? I thought touring with the Lost Generation would change my life. It hasn't."

Jamie sighed and stretched his legs out on the coffee table, and I got comfortable on the couch next to him. He handed me the remote—for Jamie, this was a rare event—and I flipped through the channels, finally settling on an old movie, something from the '40s that Grandma would have liked. For a moment, all the things I'd learned about my past while we were in Prairie Rose threatened to come to the surface, threatened to let me know that my life had, in fact, been changed. But I snuggled next to Jamie and fought those demons down; I felt like I'd been through enough for one night.

CHAPTER 36
SEPTEMBER–DECEMBER, 1988

We spent that fall and into the winter doing just what Jamie had said—waiting. We played the shows Kirsten had lined up, and continued to do our usual gigs around Philly. Jamie and I handled the sound and equipment ourselves, since I couldn't bring myself to talk to Rick. It was a bigger problem than one comment I'd made, and couldn't be fixed with one apology. I wasn't sure it could be fixed at all, and decided I'd rather remember Rick the way he had been, back when we were a team. I was pretty sure Jamie talked to Rick on occasion but I never asked him about it, and he didn't offer up any information.

Sean kept calling and telling us to hang on, that Tracy Chapman's success had the record companies scrambling for folk-rock acts and that he was sure something would happen with our album soon. Jamie and I had enough new songs by then for a second album, and I knew he was frustrated that we couldn't get the first one out, record these songs, and move on. I myself might have been more upset about it all had I not thrown myself into a much bigger project that basically took up all my time and energy. The project was the seduction of Peter Fenster.

After that night I walked him home, I saw a lot of Peter. He called me almost every day, and he started turning up at all of our shows. He'd stand right in front of the stage and sing all the words to the songs Jamie had written when he was heartbroken over Clay, so loud that sometimes Jamie and I could barely hear ourselves. Peter's volume would increase with each beer he drank, to the point where other folks in the club would yell at him to shut up. Sometimes Jamie and I would invite him up onstage to play a little guitar as a way of getting him to stop singing; Jamie never miked Peter's guitar, as he was always too drunk by then to really play.

By November, it was rumored around town that Peter and I were dating, but we weren't, not really. For one thing, even I was a bit turned off by his physical state; he had pretty much stopped washing and shaving since he and Annie had broken up, and his diet consisted of beer and pretzels. Jamie said he was starting to look like an "L.A. Woman"–era Jim Morrison, and I'm sorry to say he was only exaggerating a little.

But I saw flashes of the old Peter, just enough to keep me going. He would tell me funny stories about the bands he played with in high school, like the one that tried to do covers of the Electric Light Orchestra despite the fact that they had no synthesizers; he'd come into the record store, where I'd gotten my old job back, and pull out obscure albums and give me little historical speeches about the bands. Peter was working as a temp a couple of days a week, doing computer stuff he'd learned in college, and the days he worked these jobs he'd drop over in his nice work clothes and take me out to dinner. But as soon as we'd sit down, the drinking would start, and I'd watch as he went through the different stages—relaxation, then hilarity, then an edginess that would give way to a kind of bitter sadness at the end of the night.

We never did more than kiss that fall. He would always be the one who started it, but, whether sober or drunk, he would always stop at kissing. The thing was, the way he kissed was so different from anything I had experienced that I don't rightly know if I could have taken much more. For two years, I had watched the way Peter treated Annie—the tender way he touched her, took her by the hand, brushed his lips against hers—and now that kind of attention was being turned on me. He kissed me like I was some kind of delicate thing that could break if he wasn't careful. I took his holding off on sex as a sign of respect for me, just as Troy Wilson had held off way back when. I was sure, from the way he kissed me, that he loved me; I figured if I just gave him some time to get over Annie, he would be mine. I took it as a good sign when he invited me to his parents' house for Christmas.

But one night in early December, it seemed like every tension in my life came to a boil. Jamie and I were playing a show at Ground Zero. Peter went along with us; by then he'd taken to showing up at our place before the gigs, riding over with us and helping to set up. But there were two other people at the show that night who managed to throw my whole life into chaos: Annie and Rick.

Annie got there first, alone. She walked in during the set of the opening band, the Wishniaks, a rock band that Jamie had taken quite a shine to. I saw right off that I wasn't the only one who'd noticed Annie; Peter moved closer to me and slipped his arm around my waist as soon as she walked in. I knew that this was partly—okay, mostly—for her benefit, but I had to believe it had something to do with how he felt about me, too.

When the Wishniaks' set was over, Annie started making the rounds, chatting with every guy she knew in the bar. She finally settled on one of the bartenders, a guy named Kirk who I knew because he was a friend of Bill's. Kirk's girlfriend stood in a corner and watched Annie smiling and nodding her head at Kirk; the girlfriend was fuming. Bill, who was also there, was giving me and Peter funny looks, but turned his head anytime I tried to catch his eye. Through all of this, Peter and Annie kept stealing glances at each other. As Jamie and I set up for the show, Peter hovering at my side and helping, I wondered if there was any way this jealous ricochet could get much worse. Just as I was thinking it, Rick walked into the bar. With a girl.

We had just finished setting up, and the timing made me wonder if Rick had been watching us through the window outside, waiting until we were almost done to make his grand entrance. That way we wouldn't really have time to talk, but I'd see him, and I could wonder about this girl through our entire set.

And wonder I did. The girl was not what you'd call pretty, exactly, but you couldn't help but notice her. She was almost as tall as Rick, and dressed, as Jamie would point out later, like Elvira, or Morticia Addams: she wore a tight-fitting black dress that came down to her ankles, silver spike heels, and a black feather boa around her neck. Her hair was dyed black, too, and hung down limply around her white-powdered face. This vampire look was an offshoot of punk I had seen before, but not for a couple of years. It was like she was the last of a dying breed, maybe, or the start of her own trend. She looked out of place at our show; most of our crowd wore jeans, or thrift-store clothes from different eras.

Rick nodded to me as Jamie and I took the stage and then he made sure he positioned himself and the vampire girlfriend right in front of me, where they felt each other up and sucked face off and on for most of our set, while Peter got progressively more drunk and sang along louder and louder. At one point, Jamie whispered to me that the biker bar in Tennessee didn't seem so bad just then, and I had to agree.

After the show, Rick and the vampire girl marched right up to me as Peter and Annie stood at opposite ends of the club, staring at but not talking to each other.

"Miri," Rick said, a shit-eating grin on his face that made me want to smack him, "this is Eclipse."

I put my hand out to shake, but the girl just stared at me. I remembered having done this to Kirsten once, and was not about to be beat at my own game, not by the likes of Vampirella.

"Eclipse?" I asked. "Were your parents, like, hippies or something?"

She raised a black-painted eyebrow at me. "It's a name I've chosen for myself," she said, her stare defying me to question her further. I sized her up for a few seconds before I decided how to proceed. She was clearly older than Rick, but not much older than me—twenty-four, twenty-five, tops.

"So, what's your real name?" I asked.

"What?" A hint of alarm crept into her voice, just enough to tell me that I could crumble her act if I worked at it. I could see that Rick had heard it too; you learn a few things, living on the streets.

"Your real name," I said. "The one your parents gave you."

"That name has nothing to do with who I am," she said. Her facial expression was carefully designed to look disinterested, but I could tell I was getting to her. I also heard a hint of a South Philly accent behind the pretentiousness.

"Okay, it has nothing to do with you. What is it?" Rick was looking back and forth from me to her, uncertain of what to do.

She smirked, and glanced at Rick. "Linda," she said.

"Linda," I repeated. "Now, that's a perfectly nice name. Why'd you want to go and call yourself something like Eclipse?"

Before she could answer, Rick stepped in. "I'd think you would under-stand not liking your name, Miriam," he said, leaning heavy on the last syl-lable.

"Yeah," I said, "but I didn't go and start calling myself Moonbeam or something." I was being a bitch, I knew, but I couldn't stop myself. I did-n't like anything about this girl—the way she looked, the way she acted, her stupid chosen name. I didn't like Rick being with her.

Eclipse/Linda stared at me for a minute, and then did one of the single weirdest things that has ever been done to me, and there have been quite a few. She reached out and touched my hair, plucked a loose strand before I could move away.

"What the fuck?" I said. Rick was chewing on his lower lip.

"It's not wise to cross a witch, dear," she said, holding the strand of hair in her hand. "Remember that."

"Maybe Rick should remember that," I said. He made a face at me, the face a twelve-year-old brother might make at an older sister, and the two of them walked away. I smoothed my hair where she had touched it, try-ing to make sense of what had just happened as I scanned the club for Peter. As I moved toward the bar I ran into Bill.

"What are you doing later?" he asked me.

"I've got plans, Bill. Sorry," I said, and headed off into the crowd to try to find Peter, hoping he wasn't already with Annie.

So much went wrong in the next few weeks that I had to wonder if that girl really was a witch. For one thing, the record company deal that was supposed to get our album put out fell through. Sean kept saying that another label would come along, but he didn't sound nearly as hopeful as he had before. Then Peter started pulling away, not wanting to spend as much time with me. I was sure he was seeing Annie again, though he denied it every time I asked.

Jamie's apartment started falling apart, too. For months, it had been springing mysterious small leaks in the ceiling, which the building's owner refused to fix; we had a couple of buckets that we moved around from room to room. But just five nights after I'd met that girlfriend of Rick's, I got back from work to find the place completely flooded—the living room carpet soaked, water swirling around the kitchen, the cats up on the table, their eyes as big as saucers of milk. I looked around but could not tell where the water was coming from, and I just couldn't deal with it; I put the cats' dishes up on the kitchen table and left Jamie a note to come get me at the diner when he got home. When he came, he was mad at me for not calling the building's management company or trying to clean up myself.

And the bad luck was not restricted to things that directly involved me; it seemed to radiate out in a circle, snagging anyone who was close to me. Jamie flew out to San Francisco to spend a few days with Sean, who was still on tour, and had a terrible time; they fought so much that Jamie got his own hotel room the last night. He told me he was so depressed that he'd even called a few people he knew, looking for Clay; but either they didn't know where he was, or they weren't telling. Right after Jamie got back, Wendell sent me a note, telling me that Duke had died. This bad luck could even get an old dog down in Texas, I thought, wondering who was next.

The final straw came one night about a week before Christmas. Peter had asked me out that night on a real date, and I was hopeful that the bad luck spell was finally broken, and that Peter had decided he was over Annie. By then, he had an apartment, a little studio in West Philly. We split a bottle of wine before dinner—actually, he drank most of it—and then went out to an Italian restaurant, where he drank another bottle of wine, almost entirely by himself. I should have taken these as bad signs, but I didn't. I just kept thinking that if I could get him in bed, he would want me. Jamie had been warning me all along that Peter was completely fucked up and I should just stay away until he sorted things out, but of course I wouldn't listen.

We went back to Peter's place and got undressed. I'll admit that I was the one who started getting undressed at first, but Peter seemed more than happy to do the same. We climbed into bed, naked, and I reached out to him. I touched his sides, waiting for him to put his arms around me, but he didn't respond. Instead, he started shaking. I don't just mean trembling; I mean, all over, full-body shaking, his teeth chattering, his hands knotted into fists. I had never seen anything like this. I'd heard of seizures, epileptic fits and such, and wondered if this was one of those, but his eyes didn't roll back in his head or anything; he just kept shaking, and I kept asking him what was wrong, and he kept not answering and just shaking until finally, it stopped. I touched his arm to see if he was okay and he rolled away from me, mumbling something about sleep. Within a few minutes he was snoring.

I sat there and watched him, not knowing what to do. I was so freaked out by the whole thing that I wanted to leave; in fact, I was out of bed and starting to get dressed when I realized that I couldn't leave, he might be sick, he might need me. Instead I climbed back into bed and watched him for a while. He seemed to be sleeping peacefully. I myself dozed off in short fits throughout the night.

When I woke up the next morning, I could hear the water running in the shower. It seemed to run forever, and I was afraid at several points that maybe Peter had died in there. But I kept waiting, and finally, the water stopped. Peter was in the bathroom a good long while after that before he came out.

"Miri," he said. He was wearing a faded old Mission of Burma t-shirt and a pair of sweatpants. I was still in bed, still naked.

I started to get up, and he turned away from me. "Maybe you should get dressed," he said. "We need to talk."

I shrugged. "Anything you want to say to me, you can say right now."

He sighed and walked around the room in a circle, then sat on the edge of a small wooden chair about as far away from me as he could get. "The thing is," he said, "I'm just not ready for a relationship right now."

I'd never really had anyone break up with me before; the only actual boyfriend I'd ever had was Juan, and his leaving me was not his own choice. What a stupid line, I thought. It was no better than Clay's note to Jamie; or, for that matter, Ian Oliver's.

I pushed the covers back and sat up in the bed, hoping to make him uncomfortable with the sight of my naked body. "Who said it was a relationship?" I struggled to keep my voice even and not angry-sounding. "I was just looking for some fun, Peter. I thought you knew that."

A weird sad smile played across his face. "That's not true, Miri. You want people to think that, but it's not true."

I wasn't about to be psychoanalyzed by some alcoholic ex–local rock star who was dumping me. I got up and started pulling my clothes on, quickly. "You don't know me, Peter," I said. "You don't know anything about me."

"I know more than you think."

"Fuck you," I said. I had my underpants and jeans on and was pulling my sweater over my head.

He got up and walked over a bit closer, stopping uncertainly at the foot of the bed. "It's not that I don't like you," he said. "I like you a lot. But you're not Annie. Nobody's Annie."

I pulled my socks on one foot at a time, standing up, and pushed my feet into my boots. I laced them wildly, missing holes here and there.

"I don't want to be your fucking Annie." I grabbed my coat and stormed out, slamming the door as hard as I could.

It wasn't until I got about two blocks away that the crying started. There was so much going around in my head that I couldn't sort through any of it, couldn't grasp onto a single thought. I just kept crying harder and, after struggling for a few minutes to get myself under control, I gave up and allowed myself to cry freely, right on the street. My nose started to run and I stopped in at a Wawa to buy some tissues. I got a big box of Kleenex and just walked down Spruce Street with it, blowing my nose as I needed to and dropping the soggy tissues into trash cans or dumpsters as I passed them. People made sure not to look at me as they passed, the way they used to when I was on the streets, the way they do when they pass anything they can tell is broken that they know they can't fix.

Of all the thoughts and ideas swirling around inside me, there was one that kept bubbling up to the surface: Eclipse. The whole thing was her fault; she'd put a spell on me. It was easier to blame her than to poke deeper into those other fragments of thoughts: that Peter really had never loved me; that maybe he didn't think I was good enough for him; that somehow I had sunk to Annmarie's level, trying to get love through sex and failing, failing miserably. That Annmarie wasn't even around anymore to blame for my troubles. I pushed that last thought far, far back, for I had enough to deal with at present.

I cut down 38th Street to Walnut and walked, still crying, until I got to Rick's dorm. It tells something about my state of mind that I didn't care what I looked like. I was still holding the box of Kleenex and had five used tissues wadded up in my hand when he opened his door.

"You have to get her to take it off of me," I said.

"What?" He looked at me with concern, mixed with a kind of wariness, like he wasn't sure what I was up to now.

"Eclipse." I pulled out another tissue, dabbed at my nose to keep it from running. "The curse or spell or whatever it was she put on me—you have to get her to take it off."

Rick looked for a second like he didn't believe me, then burst out laughing.

"It's not funny," I said. "Everything's been going wrong since she put that hex on me." I told him about the record deal, the flood in the apartment, Jamie's trip to San Francisco, and Duke dying. Rick was smiling and kind of chortling as I brought each of these things up. When I got to the part about Peter, he stopped smiling.

"Miri," he said, "everybody knows that Peter's still in love with Annie."

"That's not true," I said, even though part of me knew it was. "I mean, I know he's not over her yet, but he loves me, too."

"Peter doesn't love you, Miri." He said it quietly, matter-of-factly. He should be enjoying this, I thought, but he didn't look like he was.

I sat down on his bed, pulled another tissue from my box and blew my nose. Nothing seemed to matter anymore. The one guy I had really loved since Juan didn't even want me.

"Look," Rick said, "you don't really deserve for me to tell you this, but I will anyway. Eclipse never put a curse on you. She's not a witch."

I looked up at him. "What do you mean?" I asked. "You were there. She pulled one of my hairs out."

"She just did it to freak you out. She threw the hair away as soon as we got outside."

"But what about the vampire outfit?" I asked.

Rick smiled. "I didn't say she wasn't weird. Just that she's not a witch."

I thought back on the last few weeks. "So it's just my own sucky life," I said. "That figures."

Rick shrugged.

"Are you still seeing her?" I asked.

"Yes," he said, quickly enough that I was sure it wasn't true.

I got up and threw my dirty tissues in his wastebasket. "I never meant to hurt you, you know," I said.

He looked at me full-on, and I noticed how grown-up he'd become. He was twenty now—a man, really. I realized with a pang of guilt that I'd missed his birthday when we weren't speaking.

"I know you didn't mean to," he said, his voice quiet and even. "But you did."

I nodded. There was so much left to say to him, more than I could possibly get out. I buttoned my coat up and headed for the door. In the doorway I turned and looked back at him. He'd become like Jamie; I couldn't read his face.

"You know, if you ever want to start doing sound and stuff again," I said, "we'd love to have you back."

Rick smiled. "I really just did that tour as a favor to Jamie. I'm working two jobs now and taking a ton of classes. I don't have time to do jobs I don't get paid for."

I nodded. "Just come by and hang out sometime, okay?"

"Okay," he said, and I couldn't tell from his voice if he meant it or not. I turned and headed down the hallway, then out into the cold air.

I got back to Jamie's to find him, much to my surprise, wrestling a spruce tree into a metal stand. I dropped my box of tissues and went over to hold the tree while he screwed it in. I'd known Jamie for four years and in all that time I'd never seen him put a Christmas decoration in the apartment.

"Jamie, what's got into you?" I asked when we'd finally gotten the tree standing on its own.

"Well, my mother called me this morning and said she and my Dad were invited to take some other couple's place on a cruise over the holidays. She wanted to know if I would mind if they went."

"Do you?"

"I thought I did, at first," he said, "and then I realized I felt relieved. You know, I hate going up there for Christmas. I really hate it. And yet I do it every year." He picked up a trash bag, started scooping up needles and bro-ken-off pieces of branches. "So I decided to have Christmas here. A misfit Christmas."

"A misfit Christmas?" I held the trash bag open for him.

"Yeah, I thought about all the people I know who either hate Christmas with their families or don't have families. So I called them. Kirsten. Loretta. Roger and Mark, my friends from Boston. Greg, that guy who works with me at the music shop." He took the bag from me, tied it closed. "They're all coming."

"You're really having people over here for Christmas?" I asked.

"Yeah. I guess I have some work to do."

"Well," I said, "you're gonna have one more. I'm not going home for the holidays with Peter." I told him what had happened, and he dropped the trash bag and gave me a hug.

"Fuck him," he said. "He's not good enough for you."

I knew I wouldn't be able to breathe if I started crying again, so I bit my lip and buried my head in Jamie's side. Finally I let go and flopped myself on the couch.

"You know," I said, "there's someone else we have to invite." I picked up the phone and dialed Rick's number.

The most surprising thing about it was how much fun we had. Jamie and I spent the whole week decorating the apartment. We played goofy Christmas records and drank a lot while we did it. I'd always looked at Christmas as something to be endured—my early Christmases at my snooty aunt's house; the one I'd spent with Ian Oliver, and later, my holi-days on the streets, which passed by barely noticed; and then, the Christmases in Jamie's parents' big sad silent house, his Mom clinging to some fantasy of family togetherness, his father picking at his turkey and then retiring to his study. Jamie was always depressed well past New Year's following those visits, and it couldn't help but rub off on me.

And now, we were making it into a party. Jamie's friends from Boston came down on Christmas Eve, and we spent the night baking—actually, they baked and I tasted. We got up early Christmas morning and made egg nog and punch. Loretta came with enough food for an army, and warming trays from the bar; everyone else brought some kind of dish, and a gift. We put our names in the mandolin case and each picked one out, for the presents; after we opened them we all swapped for whatever we liked best. We were all so drunk by then that no one especially cared. Rick and I got along just fine, and even Kirsten didn't get on my nerves. The guy from Jamie's music shop kept trying to flirt with me and Kirsten and Loretta, going back and forth like he couldn't make his mind up; the three of us had such a laugh about it that Kirsten snorted egg nog out her nose, which put us into hysterics. We all agreed, later, that it was the best Christmas any of us had ever had, and that something about it had felt right; it was like that was how we'd always spent the holidays. It was the shape of things to come.

CHAPTER 37
JANUARY–FEBRUARY, 1989

We had an unusually warm January, and Loretta spent several Sundays that month teaching me how to drive. We'd gone out a few times the summer before, but then I got busy with Peter that fall and pretty much abandoned the lessons. Loretta said it was now time for me to get serious about driving. At that point, I didn't care so much about getting my license; it was spending the day with Loretta that I looked forward to.

I was lonely that January. Jamie was in Minneapolis, having made up with Sean right after New Year's; Rick was working full-time between school sessions; and Peter, rumor had it, was back with Annie. I thought obsessively about him, playing over and over a Chutes and Ladders tape he had given me, like it contained some secret message that would tell me how to win him back, if only I listened hard enough. I was so lonely that I began to welcome the hang-up calls that started right after the holidays; Hank the Crank, I named the caller, and I'd chatter at his silent breathing for a good minute or two before he'd hang up the phone.

"You know, you could think about going to see somebody," Loretta said one Sunday as I told her how I'd started having trouble leaving the apartment unless I had good reason. Truth be told, since Jamie had gone up to Minneapolis I only set foot outside to go to work or to meet Loretta, but I didn't tell her that.

"See somebody?" I rolled through a stop sign at the top of the cemetery hill.

"Damn, Miri, you have to stop at those big red signs," Loretta said, laughing.

"I know." I drove carefully down the narrow road, headstones and dead winter grass to either side of me. "What do you mean, go to see somebody?"

"I mean, like a therapist."

I turned the car to the right; it was the same path around the cemetery we'd been taking for the past few weeks. I was glad I hadn't told Loretta the rest of it. I'd started having these flashes of memory: Annmarie, the look she gave me from behind the wheel of her car before she took off on me for good; Grandma, laid out in her coffin, her face looking waxy and unreal; Juan, over the phone in that prison visiting room, telling me not to come back; Peter, his strange shaking that night last month, the next day letting me know I wasn't what he wanted. It felt like everyone I'd ever loved was lost to me; even Wendell, though I'd forgiven him, was no longer in my heart, at least not the way he'd once been. The only person I loved who hadn't deserted me was Jamie, and I started to think that maybe he would, soon as he got the chance. Maybe if our album never came out he'd give up on Cloud Cuckoo Land and move up to Minneapolis for good to be with Sean. I'd had two nightmares that week in which I was on the streets again; in the last one, I was sleeping under the Walnut Street Bridge in Rick's grimy Snoopy and Woodstock bag.

The only thing I could imagine that would make any of this worse would be telling it to a therapist.

"Jesus Christ, Loretta," I said. "I don't need a fucking therapist."

"Everybody needs a fucking therapist."

I decided she had read too many self-help books. "Not me," I said. We came to another stop sign, and I hit the brake this time, too hard. The car lurched to a halt.

"Oh, I forgot," Loretta said. "Your life's been so perfect that you don't have anything to sort out."

I turned my head to give her a dirty look. "Eyes on the road," she said.

"I've dealt with those people before, Loretta. Social workers, therapists— it's all the same bullshit. It's not for me."

She was quiet for a minute as I pulled up to another intersection. "Try a three-point turn," she said.

I did the turn, although it took me more like five points, and headed back in the direction we'd come. "You haven't really dealt with your mother's death," she said.

"Nothing to deal with. She was nothing to me."

"That's bullshit." She pointed at the stop sign I was about to sail through.

I hit the brake way too hard, and we both flew forward, the Galaxie's old lap belts cutting into our stomachs. "You're starting to piss me off, Loretta," I said.

"Fine," she said. "I think we've done enough driving for one day."

The following week, the temperature dropped by more than twenty degrees, and we had an ice storm. Everything looked like it was encased in glass: the tree branches, the power lines, the parking meters, the cars tucked in along the streets. The roads were so slick that even the SEPTA buses had trouble getting around. Loretta called and said she thought it would be best if we waited until the weather cleared to go driving again. I acted like it was fine by me; I couldn't bring myself to tell her that those driving lessons were the only thing holding me together.

It became more and more difficult for me to get out of bed and make it down to the bus stop for work, and once I got back to the apartment I had no energy for anything. I stopped playing the guitar, stopped listening to music, stopped returning phone calls; I even lost interest in chatting with Hank the Crank, whose calls dissolved into hang-ups on the answering machine, which could really have been anyone. I would just sit in front of the TV, grateful for any images I could jam my head with. One night I came home and discovered I was out of cat food; my energy was so spent just from getting through the day that I sunk to the kitchen floor and cried, and it took me two hours to pull myself together enough to walk down to the corner and buy a box of Meow Mix. The next day, I called work and said I had the flu.

I picked up the phone only when I heard Jamie on the machine; he checked in every now and again, and I always told him everything was fine, and worked hard to keep the sadness out of my voice. As soon as I hung up I would break down crying.

The only time I had been in a state anything like this was those weeks after Rick left, after the Collective, when I wandered the streets until Jamie took me in. I had good reason to be depressed then; but I couldn't imagine what was wrong with me now, when I had a roof over my head and food in the cabinets. It was silly, I thought, mooning around over all these people, most of who had been out of my life for some years; and yet I couldn't stop the way I felt, I couldn't stop the crying, the nightmares.

The day before Jamie was supposed to come back, Kirsten stopped by unexpected. She'd thought he was already home, and I told her she had the date wrong, hoping she'd just go away. But she invited herself in, and once she went into the living room and glanced around I could see through her eyes how bad the place looked. Newspapers and clothing I'd once worn were strewn all over the floor; the coffee table was full of cups and mugs, some of which had what looked like fourth-grade science experiments growing in them. Three weeks' worth of trash sat in bags near the front door, waiting for someone to take them out.

"Miri," she said. "What's going on?"

I ran a hand through my hair, realizing I hadn't washed it in a couple of days and that I probably looked as bad as the apartment did. I was still in my bathrobe, and it was 2:00 in the afternoon.

"I just haven't felt great," I said.

"Are you sick?"

"Sort of." I didn't know how to explain it; I wasn't sure myself what exactly was happening to me, and Kirsten was the last person I would talk to about the things going through my head.

Her eyes continued to dart around the apartment. "Jamie's getting back tomorrow?" she asked.

"Yeah." I hoped maybe she'd leave then.

"Okay," she said, taking off her coat and draping it on the coat rack. "I'm going to take these trash bags down to the dumpster. You start picking the stuff up off the floor." She was out the door, trash bags in hand, before I could protest. I decided it would take more energy to fight with her than to do what she'd said, and so I did.

Between the two of us we had the place cleaned up by dinnertime. Actually, it was way cleaner than it ever had been; Kirsten was one of those people who scrubbed everything until it was sparkling. The kitchen hadn't really looked that good since before Clay had left.

"Kirsten, I don't really know what to say," I mumbled, as she put her coat on.

"Forget it," she said. "What time does Jamie's flight come in tomorrow?"

"Around noon."

"Okay," she said. "Tell him to call me."

"I will. Thanks, Kirsten."

She looked at me. "Are you sure you're okay?"

I didn't know how to answer her. "Yeah," I said, but we both knew it was a lie.

Jamie turned up around 1:30 the next afternoon. I had showered and dressed for the occasion. I expected him to come in telling me stories of Sean and what they'd done in Minneapolis, stories I thought would take my mind off my own troubles. Instead, he started asking me all manner of questions about myself.

It turned out that Kirsten had gone and picked him up at the airport, and on the drive into Center City had told him about what happened. And the girl had done her homework—after helping me clean up the apartment she'd checked in with Loretta, who I imagined had filled her head with all kinds of concerns about my mental state.

"Jamie, I'm okay," I said. "I just kind of had a bad month, is all."

"So what's going on?" he asked. He sat down on the couch, motioned me over.

"Well, you know, the whole Peter thing."

He nodded.

"I mean, I know it sounds stupid. It's not like I was with him for a long time, like you were with Clay. I never even had sex with him. It's not a big deal."

"Miri," Jamie said, "you've been in love with him for like two years. It is a big deal."

I thought about that for a minute. "It's other stuff, too," I said. "It's just kind of everything. I don't know." I started to cry, and bit my lip hard to try to stop it.

He pulled me over to him, put his arms around me. "I shouldn't have left when I did," he said. "I knew you were upset about Peter." He was focusing on the breakup, and I was glad to make it all about that. I didn't want to go into the other stuff: how I felt about Annmarie being dead in the ground, or my fears of losing Jamie himself.

"I thought I was okay," I said. "I don't really know what happened."

"Yeah, but you were here for me when Clay left."

We were quiet for a few minutes, just sitting on the couch.

"Let's make a deal," Jamie finally said. "If one of us needs the other, we won't leave. No matter what's going on."

"Really?"

"Really."

"Sounds good to me," I said, and we sat there together for a good long while after that, neither of us making a move to get up, not even to answer the phone. The caller hung up after listening through our message.

Jamie and Loretta did waste a bit of their breath trying to get me to see a shrink that February, but then something happened that snapped me out of the blues and sent both me and Jamie into a kind of delirious frenzy. We got word that a record label—Thick As Thieves, which was one of the biggest and best-known of the indies—had bought our old label, and wanted to put our record out. The way we heard it, one of the main reasons they bought it was for our record. They wanted to remix it and get it released as soon as possible.

We were goofy with happiness until we went to New York and met the people from the label and heard what they considered mixing: they wanted a full drum set, additional guitars, and more backing vocals. Basically, they wanted a whole different band, or so it sounded to me and Jamie.

"It'll go platinum if you just layer it some more," one of the guys said. "You have to have a beat." There were three of them, guys a bit older than Jamie who, while they weren't actually wearing suits, might as well have been.

"You don't even need a drummer," another guy said. "We can just sample a drum beat."

For percussion, we'd done on the record pretty much what we did in concert—hand smacks, foot stomps, an occasional tambourine or maraca

I'd pick up while Jamie played the guitar. Jamie felt that the way our songs were written, drums would be redundant; the rhythm was already there.

He struggled to keep his voice calm as he answered, but his cheeks were red. "First of all, the album as it is now does have a beat," Jamie said. "And sampling is pretty much antithetical to our whole philosophy of music."

I loved it that he could throw out huge words like that to these guys, who probably thought we were just a couple of stupid rock musicians.

"Then get a real drummer," the first guy said. "Adding a drummer would liven up your shows, too."

Now this ticked me right off. "Most folks think our shows are pretty lively the way they are," I said, Jamie nodding in agreement.

"We're a *duo*," he added, emphasizing the word.

"Look," the first guy said, "we think you have enormous potential. But you're shooting yourselves in the foot with this no-drums idea. Have you heard the Indigo Girls? They're a duo. They use drums."

"They use drums on only about half the tracks," Jamie shot back, "and they don't use them at all in concert."

Jamie and the record company guy glared at each other for a minute. I figured it was time for old Miri to pour on a little charm.

"Look," I said, in as sweet a voice as I could stand to hear coming out of me, "Sean Hunter produced what we have now. Why don't we go back and work with him and see what we come up with? Maybe we can get Chris Carson to come in and play percussion on a few songs." I was careful to say "percussion" because it could mean almost anything.

"Who's Chris Carson?" asked the guy who was still glaring at Jamie.

"He's the drummer for the Lost Generation," the third guy answered. He looked younger than the other two, and kinder, with short dark hair and thick nerdy glasses. I fixed a low-wattage smile on him. He smiled back.

"Can you set that up, with Hunter and . . . this drummer?" the glaring guy asked.

I looked at Jamie, and he smiled at me. "No problem," I said, thinking, hey, we've each slept with one of them.

When we left the meeting, the guy with the glasses took us aside.

"You need to hire a manager," he said. "These meetings go better when you have someone to represent you. And you really have to have someone look at the contract before you sign it."

Jamie was offended that he thought we were so naive, but I realized he was just a good guy, trying to make sure we didn't get screwed. I turned my smile up to medium-wattage on the way out so he'd remember me.

We headed up to Minneapolis shortly after that. After so many months in limbo, we had all sorts of things to think about: finishing the album and getting the record company guys to accept it; cover art, photos and the like; and hiring a manager. After our meeting in New York we discussed it for days, and finally decided to offer the job to Kirsten. It seemed only fair; she'd already done so much work for us, and she was smart enough to learn what she needed to. At least we knew we could trust her; even I had to admit that.

To our surprise, she turned us down.

"I've done all I know how to do," she said. "I don't understand contracts or record labels or organizing a real tour. You guys need a professional."

Jamie tried to argue with her, but she simply shook her head. "If I said yes, it wouldn't be fair to you. I'd be in over my head."

"You could figure it out, Kirsten," I said, hoping that my throwing in some positive words might change her mind. She smiled, raised her eyebrows a little.

"The thing is," she said, "I've applied to a couple of law schools for next fall. If I get in, I won't have time to do anything else."

Law schools? Jamie and I both looked at each other. We had no idea this was even something she'd thought of. We were both too stunned to speak for a minute.

"Well," Jamie finally said, "then when you finish you'll have to be our lawyer."

Kirsten smiled, said she'd think about it. "I may not even get in," she said. "I may be writing stupid concert reviews for the rest of my life."

I wondered then at just what point the concert reviews had become stupid to her. She'd clearly loved it once, lived for it even. We were all getting older, it seemed.

CHAPTER 38
FEBRUARY–DECEMBER, 1989

We had a fine time in Minneapolis, at least I did. Chris and I pretty much picked up where we'd left off that summer. I stayed with him, and Jamie stayed with Sean, and sometimes the four of us would go out, like a double date; I'd never been on one of those before. We went out to nice restaurants, or to clubs; I felt like I was living Lolita Clack's life, filtered through a funhouse mirror. I tried not to drink around Chris, because I knew it was still hard for him, and he seemed to appreciate this.

It was Chris who came up with the idea that would save our album, at least save it in the eyes of the record company: bongos. Chris and another drummer he knew laid bongo tracks for about half the songs. The others already had some form of percussion—the handclaps, the maracas, Jamie smacking his guitar between chord changes—and Chris just threw in a little more on those tracks, a celesta here, a wispy pattering on a cymbal there. To keep the Thick As Thieves guys from getting pissed that we hadn't used a full drum kit on any of the songs, Sean recorded a guitar solo that he mixed in at the end of the song we expected to be the first single, "Things I Know." Sean's solo would allow the record company to put a sticker on the cover that said, "Features Sean Hunter of the Lost Generation." It was thought that this sticker would help us sell more albums.

Jamie hated that guitar solo. While the song was one of our more rock-oriented songs—as Jamie said, more punk than folk—it had originally ended with some delicate interplay between our two guitars. It was a wind-down, the original ending, and the guitar solo turned it into more of a rave-up. Jamie claimed it was totally out of context of the song, that guitar solo; he said it was like letting Eddie Van Halen wail at the end of a Bob Dylan song. Of course, he said these things only to me, not to Sean.

And that wasn't the only thing about the album that broke Jamie's heart. Shortly after we came back from Minneapolis, we got word that it would be released only on CD and cassette, not on vinyl. Jamie had been fighting what looked to me to be a one-man battle to save vinyl for the past few years; he said the sound was richer, that he didn't want an average of the highs and lows, he wanted to hear them for himself. Even as it became harder and harder for him to find the new releases he wanted on vinyl, even when the prices on the few record albums that were released rose to the point where they almost cost as much as a CD, Jamie still refused to buy a CD player. He'd gotten so desperate in the past year that he'd had to buy a few new albums on cassette, something he never did. I'd known it was just a matter of time before something would force him to buy a CD player, and that something was our album. But he'd always dreamed of holding in his hands a twelve-inch record cover with his own band's name on it; and now, that dream had been reduced by more than a few inches.

Our album was due to come out in August. In the months while we waited, we played some clubs in Philly, and also some gigs the record label had set up for us, showcase-type things. We hired a management company in New York, someone the Lost Generation's manager suggested; they had a lot of ideas for us, but truth be told both Jamie and me would rather have had Kirsten. If I had thought Kirsten was annoying, these people were ten times worse. They wanted to do us a good job, but it was a business to them, an industry; and even though we weren't naive enough to think it wasn't, we didn't always want to approach things with that thought first in mind. The woman who was our publicist had some kind of fetish for foreign languages; she said *"Bonjour, mes amis,"* when she picked up the phone, *"Ciao,"* when she hung up, and, if you told her an interview she'd set up had gone well she'd yell, *"Wunderbar!"* Jamie said he was hoping to hear her greet us in ancient Etruscan some day. We went so far as to ask Kirsten again if she'd change her mind; but she just shook her head no. She was going to law school, she hoped, and that was that.

As much as the record business people annoyed me, I discovered I had a knack for charming them. I guess it came from my days on the streets; to me, working these corporate types over so they'd give us a good spot on a long night's bill, or positive publicity, or maybe push our album a little harder than they might otherwise have, was no different from scamming some lonelyheart for a free dinner. All I had to do was what I'd done back then: smile, listen to what they had to say, ask them a few questions about themselves, flirt a bit with the guys. When I was done with them they thought we were the best band since the Beatles and wanted to move heaven and earth to promote us. Once it became clear that I had a talent for handling these people, Jamie would just sit back and let me go to work, an amused half-smile on his face. I diverted most of the technical questions to him; for anything else, I just poured on the charm. Jamie said that if he'd realized how good I was at this he would have planted me in the lobby of a record company years before. He also liked to point out how my accent got real Texas when I was working these people over.

That May, Kirsten got accepted to law school at Penn, and Rick graduated from college—in two and a half years, just like he'd said. Jamie and I went to the ceremony. I expected to be bored and distracted and feeling in general like I didn't belong there; I was surprised, then, by how overwhelmed I was with feeling for Rick. When I saw him walking up in his robe to get his diploma, I started to cry. I thought about our squats in West Philly, and the one off Fairmount, and his Snoopy and Woodstock sleeping bag. I wondered what had happened to that bag. As Rick shook hands with an old guy in a puffy robe and took his diploma, I heard a girl a couple of rows behind me say, in a loud whisper, "That's him! He's so cute."

Jamie and I glanced at each other; he'd heard it too. We both looked back at Rick, who was taking his seat. His hair was long and curly now, held back in a ponytail under his graduation cap; his skin had finally cleared up, and he was tall—nearly as tall as Jamie. His brown eyes sparkled when he looked over at us; it was the happiest I'd ever seen him. Jamie and I looked back at each other, and I knew at that moment we were thinking the same thing: Rick had not only grown up, he had gotten good-looking, handsome even. Where were we when that happened?

Afterward, we took Rick out to eat at the Rose Tattoo. We had wanted to throw a party for him, but, truth be told, we didn't know any of his college friends. Rick had a whole separate life from me and Jamie, a life we didn't know very much about. It took us an hour to get Rick out of there, what with all the hugging and congratulating going on. By the time we left, he had been invited to three parties later that night.

We caught Rick up on some of the band stuff, and how Kirsten was going to law school in the fall. I asked him if he had to look for a job now, but he shook his head.

"I'm going to graduate school," he said.

"Graduate school?"

"Yeah, they gave me a really good financial deal. I'll get to teach and stuff."

"So, what does that mean, you'll get like a Master's or something?" I'd heard enough people throw the names of degrees around that I almost felt like I knew something about them.

"Maybe even a Ph.D.," Rick said.

I looked at Jamie to see if he was as surprised as I was, but he looked like he'd already known this. I wondered why I was always the last one to hear everything.

"So what . . . what do you do with a Ph.D.?" I asked.

Rick shrugged. "I'll teach, or work for a company or something. I'm not really worrying about that. I just figure, I like school and I'm good at it and they want to give me money to keep doing it, so why not?"

Now this I could understand. "I always knew you were smart, Rick," I said.

"No you didn't."

"Yes I did. I even told Jamie."

"She did," Jamie said. "Long before you ever uttered a word to me, I might add."

Rick looked sheepish. "I was such a jerk," he said.

Jamie shrugged, shook his head.

"Maybe we're both done with our jerk years," I said to Rick. "I sure hope I am." It was my way of saying I was sorry, and he got it.

"I'm pretty sure I'm done with mine," he said, and he smiled at me. It hit me just then that I hadn't heard him stutter in a long time—months, maybe longer. I wondered if that had happened at the same time he'd grown up, when I had my back turned.

Our album, which was just called *Cloud Cuckoo Land*, came out in August right before my twenty-third birthday. We got an initial thrill, of course, seeing it in stores, and we did some promo stuff the record company had set up both in Philly and in New York—in-studio things at radio stations, interviews. We played the opening night of the Philadelphia Folk Festival, and then we left on the tour the label had set up—cross-country, this time.

The shows went well in the Northeast, where folks knew us, but once we got west of Ohio it was like we'd never released an album at all. The label and our new management company had set these gigs up, and some of them were almost as bad as the worst shows Kirsten had put together. We weren't playing shit-kicker bars, but we still had nights when only five or six people came to hear us play. As we made our way across Iowa, Nebraska, Colorado, and Utah, we became convinced that our record wasn't being played anywhere west of Cincinnati. Nevada was even worse—an endless stretch of sand and cactus, and then the blinding neon of Las Vegas, where we had a crowd that talked through our entire set.

We had a few shows set up in California: San Francisco, Santa Cruz, L.A., San Diego. We were both so sick of driving by the time we hit the coast—I had managed to pass my driver's test that summer, on my second try—that we both wanted to tell the label to forget it, that we'd made a huge mistake, and we were flying back home. We wouldn't have really done this, of course, but we fantasized about it aloud.

And then, as we crossed the Golden Gate Bridge on the way to our San Francisco gig, we caught a snatch of "Things I Know" as Jamie was flipping through the radio stations. He twisted the dial so quickly that he went right past it, and had to double back to find our song again. We'd heard our songs before on college radio stations, but this was different. It was our first single, and they were playing it on a commercial rock station. Jamie winced a little when Sean's guitar solo came in at the end, but still, I could see he was happy.

The club we played that night was nearly packed; it was the best crowd we'd had since we left the Northeast. There had been a good write-up on us in the city's alternative paper, and Jamie wondered aloud if Clay had read it. Through our entire set I could see him squinting at the crowd, scanning the faces, and I knew he was hoping to see Clay out there. But the only people who turned up to meet us were some college friends of Kirsten's, who we stayed with that night.

As we headed down the coast it turned out that we had a following in California even though we'd never played there before. There were respectable numbers of people at all our shows out there; a few folks even mouthed some of the words. Our album had only been out for a month, but one of the deejays at a station in Santa Cruz told us that our demo had been floating around the West Coast for a few years.

We spent three days in L.A.; we had two shows booked, a couple of interviews and an appearance at a record store lined up. On our second morning there we picked up the newspaper to read the review of our previous night's show. The reviewer had liked us, but what was even more interesting was the ad at the bottom of the page. It seemed Ian Oliver was also in L.A., playing with a bunch of other over-the-hill rock stars from the '60s. Pterodactyl, they were calling themselves.

Jamie thought that we should stay an extra day and go see Pterodactyl and plant ourselves in front of the stage, just to see what Ian would do, if he would recognize me and how he would react. But I had a hunch that, so long as he'd read the paper that morning, I wouldn't have to go to him, and I was right; he turned up at our show that night. He was standing stage left, hidden in the shadows where he thought I couldn't see him. It made me wish I had written a song about his hairy mole that I could embarrass him with. Instead, about halfway through our set, I said, "I think everyone should know there's a real rock star in our midst. Ian Oliver is here." I didn't mean it to come out quite as sarcastic-sounding as it did. I pointed toward him, and the club's lighting guy zoomed a white spotlight in on him. Ian smiled and nodded uncomfortably and, as soon as the light was off him, bolted from the club. He moved faster than you'd think a man his age could, like he'd committed a crime and the cops were on his trail. As Ian exited the club, Jamie played the opening chords of one of Woolly Mammoth's big hits, as a goof; people in the crowd who were not disposed to care much for Woolly Mammoth started laughing, and then we went into one of our own songs. I guess it was mean, but I felt like Ian deserved it. Giving him that little dose of humiliation wiped the slate clean in my mind.

We got back to Philly in early October. The album had gotten good reviews and had been selling slowly while we were on the road, surely not making us any real money but enough that we could be taken seriously, at least that was what Jamie said. But by the time we got back, our album sales had leveled off, and we started to fear the record would sink without a trace. Jamie said we hadn't toured enough, even though we both knew that we couldn't have stood being on the road any longer than what we'd done. The big commercial rock station in Philly, WMMR, seemed to play "Things I Know" about three times and then give up on it; it was played a lot on college radio, but we expected that, by then. Jamie blamed it on everything from Sean's guitar solo to the bongos, and he'd started threatening to drag me off on another tour when we got a call from the management company: *Rolling Stone* had named us best new band, and picked our album as one of the best of the year. They were sending a reporter and photographer down to meet with us. We felt like we'd won the lottery.

The photo shoot was ridiculous; they posed us on 21st Street in front of Jamie's building, and on South Street in front of the Big Bang; they couldn't decide whether they wanted to emphasize the height difference between me and Jamie or lessen it, and so they kept having me get on and off an array of stools. By the time it was over, Jamie looked like he was about to puke, and I was certain I'd closed my eyes in every shot. Jamie said it was the single most embarrassing thing he had ever been through. We both feared that once they developed the prints, they'd recognize us as the amateurs we were, and take back the whole thing, giving "Best New Band" to some group that photographed better than we did.

But the pictures turned out great. The day the magazine hit the newsstands, Loretta, true to her word, had the page with our photo blown up, then taped it in the window with the sign she'd always said she'd put up: "Cloud Cuckoo Land played their first show here." She put "their" in all capital letters, I suppose for Peter's benefit. Loretta could sure hold onto a grudge sometimes.

Having your picture in a national magazine is a sure-fire way to root up people you'd hoped were long buried. Jamie got a letter from a guy Clay had once had an affair with, and another from a boy who used to beat him up in the fourth grade; both of these guys seemed to be under the impression that they had been best friends with Jamie. I myself got several notes from people I'd never been friends with in the two high schools I'd attended; and I received a letter on fancy stationery with a return address in Dallas to a Mary Gay Spears-Hart. I sent that one back unopened, despite Jamie's pleas for me to read it. I was curious, too, but I had a stronger compulsion to make it clear to her that we were not, and never had been, family.

There was one letter I got that I did respond to. It was from Lolita Clack; she was living in Seattle, going to medical school, of all things. She wrote a nice note about how much she liked the album; unlike the other letters Jamie and I had gotten from people in our pasts, it was clear that Lolita had actually heard the album. She said she and Jimmy had always wondered what had happened to me, that they still thought of me often. I almost didn't answer her letter, either; Lolita had always been nice to me, but still, I wasn't about to tell her everything that had happened between Prairie Rose and now. Instead I just her sent her a short note of thanks, and said maybe we'd get in touch if we toured the West Coast again.

About two weeks after the article came out, Clay left a message on our answering machine. It was short, just, "Congratulations," and for Jamie to call him in Berkeley, California, at a phone number he rattled off. He sounded like the same old Clay, haughty as ever. Jamie said he wasn't going to call him back, that he was finally over Clay, and it seemed he stuck to his word, for Clay left two more messages over the next week. The last of these accused me of not giving Jamie the messages. Jamie heard that one before I did and played it for me when I got home, shaking his head.

We played the Big Bang that New Year's Eve. Chris had come down from Minneapolis, to spend some time with me. He had recently started telling me he loved me, and the whole thing was making me uneasy; I wasn't sure how I felt. Kirsten was at the show, the first one she'd been to since she'd started law school that fall. Rick turned up with a girl; this one was very normal-looking, with short brown hair and wire-rimmed glasses, nothing at all like Eclipse. Sean was in the middle of helping an Austrian heavy metal band record an album—at least, that was what he'd said—and couldn't come down. The band was real, but I wasn't sure if they were the only reason Sean hadn't come. Their relationship was so up and down, Jamie and Sean's.

Loretta insisted on taking lots of pictures that night. "You're almost famous," she kept saying. "I want proof I knew you."

At midnight, a number of guys managed to find me and kiss me before I made my way over to Chris. He put his arms around me and stooped down to bury his face in my neck, and all around us people were shouting and blowing on noisemakers; everywhere I looked I saw the number 1990. I scanned the crowd for Jamie. It seemed to me that he should have been the first guy I kissed that year, the first year of a new decade; but he was far across the club, in a corner talking to Kirsten, and, as far as I could tell, he didn't even see me.

CHAPTER 39
MARCH–MAY, 1990

We went up to Minneapolis in early March to record our second album. By then, we had almost enough songs for a third album, too—it seemed we were always ahead of ourselves. Chris was out of town for the first week we were there, laying drum tracks as a favor to some band he'd once met on the road, and so Jamie and I both stayed with Sean at first. The three of us got along fine; in fact, I seemed to have the opposite effect on those two than I'd had on Jamie and Clay. Jamie said they actually got along better when I was around, and I could see it; Sean appeared to be taken with me, in some way that was obviously not sexual but which made him enjoy spending time with me.

Chris's desire for me was another matter entirely. He rushed the work he was doing for the other band and got back as quickly as possible, appearing not to have slept in at least twenty-four hours when he got off the plane. Jamie was afraid Chris had fallen off the wagon, but I knew better; he'd traded his obsession with drugs and alcohol for an obsession with me. I'd seen these cycles of need and desperation in Annmarie, and watching it play out in Chris put a damper on whatever affection I had for him. Despite my reservations, I stayed at his place the first two nights he was back in Minneapolis, and he wouldn't leave me alone for a minute; I could even feel him hovering over me while I slept. He was constantly trying to wait on me, jumping up to get me things, asking me if I needed or wanted anything, anything at all. It's not that I wasn't flattered by all the attention, but it was so out of proportion that I knew it wasn't just me he wanted; it was something I represented, some kind of girlfriend he thought he needed, couldn't live without. Although he took it further than I had, it was something like the way I'd been in love with Peter Fenster, and I knew what a disaster that had turned into. On the third day of my stay with

Chris I took my stuff and went back to Sean's, telling Chris he was driving me straight up the walls and that if he could pull himself together and act like a normal person then maybe I'd see him again.

Instead, Chris threw his passion into laying tracks for us. He was taking care of percussion again on this album, using odd types of drums and weird South American instruments whose names I was still trying to keep straight. Not only had Jamie resigned himself on the percussion issue, he was actually thinking about using a full drum kit on one or two tracks; this was mainly because the guys from Thick As Thieves became thrilled with the bongos after our first album's success, and were now telling us to use nothing but bongos. Jamie told Chris he didn't care what kinds of drums he used as long as none of them were bongos. Jamie had a perverse streak when it came to dealing with the record company.

Despite the fact that Chris had stopped speaking to me, the sessions went well. By the time Jamie's thirtieth birthday rolled around in April, we were close to being finished, and we all agreed this album was better than our first. The songs were stronger, Jamie had better control of his singing voice, and my guitar playing just seemed to keep getting better. We also had a clearer vision of what we wanted our sound to be; that is, Jamie had a clearer vision. This second album was more rock than folk or country, but that was okay with me; Jamie's passion for the louder, faster music had seeped into me by then. He said he wanted our third album to be heavy metal country, and he was only half-kidding.

I smoothed things over with Chris so that we could all take Jamie out for his birthday. We went to dinner and then to a series of bars; Sean and Jamie managed to ditch us at the last of these. I had to laugh when I figured out what they'd done. There was no choice but for Chris and I to properly make up, and that's what we did.

When I saw Jamie in the studio the next day, I thought at first that the way he looked was the result of a bad hangover; there was no color in his face at all. He looked like he'd seen a ghost, or like he was a ghost himself. I studied his face and decided this was no hangover; something had happened, something bad.

I pulled him out of earshot of Sean and Chris. "Jamie," I asked, "what's wrong?"

"Nothing," Jamie said. He said it in his most stubborn tone; prying anything out of him would be a real chore.

"Did you guys have a fight?" I asked, motioning toward Sean.

"Yeah," Jamie said. I couldn't tell if it was true. He had that mask on, the Emerson family mask that hid all emotions.

"What about?"

Jamie shook his head. "I don't want to talk about it. I just want to finish the album."

We spent the next few days like that, putting the final touches on the recording, me trying to get Jamie to talk about what had happened and him stubbornly refusing. Sean had the same stricken look on his face that Jamie had, but it didn't seem like they were mad at each other. They huddled together and spoke in whispers when they thought no one was looking.

I didn't mention it to Chris at first, thinking it was just some fight that would blow over; besides, Chris and I were getting along again, and when we were together, out of the studio, I put everything else aside. But it started to gnaw at me, and I asked Chris one night at dinner if he knew what was going on with Jamie and Sean.

He laughed. "I was going to ask you the same question," he said. "I figured Jamie would have told you."

I shook my head. "Sean didn't tell you anything?"

"No," he said, "but that's not unusual." He was quiet for a second while the waiter deposited a basket of rolls on our table. "He's not completely comfortable with being the only one in the band who's gay."

"Really?" I hadn't thought much about that before. I tried to imagine Jamie in a band with three straight guys. Once, I had thought this might have been something he wanted; but I knew him better now. I couldn't picture it.

"Yeah, but we don't care," Chris said. "I mean, he came out to us about a year after we started the band, but we already knew. We knew pretty much from the beginning."

"Did it bother anyone, I mean, when they first realized it?"

"Not really," Chris said. "I mean, if it did, no one talked about it. It didn't bother me." He signaled the waiter for another ginger ale. Poor Chris had been living on ginger ale since he'd gotten out of rehab. He'd told me once he'd developed a taste for it only after going sober, and he had no idea why.

"I would think some guys would have a problem with it," I said.

"Yeah, but it would be pretty stupid, in this case. Sean's the one with most of the musical ideas. He's the lead singer and guitarist. The way I look at it, anyone stupid enough to be hung up about him being gay wouldn't deserve to work with him, anyway."

I realized, at that moment, that I tended to underestimate Chris; like everyone else, I often thought of him as just the drummer, a guy who I enjoyed on occasion but didn't want to get too serious with, and who I didn't want to get serious about me. After we got back together the night of Jamie's birthday I'd asked him to cool it with the love talk; I'd told him that I wasn't looking for anything that serious, that I couldn't take it when he hovered all over me. He'd agreed that he'd come on too strong, and had seemed much more relaxed since then. I was starting to think maybe I shouldn't push him too far away; there was a lot more to Chris than I gave him credit for.

"Well," I said, "I wish I could figure out whatever this thing is going on with Jamie. I know Sean is in on it, and they're shutting me out."

"Maybe it's just between the two of them," Chris said, helping himself to a roll and offering me the basket, which I waved away.

I sighed. "I guess," I said, but I wasn't convinced.

The day we finished up in the studio, Jamie took me aside and told me he wasn't going back to Philly right away. He tried to tell me that he was staying in Minneapolis for a few weeks, but Jamie was a bad liar if it involved more than a one-word answer; I could see right off that he wasn't telling me the truth, and I badgered him until he told me where he was really headed: Berkeley, California.

"Don't even tell me that," I said, anger rising in my voice. "Don't even tell me you're thinking of getting back with Clay."

"I'm not getting back with him," he said. "I just have to go out there."

"Why?" I asked. "So he can turn your head around and convince you to break up with Sean, and move out there with him?" And leave me, I thought, but I kept that part to myself.

Jamie looked at me, but I had the sense he was looking through me, not really seeing me. "I just have to go," he said. "I'll be back home in a few weeks."

His answer was no denial, and it gnawed at me. I stayed with Chris rather than going back to Philly, to kick around the empty apartment by myself. Kirsten had the cats, and my job was pretty flexible at that point; Paul would put me on the schedule whenever I was in town. There was no reason to rush back, especially without Jamie there. I surprised myself by admitting my fears to Chris, and he tried to assure me that no matter what happened with Sean or Clay, Jamie wasn't going to break up the band; but I wasn't convinced. And without the band, I thought, Jamie had no real need for me.

A month went by before I heard from Jamie. He left a message for me at Chris's place, saying that he was back in Philly and that I should let him know when I was coming home. I called at many different times of day but couldn't reach him—I wasn't sure if he was really out or if he was just screening—and so finally I left a message telling him when my plane would arrive, assuming he would pick me up at the airport. Chris made me promise to call him as soon as I found out what had happened.

Kirsten showed up at the airport in Jamie's place. I asked her where he was, and she just shook her head.

"He asked me to pick you up, but he wouldn't say why he couldn't come himself," she said. "Something's going on with him, Miri. He's real upset but he won't talk about it."

I was secretly glad he hadn't told Kirsten whatever it was; it would have killed me if he'd confided in her and not me.

I got home to find Jamie on the couch, with the TV on, the sound down low. Nico and Artemis came up and rubbed on my ankles, then my bags.

Jamie looked up at me and clicked the remote off. The light was dim in the living room, but he looked like he'd been crying.

"Jamie," I said, sitting down on the couch next to him. "Please tell me what's going on."

He wiped his eyes with the back of his hand. He stood up, walked around the couch in a circle, then sat down again.

"I don't know how to tell you," he said. "I mean, I really just don't know how to do it." I could hear a catch in his throat every few words.

Thoughts raced through my mind, the thoughts I'd been having for weeks: he was moving to California to be with Clay; he was breaking up the band. Like Peter, he was going to freak out and bail just as we were on the verge of making it. The record company expected this second album to really sell, to take us places.

I just sat there and waited for him to go on.

"The only reason I didn't tell you before I left," he said, "was that I wanted to get the album finished before we had to deal with this."

"Okay," I said. "It's finished. So tell me now." I let a little irritation creep into my voice.

He drummed his long fingers on the coffee table for a few seconds, then picked his hand up abruptly. "I checked our messages from one of those bars the night of my birthday," he said. "I wanted to see how many people had called me." He let out a short bitter sound that was barely recognizable as a laugh. "There was a message from a friend of Clay's." He cleared his throat, looked away for a second. My hands were knotted into fists in my lap.

"Clay had been trying to get in touch with me," he said, "because he was sick. Because he was dying."

"Dying?" It still didn't hit me, though I should have figured it out by then.

"Of AIDS," he said. "He died two weeks ago."

I tried to stop the panic that was filling every empty space in my mind. "He's dead?" I asked, barely a whisper.

"Yes," Jamie said. "I . . . we made our peace with each other, before he died."

"Oh," I said. My right foot, the one closest to the door, began tapping; it was an involuntary thing. I tried to stop it, but couldn't. I wanted to spring to that foot and flee the room.

"But you're okay, right?" I said. "I mean, you tested negative and all, before he left."

Tears started to spill out of his eyes.

"Jamie, tell me you're okay."

He was quiet for a minute, and rubbed his eyes again. "Remember," he said softly, "how we were supposed to go back and get retested? And neither one of us did."

"But you're okay. You were negative when you were with Clay, and you weren't with anyone else. Not for a long time." It felt like a whole chorus was screaming off-key in my head. The pounding was so bad I could barely hear what Jamie was saying.

"Sometimes, the virus doesn't turn up for six months after you're exposed," he said, in the dry way a doctor—his father, maybe—might say it. "That's why they tell you to come back." He sighed. "And it doesn't matter how many people I was with. Clay was with enough for us both."

I stared at him, not wanting to hear any more.

"I just—I mean, I knew all that, but—I just didn't want to go back to the clinic, you know? I was negative once, why tempt fate?" He shook his head.

"Are you saying you're not negative now?" I asked. It came out all garbled, a math equation gone wrong.

He blinked hard, looked at me. "I went back to Minneapolis for a few days before I came home," he said, "and Sean and I both got tested. He's okay." His voice got softer; his gaze roamed past me, searching for something. "I'm positive."

In an instant I was back in Grandma's house. I was fourteen, coming home late from school, my lips tingling from my first kiss. I put my key in the door, opened it, called out her name. I could hear a rhythmic buzzing sound. I could smell the lemon Pledge, I could see all the rooms as I walked through them, a knot of dread tightening in my stomach, looking for Grandma. Every room of the house led to that one room where she lay dead, the phone buzzing in her hand.

"I don't believe it," I said. "They made a mistake with the test."

He shook his head. "It's not a mistake, Miri. I'd like it to be, but it's not."

"How do you know that?" I asked. My voice was getting higher in pitch. My foot continued its unstoppable tapping.

"I had it done again, here."

I was at the cemetery then, watching as they lowered Grandma's casket into the ground. Wendell was by my side. I could hear Aunt Melissa's showy wailing in the background, and Annmarie's quieter sniffles, ones she was choking down. In my mind, the one selfish thought, the thought I could never keep down no matter how hard I tried: What's going to happen to me? How will I live, now?

I gave in to my trigger foot, the one that wanted to head out the door, and was up off the couch before I could stop myself. "I have to get out of here," I said to Jamie.

"Miri, wait. I know I should have told you what was going on. I—"

"I have to go," I said, grabbing my black bag and one of my duffel bags of clothes from the floor. "I'll—I'll call you."

I knew how awful it sounded the second it came out of my mouth. I saw the look on Jamie's face, the look of pain and fear and disappointment, disappointment in me. But I couldn't stop myself from leaving the apartment, or breaking into a run as I hit Spruce Street, or continuing to run all the way down to the waterfront, where I tossed my bags onto a bench and, exhausted, buried my face in them, allowing myself to cry harder than I'd ever cried in my life.

I stayed on that bench for hours, until the sun started to go down. Finally I picked up my bags and headed for Bill's, but he wasn't home. I didn't know where else to go. I imagined Jamie had called Rick and Kirsten by then and told them everything, including how I'd run off; I was an awful person even by my own account. I'm not sure what I was thinking as I got on a bus and headed to West Philly. I couldn't go to Rick; maybe I was thinking of that parking lot under the Walnut Street bridge, the place where Rick and I had slept, years ago. Somehow, though, I wound up at Peter Fenster's building.

I rang the bell, and waited. It took him a few minutes to come down, and I sat on the step. I was in no hurry; there was nowhere else for me to go.

"Miri," he said when he opened the door. "What are you doing here?"

He was clean-shaven now, and had lost weight. He looked like the old Peter again, the one I had wanted but not the one I'd gotten.

"I need a place to stay for a couple of days. Can I crash on your couch?"

He looked at my bags, then back at me. "What's going on?" he asked. "You guys didn't break up, did you?"

"Break up?"

"The band, I mean."

"Oh." There was a cool wind blowing that night; I pulled my denim jacket tighter around me. "No, we didn't break up, but I need a little time away from Jamie. Can I just sleep here, Peter? I won't hang around much. You won't even know I'm here." I knew there was a kind of desperation in my voice; I could hear it myself.

"Umm, sure," he said, and opened the door wider. "Come on in."

We went upstairs, and I dropped my bags next to the couch.

"I was heading out with a couple of friends tonight to see this new band, the Low Road," he said. "You want to come?"

"If you don't mind, I'd rather just stay here," I said.

"That's cool. Just help yourself to whatever."

Twenty minutes later, he was gone.

CHAPTER 40
MAY, 1990

I slept all the next day, a fitful sleep without enough blankets, a sleep full of self-hatred and bad dreams. I never even heard Peter leave for work, and I only woke up when he came home that night.

"God, Miri," he said, putting his book bag down next to the couch. "You just waking up now? What the hell happened, anyway?"

I wasn't going to talk about it, to Peter or anyone else. By now, enough common sense had creeped back into my paralyzed brain to realize that Jamie wouldn't want too many people to know. And even if he wouldn't have minded my telling Peter, my part in the whole thing looked so bad that I feared Peter would just kick me out on the street if he knew what I'd done, what a completely selfish, hateful person I truly was.

"We had a fight. I can't go back there. And I don't want to talk about it." I got up and went to the bathroom, washed my face, and tried to brush the knots out of my hair. I knew Peter was a little bit afraid of me, and I was hoping that fear would keep him from booting me out for a while.

When I came out of the bathroom, Peter was putting a pot of water up to boil. He had a box of spaghetti and a jar of tomato sauce out on the counter.

"My God, a straight man who cooks," I said, and he smiled weakly. I watched as he opened the jar of sauce, poured it into a pan.

"Miri," he said, "how long do you think you're staying?"

"Not sure," I said. "Just let me know when you're sick of me, and I'll move on." I stuck my finger in the sauce, licked it off. I wasn't trying to be seductive; I was really just hungry, but it seemed to make Peter uncomfortable.

"I don't mind if you stay on the couch for a few days while you and Jamie sort things out," he said, "but I probably should tell you that I have a girlfriend now."

"I heard you were back with Annie."

"No," he said, "someone else."

I knew exactly what this meant: that I hadn't been enough to get him over Annie, but some other gal was. It pissed me off, but I didn't have the luxury of being able to blow up at him. I needed him too much right then.

"It's no problem for me, as long as you're cool with it," I said. "You won't even know I'm here. I just need a place to crash."

He smiled then, and looked more relaxed. "Sure. I just wanted you to know. She sleeps here a couple of nights a week."

That happened fast, I thought, for the last I'd heard he was still with Annie when Jamie and I had left for Minneapolis.

"Whatever," I said. I picked up a fork and stirred the spaghetti with it. "Like I said, it's just temporary."

The price for staying at Peter's that night was listening to the whole story of how he met Melody—I wanted to joke about her name but thought better of it—and all the things about her that made her so wonderful. She turned out to be a bit older than Peter—he said she was thirty-five, but when I met her I was sure she'd lied about her age by a few years. She worked as a massage therapist at some kind of New Age health center in Germantown. When I pressed him for the details of how they'd met, it turned out that Peter himself was studying to be a massage therapist. The world just kept changing all around me, and I felt more and more pushed to my own tiny island.

Four nights into my stay with Peter, I went out with him and Melody for drinks. I had to admit Melody was being pretty cool about my staying there; I guessed it was part of her whole New Age deal.

We went to a little bar off the Penn campus, one where I thought we wouldn't run into any of the band people I knew. Unfortunately for me, it turned out to be a hangout for the law school, and, while I was on my third Rolling Rock, I saw Kirsten walking over toward my booth. The way she'd been telling it to Jamie, she barely had time to eat what with all the studying she had to do; it was just my luck that the one night she took a break, I'd run into her.

Peter and Melody had gone to play the jukebox. I knew I looked a wreck; the crying fits I had during the days when Peter was at work had made my face puffy and blotchy, my eyes narrowed to half their normal size. As Kirsten approached my booth I hunched over my beer and tried to hide behind my hair, hoping she hadn't seen me. But she slid into the booth facing mine, and just looked at me for a good long minute.

"Miri," she finally said.

"Kirsten." I didn't look up from my drink.

"What are you doing?" she asked.

I knew what she meant, but I wasn't going there without a fight. "Trying to drink my beer," I said.

She sighed in an exaggerated way that reminded me of why she'd always annoyed me so much. "Jamie told me," she said.

I shrugged.

"Miri, goddamnit. I would have thought you'd be the last person to run out on Jamie when he needed you."

I took a long sip of beer, and let it linger in my mouth for a few seconds before I swallowed it. "Kirsten," I said, "you don't know anything about me. You never have."

"If I don't know you," she said, "it's because you never let me get to know you."

I shrugged again, took another sip of beer.

"It's not easy for me, either," she said, her voice cracking a bit. "I love him too, you know."

I looked up at her then, her face all open and honest the way it got sometimes. This was probably one of the things Jamie liked about her, I thought, this openness. But I wasn't falling for the bait. She wanted me to have some kind of goddamn Hallmark moment with her, and I just couldn't do it.

"Kirsten," I said, my voice getting louder, "you think I don't know what I'm supposed to do here? I know what the right thing to do is. I'm supposed to stay with Jamie until he gets sick and then take care of him as he gets sicker and then watch him die. Well, guess what? I can't do that. I can't watch Jamie die." My hands were shaking hard enough that I had to put down my beer for a second.

"You don't know he's going to die," she said softly.

"Oh yeah? You know anyone who was HIV positive who didn't die?"

"Some people stay well for a long time," she said. "There's a guy out on the West Coast . . ."

"I don't care about some fucking guy on the West Coast!" I was on my feet now, shouting. The people in the booths closest to ours turned around to look. "I care about Jamie. And I can't watch him die. I don't care what anyone thinks of me, Kirsten. I can't do it. I just can't."

I was crying by then, and Peter and Melody were headed back over to the booth. I pushed past them and stormed out the door.

I took the bus over to Bill's, the only place I could think to go. To my surprise, he was home for a change. Once he opened the door I pushed past him before he could say anything.

"Just take your clothes off," I said, "and don't even try to talk to me."

"Uh, okay," Bill said, and he did exactly what I told him to do.

Bill left for work around 10:00 the next morning—he had a new job, managing a restaurant. I decided to hang around his apartment until Peter would be home from work.

As the day wore on in that dreary basement apartment, I made a decision. Without Jamie, there was nothing left for me in Philly. It was time to leave town. I couldn't complain, really—for a girl who'd wound up in Philly purely by chance, I'd done alright in my six years there. But now I needed to move on. I'd get my stuff from Peter's and stay in a motel that night—the Divine Tracy, maybe, the place where I'd first stayed in Philly. I thought that bringing it around full circle like that would help give my leaving some meaning, would make it seem somehow fated. And when I got up the next morning I'd head directly to the bank and clean out my account, and then, cash in hand, I'd head for 30th Street Station. I'd take a train somewhere—anywhere.

I left Bill's place around 5:00 and headed over to Peter's. On my way, though, I decided to stop in at the Big Bang to say goodbye to Loretta. I was sure Jamie had told Rick, so I wouldn't dare go there, but I was hoping he hadn't clued Loretta in. I wanted to see her one last time.

From the second I walked into the Big Bang, I knew I'd made a mistake. Loretta made a beeline for me and pulled me in the back of the bar. I could tell she knew everything.

"You can save whatever speech you have ready, Loretta," I said after she'd closed the door to her office. "I just came to say goodbye."

"Oh, I can save it, huh?" she said, and she looked so mad that for a minute I thought she might hit me. I didn't much care if she did or not; there was no way I could feel any worse than I already did. She looked like she was struggling with herself for a minute, and then she calmed down.

"You'd piss me off a lot more," she said, "if you didn't remind me so damn much of myself at your age."

"I'm leaving town tomorrow," I said. "I really just came to say goodbye."

"You thought maybe I didn't know. You thought maybe Jamie hadn't told me."

I shrugged.

"You know, he's not mad at you," she said. "For the life of me I don't understand why not. I'd be mad as hell. But he's not. He just wants you to come home."

"Can't do it," I said. Something about the way she'd put it, that he wanted me to come home, made my eyes tear up.

Loretta put her hands on her hips. "So you just take off," she said, "just like that. Fuck Jamie, fuck the band, fuck everything, right?"

I stared at the "Miller Time" clock hanging on the wall. "Yeah," I said, "just like that."

"Okay, Miri," she said, "you go run off somewhere because life got tough. Go ahead. But let me ask you one thing: you hate your mother so much for taking off on you. If you do this, what makes you any different from her?"

Loretta was staring me hard in the eyes. Like Kirsten and her Hallmark moment, Loretta thought she could change my mind, make me think

more about what I was doing. She didn't realize I'd already thought long
and hard about it.

"I'm not any different from Annmarie," I said softly. "I'm exactly like
her. Bye, Loretta."

I pushed past her, out of the office, and through the bar to the front
door. She didn't try to stop me.

Peter and Melody insisted I spend the night rather than take a motel.
They still didn't know what was going on. Peter seemed to think I was running away from the band, just as he had.

We said goodbye in the morning, me and Peter. It was funny how unimportant he seemed to me now—he mattered as little as those college boys
I'd hooked up with on the road to Austin, all those years ago.

I got to the bank as soon as it opened and closed out my account. There
was a little over $9,000 in there—my share of what we'd made off our first
album, minus what little I'd spent of it. I asked for half the money—
$4,500—in cash, the other half in a check. The check I made out to Jamie.
He didn't really need the money, but it was all I could think of to give him;
it was my way of saying goodbye. I stuck it in an envelope I'd stamped and
addressed at Peter's, and tossed it in a mailbox outside the bank.

I walked over to 30th Street Station and looked over the options at the
Amtrak window. I could head north, up through Vermont and clear into
Canada. I could head west, to Chicago. I thought about trying to make it
out to Minneapolis, to stay with Chris for a while; but he was part of my
old life now, the life I was leaving behind. There was another train line, the
Southern Crescent, that went from New York City all the way down to
New Orleans. I liked that name, Southern Crescent; it was mentioned in
an old R.E.M. song, one that Jamie and I both loved. It made a weird kind
of sense, to head for New Orleans, just like Annmarie had. I wondered if
maybe it was in our Cajun blood, New Orleans; a place we were destined
to seek out in times of trouble.

The Southern Crescent train wouldn't hit Philly until late that afternoon, and I felt the sooner I got out of town, the better, so I bought two
tickets: one for the Metroliner to D.C., then a second from there to pick

up the train to Louisiana. I figured I could spend the day in Washington, walk around like a tourist and then high-tail it down south. From there, the trip to New Orleans would take about twenty-four hours.

I had an hour to kill before my train left for D.C. I bought a Coke at the McDonald's in the station and sat down on one of the big, high-backed benches. I had always loved this train station, going back to the days when Rick and I used to stash our stuff in the lockers. The way the light came in the high windows, the pigeon or two that always managed to be trapped up in the rafters, the big ancient-looking clock—you could just picture this station 100 years earlier, people coming and going in hats and gloves, the high-necked dresses that the women used to wear.

I sipped on my Coke and watched a girl walk out of the McDonald's. She sat down next to me, then got up quickly and paced around in front of the bench. She was holding a cup of ice, just ice—I'd seen it when she sat down. The girl was young, maybe seventeen or eighteen; her brown hair, which hugged her neck in a French braid, was dull and limp despite how carefully she'd tried to arrange it. She was so thin she looked like she was trying to disappear. She leaned her head back and sucked on an ice cube; the muscles and sinews in her neck stood out like exposed bones. Her clothes—pastels that matched perfectly, and a pale pink leather coat that you could tell had cost a small fortune—hung on her as if she were a child playing dress-up. She was as thin as pictures I'd seen of people in concentration camps; as thin as people dying, dying of disease.

And I could tell, from the look in her eyes, that she knew she was dying. That look—a giving in, it was, a kind of resignation. She looked hollow, this girl, like she could blow away; I remembered having felt like that, before I went to live with Jamie.

That day, when I'd had no place to go and hadn't eaten for days and hardly knew where I was, Grandma had given me a message. I wished she'd come now and sit down next to me on the bench, tell me if I was doing the right thing by leaving—the right thing for me, anyway. I closed my eyes and pictured her, tried to hear her voice, but I had trouble even keeping her image fixed in my mind. Grandma wasn't talking to me anymore. I was on my own now.

The starving girl continued to pace in front of me, still sucking on her ice. I thought for some reason about Wendell—how it had seemed like he'd felt guilt all these years for not fighting to keep me. It had been almost the first thing out of his mouth, when I met him again. He'd said it in a hundred small ways in all the cards and notes he'd sent me since we'd gotten back in touch. I wondered if Annmarie had felt any guilt, about leaving me, and how she'd felt when she was dying. Had it been worse, I wondered, dying without anyone who loved her, and knowing that she'd brought that kind of loneliness on herself?

Except for getting knocked up and doing a lot of drugs, I'd made every mistake Annmarie had ever made. I'd used people; I'd hurt them. And even though I always swore I hadn't, I'd confused sex for love, at times. Or used it as a substitute.

The announcement for my train came over the loudspeaker—the Metroliner to D.C. I'd lost all track of time and couldn't believe that an hour had passed already. I looked around for the starving girl, and saw her standing a few benches away; the sun streaming in from the skylight overhead caught the dust particles in the air around her and made her look grainy, like an old photograph. She was now holding a leash, a black-and-white spotted dog attached to the other end. It hit me that I'd seen her around Philly before, but she didn't look the same; or maybe I'd just never noticed how thin she was. She looped the dog's leash around her wrist, popped another piece of ice in her mouth, and looked staight at me. There was something in her look that said she knew me, too, and I had, for a second, the strange feeling that I was looking at Jamie; something about this girl's face reminded me of his. She could have been his sister.

With that thought, a shiver went down my back; the crowd of travelers swelled around the girl, and I lost her. I pushed through the throng of folks hurrying to their platforms, to the bench where the girl had been standing; but if she'd ever been there, she was gone now, swallowed up by the crowd, maybe, or simply faded back into that shaft of sun from the skylight, dissolved into dust motes, into nothing.

A second announcement for my train came over the speaker. I held onto the back of the bench, trying to get my bearings. While I believed that Grandma's ghost had come to visit me that day in front of the library, could the ghost of someone you'd never met track you down as well? My mind was playing tricks on me, I decided, and I slung my bag over my shoulder, turned in the direction of the train platform.

People were lined up at the escalator, headed down. I watched them, bags and briefcases in hand, as they made the descent, one by one. I searched the crowd for a glimpse of the starving girl, to prove to myself that she had been real; but she was nowhere to be found. The boarding call continued, sounding more urgent. I heard Jamie's voice—"If one of us needs the other, we won't leave"—and fought to shrug it off. I hitched my bag up higher on my shoulder and tried to make a move toward the escalator, but, for once in my life, my trigger foot wouldn't work. It wasn't that my legs wouldn't obey me, exactly; more like I was unable to tell them to move. The boarding call continued; the line at the escalator disappeared. The announcement came for final call, and I just stood there as the train left without me.

I'd like to say that I decided to stay only for Jamie, to take care of him, return all that he'd done for me; but in the end, like everything else, what it came down to was me. I could live my life like Annmarie had lived hers, taking off whenever things got rough; or I could stay and actually try to make a life. My life, the only life I'd had since I was eighteen, was here, in Philly, with Jamie. And if part of that life would be watching him die, then I'd just have to find a way to live through it. The other kind of life was not a real life, anyway; it was a half-life among shadows, a homeless wandering.

I gathered my bags and headed out the door. There was a line of taxis waiting there, and I figured, what the hell. I had thousands of dollars in my pocket; I was feeling extravagant. I waited while the driver put my bags in the trunk, and then I got in the back seat. He walked around to the driver's side, climbed behind the wheel, asked me where I was going. I gave him Jamie's address. My address.

Chapter 41
August, 1991

Jamie was standing on the bottom step of our building, boxes and folding tables full of our junk on the sidewalk in front of him, haggling with a woman over the price of a lamp. I'd seen this woman before; she was about Jamie's mother's age, and had two small, yappy white poodles she walked several times a day. I personally felt that either Nico or Artemis could beat up these poodles—they were soft-looking, nervous little animals, much like their owner.

Thanks to Jamie, so far we'd made $64 in our yard sale, and the day was still young. We were selling pretty much every piece of junk in the apartment; the rule was, if it didn't work, wasn't in good shape, or if one of us really hated it, then it was out. We were moving the next day and wanted to get rid of as much useless stuff as possible.

The woman left with the lamp, her dogs yelping at nothing in particular, and Jamie waved some singles around at me, a victorious grin on his face. "The grand total," he said, after counting all the bills twice, "is now seventy-three dollars."

"We're rich," I said, and Jamie laughed.

"Not anymore," he said. "We're actually in debt now."

It was true: we'd bought a house, me and Jamie, making the down payment with our band money. Our second album had done well, sold almost three times as many copies as the first. Not that we were selling millions or anything, but it was enough, with the good reviews we got, to keep the record company happy; we were lucky to be on an indie label that didn't expect us to go platinum right off the bat. We'd each made $27,000 in the past year; to me, that felt like a fortune.

The idea of buying the house had kind of evolved over time. It had started that spring, when we came back from two months of touring to find our apartment flooded again, this time to the point where the rugs, and some of the furniture, were ruined. We had to badger the landlord for three days before he'd even send anyone over to pump out the standing water. Once we were able to move back in we found that the water had shorted out the refrigerator, and the landlord refused to replace it. After weeks of calls to tenant boards and legal services people, Jamie and I both decided the easiest thing to do was just to move.

At first, we looked at two-bedroom apartments in our neighborhood, but then we started thinking of moving to Olde City, to be closer to the music store where we still rehearsed after closing. One night in May we had Kirsten and Rick over for dinner, and she had this idea: why didn't we all just rent a big house? It would be cheaper and we'd have more space. To my surprise Rick liked the idea too—he'd been living in dorms for years and was starting his second year of grad school in the fall. It was time to have a real home, he said.

Of course, the part of it that none of us talked about was Jamie—that if we all lived together, there would be three of us around to help take care of him if he got sick. I think we all knew this but left it unspoken. Jamie was healthy as a horse, and none of us ever mentioned our fears or worries about his future. I myself had given up worrying altogether; I was sure I'd taken about ten years off my life fretting about Jamie those first few months after I found out he'd tested positive. I spent weeks trailing him with cups of tea and herbal potions Peter's girlfriend Melody recommended to me, until he finally told me to cut it out or he was going to put me on that Southern Crescent train himself. We joked about it, now; Jamie called it "Miri's little escapade."

So the four of us began looking at houses in Olde City and Queen Village, and then Jamie heard something about Mount Airy. It was a twenty-minute ride from Center City and at first we didn't think we'd want to be so far away but then we went out there and looked around and fell in love. There was grass and trees and beautiful gardens and white folks and black folks and young women who wore yarmulkes as a feminist statement—they told me this when I asked—and everyone said hi when you passed them on the sidewalk. We almost couldn't believe we were still in Philly; it was like the best things about the city with the good things about life in Prairie Rose all mixed together. And then we started looking at houses that were for sale, and decided we could actually buy one, Jamie and me. We looked at twenty houses and found a four-bedroom stonefront one with a big weeping willow tree in the front yard and we both fell in love with it, right on the spot. It needed a little work, but it had a big backyard, and a basement we could soundproof and make into a studio, and we could work it out so that Kirsten's and Rick's rent would pretty much cover the mortgage. And there was something about the front yard, the way the light hit the porch just so in the afternoon, the smell of wild honeysuckle in the next-door neighbor's yard, that reminded me of living at Grandma's. Jamie felt the same way about one of the bedrooms; it had a window seat that reminded him of his sister's bedroom in his parents' house. It was a place for ghosts—good ghosts, the kind you welcome into your life.

"We have a mortgage," Jamie was saying, more than a little wonder in his voice. He nodded to a couple that passed by, looking over our yard sale goods. "A mortgage and a lawnmower. We're grown-ups, Miri."

"Well, I'm not mowing the lawn," I said, taking a second to fix a smile on a cute guy who was inspecting a pair of high-top sneakers I'd once brought home for Jamie. "I'm not that grown up."

"Well, I can't do it," Jamie said, his eyes sparkling the way they did when he was joking. "I'm sure my father gave me a study that said it would be bad for me."

That was one of the stranger things about Jamie's being positive—it seemed to actually have gotten him and his father talking again. He'd come down to visit us twice in the past year, Jamie's Dad had, armed with all kinds of studies and suggestions of new drug trials. Maybe it was just that this was a crisis his Dad had some idea of how to handle. Maybe it was just that he didn't want to lose another child.

"We'll make Rick mow the lawn," I said to Jamie. "Better yet, we'll make Chris do it."

Jamie laughed. "You've got to take advantage of them when they're in that anything-to-please-you stage," he said.

Chris had moved to New York that summer, after Sean decided to go solo and the Lost Generation broke up. He said he was moving to play drums with some new band there; Jamie said he'd really moved to be closer to me, and I had to admit it looked that way. He'd been spending almost every weekend in Philly with me, and was taking the train down that afternoon to help us finish packing, to help us move the next day. Jamie, who had once been suspicious of Chris because of his old drug problems, was now convinced he was a keeper; a man who'll move your furniture, he joked, is worth his weight in gold records. I myself was not making any firm decisions one way or the other; for once in my life I was not trying to force something into what I thought I did or didn't want it to be. I was just letting it happen. I guess some of Jamie's Buddhist stuff had rubbed off on me by then.

I caught the cute guy looking at us over Jamie's sneakers, and I smiled at him again. He was thin, and looked to be about my age, with curly blondish hair that reminded me of Wendell's. "Hey," he said, "aren't you guys in that band, Cloud Cuckoo Land? The sound you get from just two guitars is amazing."

I looked at Jamie, and we both smiled.

"Thank you," I said to the guy, "you should come out to our next show," and I batted my eyes, just for the hell of it. He inspected an old sweatshirt of mine—the one from Ian Oliver's 1983–1984 U.S. tour—but ended up buying, of all things, my old sundress.

"You think that's for his girlfriend?" I asked Jamie as the guy walked away.

Jamie watched him walk for a second. "It's for him."

Well, I thought, at least that old dress went to a good home.

By the end of the day, we'd made $132. I couldn't believe some of the junk that folks had bought: several ugly statues that Jamie insisted had belonged to Clay; an awful painting a friend of Jamie's had given him when he was in art school; an old steam iron with pieces of fabric melted onto the bottom; a couple of throw rugs the cats had pretty much destroyed. We sold all of our old clothing, too, and most of the shoes.

When we'd cleaned out our closets before the sale, we discovered we had enough shoes to open our own footwear store. This was mostly my fault; I'd brought many of them home from my wanderings in the city, back in the first year or two after I moved in with Jamie. I'd always had a weakness for abandoned shoes. There was one pair I'd found the spring after Clay had left, right out in front of our apartment, just sitting there like orphan twins in the middle of the sidewalk: a white satin pair of high heels, with rhinestone buckles at the toes, rounder than round. The way they'd been lined up, so perfectly, it was like some woman had just stepped right out of them, and, not missing a beat in her stride, had walked on in her stocking feet. They'd looked like Marilyn Monroe shoes to me, and I'd brought them in for Jamie, to cheer him up. But he'd just looked at them and said, "Miri, what am I going to do with these?" and gone back to his room, and then I'd worried that maybe he thought I was suggesting he was a crossdresser or something, and so I'd buried them in the back of my closet. I'd forgotten about them completely until we started getting ready for the yard sale.

The only things left by the end of the day were those Marilyn Monroe shoes, and that pair of scuffed-up high-tops I'd once given Jamie, another garbage day find. We decided to leave them out there on the sidewalk, in case anyone wanted them.

"Do we have enough time for ice cream before Chris's train gets in?" Jamie asked, arranging the shoes so it looked like they were on the move, headed off somewhere.

"There's always time for ice cream," I said, moving one of the high-tops slightly to the right, nodding my approval at Jamie's sudden work of art.

We headed down to More Than Just Ice Cream, after all these years still my favorite place for sweets. We passed Sabra, Jamie's favorite restaurant, and the gay bookstore, where I was always trying to encourage him to hang out. He and Sean still talked on the phone and seemed to be on good terms, but they had pretty much broken up. Whether it was about Jamie's diagnosis or other stuff between them I didn't know and didn't ask. I knew from Chris that Sean had tested negative twice, and was considered in the clear.

We weren't using Sean as our producer on the third album; we were going into the studio in October with a different guy, a real producer who'd worked with a lot of bands Jamie and I both liked. We planned to do some different stuff on this album; we were adding keyboards, and more drums.

Jamie had been listening a lot to this band from Seattle, Nirvana—in fact, I'd joked with him that it was a good thing we were moving, or the neighbors would surely have us evicted, loud as he liked to play it—and he'd become interested in a more aggressive sound. We were even thinking of doing some tour dates with Chris on drums, like a real rock band.

The waiter in the ice cream shop was one of our fans; we'd seen him at just about every show in Philly, and he'd even travelled to D.C. and New York to see us. We'd given him a ride back from D.C. once, two years before, when he'd missed the last train home. He was a nice guy with a shock of dark curly hair who I thought liked Jamie and who Jamie swore liked me. He was one of those people who you couldn't tell if he was gay or straight. Jamie was convinced he was bi.

He brought us hot fudge sundaes and we told him we were moving to Mount Airy. His face sank like a failed cake. "Mount Airy!" he cried. "That's practically the suburbs. You might as well move to New Jersey."

We both just smiled and shrugged and finished our ice cream. I was feeling devilish and decided to write our new phone number on the bottom of the check. I signed Jamie's name to it before he realized what I was doing.

"Miri," he said to me as we left the shop, "what if he calls us?"

"Well, then we'll know it was you he liked, and not me," I said. Jamie shook his head, but he was smiling. He just needed a little push sometimes, Jamie did.

We strolled back home down Spruce Street, just taking our time, enjoying the sunny day. From several blocks away I could hear an opera singer, practicing her scales; it was coming from the Academy of Vocal Arts, a short distance from our apartment. I'd miss things like that about the city—the sound of someone singing opera in the middle of the day, the random chance of finding an orphaned cat, a pair of shoes—but I knew this move was the best thing for both of us, especially for Jamie. He'd developed a kind of calm since we'd bought the house, like nothing I'd seen in him before. Maybe it helped him to feel his life was less threatened, more permanent, being rooted somewhere.

A few blocks from our apartment, we passed a grizzly-looking old man who was dozing in the doorway of a church. He wore grimy cotton chinos and a yellowed t-shirt that had seen better days. The bottoms of his feet were visible through the holes in his worn-out shoes. Jamie and I looked at each other, and I knew we were thinking the same thing: the high-tops, which we'd left with the Marilyn Monroe shoes in front of our building.

I grabbed Jamie's hand and we raced the remaining blocks back to our place, nearly colliding with a baby carriage, sideswiping a huge Dalmatian that was tied outside the diner. We ran up to 21st Street, panting in the heat; but both of us stopped short when we turned the corner.

The shoes, both pairs, were gone. Jamie dropped my hand and leaned forward, catching his breath. He propped himself against a parking meter.

"So much for our good deed," he said. "Weird, that they'd go so fast."

I looked down at the sidewalk and watched the feet of the people who passed us by. They wore all kinds of shoes: ballet flats and jellies and suede tennis sneakers, Dr. Scholls and Birkenstocks and strappy sandals. I shaded my eyes from the sun and looked down the street in the direction our shoes had been pointed, and imagined those two pairs, fancy and simple, thrown together by chance, making their way somewhere together.

ABOUT THE AUTHOR

Lisa Borders grew up in New Jersey and lived for many years in Philadelphia. Her late father was born and raised in Beaumont, Texas, and she has drawn on these settings in writing *Cloud Cuckoo Land*. Her short fiction has been nominated for a Pushcart Prize and has appeared in *Black Warrior Review, Washington Square, Painted Bride Quarterly, Bananafish*, and many other journals. She has received grants from the Massachusetts Cultural Council and the Pennsylvania Council on the Arts, and residencies at Hedgebrook and the Blue Mountain Center. She lives in Somerville, Massachusetts, where she teaches creative writing at the adult-education level and works as a cytotechnologist—screening cellular samples for abnormalities—in a private laboratory.

Editor's Note

This book won River City Publishing's 2001 Fred Bonnie Memorial Award for Best First Novel.

Fred Bonnie, who was originally from Maine, moved to Alabama in the 1970s. He lived in the Birmingham area, not far from us, for about twenty-five years. He was a gifted author and writing teacher and was considered a master of the short story. He loved to help authors who were at the beginning of their careers. In 2000 we published his first and only novel, *Thanh Ho Delivers*, the story of a Vietnamese girl's escape from her homeland after the fall of Saigon, and her struggle to make a new life in America.

Fred died soon after the novel came out and in his honor, with the collaboration of his family, we set up this contest. We had previously published Cassandra King's novel *Making Waves in Zion*, so we asked her and her husband, Pat Conroy, to serve as final judges. They were familiar with Fred and his work. We sent the Conroys six finalist manuscripts; they told us later that *Cloud Cuckoo Land* stood head and shoulders above the rest—quite an honor for Lisa Borders.

So we salute Lisa by publishing her first novel and we salute Fred, who helped so many writers, by introducing an important new novelist to the American literary scene. He would have been proud.